Praise for *Under a Pole Star*

"A fascinating, mysterious historical novel about a female explorer in a world of men at the end of the nineteenth century. *Under a Pole Star* is an adventure, an illicit romance, and a life-defying exploration of a land most of us know nothing about. The contrast of the lovers' blazing relationship set against the frigid Arctic and the secrets that propel the narrative will keep readers riveted in this hard-to-forget, mesmerizing tale!"
—M.J. Rose, *New York Times* bestselling author

"A tale of foul play and doomed love . . . It is a tribute to Penney's superlative descriptive skills that the book's erotic charge is so startlingly effective, and that her icy landscapes cast such a lasting, almost hallucinatory spell." —*The Guardian*

"Penney does a masterly job of melding Flora's story with the more factual accounts of polar expeditions, and many of her characters are taken from the pages of history . . . A gripping tale about the men and women who were driven to conquer the Arctic. Bound to appeal to admirers of Eowyn Ivey's *To the Bright Edge of the World*."—*Library Journal* (Starred Review)

"A terrific and beautifully written yarn that will make readers yearn to travel and fall in love in a cold climate." —*The Times* (London)

"A beautifully written tale, elegant and well-observed, full of powerful descriptions of a dazzling landscape." —*S Magazine, Sunday Express*

"Penney works hard to fill her canvas with color and conviction."
—*The Sunday Times* (London)

"A classic Bildungsroman . . . Penney explores themes of love, desire, companionship, and the difference between the three."
—*Times Literary Supplement*

"What has marked Penney out from the start is her ability to make her extensive historical research come alive." —*The Sunday Herald*

"With the nights drawing in and the temperature beginning to plummet, there's no better time to curl up with this stunningly evocative tale about an intrepid young female explorer. As immersive as it is mesmerizing, this is a novel that you won't ever forget." —*Heat*

"This is an epic love story set against the forbidding beauty of snow meadows. A perfect winter read." —*Red*

"Against the backdrop of the Arctic Ocean, explorer Flora meets Jakob, a member of a rival expedition. Science gives way to love with devastating results." —*Grazia*

"Encompassing big historical themes, vast expanses of territory, and passion in its various forms—for knowledge, for discovery, and in the shape of American geologist Jakob, for human love—*Under a Pole Star* is epic in scope and delivery."
—*Writing Magazine*

UNDER A POLE STAR

Also by Stef Penney

The Tenderness of Wolves
The Invisible Ones

STEF PENNEY

UNDER A POLE STAR

Quercus

New York • London

Quercus

New York • London

ISBN 978-1-68144-117-7

Library of Congress Cataloging-in-Publication Data
Names: Penney, Stef, author.
Title: Under a pole star / Stef Penney.
Description: New York : Quercus, 2017.
Identifiers: LCCN 2016047484 (print) | LCCN 2016058641 (ebook) | ISBN 9781681441177 (hardcover) | ISBN 9781681441160 (softcover) | ISBN 9781681441153 (ebook) | ISBN 9781681441146 (library ebook)
Classification: LCC PR6116.E58 U53 2017 (print) | LCC PR6116.E58 (ebook) | DDC 823/.92--dc23
LC record available at https://lccn.loc.gov/2016047484

Distributed in the United States and Canada by
Hachette Book Group
1290 Avenue of the Americas
New York, NY 10104

Manufactured in the United States

10 9 8 7 6 5 4 3 2 1

www.quercus.com

For Mr. Van

A glossary of Inuit words appears on p. 579

North Polar Regions, 1893

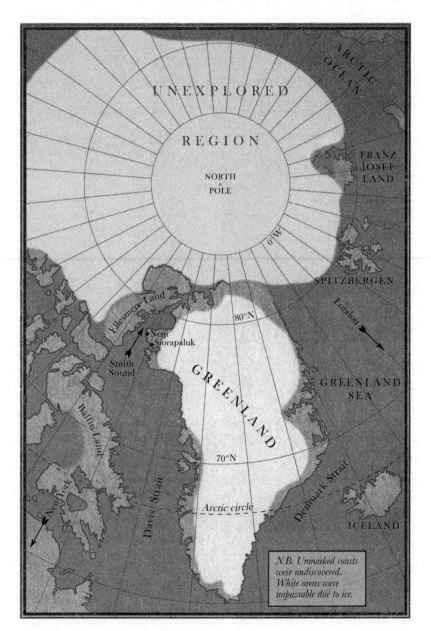

UNEXPLORED

REGION

NORTH
○
POLE

ARCTIC
OCEAN

FRANZ
JOSEF
LAND

0°W

SPITZBERGEN

London

Ellesmere Land

80°N

Neqi
Siorapaluk

Smith
Sound

GREENLAND

GREENLAND
SEA

Baffin Land

70°N

New York

Davis Strait

Arctic circle

Denmark Strait

ICELAND

N.B. Unmarked coasts
were undiscovered.
White areas were
impassable due to ice.

You see things; and you say "Why?" But I dream things that never were; and I say "Why not?"

—*George Bernard Shaw*

Prologue

McGuire Air Force Base, New Jersey, 40°0' N, 74°35' W
April 1948

The airplane, a modified Douglas C-47 Skytrain, is a fat, shining cigar of aluminum, brilliant in the sun. The word *Arcturus* is stenciled on the fuselage in a confident upward sweep. The journalist has done his homework, but there are things he does not know: for example, that grease monkeys spent days polishing the skin, and that the name has been added especially for this trip—a celestial name deemed more heroic and appropriate than the boring clutch of numbers on its tail. The Skytrain was a bomber throughout the war, but now it is carrying an overtly peaceable cargo; there are air force men, it is true—weary-eyed, beribboned, and grizzled—but there are also scientists from several universities, a camera crew from ABC, the journalist.

The film crew takes some footage of the scientists standing by the plane. When ordered, they wave and smile, raggedly, never all at the same time. The air force men stand to attention until their commander smiles—then the rest of them relax a little, but not as much as the civilians. There is one last arrival—a special guest—a British woman of advanced years, who was known, for a time, fifty years before, as the Snow Queen.

When the old lady—white-haired, erect, and rather forbidding—is introduced to the scientists, the Harvard physicist claims that his father met her many years ago and had spoken of her to his family. The Snow Queen nods and moves on, giving no indication whether she remembers the father, or was even listening to what he said. The film camera whirs, recording the handshakes. The journalist thinks that, in the resulting film, there will be a graphic of a globe, a tiny plane crawling over it, dragging a dotted line across the world. The thought thrills him.

At last they are ready to embark. Randall is nervous—not of the flight, not really, although it is his first—but because he wants to bag a seat next to the old lady. He has been thinking about this meeting for months. She doesn't look at him as he sits down, but stares out of the window. He buckles himself in, opposite the oceanographer from Harvard, behind the civilian whose field of expertise no one seems quite sure of, who is engrossed in an automobile magazine. They take off with a tremendous roaring, a steep upward trajectory that drags him back in his seat. His scalp prickles. Quite quickly, the nose of *Arcturus* levels off, the plane swings around, and fierce sun stripes the cabin, blazing off one face after another.

Randall turns to his neighbor and attempts to start a conversation, rather hampered by the din of the engines.

"I have some of your old press clippings," he shouts.

She frowns, probably because she can't hear a thing.

"Your press clippings!" he yells.

She frowns some more.

"It was such an exciting time. You knew everybody."

"Who are you?" she asks, although they were introduced on the ground.

"Randall Crane . . . Crane! Hi! I've been commissioned to write up the trip for *World* magazine."

"The journalist."

She might as well have said, "a cockroach," or, "a hernia." Something decidedly unwelcome. She looks away, through the window next to her, to where sunlight burns on a smooth field of white cloud.

"It's beautiful! Is this what the Arctic looks like?" He leans toward her, eager and also moved, made almost breathless by the strength of the light, the hot blue of the sky. After the visceral experience of takeoff, it feels as though they aren't moving at all.

"You've never been there."

"No," he admits, cheerfully. He can't help grinning. He has been told he has a winning smile. "I can't wait to see it. I hope you don't mind me saying: I've been reading about you." Does she cock her ear toward him, slightly? Flattery never fails with these old birds. "You were a superstar. You knew all the explorers, didn't you? Armitage, Welbourne, de Beyn, and the rest? It was an amazing time. All those discoveries. You were a pioneer."

"Well, yes."

"And the . . . the controversy—I've always been fascinated by what happened. What was your take on it?"

He could slow down—should, probably—but he's so full of energy; it bubbles up through him like an unstoppable spring.

"What controversy?"

"The Armitage–de Beyn controversy . . . The mystery over what happened to them. You knew them, didn't you?"

"Goodness! It's such a long time ago. They're all dead, except me." The way she says this—it is impossible to tell whether she feels satisfaction or regret. "What does it matter now?"

"Doesn't the truth matter?" He gazes hopefully at her eyes, which avoid his and give nothing away. "No one seems to know what really happened. I'd love to know what you think, as someone who was there."

"'What really happened'?" She smiles, not at him, but for herself. "You flatter me if you think *I* know the truth."

"I'd like to know your opinion. Could I talk to you about it?"

"It's very noisy here."

"Oh, yes—not here, of course. It is noisy, isn't it?"

The Snow Queen leans her head back against the seat, her eyes angled out of the window. She looks tired—but, to Randall, from his unassailable vantage point of twenty-seven years, old people always look tired. She must be—what?—seventy-seven. Older than his grandmother, Lottie. Her hair is as white as the clouds outside; her eyes, dark gray, unreadable, like boring pebbles. She wears discreet makeup, so she must care what people think. That gives him hope. He has done his homework on her, too: read her books on the north and trawled the archives for contemporary accounts. Newspaper reports from the 1890s described her as beautiful, although he found this hard to verify from the accompanying photographs—usually blurred and tiny; she tends to be one of a group of white-faced people staring at the camera, wearing hats. Lined up at the gunwale of a ship. Standing on a quay. At the front of a lecture theater. But there was one portrait, taken when she was in her early twenties: it is a studio-based fantasy, wherein the girl known as the Snow Queen poses stiffly in front of a painted icy landscape, her round, smooth face emerging from a halo of furs, her eyes fixed on an imaginary horizon. A thick snake of hair winds over her shoulder. Handsome, rather than beautiful, in his opinion. If Randall stared at the picture for long enough, he felt he could discern something in the wide-open eyes, but what was it? Arrogance? Ambition? Alarm? Almost any emotion, once he thought of it, could be imputed to those frozen features. Like most old portraits, it tantalized and revealed little.

In the seat next to him, the Snow Queen's eyes are closed. He cannot see the girl she was in her face. He suspects she is not asleep. His grandmother claims never to sleep—says you dispense with the need when you get old. Randall looks around him. Some of the scientists are dozing; some reading magazines (not *World* magazine, he notes). He is not in the least discouraged. They have hours to go before they reach their destination.

Flora Cochrane (her name has been many things, but this is the one she will have when she dies) awakens with a jolt. She was dreaming about places and people she has not dreamt about for decades. Her mouth tingles with the remembered pressure of warm flesh. A surge of erstwhile feeling has washed through her. Years since she had such a dream. For a moment she cannot think where she is. An infernal noise hammers her brain. The surroundings are distressingly bright. Then the lissome feeling in her body evaporates, and she remembers that she is old. A juddering—ah, yes, she is on the plane. *Arcturus*. She looks around to see the absurdly young man next to her; he turns toward her, too quickly. She keeps her eyes unfocused as she scans the cabin, wondering if she moaned in her sleep. No one is looking at her. They couldn't have heard her anyway.

"We're just coming down to Newfoundland, now."

He leans toward her and shouts in her ear. Flora nods minutely without meeting his eye, hoping he won't start another conversation. She would like to go to the bathroom, but doesn't remember anyone mentioning whether there was one on board. Although she was once used to it, it is still tedious to travel in all-male company. As they descend through a layer of clouds, the plane performs a series of bumps and bounds, like a small ship in a crossing sea. All very interesting, this mode of travel. They have come over a thousand miles in just a few hours. Think of all the walking that would have entailed. Even sailing, traveling at the speed of the wind, it's a distance that would have taken days. Now she leaves the wind far behind. It is as well she is speeding up, she thinks. At her age. The thought slots into her head: how he would have loved this. He would have laughed with delight . . .

"What's funny?"

The young man is smiling, tenacious. But his familiarity is less irritating than she would have thought. There is something charming and puppyish about him; perhaps it is his brown eyes, or his hair, which flops across his forehead, untamed by the pomade he uses; or his slightly buck teeth, eager to show themselves.

She shakes her head and points to her ear—the engines are roaring harder. He nods and gives her his pretty smile, biding his time.

RCAF Station, Gander, Newfoundland, 48°57' N, 54°36' W

They have landed at an airbase by a crooked-finger lake in Newfoundland, which, though far from luxurious, is designed to cater to women as well as men. They even rustle up a woman for her, to show her to her quarters and explain how to put on the extraordinary padded garment they expect her to wear tomorrow; it looks as though it were designed for giant babies, or lunatics. The woman, who has solid-looking hair and a smear of lipstick on her teeth, shows her how to put it on. There is a flap that zippers open and shut around the bottom, "For, y'know, emergencies? We recommend you practice while you're here, to get the hang of it." She is tactful enough about it, but still.

"How long is it since you were up there?" the woman asks—someone did introduce them, but Flora has forgotten her name.

"Oh, hundreds of years. During the last ice age." She smiles to show it is a joke rather than a put-down. The woman laughs, mechanically, without humor. Flora has never been good at humor. She tried it for a while, in her twenties, then gave it up.

"I'm surprised they asked me. That there wasn't anyone more . . . important."

"Not from that time. You've outlived them all," says the woman, smiling. "Good for you."

Flora is annoyed.

"You know," the woman goes on, "When I was young, I read about you and your expeditions. It was so inspiring to think that a woman could do that, even then."

"Well . . ." Perhaps she has misjudged her. "It wasn't easy. I'm sure it's not easy now."

"No. Things changed a bit during the war, but since then, when all the men came back, we've kinda had to get out of the way, if you know what I mean."

She does up the zipper with a noisy flourish. Flora isn't sure she does know what she means, but nods.

"Thank you. I think I can manage now."

"We're having dinner in an hour. I expect you'd like to get some rest before then. If you need anything, just holler."

As she closes the door, she finally remembers the woman's name—Millie . . . Mindy . . . something childish like that. She is aching to lie down. Sleep. Perhaps recapture that feeling from the plane . . . Then, afterward, maybe she will allow herself to have a cocktail. One of those sweet, deceptive things she had in New York. She stretches out on the bed with a sigh of relief.

It will be twilight for hours. The clouds have gone. The air is very clear and still. She hasn't seen air this clean for years, but then it is years since she has been this far north. Through the window, she acknowledges the faint, familiar stars as they rise. There is Arcturus, which the Eskimos call the Old Man, *Uttuqalualuk*. She cannot remember the names of the people she met earlier today, but those names learned so long ago, she has never forgotten. There, just above the horizon, is the Old Woman—Vega. The Caribou, known to others as the Great Bear. Cassiopeia: the Lamp Stand. And, just rising now, with its faint hint of red, the ghoulishly named *Sikuliaqsuijuittuq*—the Murdered Man.

She opens the window and leans out, inhaling the chill blue air. She cranes her neck to look for Draco, coiling around Polaris, and searches for Thuban, its once and future pole star. She stares until her eyes water, but it must be too early, too light, or perhaps her eyes are too tired, and she cannot find it.

Since she knew she was coming on the flight, she has been thinking again of that time. She closes her eyes and can see the valley spread out in front of her: duns and greens and grays; minute jewels of color; the lake of breathtaking blue. Impossible Valley, they called it. But it was possible, if only briefly.

Recently, her old friend Poppy fell ill and Flora had managed to see her, before it was too late. Lying in bed, looking tiny and somehow both sexless and ageless, she had talked calmly about her approaching death. She believed in heaven. She knew that she would meet her sons there: reluctant soldiers, unwitting martyrs.

Flora nodded but could not in her heart agree (though who was she to say what Poppy did or did not know, or which of their beliefs was true?). She would like to believe in heaven, of course, but that has always seemed too easy, too trite; if it were true, why would one go to all this bother down here? Besides (she thought, but did not say), heaven is here on earth. She knew; she had been there.

PART ONE

A PEG, SHAPED LIKE A WHALE

"A glass ~~vile~~vial of POISON. An iron hook. A copper penny. A length of red ribbon. A bronze pin (bent). A handkerchief with embroidry. A peg, shaped like a whale."

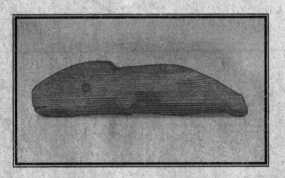

Chapter 1

This was a list of the things that Flora stole on her first voyage. There were other items, but she only wrote down her favorites. For years, until it disappeared, she kept the peg whale as a talisman—it was carved of a pale, close-grained wood, very smooth, with the merest blunt suggestions of head, fins, and tail. The eyes and blowhole were burned in with a hot awl. It fit beautifully in her fist. She had coveted it when she saw it in a boat-steerer's hand, and when she found it lying in the scuppers, she pocketed it without scruple. It was forfeit, on its way back to the sea; she felt she had the right.

Flora Mackie was twelve when she first crossed the Arctic Circle. The previous November, her mother had died, and her father did not know what to do with his only child. He was the Dundee whaling captain, William Mackie. Flora took after him in looks and brusqueness of manner, and showed no sign of her mother's grace. Elsa Mackie had been a pretty woman who delighted in her decorative capacity. Her husband was proud of her, but a whaling captain's wife in Dundee—no, anywhere—had limited opportunities for displaying her charms. She had been horrified by the process of producing Flora and was critical of the results, having a tendency to bemoan her daughter's shortcomings: chiefly, hoydenishness and a thick waist. Before Flora could talk, Mrs. Mackie had developed mysterious, lingering ailments, and left Flora's upbringing largely to a nursemaid, Moira Adam, who was efficient, but had a heart of Doric granite. In the last weeks of Mrs. Mackie's life, after the captain had come home from a successful season in the north, he and his daughter sat together in the front room while, upstairs, Mrs. Mackie consulted a succession of doctors. When she died, the widower was not so much grief-stricken as haunted by guilt—if he had stayed at home instead of leaving her for up to two years at a time, he thought, she might not have died. What if the same happened to Flora?

Other captains took their wives north, he reasoned—to himself, since he was not a man people argued with openly—so why should he not take his daughter? He had been in the Davis Strait so many times it no longer seemed to him a particularly hazardous place. People talked, although, having few friends in the town, he did not know this. He should have farmed her out to a relative, they said. He should have sent her to a boarding school, a foster home, a convent. But Captain Mackie did not know what people said and would not have cared. He had spent most of his life on board ship, where, for the last fifteen years, he had been captain and absolute ruler under God; he was accustomed to getting his own way.

So, in April 1883, Flora and her father set sail from Dundee in the whale ship *Vega*. No good would come of it, people muttered. What they meant by this, no one was prepared to say, but she was a young girl on a ship full of men, going to a land of ice, a sea of blood. It was unprecedented; it was immoral, in some way. It was definitely wrong.

Much of Captain Mackie's confidence in his daughter's safety lay in his ship. The *Vega* was a Dundee-built steam barque of 320 tons, from Gourlay's shipyard, her hull reinforced with six-inch-thick oak planks. Her bows and stern were doubly reinforced—her bows were three feet thick—and twenty-four-inch-square oak beams, each cut from a single trunk, were placed side by side across the ship to brace her sides against the pressure of converging ice floes. Captain Mackie, who had sailed in the seas around Greenland for the best part of thirty years, thought her the finest ship Dundee had produced. He was an owner-captain; that is to say, he owned ten sixty-fourths of the *Vega*, but he loved all of her, with a proprietor's love, as well as the love a captain feels for a brave, willing boat. He had captained her for nine years and was convinced that, in her, Flora could come to no harm. He couldn't have placed the same confidence in some of the other ships now—naming no names, but glancing at the aged *Symmetry*, not to mention Peterhead's wicked old *Fame*...

The *Vega* was neither large nor beautiful—Davis Strait whalers were, on the whole, small, stout, and slow—but to Flora she was marvelous: massive, dense; the weight and heft of her oak awe-inspiring. She loved the thickly varnished gunwales that she could barely see over, smooth and slightly sticky to the touch; she loved stroking the silky brasswork, rubbed to a soft, liquid gloss. When no one was looking, she straddled the enormous ice beams, unable to imagine anything that could vanquish them. And she loved her name. The rest of the fleet had names like *Dee*, *Ravenscraig*, and *John Hammond*, so the *Vega* felt to Flora like a doughty wood-and-pitch ally: the sister she had never had and, in the relentlessly masculine world of the north, a female confederate she would appreciate. And, from the first time she walked up the gangway, she even liked her smell: dark and bitter, of tar, salt, coal, and—faint after a winter in dock—a hint of her summertime carnage: the smell of fat, blood, and death.

With fifty men and a girl on board, it was a crowded ship. Often she was, nominally, alone—in the cabin, when she was working on her books—but wherever she was, she could hear a full symphony of human noises. Apart from talking, shouting, and occasional, quickly hushed swearing, all day and night there were grunts, groans, farts, laughter, cries, snores, and sounds less identifiable. Flora heard much cursing through the wooden walls. She pretended, if her father was around, that she couldn't hear it—and if it was unmistakable, that she did not understand it. In that way, the ship was no different than the streets of Dundee.

Her father did his best. She shared with him the tiny great cabin, divided down the middle by a blanket that slid back and forth like a real curtain. She had a cot slung from a beam, so that it stayed more or less level while waves pitched and rolled the ship. It had lipped sides like a tray, and she swung in it, wrapped in blankets, and later on in furs, like a sausage in bacon.

While still in Crichton Street, she had heard—she was a shameless eavesdropper—all sorts of gossip about sailors that fueled her imagination. Sailors did vague, excitingly terrible things to young girls, but on the *Vega* they were kind and deferential. Just in case, Flora had prepared herself with a weapon: a penknife that lived on a thong around her neck, under her chemise.

In her heart of hearts she did not believe that any harm would come to her from the crew; apart from their kindness, she knew she was not alluring, being plain and thickset, with a round, whey-colored face and stone-gray eyes. She had learned early in life that there were those who were caressed for their physical charm (like her mother), and those who were not; those who drew glances in the street, smiles from strangers, favors—and those who passed invisibly, like ghosts. She was used to being invisible. But it was as well to be prepared, and, in her imagination, she could be (why not?) golden-haired and fragile, with a heart-shaped face and violet eyes, like the diminutive heroine of her favorite book, *Poor Miss Caroline*. Never mind that she had never met anyone with violet eyes (nor, come to that, a heart-shaped face). There were nights when she swung in her cot, imagining assault from faceless assailants—imagining, too, her violent, blood-spattered response. She enjoyed these thoughts. Sometimes, rocked in the resounding darkness, she allowed herself to be overpowered. She enjoyed those thoughts, hazy though they were, also.

Captain Mackie ensured that Flora maintained an education of sorts. By the end of their voyage, she should have read the Bible, preferably learning the Gospels by heart, have studied the glories of God's creation in the form of the natural world, and have an idea of All the Things That Have Occurred Up to This Point. He insisted that she keep a journal describing what she had read, proving that she understood it. He bought a number of notebooks for the purpose.

Flora stared at engravings of plants and birds. *Today I studied Passiformae*, she wrote in the journal entitled, *What I Have Learned*, by Flora Elsa Caird Mackie. *They are Perching Birds. There are very many species of them. E.g., Blackbirds.* This seemed to keep her father satisfied. She worked her way through *A Child's History of the World*, and thus knew that history started with the Egyptians, followed by the Greeks and the Romans. Then there was Jesus, after which, things went downhill. *A Child's History* was tantalizing but vague. She had the impression that history got more boring the nearer it came to the present day. By their own century, long gone were gladiators, embalmed cats, and cups of hemlock, replaced by monarchs who no longer wanted to murder each other, ever-increasing agricultural yields, and the spinning jenny. Flora was disappointed. She longed to know more: How exactly did gladiators kill each other? How could a Pharaoh marry his sister? What did hemlock taste like and how long did it take to die? (Did you vomit, suffocate, or bleed to death?) On these subjects, and much else of real interest, *A Child's History* was mute.

On the second day out of Stromness, Flora took another of the notebooks and paused for a time before opening it. She was thinking about the groaning she had heard on the other side of the bulkhead the previous night. Her father slept, snoring quietly. She had been obscurely afraid, wondering if the man was ill, but fearing, in a way that she could not identify, that he was not. She did not sleep for the rest of the night.

She did not write anything on the cover of this notebook, but opened it at the back page and started to scribble in tiny, terrible writing. Perhaps she did this because, in a place where privacy and solitude were illusory or impossible, Flora had a need for secrets. So, on the day she had breezed through the order of passerines, read a chapter about the Greeks, and skimmed through part of Matthew's Gospel, she took the nameless diary and wrote, *I don't like birds. They don't have fur and I don't like the way they look at me.* The only birds she saw now were the gulls (definitely not passerines) that landed on the ship's rail—you could argue that they perched there, but somehow not in a way that counted—and stared at her with glassy, impudent eyes.

The *Vega*'s officers—harpooners, boat-steerers, and line managers— were all from Dundee and the Fife towns—Cellardyke, Pittenweem, St. Monance; but the oarsmen were Orkadians. Out of fifty men on board, eleven were named John, seven Robert. Flora made friends with the youngest Robert—a first-voyage apprentice from Dundee, named Robert Avas. Robert was a year older but some inches shorter than Flora. He had the white, pinched-faced look common to children from the fish market, but an irrepressibly sweet nature and boundless enthusiasm. He had never heard of the Egyptians, and thought that Newcastle was the capital of London. Flora was mightily impressed by such ignorance.

"I could teach you to read," she said, when they had known each other a week.

"Read? For why?" he asked, grinning.

"So . . ." Flora was taken aback. "So that you could read."

"What would I read?" he asked, genuinely curious.

She paused, wondered what would hold the most appeal. "Well . . . newspapers."

"Ach, they're fu' o' nonsense."

She shrugged. "Stories. About sailors . . ."

"I reckon I'll get to know enough about them as it is."

A tremendous noise broke over them like a wave: loud, deep cries came from the fore-rigging—the Orkneymen were raising sail, chanting a mysterious incantation that contained no words you could pin a meaning to. Flora stared at them with a kindling of unease; the Orkneymen were big—taller and broader than the men she was used to. They had sandy hair and raw, reddened skin; jutting cheeks and brows. They spoke a different language. Their chant had a glamour that stirred something inside her.

"Can you understand them?"

Robert turned candid blue eyes on her. "*Vou, vou!*" he shouted, imitating the men's weird cries. He laughed and shrugged.

The time they spent together was irregular and liable to be broken off at any moment by yelled commands; Robert would leap to his feet and scramble up the rigging, or disappear below. Flora experienced frustration at this, not envy; it wasn't that she particularly wanted to climb the rigging, but, as soon as he turned away, she knew Robert forgot her existence. He had a place in the running of the ship, which she—a supernumerary, and a girl—did not.

Her only other friend on board was the surgeon, Charles Honey. Like most surgeons on whale ships, he was a recent medical graduate without the means to buy a practice. He was twenty-three, but looked younger, with a fresh complexion and an air of bewildered innocence. For the first two weeks he suffered from appalling seasickness, and the sounds of his misery could be heard throughout the ship. At first, the sailors were sympathetic, but after a few days their sympathy turned to hilarity. Captain Mackie spoke sharply to the men, but was tight-lipped. He hadn't been able to find anyone else. Since Honey was usually on his own in the sickbay, Flora wasn't afraid of seeking him out, and since she was a little girl, and not a pretty one, he wasn't afraid of her being there. He was the least alarming of men: slight, gentle, hesitant. He blushed easily.

It was in the sickbay that she first became aware of Ian Sellar. They were beating into a northwesterly at the time, the *Vega* straining at her seams. Honey's bottles and jars rattled in their cages; on a lee lurch, a mug of coffee skated down the slope of his desk, slopping its contents but holding its footing.

Flora was perched on the sickbed, her back braced against the cabin wall, pestering Honey with questions about dissecting corpses. She had ascertained during previous interrogations that medical students did this, but he was prevaricating—he was, in short, lying to her. As the captain's daughter, she had a certain borrowed authority and he was unwilling to put her off, but he was also worried that the captain would be angry if he filled his daughter's head with nightmares.

"What force of wind is this?"

He treated Flora as a conduit for her father's seafaring knowledge, a tendency she did nothing to discourage.

"Oh about"—another lurch as the North Atlantic slapped the ship in the bows—"a force six . . . or five. Five, I'd say. It could get very much worse."

"I do hope not, or I fear for my medicines." He looked up rather wildly. The wind sang its mournful song in the rigging. Flora was pitiless.

"But have you cut up a woman's corpse?"

"Heavens, Flora, why would you want to know such a thing?"

"You have to learn about their insides, and their insides are different to a man's, aren't they?"

She looked at him, sly. It had, initially, been easy to make Dr. Honey blush, but he was getting wise to her.

"I'm sure you know far more than you let on, Miss, and you are ragging me."

"I'm not! I might be a doctor one day. I want to heal people. Without knowledge, you cannot heal the sick, can you? What do you think? Would I make a good doctor?"

As Honey opened his mouth to respond, there came a thudding outside the door, and the ship plunged into a deep trough.

"Fuckin' cunt!"

Flora made her face a blank. The door opened. A tall, loose-limbed sailor shuffled in, cradling his right arm, his face twisted with pain.

"Doctor, I . . ." He saw Flora and turned red. Flora recognized him as one of the Orkneymen, Ian Sellar.

"Miss Mackie is just going. Run along now, Flora."

"Can't I help?"

Ian Sellar released his hand with a groan.

"Ach, Sellar, what happened here?"

"Thole pin. Shoulder."

He pressed his lips together and closed his eyes. Honey sat him on his chair under the lamp, picked up a scalpel, and sliced off his shirt in one sure movement. Flora, who had gaped when he picked up the scalpel—was he going to *amputate*?—hovered behind them.

Ian Sellar was one of the younger Orkneymen, and the most perfectly made man Flora had ever seen. Where most of the men from the north were craggy and reddened, his skin, uniquely on the pink, Pictish *Vega*, was the color of honey. His features were strong and graceful; he moved with an ease that singled him out. Flora stared at his bare, golden back. She failed to understand how she hadn't noticed him before now. Honey tutted as he palpated the shoulder, where blood was spreading under the skin.

"It's not dislocated, Sellar. Just badly bruised. You'll have to keep it in a sling for a while. Flora, pass me that roll of bandage, there. No, there . . . If you want to make yourself useful, you can pour some witch hazel into that dish. It's the one in the . . ."

Flora hopped smartly to do as she was told. She was familiar with most of the contents of the sickbay. She passed Honey bandages and pins and compresses and brandy, nimble as a cat as the ship bucked under a mauling from angry waves. Ian's face was sickly under his tan; tiny drops of sweat rolled down his temples. Flora stood behind him, watching, and as the ship gave a mighty bound to starboard, she lurched toward him so that her hand brushed down the glistening, undamaged shoulder. In another moment, she snatched her hand away, stung by his heat. Honey himself had stumbled backward, with a swallowed oath. Sellar sat with eyes tight shut. Neither seemed to notice that she had done it on purpose.

After that, Flora watched for Sellar's figure on deck, tuned her ear to his uncouth accent and became adept at picking out his voice through wooden walls. Men were never alone on board ship, apart from the few minutes they spent at the head, but even had he been alone, she would not have approached him. She could not imagine what she might say.

In long twilights, father and daughter searched for Venus and Mars, Altair, Arcturus, and Polaris. Sometimes they sat up through the whole brief night and followed the stars as they wheeled across the sky. They were circled by constellations that never set: the Bears, the Dragon, Perseus, Cassiopeia, Cepheus—none of them looking anything like what they were supposed to represent, except Draco the dragon.

"Why is the Plow called the Great Bear when it looks like a plow?"

"You're not seeing all of it. The plow is just the bear's back and tail."

"Bears don't have tails. Not long ones."

"Perhaps old Greek bears had long tails."

Flora laughed derisively. Her father thought she was getting above herself.

"How do you know that Draco looks like a dragon, in any case?" he went on. "Have you seen one?"

"I've seen pictures."

"Do you think those pictures were drawn from life?"

"Of course not! They don't exist."

"So perhaps Draco is no more like a dragon than Ursa Major is like a bear."

"Yes, but . . . it can't be *unlike* something that doesn't exist because . . ." She stopped, on uncertain ground. "There *are* bears. Why do they have to make something up? They could have called it the Snake. Snakes exist."

"Are you asking me why people invented monsters?"

"I suppose so."

"Perhaps because they had never been whaling. Look in Draco's tail—halfway between the bears. There is one brighter . . . the second-brightest star."

She steadied his telescope on the yardarm. The ship was completely still; the sea like a pond. An iceberg hung, motionless, two hundred yards away, doubled in the mirror surface. The stars were multiplied, as though the *Vega* were suspended in dark space, stars under them, and infinite depth.

"Do you see? That is Thuban. Once upon a time, he was the pole star, when the Egyptians were building their pyramids. You remember the Egyptians?"

"Yes. They had a god with a falcon's head."

"They did. Whose name was . . . ?"

A fraction of a pause. "Horus."

"Yes. The Egyptians built their Great Pyramid so that Thuban shone down a shaft into the middle of the pyramid."

Flora was disturbed.

"How could it be the pole star?"

"Five thousand years ago, Thuban was the pole star. And one day—far in the future—it will be the pole star again. And it will be more perfectly placed than Polaris. Why? Because the earth moves on its axis. Like a spinning top when it's going to fall over." He demonstrated with his hand held vertically, waving it back and forth. "Very, very slowly. Now, of course, Polaris is the pole star, or rather, it is closer to the celestial pole than anything else, but one day . . . Everything changes, Flora. No matter how good, or how bad, nothing lasts forever." He moved the telescope up and fractionally to the left. "Now look there."

"I see Vega," said Flora firmly, alarmed by the conversation's metaphysical turn.

"Good. One day, very many thousands of years in the future, she too will be a pole star. And a very bright and good pole star she will be, although not as well placed as Thuban. And when she is the pole star, summer will fall in December and midwinter in June."

When Flora got over this disturbing news, she decided that she liked Thuban—once and future lodestar. She liked things to be right; not nearly right, or good enough. Best of all, she liked Vega. She belonged to all of them on the ship, but especially, Flora felt, to her. When she found out—as she was shortly to do—that the Eskimos called Vega the Old Woman, she was violently, though secretly, offended.

The Atlantic swell disappeared, quelled by the increasing frequency of icebergs. The sun came out and stayed around the clock, as if it couldn't bear to leave them. It conjured colors out of gray ice: green depths, royal-blue shadows, aquamarine hollows. The whole watery, deliquescent world glittered.

Flora spent hours hanging over the gunwale, staring at the ice. It was like watching a fire—you couldn't stop. There was a precision about ice that she felt as a new quality in her experience. Every piece was different and particular, effortlessly beautiful.

A sight she was always to remember: a peculiarly fine berg, crested and crenellated like an Alpine peak, which rotated to reveal an arch of ice, seventy feet high. It glittered white, scored with clefts that glowed deep blue above and, at its water-worn foot, a pale, silky green. A ruined masterpiece from a vanished civilization, it drew even the most ice-weary sailors to the rails.

The crow's nest called down: "If Miss Mackie would care to come up, she will see something fine."

Mackie sent Flora up ahead of him—it wasn't the first time she had been to the crow's nest on a calm day, but he made her tuck up her skirts and climbed the ratlines behind her, just in case. John Inkster hauled her up through the hole and she wriggled into the narrow space in front of him. He kept his arms loosely around her, to stop her from plunging the eighty feet to the deck below.

Above the arch, the top of the iceberg flattened into a small plateau. The sun's rays had begun to melt the ice, which formed a round pool the intense blue of a melted sapphire—and now, she could see, a little stream was carving a channel in the pool's white bank, a stream of milky blue that ran to the edge of the plateau and vanished over the other side. A blind, blue eye, weeping a single, endless tear.

"Well, Miss Flora," said Inkster, his breath warming her ear. "What do you think of our ice islands? Are they not fine?"

Flora found she could not speak. There were no words good enough. She turned full, gleaming eyes to Inkster, who laughed, but kindly. He thought it made her look almost bonny.

It was a good run, but at seventy-three degrees north, they hit the pack ice. Fog descended, blotting out the ice-choked coast of Baffin Land. Other ships in the fleet caught up: *Ravenscraig, Symmetry, Mariscal,* and *Hope* . . . They threaded their way through the loose pack to the North Water, where whales might lurk. A lookout conned the ship, peering into the murk, shouting himself hoarse. The fog smothered all sound other than the eerily slopping water and the masthead's cries.

"A fall! A fall!"

Flora was in the cabin. She crept on deck, keeping out of the way as men ran to the whaleboats hanging in the davits. She could feel the tension in the ship: running feet, bitten-off commands. She watched Ian Sellar spring into the first whaleboat, his face alive with excitement. The five men took their positions and the deck crew winched them down on to the water. They pushed off and the boat-steerer barked orders. The oarsmen swept them around in their own length and the boat shot off at a swift clip. Her father's hand landed on her shoulder.

"Flora," he said warningly, "when they come back with the fish, you get below. If I see you on deck after that, I will give you such a hiding."

"When do I come out again?"

"When I say."

"But what if...?"

He gave her a look of such ferocity that she shut up. He had sworn to himself Flora would not witness the actual business of whaling. She thought she knew all about it. She thought she was prepared. In the end, the boat returned empty-handed, having lost the whale.

The following day, they had more luck: boats were lowered after two whales; one was brought back. Flora listened to the shouts as the carcass was brought alongside. The men were cock-a-hoop. She sat quietly and saw nothing, but heard everything and smelled a stench worse than anything she had ever imagined. The reek of blood filled her nostrils, her mouth, her eyes. Another foul, chokingly awful smell—rich, ripe decay—made her retch. The men were working amidships, but she heard the drumming of feet and the laughter—louder and wilder than the men's usual discourse, as though they were drunk on slaughter.

She heard the blades' slicing and chopping, the sawing of bone and the ripping—the endless ripping—of skin; a sloshing that she hoped was water, even as she felt it was blood. Seeing it couldn't have been any worse—this way, she imagined the knives plunging into flesh and fat, the blood swilling around the men's limbs, sleeving them in red. When at last her father came to release her from the cabin, she was sickened and mutinous. Seawater had been pumped over the decks to flush out the bloody sawdust. But the whale's despoiled carcass was still near, low in the water, violated by fish and gluttonous seabirds. Heaps of gray-pink blubber were on deck, as men pitchforked it down into the hold. Blood-streaked bone hung, drying, on the yardarms.

"I told you it's not a pretty business," said her father. "Do you understand why I don't want you to witness it?"

"I don't know how seeing it can be worse than hearing and smelling it," she said. "I just imagine it. And in the cabin I can't breathe."

Her father—to his credit—took her opinion seriously. Subsequently, she was allowed a small area of freedom aft of the mizzen when the men were working, from where she could glimpse the bloody process, but not get under their feet. She appreciated the dangers—the deck became slick with blood and oil, and more than once she saw a man slip and be cut by the wicked blades.

Chapter 2

Melville Bay, 76°21' N, 71°04' W
Winter 1883–4

The men called Flora their mascot—that season, the *Vega* butchered more whales than any other ship. In mid-August, a gale jammed the ice into the bottleneck between Cape Alexander and Cape Isabella. The old *Symmetry* was caught fast. The other ships clustered around, ready to take on the crew if—when—she was crushed. The storm worsened—southwesterlies pushed the ships back into Melville Bay and piled an immense field of ice around them. Captain Mackie sat Flora down in the cabin to explain that they wouldn't be going home this year. To his surprise, she smiled.

Once he had found a floe to his liking—a thick sheet of ice the size of Barclay Park—he sent the crew out with twelve-foot saws. Flora watched as they carved out a slot that would be the *Vega*'s home for the winter. The days dwindled. At noon, the sun was so low that, if Flora stood at the rail, facing south, it hit her straight in the eyes.

She was elated. She felt she had lost her disadvantage—when a ship is in dock, sailors have no function either. She was allowed to roam where she liked, within sight of the ship. The purser made her a pair of pantaloons, and, with her hair stuffed under a wool cap, she looked like any of the shorter sailors. When the ice dock was ready, the *Vega* was warped into place, and new ice sealed her in. Visible to the west was *Symmetry*, locked in her icy cell.

Flora watched the sea change. First, it became a supple, gelatinous black paste, then a milky film crept over it. One morning, the ice pulled off one of its most seductive tricks: an eruption of crystal flowers; jagged white blooms were strewn across the dark ice as if there had been a frost wedding. Flora employed Robert and an oar to fish up some of the flowers and take them into her cabin, where she tried to draw them before they melted. Frustrated by failure, she cried.

The thickened water still heaved, like the flank of a breathing animal, but sluggishly. It congealed into porridge, which swallowed the flowers, then became big, gray pancakes that fused together, like armor plate. *Mare concretum*—the concrete sea. She couldn't remember the sound of waves.

The *Vega* was no longer a ship riding on water but a wooden cockleshell held in a medium that cracked and creaked and yelped. The pack ice could sound like a menagerie of animals in various states of distress: puppies whining peevishly, or bees swarming, or a whale groaning in agony. Or it was insensate and violent: cloth ripping, artillery fire, a grand piano falling from a second-story window. There were sounds that resembled nothing else.

The day before her thirteenth birthday, when daylight was no more than a glow on the horizon, they had visitors. The lookout shouted—there were dark dots on the ice, coming closer. Flora watched with alarm. Eskimos. The men had talked about them, so she did not feel she had very much to fear, but by all accounts they were a small, strange, greasy, murmuring people. As they got closer, one of them shouted distinctly, "*Vega! Vega!* Mackie!" Flora was profoundly shocked. These people knew her father! She did not think she would like them.

Three Eskimos came aboard the *Vega* and were admitted to a makeshift saloon on the deck, covered with canvas. Flora sat in the corner behind her father. A fire blazed in a bucket. Of the three figures, Flora could make out only one name, which was Kali. Kali was a man—he had a wispy beard and was extremely fond of tobacco. The other two had smooth faces and long black hair. One wore a pointed hat made of fur, turned skin-side out. None of them was taller than Flora. They gave the crew of the *Vega* dried pieces of something, which they chewed. One handed Flora a piece, murmuring at her. Flora sniffed it and tried tasting it. She had no idea what it was, but it was rank and hard, clearly inedible. She smiled politely. Captain Mackie handed out tobacco and produced lengths of red cloth and beads. There was smiling and talk from the Eskimos in their mumbled language, while her father smiled and spoke in English about the whales. The Eskimos nodded, but Flora did not see how they could understand each other. Before leaving, one of the Eskimos took Flora's shoulder and smiled, talking all the while. She smiled and was worried in case she had committed herself to some dangerous undertaking.

"You knew them before!" Flora accused her father afterward.

It was still an astonishing concept. While she was sitting in Crichton Street, he had entertained these people and chewed their horrible food. She gathered now that it was the dried skin of a unicorn fish. At home, he had never spoken about this.

"We usually meet the huskies when we're here. They like to trade, so we bring tools and cloth. Iron goods are precious to them, as they have no metal. And timber. I met Kali before. He is a decent fellow, for a heathen. Apilah, I have also met, although not his wife, Simiak."

"Which one was the wife?"

"The one in the hat. Only women wear the tall hats. It can be hard to tell otherwise, unless the men have beards. Most of them don't."

Flora stored this information away.

"So they are friendly? They wouldn't hurt us?"

"Good heavens, no. They are not an aggressive people—they can hardly afford to be. They know we have guns. I think Apilah wants you to meet his children."

"Why?"

"To play with, I imagine. I think you are of an age."

"But I can't talk to them."

"Come, Flora, it is just like meeting children in Dundee. It is up to you to show them good manners. Listen, I will teach you a few words."

The next day, more Eskimos came back, with two children. Apilah introduced the children to Flora. Both were shorter than Flora, with long, greasy hair. Neither had hats, so she assumed they were boys. This was a lucky guess; girls did not, she later discovered, wear the hats until they were married.

One of the boys was called Tateraq. He was sturdily built, had a round, smiling face and held himself with confidence. The other boy was Aniguin. He was perhaps Apilah's son, perhaps not; Mackie wasn't sure. He was slighter than Tateraq, and clearly, from their mannerisms, his inferior. He smiled a lot, but sometimes looked fearful, sometimes flinched.

They took Flora off with them. They had brought a sled and two dogs, which they treated with casual cruelty. The boys built snow targets and practiced throwing their harpoons. They let Flora try—or rather Aniguin, at Tateraq's command, let Flora try with his harpoon. Almost everything she did, whether clumsy or deft, produced laughter. She smiled dutifully at first, determined not to lose face, but was soon laughing with them. She had the feeling that it was not mocking; the laughter was just there, like the snow.

From November to February, it was dark. A gray light emanated from the ice as much as from the sky, sometimes tinged with blue, or rose, or violet. Flora got confused about time. She fell asleep in the middle of the day, was wide awake at night.

Strange, dreamlike things happened in this twilight. One day, she went with Tateraq and Aniguin to a place under the cliffs. It was clear, and a green aurora sizzled above them. She gaped at the writhing lights, but the boys didn't seem interested. She supposed they were as ordinary to them as rain was to her: not worthy of notice. The boys stuck hands in their trousers and, pulling out their penises, started to agitate them hard. Flora stared, open-mouthed, as Aniguin laughed, and seemed to be exhorting her to join in. Appalled, she turned and ran.

Afterward, she stayed in the cabin for days, complaining of a stomachache. Since she was rarely ill, Captain Mackie asked Dr. Honey to see her. Flora, not ill in the least, felt guilty.

"I feel better now," she announced. "I think it was something I ate."

Honey grimaced.

"Yes, the food on board is somewhat indigestible. Hardly suitable for young ladies. And the constant darkness is not suitable for anyone. But describe your symptoms to me. Your father said you were suffering from stomach pains. Has there been any vomiting?"

"Um . . . no."

"And what about . . . ?" He blushed, not meeting Flora's eye. "How are your bowel movements? Do you know what I mean by that?"

"Yes. Um . . . all right."

"So what sort of pain is it?"

"I don't know—just a pain."

"Your father did not say . . . whether . . . er, do you, er . . . have your monthly courses yet?"

He stared at the wall above her head.

"No!" said Flora, revolted to the depths of her being. Moira had warned her that this disgusting thing lay in wait for her, but she had chosen to forget it.

"It could be that it is about to begin—that would cause stomach pains."

"Oh." She wished he would go away.

"Or . . . it is just possible that it might be appendicitis. I need to make sure. If you would lift your jacket . . ."

"It doesn't hurt now."

"I will be able to feel if the appendix is inflamed. It could be dangerous."

Flora found herself lying back, lifting her jacket and tugging the various layers out of her waistband.

"I'm sorry if my hand is cold," he said, and put his hand—damp, clammy—on her stomach and pressed down. She tried not to recoil.

"Does that hurt?"

She shook her head. He moved his fingers around, pressing her flesh. She felt that she was being punished. He was looking at her face, more or less.

"And here? Does that hurt?"

Flora nodded. "A bit. It's much better than it was."

"Let me just . . ."

He pushed his hand further down toward the space between her legs, pressing and probing. His breathing changed. His fingers were now on the bony mound between her legs, and her heart quickened. She felt strange.

Without looking, Honey said gently, "How is that?" His fingers probed further.

Suddenly, roughly, Flora pushed him away, wriggling herself upright in the same movement. Her hand went, without conscious intent, to the knife hanging around her neck; she pulled it out and held it in front of her face.

Honey jerked back, eyes wide. Flora realized that the blade was still folded into the handle, and cursed herself. But her face was murderous enough.

After a second, he attempted a laugh.

"This is perfectly normal, Flora! This is what doctors do. We have to examine our patients if we are to find out what ails them. Down there is where the appendix is located. Did I hurt you?"

She looked down. He tried to laugh again, but didn't, quite.

"Well, it doesn't seem to be the appendix. Put that . . . weapon away, like a good girl. I am sure it was something you ate, and no wonder. Perhaps you should avoid the pemmican for a few days; it really is vile stuff. Although seal meat is no better."

Flora covered herself and pulled up her knees as a barrier between them. Her heart was hammering and her face was hot. Honey's face was flushed too, though whether with shame or anger, she had no idea.

"You understand, Flora? I was carrying out a perfectly normal examination. Heavens, you're a child! You cannot think . . ."

He drew back, shaking his head at the very idea.

"Flora, say that you understand what I'm saying."

"I understand," she mumbled.

"We're friends, are we not?"

She nodded, ashamed of herself. What was wrong with her that she reacted in this silly way to poor, harmless Dr. Honey?

"Well then . . . No harm done?"

She nodded and muttered, "I'm sorry."

Honey laughed, relieved. "At least the blade was sheathed!"

Flora laughed too, hating herself.

"So—ha, ha—when you speak to your father, you won't tell him . . . ?"

If he hadn't said that, Flora would ever afterward have believed she was in the wrong. But again that knell of alarm struck her, and she knew that he was begging, that he felt ashamed.

"No, of course not," she said.

Her face was a stone. She was ashamed too; it was her fault, clearly. She was bad, to make him do that. Could he tell that she had liked it?

Late that night, a storm blew up. Flora brooded in her bunk. No one had previously made her feel her femininity as such a burden and a curse. She felt betrayed, but the person she was most angry with was herself. She must have behaved with Honey in such a way as to invite what he did. And the boys . . . She unfolded her knife and pressed the tip against the skin of her inner arm. A bead of blood appeared, fascinating and frightening her.

Winds battered them from the north; the temperature dropped until the ice cracked like pistols and rang like bells. The wind howled up and down the scale; the frozen rigging clattered; ice fell to the deck with a musical clinking and susurrating; the timbers creaked; the ice growled, and groaned, and screeched. The sailors were kept busy hammering ice off the timbers and rigging, but just as quickly it built up again; every morning the ship was encrusted; it threatened to engulf them. The rest of the time they joked and sang and, sometimes, prayed. It did not occur to Flora to be afraid. She was with her father, the great Captain Mackie, in the *Vega*, the finest ship out of Dundee, or anywhere. When the storm blew itself out and the moon shone for the first time in days, everything was softened and blurred with snowdrift. It was peaceful, but the *Symmetry* had gone.

Flora had to wait several hours before the search parties returned. Not a single member of the *Symmetry*'s crew had been lost. The slowness of the ship's destruction meant they had been able to abandon ship and take most of their belongings with them. The crew was split among the remaining ships; eight came to the *Vega*.

It lightened the atmosphere to have fresh blood. Petty quarrels were forgotten. Dr. Honey was kept busy with frostbites and crush injuries. Flora spent more time with Robert Avas or reading. Captain Mackie made a visit to the Eskimo village and stayed away for two nights. When he came back, he told Flora he had something funny to tell her, but she could see he felt awkward. He said they had been asking for her—or rather, asking after Mackie's *erneq*, which he'd thought was the word for *child*, in the way that *qatannguh* was the word for both *brother* and *sister*. But it turned out that *erneq* meant only *son*, and so everyone thought—ha, ha!—Flora was a boy! There had been much laughter when he explained she was a girl, especially from Tateraq and Aniguin.

"I'm sorry, Flora. Not that you look like a boy, not at all . . . but it's difficult for them. They've never seen a white female before. And they said you were so good at spear-throwing—quite as good as any boy! Don't be so down in the mouth. When you think how many clothes we all wear—why, all they've ever seen of you is a bit of your face."

Flora was confused. She supposed it made the incident with Tateraq and Aniguin less alarming, but she didn't know whether to be insulted that they had thought she was a boy, or flattered.

For the whalers, too, it was easy to get hold of the wrong end of the stick. Relationships were particularly confusing. Flora came to understand that there were only perhaps two hundred people in the area of Smith Sound. Everyone was related or knew each other well. The population of northwest Greenland was roughly the same as that of an average Scottish street. And with their elastic comprehension of family ties—swapped wives, adopted children, half brothers and sisters—there was a dense web of interconnectedness. It was no wonder her friends rarely said "I" do this or that, but always "we" do this, or "the Inuit" do that.

Flora picked up the language quickly. She learned that Aniguin was adopted, his parents both dead. He told Flora he would have died if Apilah and Simiak hadn't taken him in. He became her closest friend.

"You're unhappy to go away from us," he said, when the ice started to break up in spring. "You must not be. You will come back. The spirits told me this."

Aniguin claimed to hear voices, and to commune with unseen beings. She thought it was something he affected to make himself more important. She understood why he would do this.

"We're friends, Fellora."

"Best friends, Aniguin. I will come back, I promise."

"Tateraq says he is going to marry you, but you won't, will you?" He looked anxiously at her.

"No, I won't marry him. Never!" Flora laughed, aghast at the thought.

"He has everything and I have nothing. It's always like this. Look, you see those two . . . ?"

Between his outspread fingers, Flora saw two stars, side by side—the ones he called the Doorway, and she, Gemini.

"They are we."

She was enchanted. The thought of being a star made her dizzy.

"You will come back, Fellora, and then we will marry. I am going to be a great *angekok*!"

He grasped a handful of sky as he said this, as if to demonstrate his power, but he laughed, and Flora laughed too.

A week after they turned for home, the *Vega*'s hold stuffed with oil and bone, there was a rent in the fog to the west, and they saw a ship. It was not one of the Scottish fleet. Captain Mackie stared through his glass until tears ran down his face. It was American, he said.

"A whaler?"

"It doesn't look like one."

There was something in his voice that was unusual.

"What is it? Why do you make that face?"

Flora had seen much this last year; perhaps he had forgotten about protecting her sensibilities. She had survived the north, had thrived; she had made friends and laughed—something he did not remember seeing at home. So he told her what he thought: there was a party of American soldiers who had been sent to live far to the north, on Ellesmere Land, the land divided from Greenland by the Davis Strait, and which Flora had occasionally seen on clear days. The men had been gone over two years and had not been heard of since. The ship was probably a relief ship, going to succor them . . . if it was not too late.

"What are they doing there?" asked Flora, who had not heard of men going to such remote regions for any reason other than oil, bone, and money. She could not see the point of sending soldiers somewhere where there was no one to fight.

"I think they are scientists. They measure the weather and look at the rocks. Or perhaps they are trying to go to the North Pole. Or perhaps both."

"What's at the North Pole?"

"No one knows. That's why someone has to go there, to find out. The last men who tried were with the British navy. They set off over the sea-ice in sleds, but they had to come back before they had gone far."

"Why?"

"They became ill with scurvy."

"Didn't they have lime juice?"

"I don't know. I suppose not."

"That was silly of them."

Flora studied the ghostly ship through narrowed eyes. Fog swirled around it.

"I will go to the North Pole when I am older."

Captain Mackie looked at her with a tinge of unease. Mostly— because he was unfamiliar with young girls and how they behaved—he did not worry too much about the masculine atmosphere of the ship and the effect it might have on her. He knew the *Vega* to be God-fearing and sober, and that every sailor on her respected him. But occasionally Flora would come out with something that struck him as a ridiculous thing for a female to say.

Flora glared. "You don't believe me. But you'll see."

"Perhaps the Americans have already gone there. And now they know all its secrets. One thing I can tell you—there are no whales there."

"Perhaps the Americans got scurvy too. If they've been gone for two years, mightn't they be dead?"

Privately, he thought it likely, but did not want to frighten her. "Oh, I'm sure they are alive."

"They might have eaten polar bears."

"Yes, indeed. Or seals. That is how the huskies live, after all—by eating seals."

Flora and her father peered at the shadowy vessel, its outlines blurring and fading, until it was eaten up by the fog.

Captain Mackie's fears were well founded. It was the ship that would later bring back the survivors of the Lady Franklin Bay Expedition: six starving men out of an original party of twenty-five. They had not been to the North Pole, and they made a mistake: they had not eaten polar bears or seals, like the huskies; instead, they had eaten each other.

Chapter 3

New York, 40°42' N, 74°00' W
1871–80

ADRIFT ON AN ICE FLOE. No more thrilling or improbable adventure could be invented than the actual experiences of Captain Tyson, half the crew of the *Polaris*, and the two Eskimo families in their employ, who took to the ice when the ship was crushed. They were part of the expedition led by Captain Charles Francis Hall, who lost his life before they had proceeded far on their way. In the gales that followed the ship's sinking, they lost their boats and had to exist on a rapidly diminishing ice floe as it was slowly carried south by swirling currents and icy gales. Time after time they tried to get to land but were thwarted by the weather. For six long months the party of nineteen lived off scraps of food and the occasional seal, shot by their native friends, before the ice floe was at last seen by a sealer off Newfoundland. Captain Tyson, on their rescue, said it was a miracle—and one that had come not a moment too soon. Incredibly, not a single life—not even those of the Eskimo children—was lost.

New York Examiner, October 12, 1874

Jakob de Beyn's fascination with ice stemmed from childhood. At the age of ten, he read news reports of the disastrous *Polaris* expedition with an excitement that seized him by the throat. The stories were wilder and more incredible than any fiction; they had the starkness of truth, and the thrill of proximity: the wharves from which these men had set sail were almost within sight. He began reading accounts of previous Arctic explorers: from Kane, Hayes, and the ultimately unfortunate Hall, he progressed back in time to McClintock, Parry, Scoresby. Not every explorer got into a pickle. The British record had been, for a long time, quite respectable, although it came crashing down with the Franklin disaster. The climate and conditions were challenging, but, even as a boy, he suspected that Franklin, Tyson et al. had been wrongheaded and incompetent. He couldn't help feeling that he could do better. How an orphan growing up in genteel poverty on the Lower East Side would ever be in a position to do so was not, at this stage, clear.

Jakob never knew his mother. She had died in an epidemic that swept the country in the wake of the War of the Rebellion, when his brother Hendrik was eight, and Jakob too young to remember. His father was an uncertain memory. Arent de Beyn was a minor civil engineer who had perished working on the foundations of the New York and Brooklyn Bridge. Working in caissons on the bed of the East River led to several cases of nitrogen poisoning; many of the construction crew suffered, including the chief engineer, who was paralyzed by the disease. (It was an unlucky bridge; its designer had been injured while surveying the site, and subsequently died of tetanus.) Less famously, Arent de Beyn was—the story went—crippled with pain on leaving the caisson one dark February evening and fell into the East River. He shouldn't have drowned, but it was dark and chaotic and hours passed before anyone realized he was missing. His sons did not attend the funeral.

Some time after that—after a period of being shuttled from one set of relatives to another—the boys settled with their father's cousin, a stern Lutheran they called Uncle Seppe, and his wife Grietje. The

Koppels, who had two adult daughters living upstate, were doing their duty to Arent and to God, as they saw it, but were unprepared for the demands of two young boys. They went to church for three hours every Sunday and said grace before every meal. Uncle Seppe was a great believer in stiffening the sinews, in making the mind master of the flesh. There was a slight suggestion emanating from him and his wife that he had failed in this duty in regard to his own daughters and was not going to make the same mistake again.

Jakob hated living there. They both did, but Hendrik had already developed reserves of stoicism and self-control that would always elude his younger brother. The elder by six years, he felt responsible for Jakob. Hendrik protected him, in part because he reminded Hendrik so much of their mother. The boys had one likeness of Annette de Beyn—a tintype photograph mounted on a card. Where Hendrik was fair and blue-eyed, Jakob had the dark eyes and grave expression of the woman in the picture. He seemed, to his brother, small, fey, delicate. Their mother had been the same—she had needed protection from the typhoid miasma, but his father and he had unaccountably, unforgivably, failed to provide it.

The first winter the boys lived with the Koppels was a harsh one. Snow gathered in drifts up the sides of houses, telegraph wires came down under the weight of ice. People, somewhere, it was rumored, froze to death in the street.

A main prop of Uncle Seppe's regime was that the boys had to wash in cold water every morning, as he did himself. Even in winter, they got their washing water from a barrel in the backyard, smashing the ice on the surface with the hatchet that hung on a rope. One day, Hendrik pointed out that they could fetch the water indoors the night before, where it wouldn't freeze. Uncle Seppe told him he could wash out in the yard from then on. Hendrik did so without complaint for a week, until the temperature dropped so low that the water in the barrel froze solid. One morning, he was still out in the yard when they started breakfast, eating in silence, listening to the peck of the ax on ice. He was chopping an awful lot of ice, Jakob thought;

perhaps he wanted a bath. Without a word, Hendrik brought the pail of ice inside and poured the contents onto the breakfast table in front of his uncle, right under his nose. Jakob, who knew something was up as soon as he saw his brother's face, felt a thrill of horror. He stopped chewing and held his breath. Mrs. Koppel, a sandy, nervous woman, gasped and leapt to her feet.

"What are you doing, wicked boy! Clean that up right away!"

"You try washing in that," Hendrik said evenly. He was twelve.

Mrs. Koppel looked at her husband. Uncle Seppe continued to eat bread and cheese, refusing to meet Hendrik's eye. There was a tumultuous silence for about a minute, marred only by the sound of Uncle Seppe swallowing, a shard of ice falling off the table, and, Jakob was certain, his own frantically beating heart. The pieces of ice—on the tablecloth, on the plates, in the butter dish—began to gleam in the warmth of the kitchen. Mrs. Koppel gave way first—she uttered an inarticulate noise and started to sweep the ice into a saucepan, knocking several pieces onto the floor, where they skittered and span into corners. Jakob, still biddable at six, dived under the table to help pick them up, but kept a particularly satisfying piece for himself: chunky, clear, with an inner universe of planes and bubbles, and sharp, curved edges like a prehistoric tool. He slipped it into his pocket and, after breakfast, while Hendrik was being walloped in the front room, he sat in their bedroom and turned it in his hands, rubbing the sharp edges smooth, studying it from every angle. He entered into that perfect, crystalline universe, where the yells from downstairs could not penetrate, until his hands were pink and frozen, and he was stricken to find that there was nothing left.

He wasn't aware of that moment being the beginning of his love for ice, but perhaps it was. It was something so strange, so other, but associated with escape, with distraction from fear, a panacea against the struggles of life. And yet you couldn't keep hold of it. The more he caressed and loved it, the faster it disappeared.

Jakob had known about ice, but he hadn't really understood it before that morning; hadn't appreciated its particular, fugitive allure. He would later remember his anguish as the shard dwindled in his hands, and the return of dreary, quotidian anxiety—there was shouting from downstairs, the tension of his brother's mutinous hatred.

Jakob didn't realize, then or later, that Hendrik's protest had been on his behalf; Hendrik wanted to protect his little brother from the ice—an instinct that was both misplaced and, in the long run, utterly inadequate against its power.

Throughout childhood, Jakob suffered from nightmares in which he was drowning. Usually, the first he knew about it was when Hendrik—they shared a bed—shook him awake, simultaneously reassuring him and whispering fiercely to shut up. The first time Jakob remembered this happening, there had been a mumbling from the other side of the wall, and then Uncle Seppe opened the bedroom door and peered in, holding a candle. He didn't step over the threshold, and kept one hand on the doorjamb, securing his line of escape.

"*Wat is al dat lawaai?*" he demanded.

"Jakob had a nightmare," said Hendrik. "He's all right now."

He had his arm around his brother, shielding him. Uncle Seppe looked wary, but finally grunted and closed the door. Neither he nor Aunt Grietje ever asked Jakob about the nightmares, nor did he or his wife ever come to the boys' door again, although the broken nights went on for years. Eventually, Jakob learned to wake himself. He could—it seemed to him—feel the nightmare coming, and could struggle to the surface, gasping for breath, before Hendrik woke up.

He knew the dreams were caused by their father's death. When he was older, he would walk to the shore of the East River and imagine what it would be like to fall into that turbid water. He stared at the massive towers of the bridge, growing with extraordinary slowness, wondering from where he had fallen into the river, for how long he had believed he would be rescued. There must have been people around. They must have had equipment. There must have been chances to fish him out, and yet they hadn't. It was dark, of course, a freezing winter evening . . . Maybe, Jakob told himself, his father wasn't conscious for very long; maybe he never realized that this stupid blunder was the end. Part of him believed that, if he did this imagining well enough, the nightmares would stop. Experience did not bear him out. Sometimes they went away for a while, but they always came back, surprising him with macabre, novel twists—now there were faces down there, or hands that gripped his ankles; on other occasions he would find himself paralyzed or blind.

Chapter 4

New York, 40°42' N, 74°00' W
1882–3

TRAGIC DEATHS ON THE SIBERIAN TUNDRA
LOSS OF COMMANDER DE LONG CONFIRMED

Having lost their ship, the USS *Jeannette*, to the ice after drifting help-lessly for two years, the party led by Commander de Long set off in three small boats for the nearest land—the New Siberian Islands. One boat was lost without trace. Of the remaining two, Engineer Melville's boat made it to shore and found a native settlement. But Commander de Long's boat landed on the uninhabited side of the Lena delta. The men set off in search of habitation, but one by one they collapsed and died of starvation and exposure. Only two men survived to tell the tale.

Brooklyn Daily Eagle, April 17, 1883

At seventeen, when the bridge was still incomplete, Jakob was accepted to study natural philosophy at City College. He left Uncle

Seppe's in an atmosphere of mutual relief and moved to Little Germany, where Hendrik and his wife, Bettina, had a tiny spare room in their apartment. Hendrik had moved out when he got his first job, and lost little time in securing a wife with her own apartment and a small stash of savings. He had two ambitions—that he would make money, and that his younger brother would rise up from their humble beginnings and bestow honor on the family name. Hendrik and Bettina were adamant that Jakob would live with them, and that he would have the time to complete his studies. By then, Hendrik had been working for years in a butcher's shop, and had now, with Bettina's help, started his own business. He had good sense and unflagging energy. His wife supported him; some years older than Hendrik, and much wider, Bettina was a German widow with a ten-year-old son. She treated Jakob like another child. She was the kindest person Jakob had ever met—so much so that occasionally he distrusted it. Surely it couldn't be real? No one could be so willing, helpful, cheerful? But she was. He was determined not to let them down.

Hendrik talked of his brother's brilliant future, but Jakob was more pragmatic; he imagined becoming a surveyor for a mining company—perhaps in the Rockies or Alaska—and knew that would make him content. He envisaged mountains he had never seen, skies untainted by smog. Endless views that contained not a single human being. He gravitated toward geology, attracted both by the opportunities it offered for travel and because it had, in its imperceptible, inexorable way, changed the world.

At City, Jakob became Jake. Within its walls, this happened a lot: names lost their edges and curlicues, become short and blunt. Alessandro became Al; Piotrek, Pete; Avner, Andy. The owners of these names were proud of their nationalities, but they did not want to be judged by them. In any case, they didn't have time for anything longer. Everything was moving fast: their education, the society around them, the relentless spread of the city. Everything was galloping. Even friendships were formed quickly.

Jakob was walking to a lecture one day when a large figure fell into step beside him.

"Hi. Saw you in Ledbury's physics class."

"Oh yeah?"

"My name's Urbino. Look—I need a favor. I'm going to miss the lecture today—gotta have a tooth out. Do you think I could crib off you?"

Jakob had to look up at the man next to him. He was well over six foot and heavily built. A big, soft face with brown eyes. A slightly anxious expression.

"Sure. I'm de Beyn."

"Oh . . . Thought you were Italian."

"No."

"Jewish? That's okay with me."

"No. Give up?"

"Mmn . . . French?"

"No." Jakob was grinning now. "Well, my mother was part French. Rest is Dutch."

"No kidding. Frank Urbino. Majoring in medicine. Call me Frank."

They shook hands.

"Jakob . . . Jake. Geology."

"You don't look Dutch."

"You don't look Italian. Is that why you asked me?"

Frank shrugged. "Actually, I asked you because you're one of the three people who don't fall asleep when Ledbury goes on about wave formation."

"And the other two told you to take a hike."

Frank came from a large family in the green reaches of uptown. He had three sisters and a brother. Anna, his closest sibling, was two years older than Frank. The eldest, Angela, was recently married, and Johnny was still at school. The other sister, Clara, worked in a store on Third Avenue, and was, for this (and, Frank hinted darkly, other reasons), considered fast. Jakob was avid to meet her, but on the first couple of Sundays that he was invited to lunch with the family, she was, tantalizingly, elsewhere.

Frank was aware, as everyone is, that when a young man brings a friend home with him, he is regarded by any eligible sisters, and by his mother, as a potential suitor. The only person not aware of this was Jakob. When he was introduced to Anna, because she was shy and awkward, he made an effort to involve her in conversation. She was also—it didn't entirely escape his notice—attractive in a quiet, serious way. In fact, they looked rather alike, thin and dark-eyed, with an expression, in repose, that suggested an intense gravity. Angela remarked on the likeness.

"You know, Mr. de Beyn, it is you and Anna who should be brother and sister, not she and Frank. Don't you think?" She looked around the table, not noticing, or affecting not to notice, Anna stiffen and look down at her plate. "Frank is such a great lump."

"Yes, you and I are like peas in a pod," Frank said, with a pleasant smile.

Angela opened her mouth in feigned outrage. As she was both very pretty and extremely good-natured, she could stand any amount of teasing.

"Angie's an idiot. We can't understand how she persuaded her poor husband to marry her," said Johnny. There was laughter and the conversation moved on, but Anna did not recover her equanimity. After lunch, Jakob glanced over to see her quietly leaving the room.

It was a mystery to Jakob whenever a woman seemed to like him. He was neither tall nor well-built, being of average height and thin as a reed. When he looked in the mirror, he saw a face that did not seem to him manly enough; in fact, it struck him as more clownish than anything else—large brown eyes, strongly marked brows, a beakish, bumpy nose, and a rather feminine mouth that smiled too often. His hair was hopelessly wavy and untamable. His cheeks creased when he smiled. Worst of all, he was eighteen when he discovered the first white hairs sprouting at his temples. He thought his face looked untidy, as if someone had forgotten to finish it. On the plus side—he was at an age where he worried endlessly about his personal balance sheet of attractions and deficits—he found it easy to make people laugh (little wit was required for this), he had a rich man's teeth, and his untidy smile was contagious. As a result, he was misunderstood. People thought that as he was talkative and humorous he must be gregarious and lighthearted, whereas really he was neither; sociability was a shield that obscured and protected his inner self. He had a wide circle of acquaintances, but Frank was his only close friend.

The next time Jakob was invited to lunch with the Urbinos, the door was opened by an unfamiliar young woman. She looked Jakob up and down—he was suddenly conscious of the unfashionable cut of his trousers and the cheapness of his jacket—before extending her hand.

"You must be Mr. de Beyn. I'm Clara."

Clara seemed like a creature from another, more favored, realm: perfectly groomed, confident, witty. Surely it was art that made her lashes so dark and her lips so red? A few weeks previously, he would have been overawed by her scrutiny, but something momentous had happened since his last visit. He had not told Frank of this—had not told anyone.

One evening, his sister-in-law asked Jakob to return a fish kettle to its owner: a neighbor who lived two blocks away. The apartment door was opened by a drably dressed middle-aged woman. Jakob knew nothing about her, other than that her husband was a taxidermist. Mrs. Gertler had an intelligent face, tired eyes, and fair hair looped into an old-fashioned bun. She seemed old to Jakob, even older than his sister-in-law. She invited him in and offered him a glass of beer. They sat in the kitchen of the apartment, which seemed otherwise empty. Mrs. Gertler asked him about his studies. He was flattered by her interest. When he finished the beer, he stood up and smiled.

"I shouldn't keep you any longer," he said.

"It's no trouble," she said. "Wait a moment, I need to give you something." She walked past him, and her arm brushed against his sleeve, although there was ample room for her to pass. It was so clearly unnecessary, he wondered that she should be so clumsy. His arm tingled.

"I told Mrs. de Beyn I would lend her this." She was holding a book of some sort, but she didn't hold it out to him. "Perhaps, when she has finished with it, you could bring it back."

She had a beautiful voice, low in tone and husky. Her accent was slight but noticeable. She held out the book. Jakob took it. She didn't let go.

How it happened, Jakob afterward could not remember. One minute they were standing in front of each other and he was looking down at the book, and at her hand, so close to his; the next, her body was against his and her lips were kissing his unbelieving mouth. In his mind, he had not moved a single muscle, and yet he found his arms were wrapped around her shoulders, and his hips, after the first few paralyzed seconds, were pushing eagerly into her. It seemed entirely clear what should be done. Then there was a noise from the hall outside and they sprang apart. He was horrified; he didn't dare look her in the eye, wondering if, despite the total lack of premeditation, it was his fault and an apology was required.

"Thursday," she said, slightly out of breath, and slowly wiped her wet mouth with the back of her hand. "It would be good if you could bring it back Thursday. Seven o'clock."

Jakob nodded, mesmerized by the suggestive gleam of saliva—*his* saliva—on her lip. He was speechless, dizzy, incapable of linear thought. She almost pushed him out of the apartment. Their eyes met briefly, affirmatively, before the door closed between them. Fortunately, the hall was empty and dark, and he stood in the shadows for a minute after she had closed the door. The book was there in his hand—recipes, in German. His heart was racing, blood thundered around his body like a river in spate, making his skin so tight he thought he would burst. There was a strange taste in his throat. He was ludicrously excited, but another, clearer, part of what he felt was fear, a conviction that something terrible had narrowly been avoided, and was bound to happen if he gave in to the demands of his body. That was what he had been taught to think. Thinking about sex—dreaming about it, fantasizing about it—was one thing, actually *doing* it . . . that was quite another. Shaken, he took a long walk before going home.

In the days and nights that passed before Thursday evening arrived, Jakob found himself thinking often of Uncle Seppe. He felt that his fear came from Uncle Seppe, and he was determined to stare at it until it withered away. He did not believe in hellfire, or even, he thought, much, in God, so he was not afraid of damnation. To be afraid of wantonness in itself was unscientific—a mere superstition. He had an inculcated fear of disease, but that did not seem a serious risk; Mrs. Gertler was not a woman of the town, and she looked as healthy as anyone. Besides, he could and would take proper precautions; he walked miles out of their district to buy sheaths and even practiced using them—a business that both repelled and amused him. Aware of his inexperience, he consulted tomes in the medical library (which were not helpful). In sex, as in everything he undertook, he was nothing if not diligent.

He indulged in endless fantasies. Mrs. Gertler had been transformed from one of the nondescript older women who lived in the neighborhood into a particular, perfectly desirable being, simply because she desired him. He dwelled at length on what he could remember of her face: an expression of intelligent melancholy; hazel eyes with brown shadows beneath—hinting at sensually sleepless nights; a soft, downturned mouth that gave her a look, not of sullenness but of a great, sad understanding. He realized how attractive she was, and had always been. Her figure was good, as far as he could tell from her dress and from those brief, incendiary moments when she had pressed it against him. His imagination went wild at this point, but having scant knowledge or past experience to go on, failed to create anything satisfactory, and petered out, inconclusive, in a lack of concrete detail.

Having persuaded himself he was not afraid, Jakob could not explain why he was trembling from the moment he approached her door. What if she had changed her mind, or denied everything? He had the book she had given him as his excuse. He prepared himself for the worst, as well as the best of outcomes. But she opened the door without surprise and stood aside to let him enter. He saw that there was something different about her: she was—his heart, and everything else, leapt—clothed in a long, oriental-style wrap. He thrust the book out to her and said hello—hating how stupid his voice sounded; she took it with a slight, knowing smile. Jakob felt himself swallow with a dry throat, but she stepped close to him, put one hand on his chest, and the other went up to the back of his head and guided his face down to meet hers. While they kissed, she began to undo the buttons on his shirt.

"Wait," he said, and held her face away from his with both hands. "Wait—what's your name?"

"Cora; it's Cora," she whispered fiercely.

Jakob felt he should say something, but the fact of her tongue in his mouth seemed to obviate the need to think of an appropriate response. And then, and then . . . she pulled apart her wrap, and the singularity of her rendered his imagination null.

"So, Mr. de Beyn," said Frank's father, over lunch, two weeks later, "have you decided what is to be your special study?"

"Yes, sir. Geology."

"And what do you hope to do with that?"

"I want to travel. I want to go places where no one has been before."

Mr. Urbino senior made a considering noise. Frank looked at Jakob. He had not expressed this precise wish before.

"An explorer?" This from Clara, sounding interested.

"Well, perhaps. But there is so much to be done, surveying this country, and it offers opportunities to go to the wildest places—that is what I want to do."

"New York is not wild enough for you?" Clara had a teasing smile, but her manner bordered on aggressive.

Jakob was suddenly aware that all eyes were on him. He felt that he was exposing too much of himself.

"It's not that New York is not enough; it's . . . too much. Too many people. I'd prefer somewhere quieter."

"You don't like people?" asked Clara.

Smiling, knowing he was being teased, Jakob shook his head.

Anna was looking at him. "I don't like people either," she said, and stared at Clara.

"Well, not a million of them," said Jakob. "I mean, I'm fine with up to . . . ten."

"What a relief," said Clara. "We're all right, then."

Johnny said, "But Clara is equivalent to at least five normal people, with how much noise she makes."

After lunch, as it was such a nice day, they went outside. Frank was the first friend Jakob had known who had a backyard garden. Mr. Urbino smoked a cigarette—as did Clara, despite her parents' stares of disapproval. Jakob turned to Anna, who was tearing the heads off some flowers.

"Why are you doing that?"

She looked around at him. The movements of her hands were sharp.

"Picking the spent heads off stops them from setting seed, so they will have more flowers."

"I suppose I should have known that, as a scientist."

"You're a geologist."

"Yes, but we supposedly apply our observational powers to the natural world in all its forms. Not very successfully, perhaps." He laughed, and was encouraged to see an answering smile. "Although, in my defense, even had I known about the seeds, I could not simply assume that was why you were pulling their heads off. You might have been someone who hated flowers."

She looked at him with a spark of animation in her dark eyes.

"I might. Or someone who loved them. It looks nicer now, doesn't it?" She trailed her hand over the bush, sending the flowers springing to and fro, and dropped the spent ones on the soil beneath.

Jakob said, "Do you ever think of leaving New York and getting away from all those people?"

"I would love to travel. But I don't suppose I will get the opportunity."

Her voice flattened, and the spark went out of her eyes. He was aware that, when she wasn't being sarcastic, Anna seemed miserable, and he felt a vague distress on her behalf. This was not a particularly generous feeling; in his newfound smugness, he had a general, more or less selfish desire that no one in his vicinity should be unhappy.

"You could study. That gives you opportunities. There is the Normal College, for one," said Jakob. He knew of the Normal School for Females because City students often hovered in a predatory fashion around its premises.

"I don't think I could teach. I want . . . I don't know." Anna stared dully at the ground. Jakob, for once, was lost for words. Then Clara was beside him with her cigarette case.

"Do you?" It was a challenge, not an invitation, and although he had never smoked before, he held out his hand to take one.

"Thanks."

He was aware that Anna had started to speak, then stopped.

Clara held a match, cupped in her fingers. He sucked at the flame carefully, determined not to cough. Anna walked away. He looked around, puzzled by her behavior, then mentally shrugged it off. For some reason, he wanted to impress Clara with his newfound sophistication, the confidence that had grown in him because he knew he was desired and must, therefore, be desirable. Clara did not matter to him, except as a suitably polished mirror for his new, worldly self.

A couple of days later, Jakob was in a good humor because only one more day stood between him and his next appointment with Cora. He was shocked when Frank burst out, in a way that suggested something long pent up, "I honestly didn't think you would have flirted with Clara like that, on Sunday. I told you what she was like!"

Jakob was so stunned he stopped walking—they were on their way to lunch. "I didn't flirt with her! I mean, I didn't think I did."

He looked at his best friend, anxious. Frank looked distinctly unhappy.

"It's not that . . . I mean, damn it . . ."

"I'm sorry. I really had no thought of doing anything of the sort. I thought I treated everyone in your family the same. Did she *say* I flirted with her?"

Frank sighed. "I don't know. I haven't spoken with her."

Jakob was at a loss.

"It was thought—well . . . maybe you didn't notice this *either*"—a slight but definite barb—"I think Anna has got it into her head that she likes you, and she was upset, after Sunday, that you didn't talk to her . . . or something."

Jakob was silent for a moment. "I didn't have that impression. I'm sorry if I said anything that, could have, um . . ."

Unfamiliar with the language of emotional nuance, he floundered. He had met so few girls of their sort that he did not know what level of friendliness was normal, or standoffish, or familiar.

Frank sighed again. "Perhaps you didn't. It seems that Anna was upset. She's sensitive, you see. More than the rest of us. And Clara—Clara always gets all the attention. It's always been like that, and, you know . . ." He forced a laugh. "Families!"

Jakob couldn't help but be flattered that any of the Urbino girls would think of him in that way, even Anna, who was, candidly speaking, the least prepossessing. They queued at the lunch counter and ordered grilled cheese and soup.

"I don't know, Jake; forget it. Unless . . . I mean, do you like her—Anna?" Frank was awkward. "I don't want to interfere." Although he obviously did. "You know, it would be okay with me if you . . ."

"Frank, on my honor, I'm not interested in any of your sisters—in that way. I mean, they're very nice, but . . . I can't get involved with anyone. I won't be in a position to get married for years, if ever."

"Gracious, no one's talking about marriage yet!"

"Well, in any case, I'm not looking for . . . that, either."

Frank watched him.

"Oh my God . . . You have a little girl!"

Jakob nearly choked. "No!" The absurdity of calling Cora Gertler a "little girl" made him smile. What should he call her? His mistress? His lover? Such words were unsayable in daylight, in a diner, with a spotted mirror reflecting their distorted selves. Unsayable to Frank. He muttered, "I don't."

Frank stared at him. Was there something in his face giving him away?

"I *knew* there was something going on. When were you going to tell me?"

Jakob shook his head, but couldn't stop himself from smiling.

"Aren't we friends?"

"Of course."

"Well then!"

"Look, there are some things I just can't tell you."

"You've . . . You *have*, haven't you? God damn!"

"It's . . . you mustn't say anything to anyone, Frank. Promise me? You see, she's married."

He looked at Frank and never forgot his face at that moment; it so purely expressed his shock, his envy, and his judgment.

Jakob's experience of the Gertlers' apartment was limited to the hours between seven and ten on Thursday evenings, long after the sun had sunk below the roofline opposite, so he knew it as a dim, twilit place. It smelled of wood polish, sauerkraut, and a sweet, limey scent that Jakob later realized was Mr. Gertler's hair pomade. On Thursdays, Cora's husband went to his social club—that was all Jakob knew about him. Cora did not discuss him, either to make excuses for her own behavior, or to complain about her husband's; Jakob knew nothing of their marriage and did not ask.

Cora never made any claim on Jakob's feelings, nor did she express any of her own, beyond teaching him, without embarrassment, how to please her, and pleasing him in ways he had never even dreamt of. He was an enthusiastic pupil, and if his lovemaking sometimes had an element of experimentation about it, it was a happy experiment. He tried things and observed how she—or he—responded. He asked questions.

"God," she said, out of breath, when he had gotten her to change position for the third time. "Are you taking notes?"

"I don't need to take notes," he said, smiling up at her from his supine position. "I just want to know which feels best, this way or . . ."

For answer, she reached one hand down to grasp his penis and guide it into her; the other she placed firmly over his mouth.

Jakob was in heaven. At times he believed himself in love with her, at others he told himself they had nothing in common outside her bedroom. He was deeply attached to her, and she seemed fond of him. But she was, from beginning to end, a mystery he couldn't fathom. She was sharp-tongued, often sarcastic. He had never met anyone so cynical, and when he chided her for it, she laughed, and cited the difference in their ages.

He felt he knew her body better than his own, had mapped every inch of her skin, from the roots of her hair to the thin, shiny skin of her instep. She was a whole country, a continent with many types of contour and landscape that he never tired of exploring. He learned the subtle, secret architecture of labia and clitoris, amazed and thrilled to find her pleasure as intense as his own. Her breasts were a wonder to him: soft and pendulous, with large brown nipples he would take in his mouth, caressing them with his tongue as they hardened and wrinkled. She seemed to take as much delight in his body as he did in hers, in his softening and hardening flesh; she would lick and suck him, and dig her nails into his buttocks as he trembled with the effort of holding back his excitement.

She teased him. "You want to do that again? But we just did that. Always the same thing—how boring, no?"

He grinned and shook his head, and nuzzled his lips down the mysterious silvery tracks on the side of her breast, paths only visible in certain angles of light.

"You don't mind them?"

"Mind?" Jakob was astonished. "Why would I mind?"

"You don't know what they are, do you?"

Jakob admitted he didn't.

"Young girls don't have them. They are . . ." Unusually, she was at a loss for the English word. "*Dehnungsstreifen* . . . Strain . . . stripes—from being a mother. Mother scars."

He knew she had had two children. He didn't want to think about them, didn't know where they were, how old they were, even if they were alive. He didn't dislike anything that revealed the history of her body, other than when she reminded him of the gulf of life that divided them.

Around ten minutes to ten—always—she stroked his back with light fingers, as though regretting the necessity.

"Time to go, *Liebling.*"

He would protest sleepily, winding himself more tightly around her body, kissing and caressing her, as if to imprint the sensation on his hands and mouth for the coming week. He wriggled on top of her, weighing her down.

"I want to stay here. I want to wake up with you."

"Ha. You're sweet. Now get up." Here, she would slap his rump, or pinch him, no longer gentle. "Or there will be"—this was one of her favorite words, used in all sorts of contexts, with relish—"a bloodbath."

Chapter 5

New York, 40°42' N, 74°00' W
Spring 1883

One lunch, toward the end of April, Frank looked up from his paper.

"Hey, it's finally opening. There's going to be a firework display. And balloonists. Should be something to see."

The New York and Brooklyn Bridge, which had been growing with infinite slowness throughout their conscious lives, was complete.

Jakob agreed, without much enthusiasm, to go and watch the festivities. He was even less enthusiastic when he found out that May 24 was to fall on a Thursday. Frank knew that his friend spent Thursday evenings with the person he persisted in referring to, with a coyness that did not quite disguise his disapproval, as Jakob's "little girl." But the occasion felt like a test of their friendship. The next time he saw Cora, Jakob mentioned it, with a show of regret, before they undressed.

"Oh, the bloody bridge. My husband is going to take me. It's going to be the biggest firework display in history, they say. It's a Thursday? Ah, well . . ." She kissed him on the nose. "That's too bad."

Annoyed that she regarded the loss of his company with so little regret, Jakob took her in his arms and muttered into her ear, "Can I see you on another day, then? I'm not sure I can go without you for so long."

"No other days. It is not possible." She had said this before, and betrayed a hint of impatience at having to repeat herself.

"I wish I could take you," Jakob said sulkily.

"Silly. How could that be?" But she saw the look on his face, and decided, perhaps, to humor him. "I like very much that you come here, *Schatz*. But this is the way it has to be . . . yes?"

She had unbuttoned his fly and was now cradling his scrotum in her hand, two fingers paddling the excruciating area behind it. Jakob closed his eyes and held his breath, his petulance withering in the heat of a force majeure.

"Yes, *Liebling*?" asked Cora, caressingly. "What did you say?"

"Yes . . . yes," said Jakob in desperation, although he could no longer remember what they were talking about.

He had never told Frank the cause of his father's death. He suffered from the nightmares less frequently now, but occasionally, still, he would find himself awake in his tiny room, sweating, heart pounding with a vague horror. Shortly after that conversation about the bridge, he had the nightmare again. He told himself that it would be a good thing to go and look at the bridge, see it for the technical miracle it undoubtedly was. Twenty-seven men died during its construction. Stone and steel marvels exacted their toll in lives; his father was one of many. He didn't know if that helped or not.

On the evening of the opening, Frank and he were part of the mass of people crammed into the waterside streets and parks. Balconies and rooftops were black with onlookers. Jakob caught the excitement in the air; from the bank where they stood, the bridge was so massive, yet so graceful, soaring away to the far shore, the taut cables forming a loom of extraordinary intricacy and perfection. In the crush, fragments of conversation struck their ears like hail rattling a window: a woman saying, "They put on special trains from Philadelphia . . ." A man gesticulating wildly, speaking rapidly in a language that might have been Polish. Someone saying that the governor had been the first person to cross the bridge. Or perhaps it was the president . . . Jakob and Frank exchanged glances, and grinned.

There was cannon fire, and the whine of a military band was occasionally audible through the rumble of talk. When the fireworks started, the crush at the waterside became worse and they decided to find something to eat. Jakob was desperate to relieve himself and was shy of doing it in the street. They fought their way back from the river and headed for a beer cellar. Frank kept half an eye out for his sister, Clara, who had said she was going to watch the festivities with friends. It was partly the thought of her presence somewhere that stopped Jakob unbuttoning his fly in the street like everyone else.

Around eleven, Frank and Jakob left the beer cellar and began to head back to the bridge, which was due to open to the public at midnight. In the stream of people—now heading both to and from the river—in light spilling from a lit doorway, he saw a face that, even before he consciously recognized it, caused a strange clutch somewhere in his solar plexus. It was Cora, walking with a heavy, middle-aged man. Her face was turned toward Jakob; she wore a brown coat and hat, and seemed older and more alien than the woman he had come to know and had assumed was, in some way, his. He had never seen her dressed in street clothes (had rarely seen her dressed since that first evening) and it reopened the gulf between them.

The Gertlers were heading away from the bridge; it was past their bedtime; they were going home, as befitted people of their age, while he and Frank were going to cross the bridge, into the future. She did not notice him. He was disturbed at seeing her, for once, without a flicker of desire. How was it possible that they had anything in common? At the same time, he was jealous of the Derby-wearing Mr. Gertler. A primal resentment took hold of him and held him until they were on the bridge itself.

"What's up? You haven't heard a word, have you?"

"Sorry." Jakob gave Frank his most engaging grin. "Incredible, isn't it?"

"It's beautiful." Frank was elated.

They climbed the stairway to the wooden promenade that carried pedestrians along the middle of the bridge. The walkway shot, arrow-straight, to the Brooklyn shore, piercing the huge tower near the Manhattan side, before leaping confidently over the great span. They were surrounded by a web of steel: giant harp strings, soaring to the tops of the towers. Crowds poured onto the bridge; Jakob and Frank had to shuffle at an uncomfortably slow pace; people kept stopping to exclaim in wonder at the view.

The water seemed far below, very black. Growing from both sides, the crowd became denser. Behind them, a man yelled out for those ahead to hurry it along. Some people turned back, adding to the confusion. Jakob and Frank kept walking, but there was a disturbance up ahead. A woman cried out in alarm. The crowd was suddenly a crush. Someone screamed, and the festive atmosphere shivered and cracked. The boards beneath their feet drummed and vibrated with footsteps. Someone shouted, "It's giving way!" and screams rose all around them. Those ahead tried to run back to the shore, but those coming onto the bridge far behind kept coming. Caught in between, Jakob and Frank seemed to be in the densest part of the crush. Jakob, suddenly and icily calm, shouted, "It's not giving way. Don't run!" and was surprised at the authority in his voice.

A woman looked at him, sheer panic and entreaty on her face, and cried, "I felt it move!"

Jakob took her arm—she seemed to be alone—and said, "Don't worry; there is nothing to fear as long as we stay calm." He raised his voice again and shouted, "Everyone keep still. The bridge is sound." A few other voices were calling for calm, but the majority of the crowd were panicking, pushing to get off the bridge as fast as they could.

Frank grasped his sleeve and shouted in his ear—he had to shout, now, to be heard—"Let's keep going—there's fewer people that way." He looked around him, over the tops of heads, and yelled, "If everyone keeps walking across the bridge, there won't be a problem!" But even his powerful voice was lost.

Jakob found himself pressed up against the woman who had appealed to him. Everyone was now crushed together, and it was difficult to breathe. The wooden deck vibrated with stamping feet, although no one could move in the crush. Jakob felt himself being squeezed in a vice of flesh and bone; there were more shouts, screams; people began to collapse. In front of him, a man's face was distorted into a terrible grimace—he was screaming at the man next to him, his face twisted with fury. No words were audible. Jakob realized with a shock that he was the target of the man's fury; he had no idea why.

It was impossible to move forward or back—it was all he could do to stay on his feet. He struggled to turn his head to look for Frank. He had no more breath to talk to the red-headed woman pressed against him. At one point, a great pressure on his back caused him to lose his footing and he felt himself start to fall, but very slowly, unable to move his feet. He and the woman were both falling, he realized, and then they would be underfoot, and then . . . He felt a hard blow on the side of his head. He struggled, almost comically helpless, and at the point where he realized both feet no longer touched the ground, a painful grip on his arm pulled him steadily backward. Frank, with the advantage of his height and bulk, stood like a rock in the roiling current and heaved Jakob back onto his feet. The woman he had been holding was gone, and he called out in alarm; as far as he could tell, nobody was on the ground near him, but he couldn't see the ground amid the press of bodies. The human mass swayed back and forth; the screams went on, although, as people were starting to realize, those screaming were all right: they could breathe.

It seemed endless, although it could have been only a couple of minutes that they were jammed into that awful pressure of bodies. Frank was holding Jakob's arm, tugging him. "Climb up there," he was shouting, jerking his head toward the steel girders. Jakob nodded, and tried to swim his way through the swaying bodies, but it was impossible to move. By the time he could make progress in any direction, the pressure had eased sufficiently to allow them to walk back to the Manhattan steps. A woman was crying hysterically, slumped against the handrail, while a man comforted her. The ground was littered with the things people had dropped—umbrellas, baskets, shawls. One of Frank's sleeves was almost ripped off. Jakob had lost his hat. His right ear sang with the blow he had taken. A dozen yards away, a clot of people loosened and revealed a dark-featured man lying on the boards. A stout man squatted beside him, shouting hoarsely, "We need a doctor here! Is there a doctor?"

Frank pushed toward him, said he was a medical student, knelt beside him, and put his fingers on the wrist of the motionless man, thumbed up his eyelids. The man who had called Frank over backed off and, when Jakob looked round, had vanished into the crowd.

"What can I do?" Jakob knelt beside him. Frank shook his head, pressing his ear against the man's chest. He started to work the man's arms, pulling his elbows above his head, then pressing them down against his chest, over and over again. Next to Frank's big body, the dark-skinned man seemed the size of a child. His features, bloodied from a cheek wound, hinted at far origins: China, perhaps. There were others watching, but fewer every minute; the crowd was thinning—people were desperate to get off the bridge. And then, at some point, a fireman was beside them, and a stretcher was brought. Frank didn't cease his movements until a uniformed man demanded of him, "Who are you?" Frank said again he was a medical student. The officer's aggressive manner softened a little. He peered into the dark man's eyes and sat back on his heels.

"He's been dead some time. There's nothing you could have done."

Jakob looked down at the dead man's face. He was older than he had assumed; though his hair was thick and black, the skin was wizened around the eyes, and his jaw hung open, revealing gaps where he was missing teeth. His clothes were poor.

Frank was panting, his brow creased, and he looked as though he might weep.

"So what do we do now?" he asked the officer.

"Do?" He shrugged. "We'll take him to the hospital. You go on home."

Frank stood up, unwilling to walk away. "But his family . . ."

"You know him?"

"No."

The fireman shrugged. "We're taking them to Chambers Street. Anyone looking for someone will go there. Go home, son." Another official joined him, and together they scooped the body onto a stretcher.

There had been more casualties on the stairs, where people had tripped and fallen, and tripped others, who fell on them in their turn. The stairs were stained with blood; in the darkness, Jakob and Frank did not see this, only read about it later. Afterward, Jakob found he could picture the bloodstains in his mind, although he knew this memory to be false.

They walked away in silence. Jakob wanted to say something to comfort Frank, who strode with his head down, looking neither right nor left.

"Let's get a drink. I think we could do with one."

Frank looked at him and shoved his hands in his pockets.

"Jesus Christ!" he said viciously, shocking Jakob, who had never heard him blaspheme. "I've been robbed! My money's gone!"

"Maybe it fell out . . ." Jakob felt in his own pockets, relieved to find his money was still there.

"I thought I felt a hand in my pocket. Can you believe that? Can you fucking believe that? Fuck!"

Noise and light spilled out of a beer cellar up ahead.

"Come on, I'll buy you a drink."

They went inside. It was full of loud voices and the smell of beer; they had outpaced news of the tragedy, and everyone was still celebrating. Jakob bought beers and they stood outside the door. Frank seemed more angry than anything, and more angry about the stolen money than the crowd's panic, or the dead man.

"I hope that woman got out all right," Jakob said.

"What woman?"

"The red-haired woman. She was next to me practically the whole time, sort of clinging onto me, until you stopped me falling over—then she'd gone."

Frank gave a twisted smile.

"You had a woman clinging to you? Some people have all the luck."

Jakob laughed dutifully, although Frank sounded vicious.

"I guess anyone who wasn't lying on the bridge must have gotten off okay."

"Fleeing for her honor, probably."

Jakob couldn't think of anything else to say. The beer was sweet and warm and made him feel sick.

After a long pause, Frank said, "What if I didn't do it right—and he would have lived, if it had been someone who really knew what he was doing?"

"The fireman said he'd been dead for a while."

"He was just a fireman."

"Yeah, but . . . they must see a lot of people who've died."

"Died of fire."

Jakob felt a mad bubble of laughter rising in his chest.

Just then, a young, inebriated couple left the beer cellar, tripping over the step on the way out. The woman fell against Frank. He had to grab hold of her and heave her back to her feet. She clung to his jacket, giggling, looking up at him with great round eyes.

"My, you're a big fella," she said. Her companion apologized fulsomely, great blasts of beery breath hitting them in the face. He dragged the woman away, both of them laughing non-stop. As they staggered down the street, Frank looked sourly after them.

"She was probably trying to rob me too. Well, too late."

"Oh, come on."

Frank seemed to have difficulty swallowing his beer. Jakob didn't particularly want his own, but finished it, since he'd paid for it.

"Frank, it'll take you hours to get home. You can stay with me."

"What, in your rabbit hutch?"

"I'll sleep on the couch."

"No. Thanks. I could do with the walk."

Jakob was relieved, and ashamed of his relief. Frank simmered with a sort of rage. Before they parted, Frank said, with a twisted smile, "That woman in the beer cellar, who fell against me . . . Do you realize, that's the closest I've ever been to a woman?"

After a moment's silence, Jakob laughed, although he knew Frank wasn't joking.

People talked about the tragedy for days afterward. Anyone who had been in the vicinity was questioned endlessly. Neither Jakob nor Frank had much to say, although it got out that Frank had tried to resuscitate the dead Chinaman. This was the cause of merciless ribbing by his fellow medical students. Jakob was horrified, until he realized the morbid teasing soothed Frank more than anything else.

After a couple of days, the final death toll was announced: twelve people had lost their lives. Their names were published in the *Brooklyn Eagle*. Frank bought a copy and showed it to Jakob, his finger resting on a name that stood out from the others.

Ah Ling. A fifty-four-year-old Chinese tobacco peddler.

Jakob scanned the article. Among the dead were two children—a fifteen-year-old girl and a thirteen-year-old boy. A newly wedded bride. Those deaths seemed far sadder to him than the old tobacco peddler's.

"It says he had no family."

"So? He didn't deserve to die." Frank's voice had that aggressive edge again.

"I'm not saying he deserved it. It's all terrible . . . They're all . . ." He shook his head. He knew that nothing he could say would be the right thing.

The following Thursday was the first time Jakob felt almost indifferent to the prospect of sex. He went, but walked past Cora into the apartment, rather than seizing her as soon as the door was closed, as he usually did. Cora contemplated him with one of her more sardonic expressions.

"What is it, *Liebling*?"

He shrugged, sullen and uncomfortable. Now that he was here, he did want to make love, but he was irritated by his body's desires. He was angry and didn't know why he was angry with her.

"I heard you were on the bridge when it happened."

Cora didn't offer sympathy—he would have been surprised if she had. She must have talked to Bettina about him, which made him suddenly furious.

"Yeah . . . well." He shrugged again, aware that he was behaving like a child, and then said, although he had determined not to mention it, "I saw you that night, in the crowd."

"And you thought, Who is that old hag?"

"No!" he lied, guilty. Cora smiled.

"I saw you too."

"Oh." He paused, surprised; what did that mean? "I didn't say anything, since you were with your husband."

"No, that was quite right. Thank you." She paused, for once uncertain. "Do you want a beer?"

He shook his head.

"Was it true? They said people thought the bridge was going to collapse, and there was a stampede."

"Yes, pretty much."

Cora shook her head. "People are such idiots. As if that bridge could fall . . . Ah well, there are twelve fewer fools in the world now. They'll be spared further trouble."

Jakob glared at her, glad that she had given him a reason for his anger.

"How can you say that? You weren't there. It wasn't the people who panicked who died . . . It could have been anyone—it could have been me—would you say *I* was a fool then?" He paced across the room in a rage, aware that he was overdoing it, but unable to stop himself.

Cora watched him. "No, of course not. I'm sorry, *Schatz.*"

"Those people . . . My father died, you know, building that bridge."

"I didn't know that. How old were you?"

"Three, four . . ." This is what he believed, rather than remembered. A shadow passed over Cora's face.

"That was after your mother died?" She must also have known this from Bettina, since he had never spoken of her. "Do you want to talk about it?"

Jakob shook his head, martyred, but sat down on the edge of the chair behind him.

"Would you rather go home tonight?"

He shook his head again, and she shyly put her arms around him. He allowed her to hold him while he remained inert for as long as he could—to punish her—and then turned his face into her bosom and put his arms around her waist. He wouldn't let her lead him into the bedroom until they had made love, roughly, awkwardly, right there in the chair.

For some reason, nothing they did that evening was truly satisfying, although there was a tinge of frenzy in his desire. He thought, perhaps—this was long afterward—because he was trying to cure something in himself that could not be cured, or forget something that did not want to be forgotten.

When Jakob was in his final year of college, Hendrik received a much-forwarded letter. It was from the public asylum on Blackwell's Island.

Jakob came home one evening to find Hendrik and Bettina sitting in a tense silence at the kitchen table. The upstairs neighbors were fighting—a not uncommon occurrence.

"What's happened?" he asked, struck with a nameless dread. His first thought was that either Hendrik, or Bettina, who was pregnant, was terminally ill.

"I got a letter. It's about our father."

Jakob was instantly relieved. Once someone is dead, you are inured to further anguish.

"Apparently . . . Ha! It says he's not dead."

Jakob put both hands on the table. Even so, he swayed. "You're joking."

"No, I'm not. Here's the letter; look . . ."

"It's a joke, Hendrik." He didn't take the letter. He had an enormous desire not to read it.

"No, it isn't. He's on Blackwell's Island. It says he's been there since 1869."

Jakob made a strange, abrupt noise—it was meant to be a laugh. He shook his head. "Then it's a mistake. Someone with the same name."

Hendrik pushed the letter toward him. Reluctantly, Jakob picked it up. The letter stated that Arent de Beyn, civil engineer, born Ede, Holland, April 1832, had been committed to the public asylum after several attacks of mania, culminating in February 1869. He had attacked a fellow worker. It was thought his mania stemmed from his experiences during the War of the Rebellion. Now, the consulting doctors felt he was no longer a threat to others or himself, and was well enough to be released into the care of his relatives—if any could be found. There was no mention of the East River Bridge, or any bridge.

"No, Hendrik—our father didn't fight in the war."

Hendrik shrugged uneasily. "I don't know. I didn't know that he did . . . but he could have."

"What are you talking about? We would know!"

"Would we? Who would have told us?"

"*He* would! He would have told *you*!"

Hendrik shook his head.

Jakob was bewildered, then he laughed with a tinge of hysteria, then he got angry with Hendrik—he, being so much older, should have known the truth, should have—

"There was a funeral. Wasn't there?"

"I don't know."

"Why would they tell us he was dead?"

Hendrik shrugged. "To protect us? If they thought he was . . . incurable. Does it matter now? It couldn't have come at a worse time—we don't have room here. I don't have time, with the business, and now, with the baby . . ."

"It's all right, Henk," Bettina put her hand over his. "We'll manage."

"I can move out. I could work full-time," Jakob said, dully.

"No! You have to finish your studies. You're not moving out until you do. Don't say that again. Ever!" Hendrik stabbed his finger at Jakob. He looked demented.

Jakob read the date on the letter. It had been written nearly three months previously. Bettina looked anxiously at her husband. Hendrik was the owner of a temper that he rarely let get the better of him, but when it came, he burned with a dark flame; there was no talking to him. Recognizing this, Jakob addressed Bettina: "I suppose we'd better go and see him; see if it's actually true."

"Blackwell's Island!" Hendrik made an expression of disgust. "Don't you see what this means?"

They both had the same thought.

Bettina tugged the hand she held. "Henk, come on. I know what you're thinking. It isn't hereditary. He's just a poor old man. Sick, because of the war."

Hendrik snatched his hand away. "You don't know anything about it."

Bettina held her rejected hand, hurt, but too dignified to show it.

"I know these things can happen. If he was in the war . . . many men became sick afterward. Jake isn't thinking that, are you?"

Jakob shrugged. He appreciated her kindness and her good sense, but it didn't help. It wasn't her father in an asylum. He stared at his brother. The thought of seeing their father was so extraordinary as to be meaningless. He had only the vaguest memories of him, perhaps not even that—just a collection of things he had been told by Hendrik. The photograph on the mantelpiece made up the greater substance of this memory. He had never had a father, in effect—why should this stranger, after abandoning them to the ice baths of Uncle Seppe, be allowed to reappear and demand their attention? After bequeathing him nightmares—and how could those nightmares be real when the death that inspired them was a lie? He hadn't finished his studies. He hadn't had a chance to get started. It wasn't *fair* . . . His chest constricted with the pressure of words he could not say, Jakob walked out of the apartment.

It was a freezing night. The bellicose neighbors had fought themselves to a standstill, and, for a moment, the noise of the city dropped away. There was silence. He walked around the corner, pretended he was somewhere else. His breath smoked in front of him, hanging in the stillness. He imagined getting away, as far as possible—not just from his family and the cramped apartment, but from the city—to a place where it was always silent, where he would be so distant and unreachable that such problems dwindled to nothing. He craned his neck and looked up to where the tenement roofs framed a corridor of sky, deep and dusty with stars. A road, leading to anywhere.

PART TWO

VEGA IN LYRA

The constellation Lyra represents the lyre that
Apollo gave Orpheus, whose music captivated every
living thing. Its brightest star, Vega, was once the
pole star. In another 12,000 years, it will become
the pole star again—by which time winter will have
become summer, and summer, winter. The name
Vega derives from the Arabic for "falling."

Chapter 6

It wasn't until Flora was eighteen that her father refused to take her north again. For some time, he had been aware—as had she—that the men had changed toward her. As a child, she had been regarded with affection and humor; as a young woman, she was dangerous, unpredictable—a smoldering match in a heap of tinder. And this despite doing nothing to improve her appearance, wrapping herself in bulky clothing that concealed everything and made her look like any other young seaman, and less alluring than some. Still, she was aware of the sidelong glances, hungry looks and muttered comments, laughter erupting from conversations that died away when she approached. Even her old friends withdrew—the ones that had been fatherly, like John Inkster, and Robert Avas, still shorter, slighter, and more childish than she was. They seemed to be trying to hide something, but perversely wanted her to know—that she disturbed them, and it was her fault.

Flora was furious. She did not want to be seen as a woman before she was seen as Flora. It was as though all her friends had forgotten her—*her*, the person they had known so well—forgotten their shared pasts, her skill with the sextant, her knowledge of the stars, her ability to swallow a fish's eyeball. She felt diminished: as a young woman, she was less of a human being than she had been as a child. How could that be allowed to happen?

On their last return from Cape Farewell, Flora walked up to the quarterdeck, where Captain Mackie was snatching an observation of a pale sun seeping through cloud. Flora took out her sextant.

"There's no need, Miss Flora," said Inkster.

"I have to keep in practice," she replied.

He shot a look at her father: worried, censorious. She ignored it, adjusted her index bar. Then the threatening clouds ate the sun, and there was nothing for her to shoot. Inkster and the captain bent their heads over their workings, excluding her.

Weeks later, back home in Crichton Street, Flora burst into furious tears.

"You cannot expect me to take you north forever," said Captain Mackie, puzzled by the daughter he had raised, and slightly afraid of this passion. "After all, I will not be here forever to look after you . . ." It was brutal, but it had to be said: "You cannot follow in my footsteps as if you were a son. You will marry; you will . . ."

He could not think of anything else she would do.

"To take you north again will only harm your chances. You have to live a more normal life. Now you are grown up, you have to learn to be more regular. Meet people."

"I meet lots of people!" cried Flora.

"I mean the right kind of people, as you well know. Not sailors. You cannot marry a specksioneer, Flora, or a boat-steerer."

Annoyingly, this made her blush, but her father's eyes were lowered, fixed on his wooden blotter, and he didn't seem to notice. He rocked it to and fro with two fingers.

"I have taken you with me, Flora, perhaps selfishly, because you are all I have left and I like to have you by me. But it cannot be any longer. Perhaps I was wrong to do it. Perhaps it was not fair to you. All I want is for you to be happy."

"Don't tell me you want me to be happy, when you are making me unhappy! I think I can better decide what is fair to me!"

"No, Flora; in this, you cannot."

The argument went on in this vein for some time, then Flora capitulated. She did this by running upstairs and throwing herself on her bed, sobbing. She was humiliated by her behavior, but that did not seem important when she had lost everything that most mattered.

She was a pragmatist at heart. For weeks she kept to her room, considering her options. The University College of Dundee was on her doorstep, and, having been endowed by the generosity of a Miss Baxter, was coeducational. Her father agreed to pay for her tuition, and, after some discussion, the college waived its formal educational requirements. For the first time, Flora realized that her unusual past was capital, just like money, or beauty—it fascinated people. Since she was entering as a science student, she was exempted from a knowledge of the classics and modern languages, and, having read all the Arctic literature she could get her hands on, she decided to focus on the new science of meteorology. It was clear to her that, in the future, expeditions would go north to amass information rather than to service the declining need for oil. And since all expeditions to the Arctic were more than anything at the mercy of the weather, she would make herself its adept.

She lived quietly, going to classes, residing in Crichton Street, looked after by her old nurse Moira, while her father was at sea, but she was not left entirely alone. Word of the girl who went whaling had leaked out. It was a middle-aged writer, R. G. Whitfield, who first brought Flora to the public's attention. He was a hack with a penchant for medieval romances, but he had a nose for a story. His senses jangled when he heard about the young girl who had spent more time in the Arctic than many explorers. In his happiest stroke of invention, he dubbed her the Snow Queen, and made it his quest to meet her.

Whitfield arrived in Dundee in February. Coming from Manchester, he was prepared for the cold drizzle that greeted him, but not for the smell of a whaling port: a stench like a physical presence. Recovered enough to ask around, he was told to go to the Whalers' Parliament, an inn near the quay, where he could find out everything about whaling. For an hour, Whitfield combed the quay and its surroundings, before realizing that the Whalers' Parliament—the name enchanted him—was not the *actual* name of the inn, which was in fact called the Ship (readers would not need to know that). As he walked into the fug—dimly lit, smelly from the fire and from the exhalations of many bodies, but still dank and with an underlying, mizzling chill—he experienced a fear that his maiden of the snows, his Snow Queen, would also smell like this. His mental picture of her (auburn tresses, dark eyes, and a pliant yet rounded figure) wavered. He nearly turned around and walked back to the station.

Half an hour later, he presented his card at the house on Crichton Street and was admitted to the front parlor. He was left on his own for several minutes, relieved that in the house he seemed to have escaped, temporarily, the mugging of the Dundee atmosphere. When a young woman came in, he stood up.

"Thank you, Miss Mackie, for seeing me without notice. It is very kind of you to allow me to interrupt you."

What did he see? A strapping girl, almost as tall as he. A direct gaze of winter gray; cheekbones still freckled by her last nightless summer, and artless coils of hair, not auburn, but a disappointing mousey-brown. Not beautiful, no, but . . . not unattractive, if she made a bit of effort. She did not comport herself as young ladies are expected to. She strode into the room like a challenge: a bold, angry element that might have damaging consequences. A wild young creature. Whitfield smiled, to cover his surprise. Flora did not smile.

"What do you want?"

"Ah . . . Well! Down to business . . . Quite."

Flora stared. She did not know what to make of this whiskery, dandified southerner, either.

"I have been looking forward to meeting you, Miss Mackie. Perhaps we could . . ."

"Oh. Yes. Sit down."

As Whitfield began to explain his presence, a stout woman came in with a tray of tea. She exuded disapproval.

"All right, Murra. That will do," said Flora sharply, when the woman was about to distribute some chunks of a blackish material. Whitfield thought her manner rather rude. (And was "Murra" really a name? Could she possibly have said "Mother"? It seemed most unlikely . . .)

"Yes," he continued. "You are a unique young lady. I think unique in the whole world."

"Really?" Flora looked as though she were thinking about this for the first time. "But I only went with my father on his journeys. It's not as though I have done anything extraordinary. Captain Penny used to take his wife with him."

Whitfield had no idea who Captain Penny was, and didn't feel he was that interested.

"But a daughter—a young girl, that is. . . . How old were you when you first voyaged to the land of Boreas?"

Flora was taken aback. "I was twelve. Captain Penny used to take his son too, so it's quite regular. No one thought badly of it."

"Oh no. Not badly, I'm sure. Far from it. But what you have done *is* extraordinary, Miss Mackie. Which is why I want to write an article about you."

She laughed, an uninhibited yelp that she quickly moderated, putting her hand in front of her mouth.

"As you may know, people have long been fascinated by the north—the snows, the extremities of cold and darkness, the incredible dangers of the whale fishery, the ice mountains . . . Leviathan himself! And, of course, the Esquimaux people and their ways, their strange diet and habits—all fascinating. But to hear about that, you see, from the sensibilities of one so unlike the common sailor or explorer . . . People would find that intriguing."

"Would they?"

"I assure you. Down south, they have no direct connection with the business of whaling. And you, yourself, being so personable—a young woman of good family . . ."

He paused, not entirely confident on this point.

"You work for a newspaper, Mr. Whitfield? Which newspaper?"

"I am published by many newspapers. The *Evening Times*, the *Manchester Chronicle*, the *Gazette* . . ." He waved his hand to indicate the legion of papers clamoring for his services. He watched her absorb that he had called her personable. She clasped her hands and assumed a slightly coy look. He was touched by her gaucheness.

"I think a series of articles, with illustrations, or photographs, ideally—certainly a photograph of yourself—would be desirable to a number of papers and journals."

"Oh! So you mean, we would go to the north?"

He saw her face bloom with hope and was sorry he had to crush it.

"Well, not *go* there, as such. I mean to interview you, if you are willing, and gather photographs from . . . elsewhere. Of course, we would take a photograph of you in Arctic clothing. Furs."

He watched her calculate again, but she looked uncertain.

"Perhaps I should speak to your father?"

"That is not necessary. Or possible, at present. When you say these articles would be 'desirable,' you mean, they would pay for them?"

"Newspapers are sometimes prepared to pay for such a thing. I cannot say how much—that depends on many things."

She was silent.

"We can, of course, come to an arrangement about terms."

"Terms . . . What, for example? Half and half?"

Whitfield nearly choked on his tea.

"Well, there may be a lot of work involved. Raw experience, you see, can be indigestible. It needs arranging, shaping, the filter of a literary mind . . ."

"But I could do it myself—write accounts, find illustrations and so on. I'm a student at the university."

"Ah? Indeed. But writing for the newspapers is a hard-won skill, and although your experience is unique, unless presented in the right way—by one who has long experience of the demands of editors—it is highly possible that it may not find its mark at all. One needs to know individual editors and what they like; one may want a certain angle, another a different length, or a different tone."

Flora sat back in her chair. She had a very stubborn, willful look, he thought. Quite unappealing, if she was not careful. But, in the right hands, and laced into a tight pair of stays, she could be made to look quite fetching.

"But, without me, you don't have anything at all."

"You have a good head on your shoulders, Miss Mackie. Of course, you're right—which is why I would not agree to less than thirty percent for you."

"Thirty percent? So seventy for you."

"That is a very favorable percentage for the subject of an article, I assure you."

Flora looked at him for several moments. Whitfield felt uneasy.

"Some journalists would write an article without even asking for permission."

She seemed to be thinking of something far away. Flora was forming an idea—vague, as yet, but growing, solidifying—of benefits other than financial ones that might accrue to her . . . Was it possible? She stared at the dark blocks of what Whitfield presumed (going by time of day) were some sort of cake. She looked as though she contemplated building something.

"If, as you say, neither of us can proceed without the other, half and half seems fair."

Whitfield sighed. "You drive a hard bargain, Miss Mackie."

She smiled then; a slow, sharp-cornered smile, which gave her a rather raffish look. Whitfield stretched his mouth in uncertain response. She leaned forward and picked up a plate.

"Won't you have some Dundee cake, Mr. Whitfield? You've come all this way."

The first article he sent to her was clipped from the *Manchester Chronicle*. There was no photograph—instead, an artist had drawn a young girl surrounded by towering bergs and apparently menaced by Eskimos. The illustration was remarkable for managing to include a whale, a ship, dogs, seals, Eskimos hunting with harpoons, a polar bear, and a storm, all in unlikely proximity. The fur-clad girl bore more than a passing resemblance to Alice in her wonderland. She bore no resemblance at all to Flora, probably because the illustrator had never seen her. As for the article, it was not actual fiction, but Whitfield had greatly exaggerated the perils of her journeys.

All this was more or less what she had expected. He was true to his word about the money, and although the articles never produced as much as he had led her to believe, in the end, it was she who owed him a debt, because without them her life would never have taken the course that it did.

Chapter 7

London, 51°30' N, 0°7' W
1889–90

"And on *no* account are you to come in through the front door. I know it's ludicrous, but just don't. A girl did that last year and they threw her out on a pretext. They talk of equality between the sexes, but don't ever think the rules are the same for them and us. They're not."

Flora's new college in London, like the one in Dundee, is co-educational, but the women and men are not supposed to meet, even though they attend lectures in the same theater, at the same time. This is achieved by having the men come in through the main door and sit at the front, while the handful of female students have to make their way down corridors and up staircases, and creep into the theater through a door at the back. Then they sit in the back row. Flora has all this explained to her on her first day by a nervous young woman called Poppy Meriwether. Despite having the name of a character in a children's story, Poppy wears steel-framed spectacles and a severe expression. She is thin, sallow, and looks exhausted. She is, if not exactly friendly, painstakingly thorough, as though briefing Flora for a military engagement.

"What would happen if we sat in the front rows?"

Poppy makes a face. "You're welcome to try. But just remember, a girl was severely reprimanded after she was seen walking home with a young man. He was her *brother*!"

She learns that women are not expected or encouraged to ask questions of their lecturers. The men, down at the front, can engage them in conversation—one might even call it banter—but the exchanges don't quite carry up to the back of the theater. Their half-heard comments and laughter are barbs. Flora feels a simmering anger at those students who exclude them—even more at the lecturers who encourage it. In her second week, she puts up her hand. The chemistry lecturer, Mr. Wallace, ignores her, or perhaps genuinely doesn't see her. Furious, and ignoring Poppy's frowns, she persists.

"Excuse me, Mr. Wallace?"

Her voice floats down to the front of the theater. Silence falls. Mr. Wallace looks up—the back of the theater is so dark, he has to squint to make her out.

"Yes? I'm sorry, Miss . . . ?"

"Miss Mackie. We can't hear you at the back. We don't know what you're laughing about. We pay our fees, and we don't want to miss anything important."

On the front benches, heads turn. Flora scans their faces—a mixture of curious, derisive, amused. One man—the one who has been talking the most—is smiling; he has wiry, dark hair and spectacles; a lively, clever face. The lecturer addressed him as "Our Israelite," which made Flora stare. Flora looks hard at Mr. Wallace, who clears his throat.

"Thank you, Miss Mackie. I will bear that in mind. Rest assured, ladies, if you pay attention in lectures, you will not miss anything you need to know."

The girl on Flora's other side mutters, "Old windbag." Flora shoots her a grateful glance, surprised to find an ally in the girl with flaxen hair and a face of Renaissance purity. She has noticed male students glancing openly at *her* in the corridors. Afterward, the girl introduces herself as Isobel Kirkpatrick. She admires Flora's courage in speaking out. Later, Poppy explains that Isobel is the daughter of a wealthy MP.

She is doing a degree as an accomplishment; she will never have to earn her own living. Poppy rolls her eyes as she says this.

A few days later, Isobel invites Flora to lunch near the university. Flora has never been in a cafe like Berardi's. Dundee has nothing like it. It sits on the corner of Chenies Street, a mysterious lair full of cigarette smoke and the sort of muttered talk that suggests goings-on of a fascinating and slightly disreputable nature. Lamps that look like jellyfish do little to alleviate the dimness. Isobel weaves through the crowd to a table in the corner. A handful of young men are talking, until one of them—a plump youth with sleek blond hair—catches sight of Isobel and jumps to his feet, and the rest break off and turn their heads toward them. Flora feels a rush of self-consciousness that is half painful, half pleasurable. Something inside her quickens under the scrutinizing gaze of the men. She is conscious that she is not as pretty as Isobel, that a couple of them slide languid eyes over her and lose interest—this is humiliatingly clear.

"This is Flora Mackie. She has just transferred here from the University of . . . Edinburgh, isn't it?" Isobel, congenial enough, has a habit of being vague about details, which gives the impression that Flora isn't quite interesting enough to remember. Flora can't believe it isn't put on.

"Dundee." She gives a small, tight smile to the table of men.

The blond man holds out his hand and makes a bow. "Welcome to London. And, more important, welcome to Berardi's. A home from home."

Flora shakes his hand and smiles. The others get to their feet.

Isobel says, "Flora, this is David Lydgate. My cousin. He's in our biology class."

"Please, sit down. We can shove over, can't we . . . This is Thomas Outram . . . Mark Levinson . . . Oliver Bennett . . . and Herbert Wickham."

Flora nods at the others, and they raggedly sit down. Isobel is next to Herbert Wickham, who is good-looking, with smooth black hair falling over a high forehead. Flora registers a tension there—is he Isobel's boyfriend? He is one of those who gave her a perfunctory, dismissive glance. David Lydgate waves at a waiter and orders tea for the girls. Conversation resumes. Flora is content to sit and listen as they discuss their lecturers, and realizes that most of the men share one or other of her classes. She dismisses Herbert and Oliver Bennett, as they seem to take no interest in her. David is friendly. Thomas Outram is fresh-faced and almost entirely silent. She discovers that this is due to a stammer, which blurs his otherwise cut-crystal diction. Mark Levinson she recognizes as the talkative "Israelite." He smiles briefly, then resumes a story about some members of staff: one, apparently, an alcoholic; another, a wife-beater. He breaks off, peering at Flora through the cigarette smoke.

"I've just realized . . . no . . . is it possible?" His voice is accusatory. She holds her breath in fear.

"What are you driveling about now?"

"I thought I recognized the name. But I didn't hear it; I read it. Flora Mackie—the Snow Queen. You are, aren't you?"

Flora is taken aback. Few students read those sorts of papers, she has discovered.

"Um, yes."

Mark Levinson smiles, eyes bright in a lean face. He doesn't look like her idea of a Jew: his nose is fine and straight, the overall impression one of ascetic intelligence. "The others don't know about these things, but I make it my business to know. This young lady," he announces to the others, "grew up with Eskimos. In Greenland. She is something of a celebrity."

"Hardly. I just went with my father."

"Is he an explorer?" This from David.

"No, he's the captain of a whaling ship."

Oliver Bennett raises his eyebrows.

"According to what I read, you have eaten things I can't even begin to imagine."

"Can you imagine rotten auk meat?"

"I can imagine it, but I can't imagine eating it. What does it taste of?"

"It's pungent and slimy, but very savory. I liked it when I got used to it."

Isobel is grimacing. "You've actually eaten that?"

"Yes. I prefer fish's eyeballs."

Herbert looks as if this is all rather tasteless. Mark Levinson laughs. She smiles, although she isn't sure if she is the butt of a joke or in on it. The others stare at her. Isobel looks as though this is exactly the effect she intended when she brought her here.

"I might have known Mr. Levinson would know about her." Then she adds, "Flora lodges with Iris Melfort."

There is an exchange of meaningful glances around the table. Herbert says, "Then you do move in illustrious circles. Is she your relative? She is Scots too, isn't she?"

"Yes, but she's not a relative; my benefactress, I suppose."

Oliver looks at her keenly, as if she has just become interesting.

"Staying with La Melfort? Well, well."

"You know her?"

"Everybody knows Iris Melfort."

"I don't know her," says Mark. "But I know *of* her."

"Mark comes from Bethnal Green. He doesn't know anybody."

Flora has never heard of Bethnal Green—presumably a country village. Mark grins, not in the least offended. He and Oliver exchange a look.

"So . . . thinking about what I know *of* Miss Melfort—I ask, of course, in a spirit of scientific inquiry—is it true that she's a sapphist?"

There is an outcry. Isobel scolds Mark with apparently sincere outrage. Oliver laughs. Herbert smirks. David and Thomas look embarrassed. It gives Flora time to collect her wits. She is shocked and angry, but knows her face hasn't changed.

Herbert looks slyly at Oliver and says, "She doesn't know what it means."

Flora fixes her gaze on one of the lamps, her face burning. "I do know what it means, and I can assure you that it is none of your business." She aims her most glacial smile at Mr. Levinson's ear.

"Touché," says David Lydgate. "Miss Mackie, I'm so sorry. Please let me apologize for my . . . acquaintances."

"It's only a joke, David," says Herbert, and Flora keeps the smile on her face, determined to appear modern and unshockable. But, later that afternoon, when she is safely on the omnibus back to Kensington, she finds that she is shaking with anger, her vision smeared with tears.

Flora didn't know what to make of Miss Iris Melfort when they first met. They had corresponded for months by then, and Iris had written to her father to assure him that she was a suitable person to shelter his daughter from the depredations of London life.

"I don't understand why she would do such a thing. She doesn't know us."

"She knows *about* me," Flora said. "She wants to help me be an explorer. She's a New Woman."

Her father sighed at the multiplicity of folly in the world.

"And what does Miss Melfort know about the Arctic?"

"Not much, I imagine," said Flora, with the insouciance of one who has received admiring letters from strangers, including two proposals of marriage. "But then, she won't be going."

Now, Flora arrives back at the house in Kensington—an imposing stuccoed edifice (Iris is very rich)—and is let in by the sort of immaculate maid she never encountered in Dundee. Iris is in the first-floor drawing room overlooking the park. Another maid has brought tea.

"What did you get up to today, Flora?"

"Erm, chemistry—the noble gases, and, in mathematics, calculus."

"Did you speak to Dr. Sullivan?"

"Yes, I did . . ."

Flora has voiced her concern to Iris about the lack of meteorology on the syllabus. Dr. Sullivan is the only staff member who has any experience in this field, having been a junior member of an expedition to Iceland twenty years ago.

"He said there is no meteorology class scheduled, and that I would do well to concentrate on my physics and mathematics, as there is room for improvement."

"Well, then, that is what you must do for now. Then, perhaps in a few months, you can . . . My dear, are you all right?"

Flora blinks back tears. "I know I've a lot of catching up to do, but he talks as though I were an idiot, and my ambitions . . ." She can't go on.

"You'll have to get used to that, Flora. Most men—and quite a lot of women—will laugh at you, will think you're mad, probably. Pioneers are always laughed at."

Flora tries not to think of the scene in Berardi's. She suspects that many people laugh at Iris, and feels an unwonted desire to protect her. She *is* eccentric, by most standards, and a pioneer in her own way: a wealthy spinster; modern; voluble; an enthusiast for fashionable causes—all the things her father would most distrust. She is somewhere between thirty and fifty, and drapes her lanky frame in startling, flowing gowns. She and her friends embrace vegetarianism, universal suffrage, and rational dress—to name only those causes Flora knows about. She is astonishingly generous. Over the past few weeks, Flora has become fond of her.

"I know. But he as good as said that, if there *were* to be an expedition mounted through the university, I'd be the last person invited to join."

"You already know that. You won't be joining anybody else's expedition. We have other plans, don't we?"

Sometimes Flora despairs of these plans. She is good at mathematics and a fast learner, but ignorant of some basic scientific concepts. She struggles to keep up, begging Poppy and Isobel to fill in the most glaring gaps in her knowledge—which they do, with varying degrees of patience. In lectures, she keeps quiet for fear of humiliation. She is painfully conscious of her lack of education, especially compared to those fellow students who have been to famous schools.

At other times, she finds those same students curiously childish: most of them live with their parents, have never traveled outside Europe; they may have learned dead languages, but have never spoken to a person from another class. They are ignorant of areas of life that Flora has come to take for granted: the whale fishery with its danger, butchery, and profit; the toil and hardships of the men; the astonishing, carnal nature of the North.

On her first voyage, walking with John Inkster, the mate who was like a second father, she came to a beach that was dark with seals; heaving with the violent motion of sack-like bodies. The massive creatures collided with shuddering impacts, alarming cries, bloodshed. Flora asked, disingenuously, what they were doing. Crimson with embarrassment, and unable to tell a lie, John told her the seals were getting married.

She has seen glaciers crumble into the sea. She has seen an iceberg, eroded to expose the skeleton of a ship. She has seen a sky with three suns: things the Herbert Wickhams of this world can only imagine.

Outside of her course work, she spends hours in the library, reading Galton and Fitzroy on measuring the weather, Beaufort on winds, Dove on storms, Glaisher on the experiments in hot-air balloons that nearly killed him. She reads Tyndall on the transfer of heat in the atmosphere, the scattering of light by ice crystals, the plasticity of glaciers. She reads Humboldt's *Kosmos* and Hall's accounts of living with Eskimos. She studies the circulation of air, the hydrologic cycle, the formation of clouds. It is not out of gratitude or obedience that she does this, nor because she cares about being a pioneer. It is because the Arctic, with its stern, patient, endless light, is the only place she has felt free.

One day, she returns to her seat to find an envelope tucked into her topmost book. It contains a passionate plea for forgiveness, and is signed *Mark Levinson*. It is over a week since she met the men in Berardi's (when she vowed never to speak to any of them again). Mr. Levinson claims he has been suffering the torments of the damned, is mortified by how rude and unkind he was, only did it for a bet, has no money, so cannot afford to turn down such dares . . . The letter is a curious mixture of contrition and defiance: absurd, yet somehow touching. She wonders if it is another joke and puts it away, determined not to waste time wondering. But somehow she cannot concentrate on the absorption rates of gases with quite the same application as before.

A week later, Iris returns from a meeting of the Women's Improvement Society on Bethnal Green Road. Flora asks, casually, what Bethnal Green is like.

"Heavens, why do you ask? It's the East End. You don't want to go there, do you?"

Flora shrugs. "I heard someone talking about it. Is it very awful?"

"Ghastly. But one goes where the need is greatest." Iris is looking at her rather sharply. "Of course, it's full of Jews."

"Oh?" says Flora.

"Is that where he's from?"

"Who?"

"Whoever is making you blush."

After a second, Flora regains her composure. "There isn't anyone. I don't know what you're talking about."

This is not part of the plan, so she tries to keep it from Iris, from everyone. There is that first encounter in the physics corridor, when he mutters, "Am I forgiven?" and she does not reply, more out of confusion than propriety. But then they meet by chance in the street, or perhaps not by chance, and end up having tea in a quiet café. He is kind, amusing; his obvious interest flatters her. He wants to make amends, he says, for having embarrassed her in public. She tells him that, if he wants to atone, he could help her fill in the gaps in her knowledge (he has prizes for physics and chemistry, so who better?). He agrees. Flora congratulates herself on turning the situation to her advantage.

Early on, he says, "You know I'm that terrible thing: an East End Jew?"

"I don't know what you mean by that."

He laughs shortly. "I'm not like the others, like Herbert and Tom. I don't come from money, or a good family. So if you wish to change your mind . . ."

"It doesn't matter to me in the slightest where you come from."

Flora watches his expression soften into a smile of great sweetness, as though she has bestowed on him an unexpected gift. She tells herself that she is not susceptible, not interested, has other, higher, priorities, but Mark Levinson is unlike anyone she has ever met.

In March, they take a ride through the City on the top deck of an omnibus. Sitting side by side, Flora is intensely aware of the inch of space that separates her skirt from Mark's trouser leg. He points out the Monument to the Great Fire—he seems to know everything about London, and many other things besides—and she leans until she brushes against him, as though she does not know she does it.

"Robert Hooke had the tower built with a shaft all the way down the middle. He wanted . . ." The omnibus jolts around the corner, and, from shoulder to knee, every inch of her is pressed against his body. He falls silent, but she doesn't ask what Robert Hooke wanted; they look up at the vertiginous tower with its frozen flames, and she feels the blood rushing in her ears, her composure loosening inside her.

Later that afternoon, he says, with a helpless smile, that he never knows what she is thinking. He calls her the Greater Northern

Sphinx. Flora laughs. If he really doesn't know what is on her mind, then she is indeed a sphinx. She glances at his neck, where the skin of his throat vanishes under his collar. The space between them makes her dizzy; she is continuously falling into it.

In April, a warm wind blows the scent of the river into the woods. Flora and Mark walk into the shade of sweet chestnuts. It is a mild spring day, so they chose to go for a walk in Richmond Park, but it has been an oddly silent journey.

"Why is it called the Isabella Plantation? It sounds romantic."

"It isn't. The word *Isabella* used to be the word for dingy yellow. It probably refers to the color of the soil."

Flora laughs, hoping to lift his spirits. "You're making that up."

"I'm not."

"Do you think Isobel knows that?"

"I don't know."

She wonders what is wrong, and if it is her fault. Mark picks up a broken switch and threshes it against the trunks as they pass. Motes of dust fleck the sunlight that fall between the leaves.

"You seem troubled, Mark. Is something the matter?"

He sighs. "It's beautiful here, and I'm with you, and you must know how much I think of you . . ."

He stops and stabs the path with the switch. He speaks in a strained murmur, staring at the impaled ground.

"If you want to know the truth . . . I don't deserve you."

"Don't be silly. You're the cleverest person I know! You have a great future—"

"I'm not worthy of you."

"You are!"

He smiles unhappily, shakes his head.

"You don't know . . . Seeing you, being close to you . . . It torments me. I want to give you everything, Flora, but I don't even deserve to say that."

He stares at her so intently his look seems to scald her.

"I don't want to torment you." She takes his hand, and he recipro-
cates by pressing hers so hard that it hurts.

"I'm ashamed . . . I can't work for thinking of you. I can't sleep. It's
driving me mad. I'm afraid that . . . Perhaps we should stop meeting."

"No! Don't say that . . ."

Flora steps toward him and puts her arms around him. She is
deeply moved to find that she can feel his skeleton—his shoulder
blades, the ribs in his back. She smells *him*, sharp and slightly musty,
as he presses her to his chest. His jacket is rough against her cheek.
She twists her head around and pulls back to look into his face. The
look in his eyes is oppressively tender. She is almost frightened—it
is too much to be responsible for that—and because, in part, she
cannot bear to go on looking, she moves her face toward his, and
then feels the peculiar, soft warmth of his mouth against hers. His
mouth moves, his tongue touches her lips. She opens them, with the
sense that, in doing so, there is no going back. It is intriguing, like a
key that has the effect of unlocking her whole body, and the sour-
sweet ache that has taken up residence inside her writhes like a
thing with its own will. She finds that she is pushing herself against
him, as if her body acts independently of her mind, which is acutely
aware of every sensation: his hands stroking her back, the soft, wet
noises their kisses make. She can, through her skirts, feel a hardness in his groin, and what she thinks about *that*, she doesn't begin
to know . . . and then, fearful, she tears her mouth away from his,
breathing hard, and he crushes her to his chest again, so that her
chin pokes uncomfortably over his shoulder.

"We can't . . ." she says, breathless.

"I love you, darling girl. Say you will be mine, one day. Please . . ."

A dark bird explodes upward through the leaves above them,
chucking disapprovingly. Mark looks around nervously. She looks at
his handsome profile, and her chaotic feelings tip and shift—just—to
the point where she says, "Yes. One day."

Their mouths meet again, and then Mark pulls away from her,
making a space between them, breathing deeply. He has his hands
on her upper arms, holding her still.

"Darling Flora . . . I think we'd better go." He attempts to smile in a normal, lighthearted manner.

"Yes." Flora takes a deep breath and looks around her. They are completely alone. The possibility of someone coming across them while they were embracing did not occur to her. Now it makes her cold to think of it.

Going back into London, they sit in silence, but a different silence, not awkward and heavy, but as if they are both so full there is no need to speak. At least, that is what Flora feels. On Albert Bridge, Mark suddenly bends forward and puts his head in his hands.

"Mark!" She is alarmed. She puts her hand on his arm. "Are you ill?"

He says, in something between a groan and a whisper, "I'm sorry. It's all wrong."

"What do you mean?" She leans toward him; there are other people on the top deck.

"I've made everything worse."

"You haven't."

He groans. "You can't love me."

"But I do. Mark . . ."

"Forget everything I said. I'd no right to ask that of you."

"No! Don't be sorry. I'm not." She puts her hand on his arm, shaking him until he lifts his head. She wants him to look at her in that way he did in the plantation. She bends toward him and whispers, "I'm glad."

The omnibus is approaching the point where they have to change routes. She says, "This is where we have to get off."

Mark doesn't move.

"Mark . . ."

He shakes his head. "Just leave me."

Astonished, and a little frightened, Flora lets go.

"What is wrong?"

"I'm sorry. Forgive me, Flora. Go, please."

She has no idea what to do. The bus pulls into the side of the road. She mutters again, "Don't be sorry, darling," and presses a hand on his sleeve before she stands up and makes her way down the omnibus stairs.

After two days, in which she does not catch so much as a glimpse of Mark in a corridor and he cuts their usual chemistry lecture, Iris calls her into the drawing room when she comes home, and pours her a glass of sherry. Flora shakes her head.

"Take it. How long have you been here?"

Flora feels a chill. "Seven . . . eight months. I'm sure I can find somewhere else, if you—"

"Flora, please. I simply mean I know you well enough to know when you're unhappy. I haven't pressed you, have I?"

Flora shakes her head.

"I don't know how anyone manages to get a degree, at the age you are, when everything is so urgent. There's a man, isn't there? Dear, I won't be angry, no matter what you've done."

"I haven't done anything!"

"Well, if you're not engaged, married, or having a baby, that makes things easier."

Despite herself, Flora emits a strangled laugh. "Ah . . . no."

"Good. Do you want to tell me what's happened?"

Flora tries, but somehow her account of her relationship with Mark, and the events of Sunday, makes little sense, even to her.

"Perhaps he's right in saying he doesn't deserve you."

Flora shakes her head vehemently. "I can't bear that he thinks so little of himself—when he's so brilliant! He is cleverer than all of us."

"Perhaps he wasn't talking about his background. How well do you really know him?"

Flora stares at her. "What do you mean? I know that he is good."

"If he is good, then he will explain his behavior. I know . . . It is not quite the same for me, as you may have realized . . ." Iris pauses, making rather a meal of lighting her cigarette. "But I know that, if people behave strangely, there is always a reason."

Flora writes to Mark after the second missed lecture. The next day, he reappears in the lecture theater and gives her a tentative look that pierces her to the core.

That evening, he waits for her, and they walk through Fitzroy Square Garden, after classes, in the dappled shade of plane trees. He apologizes, with his customary mix of sweetness and defiance.

"Your letter was so good. You are wise."

"No."

"What you said about the future: you are right; we are only at the beginning of it all. It's just so hard to be with you and . . . I want to give you a future, but I'm afraid of losing you before I have anything to offer."

"You won't lose me." She stops and looks into his eyes, and feels that sense of being impelled toward him, remembers the feel of his mouth on hers, his body responding. "I'm to blame as much as you. I understand how difficult it is."

"You're not to blame, and I doubt you really understand, but . . . thank you."

"Why doubt it? Do you think it impossible that a woman feels . . . what a man feels?"

"Well"—he smiles—"it's hardly the same."

"You know what I feel? How do you know it isn't the same?"

Mark looks at her in amusement. "All right. I don't know what you feel, objectively. But there are certain undeniable, ah, differences . . . it's agreed—by doctors."

"By men, who also don't know. I know what I feel, objectively. I long to touch you. I want to be with you. It is difficult, all the time we are together." She speaks in a fierce whisper.

Mark looks startled, then closes his eyes. "You're not making this any easier."

Flora doesn't quite speak the truth; she desires him most strongly when she is alone, when a certain distance allows her to indulge her feelings in safety; in his presence, she is constantly confused by the things he says or does. Either that, or her passion is for an ideal person who is like, but not identical with, the flesh-and-blood

Mark. She is sufficiently aware of this conundrum to be sometimes alarmed by it.

"Iris wants to meet you."

Mark's expression changes in an instant; he smiles with touching gratitude. This is why she loves him, she thinks, because beneath the moods and defensiveness is this thirsty soul that responds to kindness with heartbreaking eagerness. He covers it in an instant.

"Oh? What have you said that I can't possibly live up to?"

"I told her that you matter to me. And that you're the cleverest person I've ever met."

"Ha. So will I have to perform?"

His cheeks are touched with color.

"You'll like her. She's a socialist."

"The sort of socialist who lives in a grand house in Kensington and has a vast fortune."

"Doesn't the cause need a few like that?"

He smiles. Flora, relieved and glad, feels a wave of tenderness—his prickliness is only because his upbringing has been hard, and he has to struggle to pay his fees . . .

"Shall we walk to the park?" He looks at her sideways. "We could carry out some objective tests."

Flora pretends to think, but a warmth unfurls inside her, delicious and dangerous. The paper on atmospheric circulation she read earlier pops into her head: *Any increase in heat leads to an increase in instability* . . . although the atmosphere is only that of Regent's Park, early on a Friday evening, so there is not much danger, just . . . enough.

Chapter 8

London, 51°31' N, 0°7' W
Summer 1890

Flora moved to London so that she could study under well-known scientists, but it is not enough for an explorer to be qualified and competent—not for her—so Iris gives dinners so that Flora can meet People Who Matter. Her circle contains artists, writers, and the odd entrepreneur and minor politician. Iris admits that this is not high society, but it is society of a sort; these are people with money, and most of them are curious about Flora and her ambitions, and more polite in their incredulity than Dr. Sullivan. One of Iris's best friends is almost always present—a writer called Jessie Biddenden. She is of a similar, indeterminate age to Iris, but small and rounded, with a pretty, cat-like face and exotically slanted eyes. Sometimes Flora thinks that it is Jessie who should be the explorer; she radiates a power that Flora finds alarming—a restless, calculating energy that seems to brook no resistance. She has wondered if Jessie might be a sapphist too.

Once, there is a real explorer, Gregory Bala, recently returned from Mesopotamia. He is impressive to look at, with huge blond whiskers, and even more to listen to; he has a slight accent (he is Hungarian by birth) and a measured, grating voice that cuts through a room. With heavy, rather forced courtesy, he asks Flora about Greenland and its culture. When she answers, she can tell he thinks Greenland a place so primitive it is hardly worthy of a visit. He himself has brought back wonderful treasures from central Asia—ancient scrolls, statues, paintings. Things made of gold. And extraordinary knowledge. During a lull in their conversation, his gaze fastens on Flora's bosom and stays there for an uncomfortably long moment. Flora attempts to shrink into her chair. Then he stabs a finger toward her right breast.

"I knew I had seen that before. Did you know, Miss Mackie, that the, ah, upper part of your dress displays a Babylonian fertility symbol?"

"Um . . . no," says Flora faintly, looking down at the bodice with its pattern of interwoven loops, knowing she will never wear it again.

In such company, Flora struggles to express what makes her long to go back to the north. Sometimes she feels utterly inadequate to the task of meeting these people, which seems to call for more wit and erudition than she can, or ever could, muster. At the end of the Bala evening, when everyone has gone, Flora bursts into tears.

"Good heavens, child. Are you ill?" Iris sounds irritated.

"No. I . . . I'm sorry. I try . . . I want to do well for you. But I feel so stupid! I know so little, and these people are so clever. They speak French! I . . . I'm not up to it!"

She is thinking of an elegant woman with a tiny waist, who made comments in a language Flora could not understand, at which the table dissolved into laughter.

"Oh, really. Mrs. Harding is a table decoration—it was Italian, by the way, dear—and she only speaks it because her mother is a trollop who ran off with some catchpenny princeling. You can speak Eskimo. No one else can do that."

"But no one knows if I'm speaking it or not! It's no good if no one else understands."

Iris looks at her with fond exasperation. "You do very well, Flora. I can tell, even if you can't. And pretty Mrs. Harding is never going to fund an expedition, so don't worry about her."

"Perhaps you could invite Mark to the next one?" Flora smiles at her tentatively.

"Do you really think he would enjoy an evening like that?"

If she is honest, Flora cannot affirm that Mark would flourish in such an atmosphere. The likelihood is that he would feel inferior, and be resentful, sullen, or worse.

"I'll think about it. But not next Friday. There is someone I particularly want you to meet, and it wouldn't do for you to look too . . . attached."

"Why? Who is it?"

Iris smiles. "You'll see. You look tired. Go to bed. Have you written to your father lately?"

"He's in the north," says Flora, meaning no.

Her last letter to her father, sent before the whaling season began in May, was a masterpiece of dullness. His letters to her are no better. He never has anything of interest to report—only the weather (poor, usually), the worsening pain in his knees (depressing) and remembrances from Moira Adam and his few acquaintances in the town. He displays no curiosity about her studies or about her life generally. She tells him about her work—she wants to show him that she is doing well—and that she is meeting important people, except he has never heard of any of them. She has not written a word about Mark Levinson; has not told him she is in love.

As spring turns to summer, she and Mark reach an accommodation. On alternate Saturdays, Mark travels to Kensington, and they walk in the park, or go to a museum, and then go back to Iris's house for tea. But if Iris is not at home, they go to the house immediately, and Flora takes him upstairs to her own little sitting room. They can stand, or they can sit on the sofa, but, if sitting down, there is no touching below the waist. These rules—which Flora decided on after some confusing research in the library medical section—state that they will remain dressed, although the definition of "dressed" is elastic enough to include a certain amount of unbuttoning. Flora shuts the door and listens for the sound of servants' footsteps. When she is satisfied that no one is nearby, she walks up to Mark—he waits for her to approach him, looking very serious—and she takes off his glasses and puts them on a side table.

"Now you have me at a disadvantage," he says the first time, with a nervous smile. She sees him differently from so close: the texture of his skin, which is fine and sallow, the shadows under his eyes, his black eyelashes, the dots of stubble on his jaw and neck, the downy softness beneath his ear. She breathes in the musky smell of him. She realizes, with a revolution of the heart, that he is shaking. She kisses him softly, tenderly—his neck, his temple, his cheek, his lips—and as she reduces the distance between them to nothing, fitting her body against his; she thrills to feel his erection press into her belly, and her breasts push against his chest.

"Is this allowed, on the Sabbath?" she teases him. She knows that his father won't light a fire or join two threads together from sunset on Friday till the third star appears on Saturday evening.

"Actually, it's encouraged," he says with a blissful sigh. "Well, it would be, if we were married."

He kisses her again and she opens her mouth to his. She can't believe that, not very long ago, she wasn't sure she wanted this. His arms hold her against him, caressing her, and then she unbuttons his shirt and put her hands on his pale skin, making him moan. She has dressed, this morning, so that it is easy for him to unfasten the front of her blouse and chemise, and fondle and kiss her breasts. It amazes and delights her that what she has always thought of as her bulky, inconvenient flesh is capable of inspiring such ecstasy, and she pushes her fingers hard into his hair and gasps with pleasure. It is becoming very difficult to stay on their feet, but at some point she presses her hand against the tight worsted of his groin and rubs it back and forth, pressing with the heel of her hand until he gasps and clutches her shoulder and eventually shudders, and then squeezes her to him with eyes shut, and says he loves her, loves her.

Flora wants to do this, is happy to give him some measure of relief, but for her—for both of them—it is unsatisfactory. What she wants is to be naked with him, to feel him, to see all of him, for him to fill her up. She feels like an aching void that is curdling with frustration. And his hand over her skirt, rubbing blindly at the place between her legs, doesn't help. Sometimes she feels that she almost reaches a crisis, but cannot fulfill it. It is possible that Mark doesn't notice this lack, or he is too inexperienced to ask, and she is too embarrassed to tell him—does not know, in any case, what she would say.

The only thing she can do is wait until much later, when she can reasonably retire, and conjure up the ache again in order to relieve it. She knows how to do this because she has always known. She cannot remember a time when she did not.

At one of Iris's dinners, when Mark is not invited, she meets Freddie Athlone. He is an Anglo-Irish landowner, and he wants to be an explorer. He has never been to Greenland, but he has been to Spitsbergen and climbed its ferocious mountains. He has theories about the North Pole. And he is interested in her. Not just her background and experience, but in her, personally, although he is far older—he is thirty-one. Flora finds that she likes him—he is enthusiastic and knowledgeable. They have things in common. The day after the dinner, Iris receives a note, asking them both to dine.

"I thought you would get on," Iris says blandly. "Finally, someone who knows what you're talking about."

"I don't know what to do," says Flora. "I'd like to go, but . . ."

"But what? It's just dinner."

"I know—I just feel I should . . . Mark and I, you see . . . we've talked about getting married."

"You've *what*?"

"Unofficially, of course, we're . . . we're engaged."

Iris stares, eyebrows disappearing under her fringe. "When did this happen?"

"Not long ago."

"I thought you weren't going to do anything stupid."

"I haven't! I love him."

"Getting engaged to someone like that . . ."

"Someone like *what*?"

"Someone who, however clever he is, has no money or influence. Does he really want you to be an explorer? Is he really prepared to promote you above himself? Can he help you go north?"

Flora stares at her, not knowing how to answer.

"Are you having his baby?"

"No!"

"Are you sure?"

Flora thinks, If only you knew.

"Flora, I want you to think about what it is you want. If you really want to be Mrs. Levinson of Bethnal Green, with hordes of ringletted children, that is up to you. But do you think you can do that *and* go to the Arctic?"

"That's ridiculous! It wouldn't be like that!"

The end of the sentence trails off into a mutter. A part of her thinks, Would it be like that? What is to say it wouldn't?

Iris sighs. "Does your father know?"

"He's away. As I said, it's unofficial."

An uncomfortable silence develops.

"Let us accept Mr. Athlone's invitation. It's only dinner. Who's to say he is interested in you at all? He's fantastically eligible: he probably has dozens of women dancing around him."

"You look tired."

Flora and Mark have met in Tavistock Square after classes. He looks exhausted and worried, but then, the end-of-year exams are only a few weeks away and there is a general atmosphere of strain around the university.

"I'm fine. I've been up late, revising."

"As if you need to!"

"Of course I do!"

Mark is irritable, but Flora is used to it.

"Everyone says you'll be first in the year."

Mark shakes his head and stares into the trees. It makes what she is about to say easier.

"I've been thinking; it might be better if we don't meet this Saturday."

"Oh. All right. I have to work, in any case."

Piqued that he is not more disappointed, Flora goes on: "It's just that there's going to be a dinner in the evening. It's quite a big thing; there'll be Arctic people there, so I want to be prepared."

Mark looks at her now, a strange spark animating his face.

"Who's the dinner with?"

"A friend of Iris's. Frederick Athlone."

Mark smiles quickly, unhappily.

"Ah. The aristocrat you met recently."

"Yes. He's been to Spitsbergen."

"This is why she doesn't invite me, isn't it?"

"What are you talking about?"

The smile on his face is mocking. "Just an East End Jew; not part of that world."

"You're being ridiculous."

"Well, I don't want to stand in your way. I'm sure you'll charm him."

"It's one evening!"

"The *second* evening."

Flora sighs sharply. "Why are you being so . . . There is nothing for you to be jealous of!"

"Isn't there?"

"It's you I care about."

His face softens, as it always does when she says this. As if he is defenseless.

"Then show them you do. Marry me, Flora, now."

Flora wonders if this is his idea of a joke.

"Mark, we've got exams! One day, I will, but . . . there are things I want to do—and things you want to do. We have to do them . . . At least start."

The mocking smile is back, and she feels tears threaten.

"What you mean is, I don't have the money to help you. You'll run off to someone who has, as soon as you can. You don't really love me."

"Stop it!" The tears come, spilling down her cheeks. "You know I love you."

She also hates him. Right now, she is thinking, No, I don't want to be Mrs. Levinson of Bethnal bloody Green.

"Prove it. Marry me."

"I can't *now*! You idiot. We can't."

Mark's face is flushed; he looks strangely excited. A part of her is watching them, thinking, What on earth are these people doing?

"No, of course not. What a ridiculous idea. . . . You just liked me for a while—a little bit." He takes a step back, away from her. "But you wouldn't give up a single thing for me, would you?"

"Why should I?" Her voice comes out broken, ungainly. Then she breaks down into noisy sobs, not caring that heads are turning their way. "Mark . . ."

"I told you I wasn't worthy of you."

He draws himself up, a martyr to something she doesn't understand, turns on his heel and walks away.

In the space of a few minutes, the man she loves (and hates, perhaps equally) has engineered a bitter quarrel, or did she engineer it? Whatever happened, it is a rupture, and one that seems to be, with astonishing suddenness, final.

After the dinner, Flora agrees to see Freddie Athlone again. She enjoys talking to him; he respects her knowledge and seems eager to learn from her. And she is not immune to admiration. She is sustained by her sense of injustice over the scene in Tavistock Square. She vows she will not give in, or write to Mark, and then does—a letter in which she pours out her confusion and hurt. She gets his short answer by return.

He states that it is over between them. He asks—no, *orders*—her not to write again; he will not reply. The letter causes her so much pain that she has to destroy it, but she cannot erase the words scorched into her brain: *I am not worthy of you, that is all you need to know*, and, *Just know it is as well that things did not go any further between us.*

In a state of numb misery, she sits her second-year exams. She tries not to look for a familiar figure in the examination hall, but, on two occasions, sees his back disappearing down a corridor, which causes her to feel sick. She cannot stop her heart from jumping when Isobel mentions Herbert or one of the other friends, just in case . . . But no one talks about Mark to her, because no one knew. She discovers how good she has become at keeping secrets.

Flora has never been to Mark's home. For days, after term ends, she agonizes over the prospect of going there. She chastises herself: she is the Snow Queen; where is her courage?

The address takes her to a house in Old Ford Road: a tiny, low cottage in a terrace of identical others, close to the road. Curtains are drawn across the downstairs window. This may not have any meaning—the pavement is so narrow that people walking past could reach in and touch you.

She knocks and waits. As she is deciding that there is no one at home, she hears a noise inside and the door opens. The man in front of her is so clearly, painfully, Mark's father that she stares at him: the same springy hair—graying; the same eyebrows, the same mouth, the same jaw. He stoops a little. He has Mark's keen, intelligent face, but softened, with more humor, more resignation.

"Yes? What is it you want, Miss?"

He has an unfamiliar, foreign accent.

"I'm hoping to see Mr. Mark Levinson."

He looks down. "I'm not sure if he is here."

Flora can't prevent her eyes from flickering past him. The house is so small, this statement seems mildly absurd.

"Sometimes he goes for a walk without telling me. My hearing is not what it was."

"Oh." Flora smiles, embarrassed to be read so easily. "My name is Flora Mackie. A friend from the university."

As she says this, a movement on the stairs catches her eye. Mark is on the half-landing, in shadow. There is a pause in which no one speaks.

"It's all right, Dad." He walks down to join them in the tiny hall. She registers with a shock that he has spoken differently—his accent rougher than the one she knows.

"Do you want that I make some tea?"

"No. We'll go to the park." He addresses Flora, but doesn't look her in the face.

"Thank you . . ." She speaks to his father as Mark sweeps her outside. Mr. Levinson nods and closes the door. Mark strides away. Flora has to hurry to keep up on a pavement too narrow for two to walk side by side.

Once they have turned the corner into the next street and the park gates are ahead of them, he slows slightly.

"He looks like you." She is determined to make him look at her. "Mark . . ."

"Why've you come? I told you not to."

"Because I don't understand."

He keeps walking.

"And I miss you."

She has sworn to herself two things—that she will tell the truth and that she will not cry. The second of these is already proving a difficulty.

Mark sighs. "I'm leaving. I'm withdrawing from the university."

Flora stops walking, and has to start again, as he hasn't broken stride.

"You can't! Mark . . . You're going to do so well."

"No. I flunked the exams." He speaks in an uncharacteristically dull voice.

They have passed through the gates and are walking under the trees.

"You don't know that—the results aren't out. I'm sure it's not as bad as you think."

Mark slows and stops. He hasn't shaved this morning, which gives him a shabby, piratical air. She is already feeling relief—if this is all it is—a worry about results . . .

"How are you getting on with the rich explorer?"

Flora feels the sting in his voice, but is glad to be irritated. "We get on. Not romantically. We're friends, just as I'm friends with David, or . . . or Isobel. Is that so hard to believe?"

"This has nothing to do with you. I'm leaving because I must. I have to earn a living."

"But why? Is your father ill? You have to finish your degree—you have only one more year, Mark! Then you will earn a far better living than if you leave now. You know that."

Mark looks around, down the path, anywhere except at her. His hands are jammed into his pockets, his shoulders hunched.

"Sometimes things happen that are not what one would choose, but that is the course one must take."

"You must know that, if things are difficult, your friends would help you. Iris could find you the money, if you really—"

"Don't! Things have changed. I'm leaving. It's what I want."

"I don't believe you!"

"Well"—he smiles bitterly—"that is a statement about you."

"Mark, for heaven's sake . . ." She grits her teeth with irritation. "You know what I'm saying is true. You can't give up your degree. This is mad."

"No, it isn't. Now. I have . . . responsibilities."

She stares at him and makes an impatient gesture.

"What responsibilities?"

He looks her in the face for the first time, and she is heartened to see pain in his eyes. He is not decided, she thinks, not entirely.

"I didn't want you to hate me, but it's better that you do. God knows, I deserve it."

He looks away and swallows, with difficulty.

"I'm getting married."

Flora thinks for a moment that something or someone has hit her. The world tilts dangerously.

"I'm going to be a father."

Flora always thought she was clever. And that cleverness made her safe: she could have what she wanted and not pay a cost. She thought she had managed things well. But this is a cost she never imagined.

She says, at last, in a voice she doesn't recognize, "It's only been a few weeks."

Mark speaks to the ground, his voice barely audible. "It was before we were . . . really together. That doesn't make it better, I know. I'm sorry. You see, I'm not worthy of your concern."

A few feet from them, a squirrel works busily at something in its front paws. Flora stares at the creature, intent on its trophy, glossy eyes bulging out of its head.

"You mean, all the time when we . . ."

"No. No! Not at all."

"Who is she?"

Flora fights down the knot in her throat. She is getting angry, at least. She nurtures the anger: an attempt to stop anything else from overwhelming her.

"Someone from around here."

"Do you love her?" Her voice comes out harshly. She didn't mean to sound quite so vicious.

"I'm doing the right thing. I did something wrong and I'm going to make it right. It's the right thing to do."

"It is not the right thing! For God's sake. If you don't love her—if you've made a mistake . . . You shouldn't have to pay for it with the rest of your life!"

"What do you suggest? That I abandon her to her fate? She doesn't deserve that. And it's my child."

"There are . . . places. Charities . . ."

"Run by your wealthy friends, no doubt."

"If you don't love her, don't marry her. When were you ever in such thrall to convention?"

"You wouldn't say that if it was you in that position."

Flora is panting as though she has been running. She feels dizzy. "I wouldn't be in that position! But if I loved you, I wouldn't ask you to ruin your future. And I wouldn't want someone to marry me out of pity and resent me ever after. She doesn't deserve *that*."

For a terrible minute, she thinks he is going to cry. He looks so stricken, so young—she feels twice his age.

"Marry, if you must, but don't leave. Finish your degree. I will help you get money."

"It's impossible . . . You couldn't."

"Iris would help."

Mark laughs savagely. "Do you think she would help such a cad? After what I've done?"

"If I asked her to, yes."

The bitterness goes out of him then—it leaks out, slowly—and the fight. And the fire.

"Don't, Flora . . . I can't bear it. I'm so sorry. Go home and forget about me. I'm not worth it."

Flora feels two tears run down her face. "Think about it. Mark . . . Don't just . . ."

"I have to go, Flora. I'm meeting . . . my fiancée. We'll be married soon. Two weeks."

With another look at her—a dull look of defeat—he turns toward the gate. Flora turns to walk with him. She cannot countenance being left behind.

"You're spineless," she hisses, her voice uneven. She wants him to be angry. A sarcastic, defensive Mark—that is familiar, and bearable.

He flinches. "I'm doing the right thing. You have to accept that."

"No," she says, in that alien, treacherous voice. "Not accepted!"

But she stops walking.

He feels her stop and pauses for a split second, then walks on with a broken stride—a jerk, as though snapping the thing that stretched taut between them.

Flora sinks onto the nearest bench. She thinks she is going to vomit. After a minute, it passes.

She walks back to the house in Old Ford Road. When Mr. Levinson opens the door, she puts her hand on the jamb.

"Miss Mackie . . . Mark isn't with you?"

"He's gone to meet his fiancée. I told him he mustn't leave. If it's money that's stopping him from finishing, his friends will help. I want you to know that. He mustn't ruin his life."

She speaks fast, not daring to stop.

"Ah, Miss." Mr. Levinson purses his lips with a weary smile. "Thank you, and please thank his friends for their kind offer. It's not a matter of money. Mark has made up his mind. It's pride with him. Always pride."

"Just tell him, please."

He shrugs, but nods. His face is so much like Mark's, but without the anger or pain, that she can't bear to look anymore.

"Miss Mackie . . ."

She turns back to the doorway.

"I think you and my son were good friends?"

Flora doesn't trust herself to speak.

"I am very sorry for your trouble."

Chapter 9

The *Clarion* is pleased to announce that the United States northwest Greenland and Ellesmere Expedition is due to embark. The expedition leader, Mr. Lester Armitage, is taking a party of scientists with the aim of increasing America's knowledge of the North. Mr. Armitage is thirty-four years old, and his admirers are confident that no man is his equal in the undertaking he proposes. Yesterday, he told the *Clarion*'s representative of his regret that America has slipped behind in the race for knowledge of this icy realm. Since the "regrettable incidents in the recent American record," there have been no more attempts from this side of the Atlantic to explore what is not only virgin territory not far from our shores, but territory that may in due course lead to considerable commercial exploitation.

Clarion readers will no doubt recall the Hall, de Long, and Greely expeditions, which led to terrible loss of life in the de Long and Greely cases, and to a miraculous escape from disaster in the other. Mr. Armitage was keen to point out that problems on previous expeditions stemmed from poor planning, and from having overlarge parties of

men, many of whom were not Americans, which led to serious disagreement. Mr. Armitage, in taking a small party of "red-blooded
Americans," intends to avoid such schisms, and, furthermore, believes
that meticulous planning will reduce the risks to almost nothing. His
ambition is to map, explore, and unlock the secrets of the north, and
thus advance the sum of human knowledge—and do it in the name of
the United States of America.

Brooklyn Clarion, March 1, 1891

Despite the recommendation, Lester Armitage's first impression of
the new candidate is not favorable. He is failing to digest yet another
hurried lunch, and returns, chewing a dyspepsia tablet, to his office
in Gramercy Park, whereupon, hearing a cough, he pauses inside
the door and shuts it noiselessly. Whenever possible, Lester likes to
watch people while they think themselves unobserved. The reason
he gives himself is that he is only too aware of the disasters of previous expeditions, which arose largely, his reading suggests, from a
poor choice of men. Given the hurried nature of these interviews,
Lester needs all the help he can get.

The young man now awaiting him in the corridor is reading
from a small volume (reading indicates mental resource), a hand-
rolled cigarette clipped between his fingers. Stalk-like limbs crossed,
the toe of one boot jittering (nervous type), his face is lean, hair
unruly—a dandelion clock, all the more so for being liberally sprinkled with gray (congenital weakness?). Despite the gray hairs, he has
the slenderness and energy of youth.

He opens and closes the door again, and walks out of the shadows.
The man looks up, unfolds his legs, closes the book with a snap—it
is Tyndall's *Glaciers of the Alps*, Lester notices—and stands up. He is
shorter and slighter than Lester, but most men are. A smile of great
charm creases his face. "I'm here to meet Mr. Armitage—is that you?"
he says, with a guileless confidence Lester envies and therefore distrusts, but which somehow, on this occasion, disarms him. "I'm the
geologist. Jakob de Beyn."

"I'm Armitage. Come in."

He leads the way into his office. His desk is piled with stacks of paper and cardboard files. Wooden crates are stacked against the walls. There is barely room to pick a way to the desk. Lester sighs with the impatience of the terminally busy and waves to a chair piled with papers. Jakob picks up the papers and, not finding any free space, sits with them on his knee, waiting. His countenance is open, his features expressive of intelligence and good humor. Lester allows a long pause to develop before speaking.

"Why did the Greely expedition fail?"

Jakob was warned to expect a grilling. He has recently read Greely's account of the expedition, as well as all other Arctic works he could get his hands on. Theoretically, there is not a great deal to absorb, but he plowed manfully through his share of crystalline palaces and faerie cathedrals afloat on the deep. He has names and facts at his fingertips. He very much wants to go to the Arctic.

"Scientifically, I would say it did not fail. It . . . they amassed more data and mapped more new land than any previous expedition at that latitude. Of course, an expedition can only be said to be truly successful if every member returns alive. But it seems to me that most of the problems were in the organization of relief. They planned to rely on supplies being brought in from the south, and those supplies failed for reasons outside their control. The key must be to be self-sufficient, as the Eskimos are, and as Hall demonstrated is possible in his first years in the Arctic."

Lester stares at him from disconcertingly pale eyes. Jakob searches for something else to say.

"Smaller numbers would help—and forming good relations with the local Eskimos."

"You have read up on the subject?"

"As much as I could, yes."

Lester seems to unbend a little.

"So why do you want to go to such a place?"

As the interview progresses, Lester finds himself revising his initial impression of a slight, nervous weakling. Though not an obvious athlete, the man seems tough. He has recently returned from a third geological survey in the Rockies and has climbed several peaks, trekked through virgin country, in the mountains, in winter. He has walked on glaciers and come up with an improved design for footwear to prevent slipping on an icy surface. His qualifications and experience are more relevant than those of most of the candidates he has met. As important, he establishes that the man's family is Dutch Calvinist, which is acceptable. In fact, Lester forms the opinion—not due to anything Jakob says, more wishful thinking—that he is associated with one of the old *patroon* families; a minor branch, perhaps, of one of the clans of merchants who built New Amsterdam. Being the right sort is of equal importance with athletic, scientific, and moral prowess; in fact, it entails them. The other men he has chosen are all, in their different ways, impressive and roughly—as he would put it—of the same caste.

Of his party, Armitage is particularly pleased with the inclusion of Jefferson Shull. The former college athlete is blond, strapping, affable, and has the confidence of old money. Even ignoring the Shull family's donation to the expedition coffers, Lester would have found it hard to turn him down, as he is so much the type Lester wants around him. Shull recently graduated from Harvard with a degree in law, which will be neither here nor there in the Arctic, but he has a marvelous physique, has hunted, sailed, and traveled from a young age, is a crack shot, and gives the impression that nothing and nowhere on earth is beyond him.

Louis Erdinger, the physicist from Philadelphia, is stocky and tireless. He is not exactly affable. In fact, he is humorless and socially awkward, but then he is a genius; everyone says so. He graduated summa cum laude from Cornell and is already, at the age of twenty-six, widely published. He is in line for a professorship. Everyone says (those same people who proclaim his genius) that his participation is a coup for the expedition.

And the most recent recruit, Frank Urbino, who is to be their doctor, is a giant of a man. He was famous at City College for having run four miles with a full firkin on his back. Despite his name, he is a thoroughgoing American; Lester's wife, Emma, was at school with Urbino's sister Angela (a charmingly attractive woman). He is a first-rate doctor and a man it seems impossible for anyone to dislike. He is also energetic and unstintingly full of intelligent suggestions, whether they be for an improved design of sled packing-cases, or approaching a certain man on the New York Board of Trade, or the idea of a mountaineering Dutch geologist.

As for Jakob, his first impressions of Lester Armitage are positive. Frank described him as a bit of a cold fish, but impressively driven and organized. All true, but Jakob suspects the coldness is due more to extreme personal reserve than a lack of feeling. He is certainly driven—he works fifteen hours a day, either in the office, or giving lectures and attending functions where those with money to spare may be persuaded to spare it in his direction.

Physically, he is imposing: tall and broad-shouldered, with a lean face, full mustache, and a military, even an ascetic, demeanor. His appearance is a huge point in his favor: he looks like an explorer, or perhaps he fits people's idea of what an explorer should be like. Even his stiffness with potential funders is an asset. They find him serious and credible, and that lack of ease means that he does not seem to be begging, or manipulating them. They listen, impressed by his awkward sincerity, his intense patriotism. They open their wallets.

Interview concluded, Jakob leaves the office cautiously confident that he has made a good impression. He concealed his nervousness, he thinks, displaying his experience and enthusiasm, and restraining his impulse to smile too readily—he thinks it makes him look weak. The ever-present fear of being questioned about his father went unrealized; Armitage seemed content to hear that his family was Protestant. Jakob told him, as he tells everyone who asks, that both his parents are dead.

The idea of the north is hugely appealing to him, even more than the mountains of the west, which he loves, but knows his work is helping to tame. Prospectors and mining surveyors like himself are everywhere, scraping and poking at the wilderness, and they are followed by entrepreneurs, builders, saloon-keepers, prostitutes, and countless others. He knows one town, in an exquisite valley encircled by snow-capped mountains, which in four years has swelled from a single street into a rambunctious Sodom full of underscrupled profiteers, the streets a welter of mud, the mountains scarred by mining and logging, reduced to a source of precious metals, timber, and hiding places.

Jakob has been back at his brother's house only a few weeks, but he feels as though the city contains twice as many people as it did last year; the streets are crowded with ever more horses and vehicles. After the vastness and silences of Montana, the constant noise irritates him; fumes from a million fires scratch his throat and threaten to choke him. The sky, which stretches forever over the mountains, is chopped into narrowing rectangles and vanishing squares; it seems pallid, dirty, confined. And, not to put too fine a point on it, he needs a job. He has not saved much out of his last fee, due to an unconscionable stupidity that he doesn't like to think about, and he is chafing at the lack of funds. He wore his traveling clothes to the interview, not because he wanted to pose as the rugged frontiersman, but because he has no others that do not make him feel shabby, or out of date, or both.

Jakob and Frank have not set eyes on each other for a year. They have exchanged letters—with increasing frequency since Frank mentioned the Arctic expedition he was joining, and recommending Jakob for—but the last time they met was a hurried lunch before Jakob left for Montana the previous spring.

It is the day after the interview. The lunch counter hasn't changed, except that a new generation of students eats the grilled cheese.

Jakob walks over to Frank, limping slightly; looks him up and down, and feels Frank do the same to him. As they shake hands, both burst out laughing. Frank grimaces.

"I know, I'm as fat as a pig! It's all the damned paperwork. I don't get a chance to do anything else."

"You'll be well set up for a starvation winter. Or perhaps not—we'd eat you first."

"What's up with the leg?"

"I fell off a glacier. Cracked a bone in my ankle."

Frank's mouth opens slightly.

"What did Armitage have to say about that?"

Jakob grins. "I didn't tell him. It'll be fine in a week or two. So, when did you get involved in this business? I must say, I was surprised when you told me you had joined an expedition; I didn't know you were interested in this sort of thing."

"Ah, well . . . Things change." Frank waves his hand airily: a gesture that strikes Jakob as uncharacteristic. "Practice work is all very fine, but there isn't enough of a challenge. I got bored, I suppose. I'm not like you—I'm sure, in future, it will be enough for me—but right now, I want to prove myself. I want to do something I can be proud of, tell my grandchildren."

He says the last phrase a little self-consciously. Jakob raises his eyebrows.

"You're thinking about posterity?"

Frank laughs shyly and looks down at his hands. "I didn't want to tell you in a letter, but . . . I'm engaged to be married!"

"Congratulations!"

"You look shocked."

"Not shocked, just . . . surprised. You could have written me!"

"Well, you know it's been such a whirl. So sudden . . ."

"That's wonderful. When did this happen?"

"Not long ago. I first met Marion, my fiancée, ah, last autumn, and when I was offered a place on the expedition, I thought, either I don't go, or I go, but I don't want to leave things uncertain, because, when you have met someone who is just perfect . . ."

He shakes his head, grinning bashfully. Jakob feels ashamed of his first reaction.

As Frank tells, rather incoherently, the tale of meeting Miss Marion Rutherford at a neighbor's dinner, or tea, or at any rate at someone's house, Jakob experiences an unfamiliar twinge of envy. In college, he was used to being the one envied. He himself has recently escaped a sentimental encounter that left him not only bruised but ashamed—the whole thing so ridiculous it doesn't bear thinking about.

"You'll meet her at lunch on Sunday—you'll come, won't you?"

"I wouldn't miss it."

"Anna and Clara will be thrilled to see you—my parents too. And what about you?"

"What about me, what?"

"Come on . . . Are you still seeing that actress—she was an actress, wasn't she?—from before you left, last year?"

"Oh . . . no. I've been away nearly a year. You know my work; it's not exactly compatible with any kind of . . . settled life."

"Don't you sometimes think it would be nice to have a home of your own, and someone waiting there for you, warming your slippers?"

Jakob laughs. "I don't possess slippers."

"Wait till you meet Marion . . . We'll find someone for you."

There must have been something in Jakob's face, because Frank's assumes a knowing leer.

"Or have you fallen for a respectable girl at last?"

There is another reason, beyond the nobility of a quest for knowledge, beyond even Hendrik's silent reproaches when he leaves for the asylum to visit their father, that the idea of a long, remote journey appeals to him.

The previous spring, Jakob went to Montana to work for a mining company. He hired a guide and spent the summer surveying in glorious mountain scenery. He was captivated by the peaks, the lakes, and, most of all, by the glaciers he glimpsed from the high passes, and once his survey was finished, he decided to stay. He could write his report as well there as back east, and he had an urge to climb in winter, to test himself against the ice. He also itched to experiment with his latest passion: he had bought a new, lightweight camera and wanted to photograph the winter landscape in some way—as yet unknown to him—that did not diminish its chaste splendor.

Jakob bribed a guide to accompany him on a trek up a modest glacier. They proceeded slowly—neither having done such a thing before—with the guide threatening to turn back at every step. Jakob, who had been congratulating himself on the efficacy of his improvised footwear, became incensed by the man's whining. He turned around to tell him to shut up, slipped, fell, slid, thought, Oh, hell, and was brought up short by his foot striking a rock that stuck out of the ice like a purplish thumb. He lay on his back, dizzily aware of pain, noted that the rock was a Precambrian mudstone erratic, speculated how it had ended up on top of the ice, and heard the guide laugh. He tramped over to Jakob and said, in tones ripe with satisfaction, "You gone done't now."

When he tried to stand, he found his ankle was too damaged to walk on. The guide helped him down off the glacier and then left him to fetch a mule. Jakob spent a sleepless, very cold night by the side of the glacier, cursing himself for his folly, but also working out how to adapt his footwear so that such an accident was unlikely to happen again. A day later, his leg splinted with pine branches and in a lot of pain, he was carried by mule into the nearest place that boasted a hotel and a doctor. The doctor made him pay his fee up front, then looked at the ankle and told him it was broken, which he already knew. He set it in plaster of Paris (Jakob had to pay extra for this) and said he would need to rest it for two weeks before attempting the journey home, or it might never heal properly.

Highlandville was a gaudy, gimcrack place: a town that had mushroomed out of nothing on the strength of placer gold. It had little choice in the matter of lodgings, all of them ruinously expensive.

Bad-tempered and bored, Jakob sat in his room—small and noisy, but still costing a railroad king's ransom—with his foot raised on a cushion, and worked on his report, or stared at the mountains he couldn't climb. In the evenings, he hobbled downstairs to sit at the bar and drink a couple of beers while watching the miners and whores come and go. Several of the women approached him, touting for business, but lost interest when he explained that he was not a miner and had no gold.

One whore came to sit beside him more than once, asking if he wanted company, and, more than once, he smiled regretfully, but she didn't go away. Her name was Swedish Kate. She was a good-looking girl of thirty, with chestnut hair and an accent that made him want to laugh. Despite his protestations of poverty, she would join him to talk for a while before going off to find herself a paying client, looking over her shoulder with a teasing smile.

Jakob, worried about money, resolved not to give in to the temptation on offer, but self-pity and loneliness bore down on him, and seeing Kate come swishing into the bar in yet another low-cut dress made it harder and harder to hold on to his resolution. Over the course of a few days, he found himself hobbling down to the bar in the hope of seeing Kate—just for the company, because she was smart and sympathetic, as well as pretty. His report bored him; he ran out of prints to develop. When, one evening, he saw her with a particularly obnoxious miner, he was run through with a lance of jealous fury, and realized his resolution was going to fail.

On his first survey, four years earlier, when he had arrived, wide-eyed and relatively innocent, in Wyoming Territory, he had been squeamish about paying for sex. Now it no longer bothered him. For a start, the choice was stark: you either paid or went without. The word *whore,* which once had shocked and scared him, ceased to be a deterrent when he found that almost every woman he saw in the mining towns was in some way for sale, and also that they were not, as he had been brought up to believe, a race apart, but ordinary people wresting a living out of difficult circumstances.

Once you realized that, and talked to them in the way you might talk to any woman you met in polite society . . . well, Jakob could see no reason why (taking precautions, of course) both should not have a perfectly good time. It had also occurred to him before now—as it has occurred to men the world over—that a woman's company is never to be had for free, no matter what their background or morals. You could not marry without income and expectations. If you wanted a woman, you had to provide for her, whether it was for an hour or for a lifetime. Sometimes it seemed to him that Cora Gertler was the only woman who had truly expected nothing of him in return.

When Kate came into the bar the next evening, she could see from his face that something had changed.

"What's up? Look like you got the toothache."

"Nothing." He tried to clamber on to his dignity. "My leg's bad today, that's all."

"I'm sorry. So it's not that you were jealous about last night? I saw your face." She grimaced. "He was a pig."

"Oh, no . . ." He shrugged valiantly. "Why would I be jealous?"

Kate leaned forward. He was aware of the smell of sherry on her breath, and a sweet, heavy perfume on her skin.

"I'd be jealous if I saw you talking with one of the other girls. You know I work for Mrs. Hensley; I don't get to do the picking. If I did"—she spoke even more quietly—"I'd pick you."

In front of him, only inches from where his hand was resting on the table, her bosom swelled out of a tight bodice of dark material. It moved with her breath. He fought a sharp tussle with his better judgment.

"Come upstairs with me."

"Jake, I'm working." She said it gently, but firmly.

"I know."

They went to his room and, as he sat on the bed with his leg stuck out in front of him, she undressed, smiling, fulfilling all the promises his imagination had made him. He apologized for the difficulty in pulling his pant leg over the cast on his foot, so they left it, giggling. She seemed to him entirely lovely, with no trace of artificiality. He wondered, briefly, whether she made every man believe she really wanted to be with him.

Afterward, she lay beside him, breathless.

"My," she said. "Quite the ladies' man, aren't you?"

"Oh, no, not really," Jakob protested, delighted.

"Well, it's not the first time you've done that." She pushed herself up onto her elbow—a lithe, glowing odalisque—and kissed him. "Promise me you won't go with any of the other girls. They don't deserve you."

He shook his head. "No. I won't. I mean, I don't want to."

"You're nice, Mr. Jake de Beyn. I would go with you for nothing, but I have to account for my time." She traced a finger down his chest.

"I know. It's all right." Jakob, calculating, was already writing off his fee for the last few months.

"I could see you sometimes in my time off, if you'd like. I have Wednesday and Sunday afternoons."

Jakob was touched. "Really? Well, that doesn't seem fair. What if . . . we could do half and half?"

On their third Sunday, an early snowfall beat against the window of her room. A fire popped in the grate, a bowl of artificial flowers sat on her dressing table, the curtains were red velvet. Kate looked out at the darkening sky.

"Last year, the railroad closed mid-November. You never know when it's going to hit."

Jakob was silent. Kate got up and poked the fire, sending sparks up the chimney. Lying in her bed, he contemplated the domesticity of the scene, which seemed less tawdry than in daylight, and was struck by how much he didn't want to leave.

"I wish you could stop all this!" He spoke with unaccustomed violence. Kate sat on the bed and took his hand with an amused smile.

"What would I do instead? Dig for gold in the hills?"

"I could help."

"Oh? How?"

Jakob was surprised by what he said next. "You could come with me, to New York."

She raised arched eyebrows.

"Are you asking me to marry you, Jake? You wouldn't be the first."

He was shocked by this revelation. And tongue-tied. He was twenty-five, but still thought of marriage as something beyond the horizon. It was for people who got up at the same time every morning to go to work in the same place, saw the same things, the same faces, day after day. After a couple of seconds, the silence had become awkward.

She smiled, and said, quite gently, "I didn't think so."

Jakob didn't want to be a heel as well as unoriginal. "No, wait," he stammered, his heart bounding in his chest. "We could marry—why not? Marry me, Kate. I mean it."

He seized her hands, lightheaded and reckless and excited by the feeling. He was always so circumspect—why not do something different, for once? Kate was laughing.

"Why not? Well, I still have a husband, as far as I know. But, also . . ." She grew serious. "I don't know that I will ever marry again. Men are different from women; before they have you, they are sweet, but once they own you, they treat you like dirt. My husband didn't hit me until I married him."

"I don't want to own you, Kate. I want to make you happy."

She smiled, a little sadly.

"I believe you. I don't need saving, Jake."

"That's not . . . I love you."

He had not said this to anyone since Cora Gertler. As he said it, he had a strange, hollow feeling in his chest: he fancied that he could feel it becoming true.

Kate sighed and put her hand against his cheek. "Dear Jake . . . You are young."

Jakob swallowed. This was not, he felt, how a marriage proposal should go.

"I'm twenty-five. You don't have to patronize me."

"I'm sorry. You're right. I like you very much, but I know that men say things sometimes in bed . . . things they don't mean when they're dressed."

"I'm not like those men," he said hotly, wondering, as he said it, how exactly he was different.

"Besides, I don't think we would suit each other."

Jakob was hurt. He wished he had never begun this, but now that he had, he felt bound to continue, or else appear idiotic.

"I know we haven't known each other long, but . . . we get on so well. Not just here, but talking, and—"

"Jake, have you forgotten I'm a whore? This is my job. I'm not honest."

With huge reluctance, he said, "What do you mean?"

Kate looked down. "Well, do you really want a wife who doesn't like to make love?"

Jakob was so surprised, he laughed. "But you do . . . I mean . . ."

Kate looked at him. "I pretend, Jake. That's what I do. Some men don't care . . . But with someone nice, and especially with you . . ." Seeing the look on his face, she dropped her eyes. "I like being with you, and you try so hard to please, so I pretend. I want you to be happy. But . . ." She shrugged. "When I retire, I look forward to sleeping alone."

Jakob, naked except for his pants tangled around the cast, wondered how to get up and leave without being completely absurd. He must have looked so woebegone that Kate said, over and again, that she was sorry. It wasn't his fault, it was hers; and it wasn't that she *hated* it, it was just, well, nothing to shout about. Such a silly business . . . But the damage was done. When she tried to kiss him, he pushed her away, his throat ominously tight. He dressed in silence, feeling as miserable as he had ever felt in his life. As miserable as when Cora announced she and her husband were moving to St. Louis, and he had burst into tears. He knew, even as he pulled on his sock and found his errant crutch under the bed (how odiously long it took to get dressed when you had been told such a thing!), that it was his vanity that suffered, as much as his heart, but that wasn't any comfort.

He left without speaking and limped back to his hotel. It was only across the street, but he managed to soak both feet in the slurry of snow and horse shit. He bought a pint of whiskey from the bartender, took it to his room, and drank until he could barely stand.

He didn't see her again. When he was sober, he still couldn't bear to contemplate what she thought of him. To recall their conversation made him cringe; he was vain, egotistical, ridiculous. Since the age of eighteen, under Cora's tutelage, he had prided himself on his skill as a lover. Now that pride was bile in his throat. If Kate had fooled him, did that mean other women had fooled him also? Even Cora—was it possible? He felt his gorge rise, but after eating nothing for two days, retching over the washbowl produced only strings of gluey saliva. He imagined Kate relaying their words to her whore friends, their derisive laughter. In a temper, he began to pack his belongings, stamping around his room, which had become vile to him. His ankle hurt and he dropped the salts of silver—her fault, of course!

That day, he received a letter from Kate, poorly written and badly spelled, saying she missed him and begging him to pay her a visit. Although the note had the flavor of honesty, he didn't respond. Her illiteracy did more to put him off than her profession ever had. Instead of going to see her, he told himself to pull himself together, took up his bags, and left Montana on crutches, nursing his wounds. Two days later, blizzards closed the railroad for the winter.

Four months on, his ankle is almost as good as new, but his heart and ego are still bruised and tender. He is tormented by his inability to judge whether Kate had played him for a sucker all along—whether everything she said and appeared to feel was an act. He was really attached, and was sure that, in some way, she felt the same.

Whatever the truth was, it no longer matters—he is in New York; she was only a whore—it was foolish and naïve to become attached. He attributes his feelings to a kind of cabin fever: a sentimental malady brought on by boredom and altitude. He resolves to be more circumspect. The prospect of a long and arduous expedition, to a place where surely no woman can entangle him, is a seductive relief.

Chapter 10

New York, 40°42' N, 74°00' W
March 1891

A few days after the lunch with Frank, Jakob receives a letter. He tears it open; the letter offers him the post of geologist on the United States northwest Greenland and Ellesmere Expedition. Feeling better than he has for weeks, he dashes off his acceptance.

He tells Bettina, his sister-in-law, that he won't be cluttering up her house for much longer. She is horrified to hear that he is going so far away.

"Why? Where are you going?" asks Vera, his niece, now six years old.

"I have a job, and to do it, I'm going very, very far north, where there is snow all year round."

"Will you make a snowman?"

"I expect so. A big one. I tell you what, I will make a snow Vera and take a photograph of it, just for you."

"Yes!" Vera claps her hands.

"And you will be gone for two whole years! Do you know how we worry about you when you go off to God knows where?" Bettina says.

"Really? When I am away, I never think about any of you at all."

"Ach, you are a terrible man. Vera, your uncle is a terrible man."

Vera giggles and climbs on Jakob's lap. The heavy metal caliper bangs his kneecap painfully.

"She's right. Listen to your mother."

"Hendrik lies awake at night. He still thinks you can't look after yourself."

Jakob smiles and jiggles his niece. His brother gives no outward sign that he worries about anything other than the price of beef. He has worked hard at building up his business, and now supplies meat to a number of restaurants. He has become substantial around the middle and looks like the steady, respectable paterfamilias he is. He and Bettina have two children, Vera and three-year-old Willem, as well as Carl, the son from Bettina's first marriage, who is apprenticed in the business. But there is always room in their house for Jakob. They live in a four-story brownstone now, in a quiet part of Brooklyn. They keep a room on the top floor that they refer to, even when he isn't there, as "Jakob's room." Jakob takes this entirely for granted.

"He should know better by now. I'm not the one crossing dangerous streets and surrounded by sharp knives . . ."

Bettina shoots a warning glance toward her daughter, who is agog.

"Where are dangerous streets?"

"Nowhere. Uncle Jakob is joking. Isn't he?"

"Yes. And now, since I have a job, I'm going to buy some new clothes. Your uncle feels like a bum. Frank Urbino has invited me to lunch on Sunday."

"What's a bum?"

"A bum is a man who sleeps outside. He has nowhere to wash."

Vera pulls a face and shrieks with laughter.

"Be quiet, Vera. That will be nice, to see your friends again." Bettina gives him a meaningful smile. She makes no secret of her desire for Jakob to meet a nice girl and settle down, preferably nearby.

"Yes," he says, wondering if it will be.

When Sunday comes, Jakob knocks on the Urbinos' front door, experiencing an unaccountable nervousness. He is wearing his new coat, which makes him feel uncomfortably formal. But Frank opens the door and smiles with such genuine pleasure that Jakob has a lump in his throat as they shake hands. Frank seems unnaturally excited, as if he is nervous too.

"Come on through."

Frank leads Jakob into the dining room, where he sees Anna and Clara. Angela and Johnny are not present, but there are two more young women, unknown to him, one dark and one fair, both standing with hands folded neatly in front of them.

"Let me introduce someone very important. Marion Rutherford, my fiancée. Marion—my best friend from City College, Jake de Beyn."

Frank beams with pride as he presents the fair-haired girl. Jakob professes his delight, proffers congratulations, and says how lucky Frank is. She thanks him and says she has heard a lot about him. Neither could possibly have said anything else. Jakob is astonished by the powerful antipathy he feels toward her, but cannot say from what it springs.

He greets Clara and Anna with real pleasure, and is inundated with questions about his trip. He thinks Anna seems better than the last time he saw her, when she had barely spoken. Frank had not said as much, but he suspected there had been some sort of breakdown. Clara is everything he remembers—polished and confident—her face perhaps a shade more defined by art than formerly. The other woman is a friend of Clara's from the store where she works—Lucille Becker. She has a dark-complexioned, humorous face and a monkey-like grin, and her lack of obvious attractions makes him feel at ease.

By contrast, Marion Rutherford is a small, pale girl with a neat figure. She is undoubtedly pretty, but the more they talk, the more Jakob is puzzled by Frank's evident adoration. He grew up with lively, intelligent sisters; it would not have been surprising if he had chosen a girl who in some way resembled them. But Marion seems their polar opposite, not only in looks, but in her passivity—a dampening lack of spirit. She seems deficient in some vital energy; more than that, she seems to drain it from those around her; Jakob feels himself becoming dulled in her presence. When he asks her questions, she replies in lengthy, complex sentences. She constantly glances toward Frank with a satisfied, expectant air, and Frank, ever alert for the turn of her head, smiles at her proudly. Jakob finds himself wondering if she has any passion; it is difficult to imagine. He could always be wrong (what does he know about women, after all?) or perhaps Frank, who has lived an unusually ascetic existence in many ways, finds that very insipidity reassuring. Whichever it is, something about her depresses him.

He slips out to the garden for a cigarette, and finds Clara and her friend already there. It is a relief to be outside. Clara gives him a searching look as he joins them.

"So what do you think?"

"What do I think about what?"

"Oh, come on . . . The intended."

"I've only just met her. I hardly know the first thing about her."

"I was listening: you know all there is. We've been searching for something more for months. But . . ."

She widens her eyes and lifts her arms expressively—nothing! Jakob is momentarily speechless. The Clara he knows might be acerbic, but she isn't usually unkind. Lucille gives her a warning glance. They make small talk for a minute or two, then she says, "Frank was always rather naïve. But he has a great capacity for love and loyalty—as you know. I don't want him to be disappointed."

"Perhaps he won't be. I gather they aren't going to be married before he leaves."

"No. He may yet come to his senses."

Jakob laughs. "That's not what I meant." He takes a drag of his cigarette. At the risk of shocking Lucille, he says, "I doubt that two years in the frozen north will cool his ardor."

It is Clara and Lucille's turn to laugh.

"No, worse luck. And we've had to promise him we will gather her to the bosom of the family in his absence . . . It's only just over a year, isn't it?" She sounds genuinely anxious.

"If we leave in May. We'll have the following season there, and should return next September or October. That's the plan."

"Barring accidents."

Jakob smiles. "All plans are barring accidents."

Clara looks back at the house and says, "We'd better go in, I suppose."

As she mashes out her cigarette with the toe of her boot, she takes him by the arm in a way that is unusually intimate, even for her. Tactfully, Lucille drifts away from them.

"I wanted to ask you: you will look out for Frank, won't you? After all, it's your fault, this adventuring."

"What on earth do you mean?"

"You must realize . . . he wouldn't have gone in for all this if it weren't for you."

Jakob is astonished. "That's ridiculous! He's been a member of the expedition far longer than I have. It was he who introduced me . . ."

Clara gives him an indulgent, elder sister's smile.

"I know, but he was always talking about the things you were doing, the wonderful, exciting places you were going to. I think he feels that his life has been boring and staid by comparison. Dear Frank—he wants to do something big and . . . newsworthy"—she laughs briefly—"before it's too late. He even says he wants to do something 'worthy of' Marion. God knows why—Marion doesn't like it, or even understand it . . . but I suppose you do."

Jakob is troubled to hear this, although he suspects her of exaggeration. "Of course I'll look out for him. But it isn't going to be dangerous. There are people who spend their entire lives where we are going."

"They didn't prevent the Greely tragedy."

"We learn from others' mistakes. Armitage knows what he's about. It's really no different from going to the mountains here."

He is equivocating and she knows it. Clara releases his arm and draws away from him as they reach the doors. "Look at you," she says. "You can't wait. Just promise me."

"I will look out for Frank, I promise," he says, sure that no one is extracting such a promise on *his* behalf.

Marion extracts the same promise before he leaves, which makes Frank laugh out loud. He puts his arm around Marion's slender shoulders and looks fondly down at Jakob from his half-foot height advantage. He repeats what Jakob told Clara: "You have nothing to worry about, dear little girl. There will be no danger. None at all."

Chapter 11

London, 51°31' N, 0°7' W
Summer–Autumn 1891

On the eve of her marriage, Flora Mackie writes a letter to her father, far away in the Davis Strait. She informs him of her impending wedding, expresses sorrow that he will not be there to give her away, apologizes for the hastiness of the arrangement, and assures him of the wisdom of her decision. By the time her father reads the news, which will be this autumn, or even the next, it will be too late to object.

She has made a bargain. She renounces expectations that other young women might see as their right—emotional luxuries like romantic passion, along with ease, dependence, restricted and domestic responsibilities—in return for a career and the opportunity to return to the north. She will achieve this by marrying Freddie Athlone. She does not think that she is in love with him, and doubts, despite his claims, that he is in love with her. They complement each other, and she is fond of him. Perhaps, one day, she will love him.

He proposes just before her final exams. His proposal is unusual; not so much a declaration of love as a prospectus. He outlines their joint expedition to Greenland: a venture that requires her presence as the celebrated Snow Queen, and his presence as the driving force that will brook no opposition. He has energy, will, connections. She has something that no one has seen before. Neither his proposal, nor the form it takes, comes as much of a surprise; they have been talking of exploring the north ever since they first met. Flora takes a day to think it over, but her answer is never in doubt. She tells Iris after she has accepted.

Iris hugs her.

"Darling, I'm so glad. It's rather soon, but, if you're sure . . ."

Flora smiles calmly. "I'm sure."

Iris looks her up and down. "You're going to do great things, Flora."

Flora laughs. This is what she wants to hear. Then Iris surprises her by her suddenly serious expression.

"I know I've encouraged you in this, but you're not beholden to me. It is what you want, isn't it?"

"It's what I want. I'm not as naïve as I once was."

This is as close as she ever comes to referring to Mark Levinson.

Flora takes her natural science degree, coming sixteenth in the year. She has achieved what she wanted; she is as good as anyone else—or, rather, she now has proof of it. Over the last year, she worked hard to relate her studies to the field she wants to make her own. She suspects that she does not have the mind of an innovator; she lacks the overarching vision, the capacity to make intuitive leaps. What she can do—and perhaps this suits her ambition better—is endure. The more she learns and thinks about the science of weather, the more she appreciates the importance of simple accretion of data—unspectacular and repetitive. No lightning flashes of inspiration, perhaps, nothing extraordinary, but the day-by-day keeping of the record, a constancy of endeavor that gathers value and meaning the longer it goes on. Perhaps her marriage will be like that, also.

Isobel and Poppy react with astonishment when she tells them she is to become Mrs. Freddie Athlone—but then, she has hardly spoken of him. They congratulate her in rather stilted tones. Isobel, who broke off her engagement to Herbert Wickham the previous winter, seems particularly aggrieved.

"But don't you see?" Flora says. "It's to further my ambitions, my career, that I'm getting married. We'll be partners. We're planning to leave next year. Can you imagine how impossible it would be to do that on my own?"

"Yes, we see that. But do you love him?" asks Poppy.

"Of course. What's more to the point: I like him."

"You like him?"

Isobel stares at Flora with a penetrating gaze. To everyone's surprise, Isobel came fourth in the whole year, and won the prize for astronomy. Over the past year, she has become fierce in her devotion to female independence. She, who has always seemed quite without serious ambition, did far better than Poppy (Poppy is still smarting from it). No one says—who knows how many of them are thinking it?—that, if Mark had still been at the university, he would have outshone them all.

"But what about babies?" Poppy asks.

"Oh, well!" Flora affects a worldly disdain. "There are ways of avoiding them, of course, if one wants."

Freddie has talked about this—in delicately vague terms. They agree that there will be no children, at present, and she assumes that he—a man about town—will know how to ensure this.

He is older than her, of course, but only by twelve years, and he is not bad-looking—with pale skin, high cheekbones, thinning, wavy hair, and eyes that are russet-brown. Altogether, she sometimes thinks, there is something fox-like about him. But Flora likes his face, likes the fact that he blushes easily and hates it. She also likes the fact—she has been told several times—that he is a catch; many young ladies have tried there and failed! And he has a quality that, to her, is of inestimable value: he defers to her greater knowledge of the north. He is as enamored of her peculiar history as he claims to be of her person. Flora thinks they understand each other very well.

At first, Flora does not share Freddie's confidence about their great plan. But, once it is made public, one after another, newspaper editors, sponsors, manufacturers, and advertisers light up with the reflection of his enthusiasm, and chuckle and shake their heads and take out their checkbooks. Freddie and Flora sign a sponsorship deal, a newspaper deal, a publishing deal.

In Manchester, the new editor of the *Evening Record*, R. G. Whitfield, reads about the expedition—the Snow Queen is in the newspapers again, after three years—and writes a letter that is vitriolic in its wounded pique. It almost, but not quite, goes so far as to say that she will owe him money from any profits they eventually accrue. Flora shows Freddie the letter.

"You don't need to worry about him. He's a nobody. You owe him nothing."

"Perhaps not," Flora says, "but if it weren't for him, I wouldn't be here."

She means to reply, in a mollifying way, but instead forgets about him, caught up in the deluge of plans. Freddie has a kind of genius for this. There is no one else in the world, she thinks, who could have gotten her north again, as joint leader of an expedition. She is happy and grateful, and sometimes she prods her heart, pokes her feelings: What is it, exactly, that she feels for Freddie Athlone? It is nothing like the wild, confused craving she felt for Mark. She doesn't feel raw with him. She doesn't feel as though he could hurt her. She is determined never to be hurt like that again.

They marry in August. Since it is all rather irregular, as well as hasty, there is little in the way of traditional ceremony. They marry in a Unitarian chapel, since Freddie is Catholic, and Flora Presbyterian—both, nominally. There are few guests. The only other Athlone present is an elderly cousin who is drunk by ten in the morning. Iris is there, of course, and Poppy and Isobel, and some of Iris's friends, like Jessie Biddenden and Lionel Fortescue, the actor (vying with Freddie's cousin in signs of early inebriation, and, Flora can't help noticing, wearing something that looks suspiciously like rouge). Freddie is accompanied by a couple of old friends: men she has not met before. There are no bridesmaids, or flowers, or other sorts of pomp, because they are saving every penny for the expedition. There has been so much to do, meeting sponsors, assembling a wardrobe (for the Arctic, rather than the wedding), interviewing prospective team members, drawing up lists and making calculations, that the wedding feels like just another task to be ticked off the list. As a result, Flora is only a little nervous.

With her father absent, Flora walks down the aisle by herself, which she thinks is appropriate. As she does so, she is overwhelmed by a dizzying sense of unreality, as though she is in a play and has not learned her lines. In more than one way, she is pretending: to be grown up; to love a man she doesn't know very well; to be an explorer. The effrontery of it terrifies her. She reminds herself that she does have the right: they are writing their own lines, making a new plot, and anyway, one day, she will come to love him.

After the ceremony, there is a toast to the new couple, and then the guests disperse, with a feeling of anticlimax. Freddie takes Flora to a smart restaurant in Piccadilly for lunch. Despite the occasion, it is not romantic. Freddie brings his perennial list of jobs to be done. When she makes him put it down, he finally takes her hands in his.

"Dearest girl, you make me very happy, and one day, I promise, we will have a proper honeymoon. But tonight I have to go to Birmingham. There is a manufacturer I must see tomorrow."

"I know. I'll come with you." She smiles. "I want to learn as much as I can about the business side. And anyway . . ." She strokes his arm, thinking it feels thin and frail through his sleeve, imprisons his hand in hers and leans toward him. She has had two glasses of champagne, and they, on top of the excitement of the day, have made her bold. "You can't go alone. I forbid it."

"Dear, I hardly think Birmingham is a suitable place for a . . . wedding night."

"I don't care about that. I'm your wife. I want to be with you."

She stares into his russet-brown eyes, trying to put her meaning into her own, so that he will know what she means—know that she is not afraid.

The trip to Birmingham, to interview makers of wool underwear, gets off to a bad start. Their train is late, and they don't arrive into New Street until after nine o'clock, tired and hungry. Freddie takes a suite at the Queen's Hotel. They have a late supper in the restaurant. He drinks several glasses of claret, which, although she is used to his finishing off a bottle most evenings, strikes Flora as a sign of nerves. She is nervous, of course, but assumed that, because he has done this before (she has assumed rather a lot, perhaps), he would be more confident—and, one would hope, somewhat eager. At last, she takes his hand.

"Dearest, are you all right?"

"My poor girl, I'm sorry. I'm feeling a bit crock, that's all. I suspect it was the crab at lunch. I think I'd better go up. Do you mind awfully?"

They go upstairs in the gilded, cage-fronted elevator. Distant laughter follows them down their corridor, fading into muffled luxury at the door to their suite.

Once inside, he apologizes again—he is very pale—and disappears to the bathroom at the end of the corridor. Left on her own in the bedroom, Flora undresses and puts on her new nightgown—a silk-and-lace confection, chosen by Iris. She brushes her hair, arranging it over one shoulder and then the other, rather pleased with the effect. Downstairs, she was nervous yet excited; now, she is frightened but determined. She washes in the ornate basin. She does all this very slowly, but at last she can think of nothing else to do, and Freddie has not reappeared. Eventually, she puts on a robe and goes to knock on the door of the bathroom. There is no answer. She tries the handle and finds that it is locked.

"Freddie? Are you all right? Freddie?"

She knocks again, but does not want to seem desperate—like a music hall sketch, except that, in the sketch, she would be old and bald, with a false leg, and he, young and terrified. Is she really that unlovely? The image of Mark comes to her; she pushes it away.

She hisses his name at the keyhole. No reply. Should she ring for someone? Who would come? And what would she say to them? At last, unanswered—but, at least, unseen—she creeps miserably back to her room and gets into her bridal bed, alone. She lies awake for what feels like hours, hearing the clock dragging leaden minutes past while her husband does not come and does not come, wondering if this whole, hastily constructed edifice is crumbling around her. She wonders, in her small-hours madness, if he has run away, or is dead. If she is not a wife, will she not be an explorer, either?

In the morning, she discovers that they have both survived the wedding night—Freddie slept on a chaise in the adjoining room. He is apologetic, but seems better, blaming the seafood for his bad night. Flora is reassured—what is one night, after all, out of a lifetime? One day they will laugh about it.

The manufacturers of underwear are suitable, so the trip is not an entire failure: the marriage may be unconsummated, but they have free combinations. When they arrive back in London, they take a hansom back to his rooms, and he gradually falls silent. Flora's belongings have been sent over, and form a small pile in the room that is to be hers, looking out of place. Flora starts to feel nervous again as bedtime comes nearer; she is worried by Freddie's distracted air. Much as she tries not to think about him, she cannot imagine Mark—the Mark of the early days—being distracted and distant at the prospect of going to bed with her.

She goes up to her husband and shyly puts her arms around him, then turns her head to brush her lips over the skin of his neck.

Freddie, standing very still, strokes her hair, then takes her by the shoulders and, quite gently, pushes her away.

"Dear, I've been thinking . . ."

He smiles. She smiles back, not because she feels like it, but because she feels this is the right thing to do.

"This is not a very suitable place for a young lady to live, at the moment, I'm afraid."

"Freddie! I'm your wife! If it's suitable for you—"

"I know. Perhaps, for the present, you should continue to stay with Miss Melfort—just for the time being."

Flora can't help herself. Tears come to her eyes.

"What have I done wrong?"

"Dearest girl. You haven't done anything wrong. Far from it."

"Then wh-why don't you like me?"

"I like you very much."

Freddie sounds so sad that she is inclined to believe him. He sighs heavily.

"It is I who have done wrong."

She looks at him in alarm. He avoids her eye. Oh, God, she thinks. Whatever he says next, it will be awful. It occurs to her that this is what marriage is: it means that she can come up with no excuse not to hear what he is about to say.

"What do you mean?" Her voice sounds much calmer than she feels.

"My dear, I'm ashamed. As you know, I'm considerably older than you."

"Freddie, I don't expect that you have had no past. I know . . . Well, you know what I mean."

Freddie puts his arms around her and crushes her in an embrace. Her ear is pressed against his Adam's apple, but Flora doesn't move.

"You're a dear girl and I don't deserve you."

"I don't mind, so you mustn't either . . ."

"God, I wish it were only that. It is that—a long time ago—I . . . contracted something. I truly thought that it had gone for good, but just before the wedding it reappeared. I didn't want to lose you. But I don't want to do you harm, so . . ."

He drops into a chair, buries his head in his hands, and starts to sob. So people really do that, she thinks. At length, she puts her arm around his shoulders.

"I'm so sorry," he says. "If you wanted an annulment, you'd be entirely within your rights."

"No! I love you, Freddie."

He doesn't stop crying. She wonders what will happen now. There is a small, selfish core in Flora—perhaps not so small—that is luxuriating in the relief that it is not her fault.

"You'll find a cure." She says this without knowing what is wrong with him. "We will." She tightens her grip on his shoulders. "We have our whole lives."

Afterward, life continues much the same as before she was married. They are so busy and purposeful, she has no time to think about whether their marriage is normal, or whether she is happy. The days rush past in a round of letter-writing, meetings, and paring away at the budget. Can they do with less of that? An inferior version of this? Without that altogether? At night they go to separate bedrooms. Sometimes she puts her arms around him. Sometimes he embraces her, or kisses her on the forehead. Sometimes she feels disappointed, but perhaps also relieved. Admittedly, she married him without desire, but she believed she would come to feel it. Since that is not to be, she puts it out of her mind.

One night in October, Freddie comes to her bedroom and knocks on the door.

"Is something the matter, Freddie?"

He led her to believe that he would not trouble her in her room—this, after she suggested, with great embarrassment, that they could do *something*, if not *everything*. His response had been, "Dearest, that would be worse than not being with you at all. I don't think I could stand it. But thank you for thinking of me."

He didn't seem to realize she might also have been thinking of herself.

"No. Quite the reverse, actually." He walks over to the fireplace and stares into it. "Are you too tired to talk?"

"No." Flora has been brushing her hair at the dressing table, and golden brown strands float, crackling, around her face. She smooths them down.

"Come and sit by me."

Flora draws up a stool so that she can sit beside the armchair. He seems on edge. She turns her head toward the fire, and feels, with a shock, his hand stroke her hair.

"You know what you said before—the . . . the kind offer you made."

She nods, staring at an ash-skinned coal, about to topple from its perch.

"It was out of the question then; I simply wasn't well enough. But . . ." He clears his throat. "You know I saw a new doctor recently."

"Yes."

"The symptoms I was suffering from have quite gone. I asked him whether it would be injurious to you, if we could . . . do as you suggested. And he said that it was possible. With precautions, and, um, certain . . . methods, it should not be injurious at all. Advantageous, in fact, given what we, er, talked about, before."

"Oh?" The silence stretches out between them, but he doesn't elucidate. The cinder falls, making her jump.

"Perhaps I should leave you to think about it."

Flora, who has no idea what she is supposed to be thinking about, slips off the stool and kneels in front of him.

"Don't go," she says, and put her hands on his knees. It is the first time she has done something so intimate. She feels no desire at this moment, but she strokes his thighs and lifts her face toward him, so that he can lean down and kiss her. Instead, he averts his eyes.

"I shouldn't kiss you. There is a slight risk in that."

"Oh."

He stands up, and helps her to her feet. He smiles, but there is an unusual tension in his face.

"Dearest, would you go to bed, as you normally would?"

Flora does so. Her heart is racing. Freddie turns down the lights, takes off his dressing gown, and comes over to the bed.

"Turn your back to me."

She rolls onto her side and, with her face to the window, feels him get into the bed behind her. Creakings and rustlings ensue. She feels his hand on her shoulder, stroking her arm through the fabric of her nightdress. He maneuvers closer to her, and slides his hand around to knead her breast. Her breathing quickens. She can feel the heat of his body through their nightclothes and excitement flickers inside her. Then his hand grasps the hem of her nightdress and pulls it up; almost in the same movement, he pushes her onto her stomach, so she is spread-eagled on the bed. He has her nightdress bunched on the small of her back, and clambers on top of her, spreading her legs.

She wonders what on earth is so wrong that he doesn't want her to look at him. It must be awful . . . but her face is pressed sideways into the pillow, so she can only see through one eye, and the vision of that is obscured by her hair; nor can she move, and then something hard nudges between her buttocks. The first thing she feels is a thrill of relief—he does desire her! She tries to lift her hips to help him, because he seems to be in the wrong place, but a hand on the base of her spine pushes her down. And his erect penis seems to be trying to force its way into her anus. She tries to reach behind her to guide him better, but her arm is stuck and she cannot move to free it.

"No, no, like this is better," he whispers, his breaths coming fast in her ear.

She feels a surge of panic, and struggles, but his weight presses her down into the bed.

"Let me, dearest, oh, let me," he mutters, and so she lets him.

It burns like fire as he forces it into her, and she yelps with pain. It feels wrong; she is skewered, a pig spitted for roasting. Pinned down by his weight, she can hardly breathe, but is terrified of moving, in case it makes it worse. He begins to thrust into her and there is a tearing sensation; she grits her teeth, but it hurts a great deal and she is so shocked that *this* is what he wants to do that tears squeeze through her shut eyelids, wetting the pillow.

She pushes down her juddering breaths, but the burning pain goes on, tearing in and out and in again with rough, sharp thrusts. It hurts where he entered her—a sharp, bright pain—and it hurts again deep inside her—the dark ache of some bruised, protesting organ. She is barely aware of his groans, his accelerating gasps, and then, after an age—perhaps just a minute—of pushing his way into her, it seems to be over. He has stopped moving. She holds her breath, locked rigid. She is trapped underneath him as he lies, heavy and panting, on top of her, and then, mercifully, he withdraws. There is more burning, but the worst of the pain is over. Freddie rolls off her to lie by her side, but she doesn't trust herself to move or show her face. There is a painful throbbing in her lower belly; she wonders if she is injured in some awful way. Tears run from her eyes without stopping.

At their wedding, they had said to each other, "With my body I thee worship," and the words, in his mouth, had made her tremble with anticipation. But she revolts. How can causing her this pain be worship?

They lie in silence for a minute, and then Freddie puts his hand gently on her back and strokes her.

"Dearest girl . . . thank you," he says.

Flora pulls herself to sit on the side of the bed, still facing away from him. She dashes the tears off her face, but more come. She is miserable, but also she is angry, because he has turned something she wanted and longed for into something . . . like this.

Some time later, as she lies awake in the dark, she says, "Does it have to be like that?"

"It's what the doctor recommended. There's no risk of infection that way."

This does not make sense to her.

"But if you wear something, doesn't that prevent infection?"

Freddie sighs, rather sharply.

"Dear, in these matters, a wife is guided by her husband. Be guided by me. I know the first time can be rather . . . uncomfortable, but it gets easier. Many women enjoy it—even prefer it! It makes a lot of things easier."

Flora cannot think of anything to say. Freddie rubs her arm through her sleeve.

"I'm sorry if it was a shock. It will get better. It will be all right. You'll see."

But it is not all right, and Flora does not see. When he comes to her again, a few nights later, she rolls over and waits, lying completely still. She hopes it will be easier this time—she wants to make him happy, to give him what he wants. But it is not easier; it is just as painful as before.

"I'm not trying to hurt you!" Freddie says in frustration. "You must try to relax." And, after another minute, sounding cross: "Stop resisting—you're making it worse for yourself."

Flora wants to say that she is trying, but how can she stop resisting something that hurts so much? When he pins her down on the bed, she feels rising panic, like an animal caught in a trap.

After some muttering—she doesn't catch what he says, but she seems to have put him off rather, and his penis feels less hard— he starts again, and this time mutters in her ear, "Say, 'Fuck me in the arse.'"

His Irish accent is suddenly noticeable in the word *arse*. She is so shocked, she can't say anything at all, and he says it again, louder.

"Say, 'Fuck me in the arse!'"

So she does. But this time, while he fucks her, her sobs are audible. When he has finished, she cries hopelessly, aware that their marriage, and everything that goes with it, may be over.

The next morning, she apologizes to Freddie—for crying, for not being sufficiently wifely. She does not mean her apology: the blood on her nightdress is surely proof that it is not her fault. Freddie, in turn, apologizes to her: he does not want to distress her; perhaps it would be better if they just went back to the way they were . . . She nods, relieved and ashamed.

She does not think his apology any more sincere than hers: his manner implies that her reaction was unusual and missish. But he is inconsistent: sometimes, in the days that follow, he appears to regret his behavior, and is sweet to her; other times, he is moody and resentful.

Flora longs for advice, but cannot think whom she could ask. Iris, she suspects, is, for once, not going to be of help. And even with Iris, she does not know how she would put such questions into words.

Chapter 12

London, 51°31' N, 0°7' W
February–May 1892

"THE SNOW QUEEN" TO SAIL FOR THE NORTH AGAIN!
MR. AND MRS. ATHLONE TALK ABOUT THEIR PLANS

... The "Snow Queen," who came to our attentions three years ago while still a young girl, is now embarking on the second part of an unusual career. She has recently acquired a harmonious new title, which we find suits her very well: that of "Mrs. Frederick Athlone." She and her husband are due to set sail for the Arctic in Spring, there to undertake sixteen months of scientific research which will, Mrs. Athlone states, set an example for the fair sex, while the fruits of that research will benefit all. "The most northerly married couple in the world," as Mr. Athlone calls them, are to share leadership of this unique and perilous endeavor, and the *Record* wishes them all the best, and awaits the eventual outcome with interest...

London Evening Record, February 2, 1892

Freddie has finally found a ship—an old Hull-built whaler called the *North Britain*. After much debate with the sponsors, who all want to call the ship after their august organs (the editor of the *Northern Chronicle* was particularly tenacious), it is renamed after that cheapest and most useful of Arctic commodities: *Resolve*. They will need a great deal of that, to make up for all the things they can't afford.

The personnel of the expedition is slow in coming together. Few men are prepared to sign up to an endeavor where one of the leaders is a woman. This is hardly a surprise, but at last Freddie engages a doctor, Maurice Seddon, who, as well as acting as the expedition's medic, is an accomplished ornithologist and photographer. They meet in the expedition's offices (a room above a newsstand on Cromwell Road). Dr. Seddon is a serious man who, at twenty-eight, has climbed extensively in the Alps and Norway. The only time Flora detects any enthusiasm is when he shows them photographs of enormous, ugly birds called *lammergeiers*, taken in Austria. She is impressed by him but cannot warm to him. He has a neat face with a small mustache and marble-like blue eyes. He displays no evidence of humor. She tells herself this does not matter, although, knowing how long the winters in Greenland can be, she has her misgivings. Freddie is trying to secure the services of a geologist called Ralph Dixon, desirable because his specialism is glaciology. A Cambridge graduate, he is still an uncertain prospect, saying that, at present, he is partially committed to a Belgian expedition to Spitsbergen, whose financing seems at least as shaky as their own.

"So find someone else. There must be dozens of geologists who would leap at the chance to join." This is what the *Northern Chronicle*'s editor assures them. People will fall over themselves to volunteer. They advertise. Volunteers are certainly numerous and varied. They receive letters from schoolboys, students, women (often suggesting that all the expedition members should be women, to save on tents and awkwardness), retired doctors, crazed enthusiasts—like the man who wants to start an Arctic colony as an experiment in utopian living . . . Freddie estimates that a quarter of the volunteers are insane. Flora thinks he exaggerates, but only a little.

When Captain Mackie received the news of her marriage, he wrote her a tepid letter of congratulation, leavened with warnings about hasty decisions. It was better than she had expected. In her lowest moments, the previous autumn, she had imagined her marriage being over and her father spurning her in anger. Now that neither fear has been realized, she invites her father to London so that he can witness the rechristening of the *Resolve*. It will also be the first time he has met his son-in-law. She has not seen her father for over a year, and the prospect of his arrival makes her nervous. Even though he seems, in his letters, resigned to her "antics" (as he terms her expedition), and acknowledges that her upbringing played its part, he does not attempt to disguise his disapproval. Flora wants him to be proud of her, to admire her achievements as so many people—she is constantly told—admire her: she is a trained meteorologist—how many of them are there in the country? She will be an explorer in her own right!

When Captain Mackie arrives, Freddie shows him a scrapbook of their press clippings over a cup of tea. Flora awaits the reaction with a sinking heart. (She told Freddie this sort of acclaim would not impress him, but he refused to be put off.)

"Hmm . . ." her father says, flicking through the pages. "You have been getting a lot of attention."

"My father finds such attention undignified," she says, trying to make light of it. Freddie, who can see that as well as anyone, smiles at him.

"Believe me, sir, I understand—and, were I fantastically wealthy, we wouldn't need to court it. But it is a means to an end—the end being our expedition. Flora's expedition. It's a bargain we have to make."

He smiles at Flora, and she feels a wave of gratitude.

"He's right, Daddy. After all, I cannot be a whaler, or a naval captain."

"I know, Flora. Perhaps I'm old-fashioned, but I find it a pity that an endeavor of scientific value is overshadowed by this"—he glances at some particularly egregious headlines—"puppet show."

"Well, yes. But, despite them, sir, you must realize that there is no one in the country better qualified to lead this expedition than your daughter, and that, of course"—Freddie glances at Flora—"is largely thanks to you."

The next day, they take Captain Mackie to Limehouse Reach, where the ship is in dry dock. Flora has not seen the *Resolve* for some weeks, but it is apparent that not one of the requested adaptations has been made, or even begun. Captain Mackie walks around in silence, every flaw glowing like a beacon on a dark night.

"This is the old *North Britain*," he says as they go below.

"That's right, sir," says Freddie, determinedly genial. "She has proved herself in many winters in the north."

"Yes. I've seen her there," says the captain. "Gripes. She was stove amidships a couple of years after."

"She was re-sheathed two years ago," says Flora, aggrieved that her voice comes out sounding petulant.

"She has splendid headroom, don't you think?"

They are in the main cabin. Freddie pats the timbers above his head. The clearance below decks in the *Resolve* is six foot, five inches. In the *Vega*, it was five foot four.

Mackie grunts, perhaps approvingly; more clearance means less stability, so probably not.

At breakfast the following day, Flora's father swallows his last mouthful of kipper, takes a draft of tea, lays his knife and fork side by side, and dabs his mouth with his napkin. Then he clears his throat. Flora and Freddie look at him.

"I must speak to you about the ship," he says.

"We know there's much work still to be done," says Flora.

"I'll get on to the agent today," says Freddie. "We have months to go, so—"

"Mr. Athlone, there is not enough time to do all the work that should be done. If you intend—as I believe you do—to go north of Melville Bay, you will need a triply reinforced hull. The bows should be raised by three feet. There is rot in her cross braces and she has wormy knees. She should be completely stripped down. I'm sorry to say this, but the *North Britain* has never been a good boat and I do not like to think of you entrusting your lives to her."

He looks at Freddie as he says this.

"Mr. Athlone, Flora is my only child. When she came north with me, I knew that the ship we sailed in was the stoutest in the fleet. I would not have taken her otherwise."

"Of course, sir. But there will be a good deal of reinforcements of the nature you recommend. I would not risk Flora for the world." He takes her hand as he says this.

"What is your knowledge of ships, Mr. Athlone?"

Freddie looks him in the eye.

"Very poor, sir, but we have an agent who knows a great deal. And a good captain overseeing the work."

"But they've not done what they were supposed to have done."

"Father, please, there are always snags. There have been holdups, I know—they were unavoidable—but we will see to it. I will not go to sea in a ship that isn't safe. Nor will Freddie."

"Any advice you can give us would be gratefully received," Freddie says. "It would be wonderful to have the benefit of your expertise."

Mackie promises to speak to a man he knows. He will do what he can to galvanize the works. This is all well and good, but the real problem, as Freddie and Flora know all too well, is that there is not enough money. Even with sponsorship, donations from private sources, the publishing deal for the book Flora will write, the exclusive newspaper contract, and an unknown amount of Freddie's personal fortune, they are desperately short. The shipyard refuses to work without money up front, and no matter how Freddie rails at them, Flora can see their point.

Flora and her father walk out of the office one afternoon two weeks later and take a hansom to the docks. The rechristening ceremony is due to take place soon, but that, as Freddie pointed out, is not the same thing as a launch. As long as the side of the boat closest to the cameras looks all right, that will do.

As they rattle along the Embankment, her father clears his throat: a noisy affair—one that usually precedes a long-gestated remark.

"I suppose, if you cannot raise the necessary funds, you will be obliged to put off your journey until next season."

"Freddie will find it. He's a genius at such things."

"I'm sure . . . but I'm concerned for you. Has anyone on this expedition been to Melville Bay, other than yourself?"

"Captain Traill is a whaler. And most of the crew will have experience with ice."

Her father sighs.

"I know you want to go back, Flora. I understand. But I am worried. You will be on a boat full of men . . ."

"I will be with my husband—it's not the same."

"I don't think you understand. The *Vega* was unusual. I knew the crew inside out, and they knew me, and even then . . . If you are scraping a crew together, even the best captain cannot guarantee perfect discipline. I don't think you knew how close you came to . . . something for which I could never have forgiven myself."

Flora feels a cold finger of alarm, but shrugs. "Something terrible could happen to me here, down any side street, or in Dundee . . . There are risks everywhere. I know what I'm doing. You think of me as your child still. But I'm grown up."

Her father looks tired. This sort of conversation is painful.

"In the end, Flora—you may forget this, but others won't—you are a young woman, and they are men. It is Freddie who will set the tenor of your undertaking."

Flora looks at him in surprise.

"You've never called him Freddie before."

"You don't want me to?"

"No, I do. He's your son-in-law."

She smiles. She feels that she has won a victory—a tiny one, but it cheers her.

"I've been practicing marksmanship. And, once we're there, Aniguin will help me."

Flora has not heard of her friend for four years. Her father grunts.

"If he's still alive."

When they arrive at the dock and see the *Resolve*, Flora's heart sinks. Despite promises, nothing appears to have been done. Flora looks at her little black ship and feels a frustrated tenderness. It causes a wrenching in her gut, like the runt of a litter: the poor thing isn't really up to it, but doesn't she deserve a chance? She is small and battered and ugly; her lines are not quite true; her mainmast is too tall, her bowsprit too short.

"Come," says her father.

They make their way to the shipyard office, where their agent is bleary-eyed behind piles of paper. Her father takes out an envelope and hands it to him.

"Flora, see this. I'm giving Mr. Smedley a check for two thousand pounds to make the most pressing repairs and give the *Resolve* a new engine. I'm sorry it's not more. But she will be seaworthy, at least."

Flora gapes at him, and her throat tightens. For a minute, she can't find her voice. "Daddy, you don't . . . How can you afford it?"

"I haven't sailed for thirty years for nothing, Flora. I don't want to see you drown."

Flora feels a part of her should stop him, but she knows she won't even try. "I don't know when we can repay you. It will take time . . ." She doesn't want to cry in front of the agent, who already doesn't bother to hide his contempt for her. She pushes down the lump in her throat, and smiles. "That's wonderful. You see, Mr. Smedley; I told you not to worry."

When they go outside and look at the poor *Resolve* again, Flora sees an entirely different ship, one with strong, sturdy lines, which—once her hull is re-sheathed and her mast trimmed, a new engine installed, knees replaced, and braces strengthened—will be an entirely suitable vessel for an expedition. All it takes is a shower of cash.

Flora squeezes her father's arm through his sleeve. She whispers, "Thank you."

Despite his gift, they run out of money before all the improvements are carried out, and Freddie is compelled to sell a place on the expedition to a young man by the name of Edwin Daneforth. He has no noticeable skills other than an athletic physique. He is not a scientist. He has never been north of a Perthshire grouse moor. But he is willing. He is keen on photography, and it turns out that a condition of his family's handsome donation is that he be appointed the official photographer. As this position has already been promised to Maurice Seddon, it presents a small difficulty. Seddon is not happy, but is mollified by the assurance that he will still be able to take photographs of birds. At last, Ralph Dixon signs a contract to be the expedition's geologist, Belgian financing having collapsed entirely.

On May 18, they weigh anchor. Flora stands in the bows of the patched and primped *Resolve*, staring over the gunwale (raised a compromise eighteen inches), adding her will to the momentum of the ebb tide. They ghost downriver, the seamen's marks sliding past, insubstantial in the predawn murk: Limekiln Creek, Halfway Reach, Erith Rands. The crew is new and unfamiliar; Captain Traill, on the quarterdeck, clicks his tongue as one green hand collides with another.

They pass Northfleet Hope with listless slowness; still landlocked, the ship moves sluggishly, deep-laden, through mud-colored water.

Before he left London, Flora's father surprised her with an embrace. They have never been demonstrative, and she laughed in surprise.

"Promise me you won't do anything rash."

"You don't need to worry; I'm your daughter."

"Good luck, my dear," she thought he muttered, although she couldn't be sure, and couldn't speak to ask.

At the bend of Lower Hope, a quiver runs through the timbers of the ship; the *Resolve* seems to stiffen and gather herself, like a pointer catching a scent. The river broadens; the eastern horizon flattens and softens into the indistinct gray of the North Sea, and Flora, one hand on the gunwale, feels her heart lift with the rhythmic movement of the hull, the heartbeat of the open sea.

PART THREE

REGELATION

Snowflakes are not made for solitude; each, with outflung arms, tangles and meshes with its neighbor; over time, they compress, become ice. But ice is mutable, even in the deepest cold. Inside a glacier, pressure and affinity will melt ice at temperatures far below freezing, so that two pieces, in contact with each other, melt and refreeze as one.

Chapter 13

The sky is like the inside of a shell. To the west, where the sea is visible between floes, the water is as flat as a pond, as mysterious as an old mirror: mercury streaked with lead. The sun, his constant companion, is swathed in fine cloud, a blurred disc of nacreous light, too weak to cast shadows. He pauses at the top of the hill to get his breath back; despite being shirtless, he is sweating. He has walked for hours. It is one o'clock in the morning.

To the north lies the land they have spent the past weeks chiseling out of the unknown: 384 miles of new coastline. Fjords, headlands, mountains they have measured and plotted. Most of the features are named for sponsors—their map is sprinkled with the names of brewers, railway barons, and financial speculators—but, far to the north, there is a bay called De Beyn Inlet. He will probably never see it again, but he has photographs. He likes the fact that the number of people who will ever set foot there is vanishingly small.3

Shimmering on the tarnished mirror is the uncertain specter of more land—which could be either a continuation of Ellesmere, or—tantalizingly—an as-yet-undiscovered island. He shrugs off the heavy pack, pulls out his Kodak, and takes a picture of what he sees—gray on gray. He notes down: position, direction, weather, time.

Time is easy to forget—clocks and calendars have little meaning when it is always day; you eat when you are hungry, sleep when you are tired. But they have to adhere to a schedule, keep the record. Easy, in the endless light, to lose an hour here, a day there; but without accurate dates, they do not know where they are. Navigation would be inaccurate; mapping, meaningless. They have to impose a rhythm and structure on this subtle place, because, if they did not, they could not say truly that they had discovered anything.

Far down below, a dot moves around by the tents, squats by the campfire—probably Johannes, their half-Eskimo, half-Danish interpreter. Hopefully, it is his day to cook—Jakob's stomach growls at the prospect of fresh steak. He hoists the rucksack of rocks back on to his shoulders—his sunburn is painful, but even that is somehow a pleasure—and sets off down the slope. Intermittently, he hears the dogs bark. Rhythmically, the crust of snow yields to his boots. At every step, he thinks, I am the first man to tread on this piece of the earth. He is aware that, at this moment, he is completely happy.

A naked physicist is in one of the tents—Louis Erdinger, hunched over his notebook. Jakob squats outside the open tent flap and says, "Knock knock." Inside the tent, it must be eighty degrees.

A week ago, Erdinger told Jakob he couldn't wait to get home. He had three more years in which to do useful work, and then . . . He shrugged dismissively, implying it would all be over. Jakob was alarmed—was he ill?

"No," said Erdinger. "In three years, I'll be thirty and my brain will be mush. I've got to do my best work now."

Jakob thought he was joking.

"It's all right for you," said Erdinger. "You're only a geologist."

Jakob knew he didn't mean to be insulting.

Erdinger says, "Pass me that shirt," as if Jakob has been gone ten minutes instead of three days, and he is struck afresh by the oddness of the physicist's face—flat, square, and decorated by a perfect equilateral triangle of a nose. The square is red and peeling. The rest of his body is pink with sunburn.

"What are you laughing at?"

"I don't know. It's such a beautiful day . . . morning . . . night." Jakob grins at him. "I'm going to get Johannes to cook some steak."

"Shull's disappeared again," says Erdinger, from under the shirt.

"I expect he's following musk oxen. They don't run to timetables."

Erdinger grunts, indicating his contempt for imprecision, even on the part of beasts.

Camp Hendrik consists of three tents above a river that rushes down from the ice cap. When they chose the spot, they followed their custom of taking it in turn to christen the place. Thus far, they have pitched and struck Camp Herta (Erdinger's mother), Camp Edith (Shull's mother), and Camp Annette (Jakob's mother), followed by a bevy of sisters and sweethearts. They toast each person so honored with cups of tea and a certain amount of teasing—especially at Camp Jane (Shull's choice), which a sudden downpour turned into a quagmire. This spot—one of their last camps on Ellesmere—Jakob has named for his brother.

"What does Hendrik do that merits such a fine spot?" asked Shull, with an arch smile.

Irritated—partly because a mosquito had just bitten him on the eyelid—Jakob said snappishly, "He's a butcher," and enjoyed the look of shock on Shull's face.

Erdinger laughed. "You see, Shull, de Beyn and I are men of the people. No silver spoons for us."

"I didn't say anything! It's a . . . very fine profession," mumbled Shull, before Erdinger could go on to remind him, as he tended to do, that Shull's family had bought his way onto the expedition.

"Hendrik put me through college," said Jakob. "If it wasn't for him, I wouldn't be here."

This valley, more than any other they have found over the past weeks, is a blessed place. Effectively the head of an inlet, it is now almost bare of snow. With the sun wheeling endlessly around the sky, it gets as warm as a New York spring—on several days the temperature has broken sixty-five degrees. To men acclimatized to cold, the temperature is tropical. The river swells and shrinks according to the time of day—a trickle in the morning; a torrent by late afternoon. Its gravel banks have become a green haze of mosses and grass, powdered with tiny flowers—cinquefoils, saxifrages, mountain avens. From a distance, they are all but invisible—swallowed up in the overall dun of the land—but, close to, they are minute jewels of vivid pink, white, yolk-yellow. And there are animals: foxes, Arctic hares, ptarmigan; caribou and musk oxen.

In spring, after crossing the frozen strait from Greenland, Jakob and Erdinger left Camp Susan to climb a nearby mountain. At least, the mountain appeared close. But, as happened time and again, the clarity of the air deceived them—the summit took far longer to reach than they had reckoned. It was a clear day, and the view from the summit, when they finally reached it, stunned them into silence. A range of snow-covered peaks to the north was the Victoria and Albert mountains, but beyond them they could see still higher summits. A curving peak like a raptor's talon, perfectly white, poked above its neighbors. They looked in awe.

It was one of those rare, windless moments when the silence was strangely absolute; Jakob was aware of his heart pumping, his breath rasping, Erdinger gasping beside him. Directly in front of them, a dozen brownish-black beasts were scraping away the snow to find something edible beneath. They seemed indifferent to the interlopers. Jakob could hear the animals' slow tearing, smell their rank odor. He seemed to hear his own blood pulsing through his veins.

There was something supremely dignified, magisterial, about the musk oxen. The largest, a bull, slowly walked toward them and stopped. It appeared to float over the snow, the long hair on its body swaying like robes of state. It regarded the men from one small brown eye: a bright boss in the blunt shield of its head. Finding them of no interest, it turned and walked away.

Later, Johannes shot him. Jakob was sorry, but they had to eat. He also shot a cow, milked it, and they savored the warm milk as though it were a rare vintage.

Johannes has perfected a way of frying meat so that it is charred and crusty on the outside, bloody and almost raw in the middle. Jakob falls on his steak—tough but delicious. Sweetness, blood, charcoal, and salt explode in his mouth. He closes his eyes. He has learned this about life in the north: when you are perpetually hungry, tired, uncomfortable, and (usually) cold, the sensations of warmth, comfort, and taste are overwhelming. It's the same with the landscape: at first a vast monotony, its colors and treasures hidden by scale, you have to squat down to appreciate them, and then their delicacy moves you beyond measure. As for the ice, it confounds with its indifferent beauty; there are so many ways to look at it, and each reveals something new, whether from a distance, when it suggests fabulous, ruined cities, or squinting at the universe in a snow crystal, or the changing reaction of either with light that teases you with colors you can neither describe, nor photograph, nor forget.

"Good," mumbles Erdinger, mouth full. Jakob eats in voluptuous silence. Johannes sits by the fire, legs straight out in front of him, his eyes on the middle distance, and sucks on his pipe.

When he is finished, Jakob lights a cigarette, lies back, and sighs with contentment.

"I saw more signs of the Paleocene forest: there are trunks three feet in diameter!" He shakes his head in mingled frustration and delight.

Johannes coughs. His pipe shifts from the center to the corner of his mouth: the signal for approaching speech.

"Te Peyn—tomorrow we go back?"

"Not yet, Johannes. Another three days. Maybe four. I want to make a dash to the south—see if we can get close enough to see the land over there."

Armitage has instructed them to return to winter quarters on the Greenland side of Smith Sound no later than the last day of June, so they will have to set off soon.

"Snow is coming." Johannes gestures at the western sky.

The others look—it is clear, though tinted with yellow.

"When?"

"Soon—one, two days."

"How can you tell?"

"The water is different. The wind has changed."

There is hardly any wind; a cool breath, welcome in the sun.

"The wind is *ooangniktuq*."

"Does that mean there will still be ice in the strait?"

Johannes glances upward. "I will ask the Lord."

A few hours later, Jakob is shaken awake. The sky is the congealed gray of an oyster's flesh; the wind drives snow into their faces. Instead of being able to see all the way to the coast, they can barely see each other. They strap down stores and sleds, pull stoves and food into the tents, and crawl into their sleeping bags to wait. Moisture freezes on the inside of the tents. When the blizzard dies down, two days later, plates of ice fall on them, and the valley outside is white and silent—no animal, bird or plant is visible, nor sign that they were ever here. The only thing still moving is the shrunken river, grumbling darkly through a land in which life appears not only wiped out, but inconceivable.

Jakob looks around at the valley as they leave it. Fog obliterates the horizon. The new land he may have seen from the hilltop has vanished into the whiteness of the sea.

Chapter 14

Return from Cape Dupree, 82°34' N, 46°12' W (disputed)
June 1892

"Right! Right! God damn you!"

Armitage is cursing the sled, Frank is almost sure. He throws his weight to the right, the drag of the sled causing the rope to bite into his shoulder and squeeze him cruelly around the waist. Armitage hangs on the other rope. Metek, the hunter, holds the sled itself, guiding it as they lower it down the slope of wind-scoured ice. The gradient is so steep, the dogs have had to be uncoupled, and the sharp frenzy of their barking comes and goes under the shriek of the wind.

Metek holds up his hand—stop! He points below—a dark line in the snow across their path: a crevasse. At the same moment, Armitage loses his footing and slides for a heart-stopping number of seconds toward the blue crack. Frank drops to the ground, his heels dug in against a block of ice. Cautiously, he lifts his head: Lester is spread-eagled, face down, a dozen feet from the crevasse; Metek has tipped the sled on its side, turning it into an anchor and saving Armitage a nasty fall. Their leader pulls himself back up the slope, eyes hidden by his ice-clotted hood, his mouth a black hole. Words are coming out, but Frank can't make out what they are. Perhaps he is angry with Metek about the sled, again: most of the gear has fallen off; the lashing on one of the runners has come loose . . .

Frank drags himself to a sitting position, and the wind slams onto his back like a falling wardrobe. It is unbearable, but apparently necessary, that he must once again get up and repack the sled. Necessary, but surely impossible, that Metek can once again mend the crumbling sled runner. Unbearable but true that their stove leaks, that fuel is so low they can barely heat what food they have and that their clothes are frozen hard on the outside and wet on the inside. Completely unbearable that they are still several days from their base on the coast, and that he is clinging onto a glassy, treacherous slope of ice in a torrent of wind and snow. He despairs of ever seeing home, family, fiancée again. Not for the first time on this trip, Frank wants to cry. Luckily, it is too cold for tears.

Lester Armitage, Metek, and Frank have been on the ice cap for ninety days. The younger hunter, Tateraq, turned back after thirty miles, leaving them one sled and twenty dogs. The others went on.

They have been to the north coast of Greenland and back, 870 miles, walking every step. Every mile was painfully won. Sometimes the snow was so flour-soft they floundered, thigh deep; sometimes it was like coarse sand and the runners could hardly slide through; sometimes there was a glassy crust that sliced the dogs' paws and the soles of the men's boots. Wind-carved ice ridges lay across their path: huge, concrete-hard barriers they could not chop through, but had to haul the sled over—and if they couldn't, they had to unpack, pull the sled over, climb back, drag the gear over, repack, untangle the dogs' traces, go on to the next ridge a few yards farther, to be repeated, over and over . . .

Sometimes Frank wondered if Armitage was losing his mind. Sometimes he wondered if he was losing his: when visibility was poor, which was often, it was easy to succumb to the illusion that they were walking and walking, but never advancing through the featureless grayness. Such times, on top of the weariness, uncertainty, and discomfort, were soul-destroying. But there were, it was true, other times—moments—when the sun burned off the fog, and they struggled out of their snow *illu* in the morning to find themselves under an aching blue sky, to view never-before-seen mountains glittering in the distance, and Frank would, at least briefly, be heart-glad he is here.

After forty-four days' outward march, they reached the top of a wind-scoured cliff. From its foot, a plain of ice stretched northward, as far as they could see, through drifting fog. The frozen sea looked an awful place—tortured into a chaos of ridges and hollows, even worse than those they had encountered on land. The prospect of setting out across that unstable wilderness was appalling, and they were still, by Lester's most optimistic calculation, more than 400 miles from the Pole. They celebrated their arrival at the north coast with an argument about the cliff's height—necessary to calculate the distance to the horizon. For lack of stones (even, ironically, snow) to drop over the edge, they sacrificed an empty tin, weighted with dog shit, but it bounced off the uneven rock face and vanished without sound (Frank profoundly glad he hadn't been the one to throw it). Lester thought the cliff was 700 feet high. Frank thought it more like 500—which made the horizon either thirty-five miles away, or less than thirty. The disagreement was moot: with the dense, shifting fog, they could see only a mile across the ice. Lester wanted to wait for the weather to clear, but food was short, and fuel shorter. After a miserable twelve-hour wait, in which no one was allowed to sleep, he gave the order to return. Otherwise, Frank believed, he or Metek might have pushed him over the edge.

On their return, the dogs began to die, their bodies fed to the survivors. The men could not eat the meat, not knowing what they had died of. Nor could they find the caches of food they had made on the outward journey, so had to go on short rations.

Now, at last, they have reached the glacier that will lead them down off the ice cap and back to their base. Still over fifty miles to go. They have hardly any fuel—enough, perhaps, for two nights of melting snow to drink. They are cold and starving, and desperately thirsty. Only six dogs are left alive. Frank has frostbite on his cheeks and hands. Metek is suffering from diarrhea. Lester has frostbitten feet. Frank, who took an oath to alleviate suffering, can do nothing about any of this.

Lester is shouting again. Frank sways to his feet and clambers, crabwise, down the slope to the grounded sled. Metek points to the runner—not only is the lashing loose, but the runner itself has split. Frank looks at Lester. For a moment, he thinks his leader is crying; his face is a mask of wounded disbelief—the face of a man whose world has, for a long time, been conspiring against him.

He turns to Metek and screams at the top of his voice, "Can you mend it?"

If Metek is at the end of his tether, he does not show it. He nods, *ieh*; he is a wizard with such things, has saved their lives on a daily basis, but he needs more leather thong, perhaps a tin, if they can spare it . . . Understanding at last, Frank squats down and starts to search—with the numb, slow movements that have become habitual to them—through their meager belongings for something that will get them home.

Chapter 15

Jakob's party reaches the Greenland coast on June 30, as instructed. When they are still a mile from the ice foot, they see a sled come galloping out to meet them. They wonder, for a few excited minutes, if the welcoming party is Armitage and Frank. Then they see that the sled is driven by two hunters: Omowyak and his son Sorqaq. The Eskimos hail the Americans and tell Johannes, cheerfully, that they thought they were dead.

"We have been gone for twelve weeks," Erdinger says, puzzled, "which is what we planned."

"Such terrible weather!" Johannes translates. The others look at each other with the first stirrings of alarm.

"Armitage and Urbino—are they back yet?"

"No. Not here. Still up there." Omowyak and Johannes point toward the ice cap. Jakob can understand most of what Omowyak says, but it is as well that Johannes translates to be sure what he says next.

"There have been bad storms. On the inland ice—no game. Tateraq came back because there was nothing to eat. They are probably dead."

"They could just be late coming back."

Johannes and Omowyak confer. Omowyak is emphatic.

"Dead. Yes," repeats Johannes.

On their first day back, they light the stove and burn some precious coal for hot baths—an intense, almost erotic pleasure after months of cold water. Jakob shaves off his beard, which makes him laugh, as beneath it the skin is pasty, while the rest of his face, like his body, is deeply tanned. Erdinger goes in search of Mikissoq, his paramour of the previous winter, and returns in a sulk, having been supplanted by another. Adding injury to insult, he is bitten by a dog, and his hand swells up with an infection. They obsessively watch the shoreline of the fjord for any movement that could be their returning colleagues.

After four days, Jakob and Shull, with two local men, Omowyak and Ayakou, who is Metek's cousin, set off in search of the northern party. Armitage's route was to take them up the glacier on to the ice cap, then strike across the interior until they reached Sherard Osborn Fjord, far to the north, and beyond.

Their map shows a white blank covering most of Greenland. The only words on it read, *The Interior is entirely covered with Ice.* Ice with a capital *I*. To the north and east, the land shades into a blur: Armitage, Metek, and Frank have walked off the edge of the known world.

The two sleds struggle onto the broad foot of the glacier, which forms a highway, of sorts, onto the ice cap. From a distance, it looks smooth and flat, its gradient gentle, but up close, it is a wilderness of towering blocks and hard, scoured ice, crisscrossed with open and hidden crevasses. They know how to avoid some of the worst areas, where the glacier bends around a sandstone bluff, but cannot avoid the rugged chaos at its higher reaches, where it spills off the ice cap itself and starts to fall, with infinite slowness, infinite patience, toward the sea.

The glacier on which Jakob broke his ankle was a sylph compared to this behemoth. It is in every way different: the scale, the latitude, the surrounding mountains. He finds himself wishing for the time to draw and measure, to live with the creaks and booms that ring out so suddenly below them—to understand its secrets. When they have to bridge a particularly deep crevasse with one of the sleds, Jakob stops halfway across and stares into its blue depths.

"A moment. It's fine," he calls. He lies across the sled so that his head hangs down into the crevasse itself, feeling its chill exhalation; within inches of the surface, the warmth of the sun is gone. The sides glisten. The color of the ice shades from silver and palest blue to mint and cobalt, before vanishing into a throat of blackness: the home of cold. A dozen feet below, there is a turquoise gleam in the darkness. A hidden chimney? A patch of particularly clear ice? Meltwater, perhaps, forming on the surface, finds a weakness, freezes again . . . Questions run through his head, theories . . . He leans farther, stretches downward, and, in the few moments' windless silence, he hears whispering. He holds his breath, straining—and recognizes the faintest of rustlings as ice crystals sublimate—something once thought impossible—and transform directly from their solid state into vapor. It sounds like language, the ice making him a whispered invitation he can't quite catch. He has to resist the urge to step off the sled and clamber down.

On the fourth day, before they reach the top of the glacier, Ayakou, who is leading, shouts and points up ahead.

"*Qamiut!* Sleds! Sleds!" he shouts, giving a whoop of joy. Neither Jakob nor Shull can see anything through their eyeshades, but hope and relief surge through them, the backwash of their former fear suddenly overwhelming. It is fifteen minutes before Jakob can make out black dots on the rough surface up ahead. Longer still before one of the dots yells and waves. Then, somehow, they are upon them, and three wind- and frost-blackened faces, bearded and clotted with balls of ice, crack into grins of welcome and relief. Jakob throws his arms around Frank in his joy at seeing him again. He even hugs Armitage. They laugh and talk in parched, rasping voices. Frank's shriveled lip splits, and a bead of blood runs slowly, gruesomely into his beard.

In Neqi, when the men remove their clothes for the first time in months, Jakob is shocked again at Frank's appearance. His friend, who has always seemed indestructibly massive and strong, looks ghostly, gaunt, and shrunken. His face is a terrible sight: the skin blackened, raw, peeling; his eyes red and weeping. His left hand is unusable. They weigh themselves: Frank has lost thirty-seven pounds; Lester twenty, but he was lean and stringy to start with. Metek refuses to be weighed, melting quietly away as soon as they have unpacked, anxious, perhaps, to inform his wife that she is not a widow.

Amid the general high spirits, Armitage is in a strange mood. He is adamant that they did not need rescuing, so Erdinger and Jakob and Shull agree: of course they only came to meet them; their own journey had been easy; couldn't believe how different conditions were on the ice cap; astonishing feat . . . Lester's eyes, always disconcerting, now seem incapable of focusing on their faces; instead, his gaze roams the air above their heads, distracted.

"Tateraq should be horsewhipped. I paid for those dogs. We had an agreement."

"Perhaps he thought you hired them. He lost several of his own dogs first. In any case, we won't need dogs again, before the ship comes . . ."

It doesn't matter what anyone says, Armitage seems to take no pleasure in what they have accomplished. Despite the success of his journey—of both journeys—he is morose. He spends the following days sitting in his private alcove—a corner of the cabin enclosed by boxes—staring at the picture of his wife, writing in his diary. Then he rouses himself, and takes Johannes and Shull to visit a village down the coast. He intends—with bribes and promises and, if necessary, threats—to secure many more dogs, for next time.

In his absence, a certain rhythm reestablishes itself. It is too late in the season for sled journeys—the sea is liquid, the remaining ice thin and dangerous. The men wait for their ship, the *Sachem*. Jakob sorts through his rock samples, checks his field notes, and makes fair copies. He has always found such work soothing.

Luxuriant grass now covers the ground between the shore and the cliffs, tempting the men to stretch out on it whenever the sun shines. They go fishing and scoop up samples of seawater; they spy on the busy, invisible world under the microscope. They watch seals mating on the beach. They accompany the young boys when they scramble up the cliffs to look for auk's eggs and catch the birds in their homemade nets.

A small, eroded iceberg grounds itself opposite the hut. It is tall and thin and reminds them of a shy, hopeful panhandler. Every day, when the tide goes out, the base is a little more undermined. Erdinger names it Bert Bergman, and they place bets on when it will fall over.

"I stopped writing anything in my diary. I mean anything . . . extra."

Frank is stretched out on a patch of shingle by the water's edge. He has been lethargic since his return, spending much of his time eating and sleeping. A weak sun warms his face, which sloughs blackened scabs where he was frostbitten. Jakob sits next to him, clumsily mending his fur boots. A few yards away, Bert is fretted and stooped, as though he has a stomachache, but glimmers greenly like a friendly ghost. Jakob has grown attached to the presence; he will be saddened when it finally collapses. He finds what looks like a maggot egg nestled in the seam of his *kamik* and pokes at it with the needle.

"What do you mean?"

They speak slowly and indolently. When the sun isn't going to set, where is the hurry?

"You know . . . I knew he was going to demand my diary at the end of it all, so I couldn't say what I really thought, but sometimes, I sometimes thought he'd lost his mind. He would push on so hard, it was as though he didn't care whether he made it back or not. I don't care what a man chooses to do with his own skin, but if he is responsible for others, he can't go on like that."

Frank looks uneasy; he glances toward the hut; his voice is hardly more than a mumble.

"Metek and I wanted to mark our food caches with cairns and a good spread of flags, in case we missed our trail on the way back. *He* said that was a waste of time; we wouldn't need them, and so forth. Implied we were fussing like old women. Of course, on the way back, there was so much snowdrift, we couldn't see our trail at all. We couldn't find the caches. Not one. We were out of food when you found us. We were damn lucky. He asked for my loyalty, my obedience. I gave him those. Certain risks you accept. But I didn't come here to die of someone else's . . . pig-headedness. Does that make me a coward?"

"Of course not. Did he say that?"

"Not in so many words."

"What was the north coast like?"

Frank snorts. "The fog was so thick we couldn't see much. The ground sloped down for a long time and then fell away sheer to some sea-ice. Visibility was terrible. We stayed for twelve hours, waiting for the fog to lift, but it didn't. It may have been the north coast, but we could only see a couple of miles. It could have been the shore of a fjord. There was no way of telling."

"You took photographs, didn't you?"

"I don't know how much you'll see. They won't prove anything."

"Lester said the coast was turning southeast there."

"As far as we could see."

"It was an extraordinary journey, Frank. You've gone somewhere no one has been before."

Frank is silent for a long minute.

"Don't repeat this to anyone, Jake; promise?"

"Of course."

"We didn't know where we were. We never stopped long enough to take sights. I think he took two longitude sightings the whole trip."

"But . . . you took sightings at the coast?"

"There was no sun. It was dead reckoning."

Jakob tries to conceal his shock. Not knowing where you are—and not being able to prove it—is the explorer's cardinal sin.

"I think that's why Lester's been so"—another swift glance around him—"strange. He knows that he . . . not failed, exactly, but he was negligent, and he knows it."

Jakob thinks back over their work on Ellesmere. Both he and Erdinger took sightings, and checked each other's calculations. He is fairly sure he cannot be accused of negligence. However, that is no comfort to Frank. He wouldn't have thought Armitage capable of such amateurishness.

Frank says quietly, "I thought we weren't going to make it back."

"But you did."

Frank gives a great sigh.

"I thought a lot about Marion up there. How stupid it would be if I died for this. I realized that I'm"—he laughs—"not very brave. When I get home, I'll be happy to sit in a consulting room and live a safe, comfortable life, surrounded by friends and family."

"Nothing wrong with that. That's nothing to do with bravery, or lack of it."

"But it's not for you."

"I wouldn't say that . . . but I do want to come back."

"Lester's coming back." Frank looks up at Jakob. "Would you come back with him?"

Jakob shrugs. "It depends. If the geological work goes well, I might be able to get up something in that line on my own."

Frank shades his eyes with his hand and they fall silent. A voice calling out makes them turn their heads away from the sea. Two Eskimo women approach them. One of them is Meqro, a quiet, cheerful girl who was briefly Frank's mistress in the spring. The other is a young widow, Ainineq. Both are smiling. Meqro sits down close to Frank, who sits up and grins shyly.

Ainineq squats beside Jakob and looks at his handiwork.

"This is very bad," she says, laughing. "You let me do it!"

"I want to learn how to do it myself."

"Pah! You are a man," she says, smiling dismissively. "This is for women."

He surrenders the boot, watching her as she takes the needle and thread and begins to repair his work.

Chapter 16

Neqi, 77°52' N, 71°37' W
July 1892

Last summer, when the *Sachem* had struggled through the ice of Smith Sound and dropped anchor in the bay off Neqi, the villagers came out of their houses, stared at the tall strangers who were not *upernallit*, and asked warily, "Are you flesh or are you spirit?"

The Americans answered, as Johannes had taught them, "We are flesh. We are men." It was what you said, to reassure them that you were not demons.

Word of the big house the *kallunat* built spread fast; Eskimos arrived from up and down the coast, and a straggling camp of rawhide tents—*tupiks*—sprang up nearby.

The Eskimos brought narwhal ivory, meat, and furs, and the Americans, who had been counting on this, exchanged them for utensils, tools, trinkets, and wood. Some of the men were put on a retainer to hunt over the winter, and some of the women were employed as seamstresses and general servants. The most useful thing they did was to prepare seal and bear skins and sew them into the men's winter clothing: bearskin trousers, sealskin boots, seal-gut parkas. These were beautifully made, warm, and weatherproof. Their cooking and cleaning were haphazard, to say the least.

The curiosity displayed by both sides to the other was most apparent with the women. They had an extraordinary lack of shyness. When the sun shone, or when sitting in a tent warmed by a lamp and the exhalations of many bodies, they would whisk off their parkas and sit almost naked, clad only in fox-skin shorts, with a total lack of self-consciousness. The men did likewise, stripping down to their bearskin breeches. The Eskimos took no notice of what was, to them, a practical measure to dry out clothes that had become damp with sweat, so Jakob and the others averted their eyes, and tried to do the same.

Forces ranged in defense of conventional morality were the lack of privacy (an unheard-of concept) and the lack of water for washing (equally unheard of), which meant that the Eskimos carried with them a pungent fug of sweat and seal fat. Effective at first, the deterrent lessened the more the Americans became used to it. Endangering virtue on the other side was the women's flirtatious friendliness; and the women Lester chose as domestics were personable and seemingly available. The men had heard rumors of wife-swapping and the wantonness of Eskimo women—Jakob had assumed them exaggerated, but they seemed to be true.

One of the servants, Natseq, was a widow with two young children. She was plump and bronze-skinned, her habitual expression one of gentle irony. She had hardly spoken to Jakob until, one night in autumn, after they had gone to bed (the Americans slept in the one big room of the house, divided by curtains—Armitage alone sheltered behind a wall of packing cases), Jakob was woken by someone climbing into his bunk. Gray light pervaded the hut from the snow outside.

"No talking," she whispered, and he saw her teeth flash in a smile. He guessed why she was here, was in equal measure surprised and excited.

"Natseq . . ." he muttered. Blood rushed in an avalanche to his groin; it was almost painful.

She lay down beside him under the blankets—his bunk was only three feet wide, so he could feel her warm skin, smell her ripe human scent. Apart from her shorts, she wore nothing. He thought, I'm half asleep; it's not as though I have any say in the matter . . .

"This night, Te Pey," she whispered, "I see your life is hurting you."

Jakob could think of nothing to say to this, and was not about to disagree with anything she said. Natseq placed a bare leg over his. One of his arms was around her shoulders. Her warm hand rubbed his chest, tickled his belly, his muscles tensing in anticipation, then slid downward and encountered his swollen penis, which leapt at her touch. He shivered with an almost unbearable delight. It had been a long time, and he was instantly on the brink of eruption. He prayed that he wouldn't embarrass himself.

"*Marmarai,*" she murmured. Jakob knew that this word, mumbled appreciatively over anything from a pipe of tobacco to a morsel of decomposed auk flesh, meant something like, "Mm, it's good." He remembered hearing a young boy say it as he licked the results of a sneeze off his hand. That helped a little.

It was strange—not off-puttingly so—but strange nonetheless. He tried to kiss her on the mouth, but she turned her head away—no. She rubbed her nose against his face but avoided his lips. He caressed her smooth, plump body and eased off her fur shorts with her full cooperation, but when he tried to put his hand between her legs, she batted him off, hissing, "*Naamik, naamik!* No!" And when he kissed her breasts, he was startled to find his lips were wet. He looked at her in surprise—he had forgotten, in his befuddled state, she had a two-year-old child. He could see her black, heavy-lidded eyes looking at him, gleaming in the almost dark.

"*Marmarai,*" she whispered again, laughing silently, and pulled his head back down to suckle her.

Jakob would have felt a certain unease—guilt was perhaps too strong a word—over his liaison with Natseq, except that his colleagues were doing the same. Everyone knew everyone else's business. Armitage had taken for his companion a beautiful young woman named Ivalu, despite the fact that she was married to the local witch doctor, and despite the fact that he had a photograph of his wife hanging on a nail in his alcove. Erdinger was promiscuous and indiscriminate (not, Jakob told himself, that his own discrimination had played much of a part). Not all of them succumbed; the handsome Shull—as much a magnet for female attention here as he must be in New York—laughingly fought off a number of local girls. And Frank, for the first months, at least, told them he was about to be married, and couldn't do such a thing, no matter how charming they were.

In early winter, a party of hunters returned to the village with sleds piled high with walrus carcasses. There was much shouting and laughter—it seemed there was no greater happiness to the Eskimo than heaps of raw meat. The snow around the village was red with butchery. Then Jakob understood how stark was their equation of life. More than one of the locals said to them, "This winter we will eat—we will live!" An empty sled meant hunger. In that liminal zone between survival and extinction, he thought he understood why a woman would climb into a man's bed without compunction. If, in a few months, we may be dead, why not enjoy ourselves?

The evening of the hunters' return, at the feast, the Americans had to be reminded of the hunters' names, and Jakob was horrified when one of the men was introduced as "Sadloq, husband of Natseq." At first, he thought it must be some other Natseq, but then he saw them rubbing noses affectionately, and Sadloq picked up the little girl and carried her around on his shoulders. Appalled, Jakob seized the first opportunity to speak to Natseq in relative privacy, and said, "Natseq, I thought your husband was dead! I wouldn't have . . ."

Natseq stared at him, a smile breaking out. "I not widow. Sadloq away hunting. Ainineq is widow. Her husband, Kali, die last year, hunting bear. Sadloq is alive. You only like widows?"

"No, I like you very much. I mean . . . I thought you didn't have a husband, so we could . . . I cannot take another man's wife. It is wrong."

Natseq was puzzled. Jakob was aware of his hypocrisy; a few years ago, it hadn't bothered him that Cora Gertler was a married woman, but then, he was eighteen, and he had never met her husband, who seemed, in any case, irrelevant. A middle-aged taxidermist—who could take such a man seriously, or pity him, or fear him?

But he was mortified, having met Sadloq, a friendly man his own age—and in this fragile, beautiful, lethal place, where everyone knew everything, and every man killed for his living.

He told her that he was sad, but that they could not go on now that he knew the truth. Natseq assured him that Sadloq was happy for them to continue, but Jakob could not really believe it.

The most surprising thing was that Frank, after months of celibacy, had given in to temptation and formed a relationship with Meqro. He had believed, he told Jakob, in keeping himself pure for his future wife, but now he was afraid that he might never return from the north—and then . . . he had never . . . Surely, under the circumstances, he would be forgiven? He seemed put out that Jakob had given up sleeping with Natseq, as if Jakob's abstinence were an adverse comment on his own behavior.

"For heaven's sake, Frank. I don't blame you. I'm hardly going to lecture you on morality. Needless to say, Marion will never know."

After that, Jakob decided to withstand all further attacks on his virtue (the thought makes him smile). He is aware that he does not understand the Eskimos. Though he has seen no direct evidence of jealousy, he has witnessed plenty of marital strife. Just yesterday, he was walking past the tents when he was shocked to see a man dragging his wife out of their *tupik* by her hair. Both were yelling at the tops of their voices. The man was Metek, whom he had always held in high regard. Neither he nor his wife paid Jakob any attention when he remonstrated. When he seized Metek by the arm, and they finally stopped, both hung their heads, looking sheepish.

Feeling absurdly pompous—the more so as Metek's head barely reached his chin—Jakob said, "This is no way to settle an argument. Look—good heavens, you have pulled out Ilaitsuq's hair!"

Metek and his wife stared at the ground. Metek dropped the handful of black hair with bloodied roots and grunted in apparent capitulation. Having delivered himself of a little homily on marital negotiation, Jakob went on his way, rather pleased with himself. Before he had gone thirty yards, the shouting started again.

In mid-July, the hunter Omowyak comes to visit, bringing news: at a village a few miles down the coast, another white man's expedition has arrived. After much laughter from Omowyak, Johannes further states—although none of them believe him—that the leader of this expedition is a woman—yes—with breasts and a vagina (Omowyak mimes this; Johannes does not translate), and furthermore—*ieh!*—one who is a friend of the Eskimos.

The Americans decide it must be some sort of joke, but the mere presence of another expedition in the area is intriguing. Armitage receives the news with a clenched jaw; he regards other explorers as he would burglars in his house, but the thought of meeting English-speaking men after more than a year is the cause of jollity in the rest of them.

"I'm too busy to leave, at present. What if the ship arrives while we are gone?"

Depending on ice conditions, the *Sachem* is due to come and pick them up during July or August.

Erdinger, Jakob, and Lester are sitting at the table in the hut. The weather is gray and squally. Although there is still plenty of daylight, it feels as though winter is lying in wait. Lester broods, swirling his mug of substitute coffee.

"I think you and Erdinger should go. Make inquiries."

"Surely you want to meet them yourself?"

"I will give you a note for the leader. I suggest you bring them here."

He seems to think this would show respect to the more senior expedition. Jakob, not entirely happy with his task—Lester will blame him if they come back alone—goes to look for Frank, who is sitting on the beach in the sun. He looks around with a smile. He has a notebook on his lap and is attempting to draw an iceberg.

"You're going now? I hope you bring them back—with this mysterious woman, if she really is a woman!"

Johannes has sworn on his Bible that this is the case. Johannes does not joke about his Bible, so they are curious, although they still do not believe him. It is clearly impossible.

Chapter 17

Siorapaluk, 77°47' N, 70°38' W
July 1892

Jakob and Erdinger are spotted while still some distance from their destination, and two figures come to meet them. One, Pualana, is a mahogany-faced, elderly man, who often visited over the winter. The other, Ayakou, is his son.

Questioned about the newcomers, Pualana affirms that their leader is indeed a woman—*angut*—and refers to her as one of the *upernallit*. Jakob thought that was the word they used for British whalers; he is probably mistaken.

As they approach the village of Siorapaluk, more people come out to greet and inspect the visitors. Laughing, they point to a spot a little farther down the bay, to where there are tents and the skeleton of a wooden building. Three men put down their tools and come to greet them.

The British introduce themselves as Ralph Dixon, geologist; Maurice Seddon, doctor; and Edwin Daneforth, photographer and biologist. Dixon, a big, untidy man, says, "Come and have some coffee; you must meet our leader, Mrs. Athlone." He lays distinct emphasis on the name, and gazes at them as if daring them to make some comment. As he leads the way to their tents, a figure gets up from a seated position and waits for them.

Jakob's first, amazed, thought is, For heaven's sake, she's only a girl. Mrs. Athlone is tall—almost the same height as he—and strongly built, with a youthful, watchful face. She cuts a bizarre figure; her clothing—trousers and canvas shirt—is of the same pattern as that of her colleagues. She has been talking to the *angekok*, Aniguin, husband of Lester's mistress. Mrs. Athlone holds out a hand to Jakob without smiling, and says, in a quiet, clear voice, in an accent he is not familiar with, "I am Mrs. Athlone, leader of the First British Northwest Greenland Expedition. How do you do?"

Jakob and Erdinger shake hands and introduce themselves. Jakob wishes Frank were here; he feels as though he might laugh at any moment, out of nervousness at the oddity of the situation.

Dixon goes to prepare coffee and biscuits. Mrs. Athlone and Aniguin speak quickly in the Eskimo language; she sounds fluent: another surprise. Erdinger seems struck dumb by the whole thing. In growing silence, Jakob says, "Pualana told us that you were an '*upernallit*,' which I always thought meant a whaler. I must have misunderstood."

"No, you didn't, Mr. de Beyn. I first came here ten years ago, with my father, a whaling captain from Dundee. I met Aniguin then." She inclines her head to the *angekok*. "We played together as children."

"Good heavens!" It is the only thing Jakob can think of to say. "I'm sorry, it's just very unusual." He smiles winningly at her, hoping she won't be offended. She doesn't smile back.

"You speak the language fluently?" he asks.

"I wouldn't claim that I was fluent. I have forgotten much. Aniguin is reminding me of it."

"Ah."

Jakob wishes Erdinger would say something, but he is staring at Mrs. Athlone with a meaningless smile on his face, like an idiot.

"Mr. Armitage is not with you?"

"No, he's not long returned from a journey on the ice cap, but he's anxious to meet you. There's a great deal to do before our ship arrives. I have a letter from him." He hands it over.

He watches her as she turns away, opens the letter and bends over it. Her head is bare, and a braid the color of wet sand is coiled at the back of her head, revealing an elegant neck. Her face is broad, somewhat heavy in repose. She can't be older than him—younger, surely? She is not unattractive, although painfully serious. He tries to imagine her in feminine clothing, or smiling.

She reads the letter twice through, then folds it up and puts it in her pocket. Dixon reappears with a coffee pot and cups—Jakob is delighted to realize that they have real beans; he hasn't tasted decent coffee for months.

Dixon hands round chunks of biscuit. Jakob tries not to eat too ravenously, although it has been hours since they ate. Erdinger has no such qualms.

Mrs. Athlone puts down her cup. "Mr. Armitage regrets he is too busy to come and visit, and invites us to pay a visit to your quarters. However, we, too, have much to do." She glances at the half-built house. "We don't know how long this weather will hold."

"Of course. Our ship is not expected until mid-August. I'm sure you could wait until the house is finished, if that suited."

"Or, perhaps, two of us could come back with you, for a brief visit. How far is it?"

"We're at Neqi—about twenty miles north."

"Ralph, could you continue here with Edwin? We can persuade some of the men to help you."

She turns to Aniguin again and speaks to him in his language. Jakob knows that Aniguin speaks good English, so feels a little slighted by her . . . showing off, you could call it, if you were being uncharitable. Dixon agrees they can get on perfectly well. He is the one that Mrs. Athlone's eyes go to most often, Jakob notices—the one, he imagines, she relies on for support.

"I think we can accommodate Mr. Armitage's wishes." There is the faintest sting in her voice.

Jakob tries to ignore it, his voice becoming louder and more genial in response: "Wonderful. We look forward to showing you some American hospitality, although I'm afraid we have run out of real coffee. Ha ha!"

Jakob wishes he did not smile and laugh so much when he is nervous; it gives people the impression that he is keen to be liked, when the truth is, he doesn't care. Mrs. Athlone nods and gives him and Erdinger a small smile, but it looks like an effort. She certainly knows how to talk down to people, Jakob thinks, and decides that she is not very attractive, after all.

Jakob and Erdinger pitch their tent a little way from the British camp. Cloud covers the sun and the temperature drops. Rime forms on the inside of the tent with their breath.

"Jesus," says Erdinger, who finds relief from tension in coarseness. "What a setup! Have you ever come across anything so cock-eyed? Do you think they take turns—once every three nights?" He laughs. "I guess not—have you ever seen three guys look so miserable? How they hope to get any work done is beyond me. I guess Armitage can stop worrying: the whole thing's a farce."

"I thought you were an egalitarian? 'Equality for all.'"

"For all men. I wonder why they let her get away with it."

"Probably the same reason we let Armitage get away with it. We're paid to."

"But, Christ, why is *she* the leader? At her age? And where's the husband? If there is one. Makes you wonder, doesn't it?"

Jakob grunts, to discourage him, but can't stop his mind running along similar lines. He too wonders about the absent Mr. Athlone, and about their sleeping arrangements . . . but that is a dangerous train of thought. Erdinger, next to him, begins to breathe more heavily, and there is a rhythmic rustle in his sleeping bag. Ostentatiously, Jakob rolls toward the tent wall and pulls the hood of his parka over his head.

In the morning, frost smoke rises from the fjord. The British have chosen a picturesque spot: Siorapaluk lies on a grassy, sandy bay, sheltered by smooth red hills—far more enticing than the cliffs at Neqi. Jakob walks over to the half-built house to talk to Dixon, and they spend an hour discussing the work Jakob has done, and what, in turn, Dixon hopes to achieve. Jakob learns that Mrs. Athlone is also a scientist: a meteorologist who is studying magnetic variation of the aurora. They will do some exploring, he understands, but mainly to the south, along the coast of Melville Bay.

"What I really want," says Dixon, glancing up the bay, "is to get onto the glaciers here. I don't think anyone has done any work on them."

"Yes, you need several years here. Think what you could do . . ."

They smile in understanding.

Before they leave, Jakob pulls out a small fossil he brought with him, and presses it into Dixon's hand.

"From Ellesmere: 80°32′ by 86°13′, if I remember right."

Dixon looks at the ovoid creature that left a record of its existence printed on a piece of shale, and an unbecoming blush spreads over his cheeks.

"But this is one of your specimens. I couldn't accept such a thing."

"I have so many. It's a shame you can't come too. I have photographs of the glaciers on Ellesmere; I've been experimenting with techniques to photograph the ice. Not entirely successful, but you might find them interesting."

Dixon looks torn. "I'd like that very much, but it's imperative we get the house finished." His glance goes toward Mrs. Athlone, who is by the tents with Seddon, supervising the loading of a sled.

Jakob follows his gaze. Casually, he says, "Is Mr. Athlone involved with the expedition in some way?"

"Oh, yes. He is . . . was . . . joint leader with Mrs. Athlone. But—most unfortunate—he had an accident before we reached Godthåb. It was sufficiently serious that he has had to stay there while he recovers. Terrible business, poor man. I should say, though, that he was never *sole* leader of the expedition. It may seem strange, but, among us all, Mrs. Athlone is by far the most qualified to be here."

"Yes, of course. But how unfortunate, as you say. Poor fellow."

Dixon seems unwilling to say more.

"He will recover fully?"

"Yes, we hope."

But he looks troubled. Jakob wonders if Dixon was chosen partly for his decency. He wonders what the unfortunate man is like, and what was the "terrible business" that befell him. He wonders about the serious girl now walking along the shore to her tent, as if she carries a heavy burden. There are many things he is curious to know, but time and protocol prevent him asking.

Chapter 18

Neqi, 77°52' N, 71°37' W
July 1892

They already knew there was going to be an American expedition in the area. And they know the leader, Lester Armitage, by repute, as his fund-raising efforts came to the notice of British newspapers. In fact, his publicized intentions worked in their favor, as his quoted saying that Smith Sound was the "American route" to the North Pole helped to unlock patriotic British wallets. Flora, who feels a certain proprietary interest in the area herself, anticipates their meeting with mixed feelings.

Aniguin walks at her side. She wishes Ralph were here, but he is so much more use, practically, than Seddon, that it makes no sense to leave the doctor in charge of building. There is also the consideration that Daneforth and Seddon do not get along well if left together, and any task left to them slows down drastically. This is what much of leadership boils down to: the tedious juggling of conflicting egos. She wonders, as she is constantly wondering, what Freddie would have done, whether she has made the right choice. But Freddie is a thousand miles away, lying in the governor's house in Godthåb, and she has to decide these things for herself.

Now, as they round the last cape between the British and the American bases, Mr. Erdinger walks on his own, up ahead. He has said hardly a word to her. Perhaps he is uncomfortable meeting strangers, or women. That is the charitable verdict. The uncharitable one is that he is rude. Maurice walks with Mr. de Beyn, who seems friendly enough, although somewhat lacking in gravitas. Perhaps it is just his odd laugh, which is high-pitched and somewhat infectious. He is laughing now. She cannot imagine what Seddon could be saying to provoke it. Perhaps Mr. de Beyn is one of those who laugh at their own witticisms.

"Why do white men no longer come for the whales, Fellora? Some do, but not so much as before."

Having walked in silence for an hour, Aniguin returns to a question that has been puzzling him.

"The price of whale oil has gone down, Aniguin. People have found other ways to light their houses."

"What ways?"

"They have found gas . . . An air that burns. It comes from coal . . . the black rocks that burn, you remember, that we used in the engine of the *Vega*?"

Aniguin ponders.

"That is a clever thing. Is there not the black rock on *Umingmak Nuna*?"

This—the land of musk ox—is the name they give to Ellesmere Land.

"I have heard so. It is difficult to turn the rocks into air, I think. Harder than hunting for seal."

"I should like to see such a thing."

"If you come back with me to London, Aniguin, you could see those things and more. People would be happy to meet you. You could bring Ivalu."

She now sees, set back from the shore, the alien outline of the Americans' hut. From the *tupiks* come shouts, and people stream out to see the newcomers. Flora looks for familiar faces. It has been years since she was here, but one by one she picks them out. There is her friend, Meqro, who must now be around twenty, and her father, the bearded and wild-looking Ehré, who terrified her when they first met. Meqro screams, "Fellora! Fellora!" and trots toward her, wreathed in smiles. Flora holds out her hands to her old friend.

"Meqro. I'm happy to see you."

"I too am happy, Fellora. Deeply happy," Meqro mumbles, and then retreats into shy smiles as others crowd round them.

Aniguin says loudly, "I said Fellora would come back. I saw this would happen."

Ehré says, "He did say that. You saw true, Aniguin."

Apilah, Aniguin's father, ambles over. "Where is Mackie, your father?"

"My father is at home. Perhaps he will come back next year, but the whale fishing is not so good anymore."

"Is this your husband?"

This question comes from many sides, as the Eskimos peer at Maurice Seddon.

"No, no," Flora wants to protest strongly, but smiles as she says it. "This is Dr. Seddon. He is a great *angekok*. I have a husband, but he had an accident on the ship. There was a bad storm, and he fell and broke some bones."

Her hand goes to her hip. According to Maurice, Freddie cracked his pelvis, and possibly a vertebra, when he fell through the open hatch during the storm. A hatch that should have been battened down. An accident that should not have happened. Now he has to lie still for months, just to have the chance of walking again. He should be in a hospital, but there are none. The governor's house in Godthåb was the best they could do.

The door of the wooden house opens and two men stride out. Both tall and weather-beaten, with scars of recent frostbite on their faces; one is big, with black hair, the other lean, gingery, lantern-jawed. She instantly knows which one is Armitage: the red-haired man radiates a steely, formidable energy. She notices Aniguin's wife,

Ivalu, more beautiful than ever, walk out of the house behind them. Flora has heard rumors . . . Ivalu comes up to Aniguin and they touch noses with every sign of affection.

"Mrs. Athlone. A pleasure to meet you."

Lester Armitage extends his hand, unsmiling. "Come in and take a cup of coffee." His grip is firm; his eyes bore into hers, pale blue in a gaunt, ruddy face. His is an impressive presence: intimidating, even. A natural leader. She pulls herself more erect and does not smile. She wonders how she appears to him.

He leads the way into the house. Flora and Seddon sit at the table. Flora hands over her gift of coffee beans and Meqro is instructed to do her worst. Armitage leans across the table.

"You will not think me forward if I ask what your intentions are. After all, it makes no sense to duplicate work already done, or projected to be done."

Armitage turns his head from Seddon to Flora, and back again. His voice is rather high, his accent clipped; he sounds, to her ear, almost English, in contrast to the others, in particular de Beyn, who speaks with a more drawn-out, recognizably American accent.

"Of course. Perhaps you could tell us what you have achieved?"

Flora smiles, but cannot help being reminded of his appropriation of this part of the world "for America"—the idea, after centuries of British whalers coming here! Seddon's face is unreadable. She is grateful for his presence; he has a formidable quality of his own.

There is a pause before Armitage speaks. "We have undertaken exploratory work to the north, both inland and along the coast, and made several discoveries there. Another party has mapped the west coast of Ellesmere Land, in effect filling in the gap between the Nares and Greely expeditions."

"That is impressive. Would you be so kind as to let us see your maps? That would be the best way to ensure that we don't go over old ground."

Armitage stiffens. "I don't think our maps are in a sufficiently finished state to be shown. I wouldn't want to mislead you. And yourselves? What is your program of work?"

Flora hesitates; their original program, since Freddie's accident, is in tatters. She takes a breath and reminds herself that she is a scientist, whereas, as far as she knows, Armitage has no qualifications of any kind.

"The primary purpose of our expedition is in my own field of meteorology. I'm concerned with magnetic activity and the aurora. We are setting up a series of weather stations on the coast and on the ice cap, and intend to keep the record for at least a year. We also have a geologist and specialists in animal biology, so it would be useful to know where your men have done such work."

Armitage's jaw works, as if he is chewing on something unpleasant. Flora wonders whether she should appeal to his sense of chivalry and explain what has befallen Freddie. The Americans are due to leave shortly; any discoveries they have made will be publicized long before she reaches home.

"You're due to be here for a year?"

"That's what we planned."

"So, until next August?"

He is looking at Seddon. Flora says, "Depending, of course, on the ice."

"It would be as well not to leave it too late; ice conditions are unpredictable. During some summers, Smith Sound does not open at all."

Flora smiles. "My father is a whaling captain, and I spent many years here with him."

Armitage stares in astonishment, to her satisfaction.

"The winters are quite a different matter to the summers," he says.

"I spent four winters here, so I'm aware of what we can expect."

She manages a light laugh, but still, for a second Armitage looks ferocious.

"My biologist is away at present, but I'll have one of the men run through the main points of their journey with you. I believe you have friends here; I'm sure you would like to spend some time with them."

He stands up, his chair scraping against the wooden floor, so Flora and Seddon do likewise. Almost as an afterthought, he says, "You will, of course, stay for dinner."

It is a relief to get outside. Flora sees Urbino and de Beyn talking with some of the Eskimo women. They are laughing. Meqro breaks away and comes toward her.

Flora and Seddon follow Meqro to her *tupik*, which she shares with her parents. Flora longs to talk to Meqro in private, but their homes are not constructed with privacy in mind; everything is communal—eating, sleeping, hunting, sewing. Even marital intimacy, as she remembers learning during her first winter, often takes place with only the thickness of a reindeer hide for shelter.

They sit with Ehré, Kagssaluk, and Meqro, and pick barely boiled chunks of seal meat from the pot over the lamp, which Seddon does neatly, with immaculate manners, and Flora with nostalgic pleasure. They tell her news: what children have been born, who has died, what the hunting has been like, how grateful they are to the Americans. At length, Flora says, "Meqro, perhaps you will show me again how to clean a hide. I have forgotten."

She says to Seddon, "Maurice, I'm going to talk with Meqro for a while. Will you be all right?"

"Of course," Seddon says. Since coming north, she has called him Maurice, not because there is any real intimacy between them, as with Ralph, or even the semblance of it, as with Daneforth, but because it helps her to feel in command.

She sits on the gravel beach with Meqro, who fetches a seal skin and her *ulu*, her crescent-shaped knife. Flora lost her own, a present from Simiak, years ago, so she watches as Meqro scrapes membrane and fat off the inside of the skin. She is quick and skillful. Flora asks about the children she used to know. Many are married. The village's greatest hunter, Kali, was drowned hunting walrus, leaving his wife with two children. They were weaned, so did not have to be smothered. It is clear to Flora that they have missed the whalers and the goods they used to bring. Times have been hard. They are happy the Americans are here; Meqro and some of the other women have been working for them. Flora is not particularly surprised when Meqro confesses, with much giggling, that she is "friends" with the tall doctor, whose name is Frank.

"I remember when you liked Tateraq. I thought you would marry him."

"Huh. He was no good." Meqro shakes her head. "He tried to get Ivalu. He wanted the prettiest girl—I was not good enough. He was angry when she married Aniguin. Always fighting, those two. Then he came back to me, and I said no."

She shrugs, good-humoredly, and tells her that Ivalu, though married, sleeps with Armitage, and a girl called Mikissoq, whom Flora remembers as a small child, is the consort of the silent physicist.

"And de Beyn?" she asks.

"Te Peyn was friends with Natseq, but not now—he only likes widows!" She laughs, amused. "Ainineq is widow, but she is too old. And the other one, Shooll . . . Oh, Fellora, you must see him: so tall, and his hair is like the sun . . . but he does not like our women. I don't know why." She giggles, bending over her skin.

"They are good to you?"

"Oh yes, they give us many good things," says Meqro. "They gave my father a gun, and they give me needles and buttons and other things. Fe-rank is so nice. He's like a giant."

She smiles, and then, perhaps thinking of Flora's misfortune: "Your husband is handsome fellow?"

"Freddie? Yes, he is." Flora is surprised, having never thought this—or its converse—of him. "He is handsome, and brave."

"You are sad he is ill."

"Yes, I am sad."

"He will be well again?"

"I hope so. Dr. Seddon is very clever. And there is another *angekok* in Godthåb, in the south, who is looking after him."

"Still, you came to see us. I'm happy."

"You remember the English word, Meqro? You used to be good at English."

Meqro murmurs that she does not.

"'I am happy.' *Qooviannikumut* is 'happy.' You can say that to your Frank—if you want."

They laugh.

Gravel crunches behind them. If Mr. de Beyn is surprised to see Flora sitting on the ground in the Eskimo way, her legs straight out in front of her, he hides it.

"Shall we go inside, Mrs. Athlone? It is rather windy for maps."

In the hut, Armitage gets up from the main table.

"Mrs. Athlone, I will leave you with Mr. de Beyn. You may take this map—he'll mark on it our areas of work. I have much work to do, so if you'll excuse me . . ."

He goes no farther than the far end of the house, behind a packing-case partition, from where he must hear every word. Flora finds it hard to interpret his behavior as anything other than a snub. De Beyn, who seems awkward, as though he too is aware of this, takes out some notebooks, spreads a section of hand-drawn map on the table, and smiles at her.

"The maps are far from finished," he says. "But, briefly . . ."

On the old map, he outlines his journey across Smith Sound and north into Grant Land, the northern part of Ellesmere, and sketches in the main features of the previously unknown coast, deeply crenellated with fjords and headlands.

"We left here at the end of March and came back three weeks ago."

"You covered a lot of ground."

De Beyn makes a dismissive gesture, but looks pleased.

"We were lucky with the weather. We didn't walk every step of the coastline, but we triangulated each fjord and the visible peaks."

"This is tremendous work—to fill in the gap between Nares and Greely in that time."

Flora is impressed. Her next thought is, We will never equal this.

"This was the limit of your journey?" She puts her finger on the southern coast of Grant Land. It marks the limit of what is known: nothing but white space between it and Jones Sound, far to the south.

"Yes. We managed to join up with the western limit of Aldrich's explorations, here . . . I have some photographs I could show you; it's tremendous, the landscape there; the glaciers are"—he shakes his head—"on a smaller scale than the mainland, but somehow more sublime . . ."

He becomes animated as he talks about the glaciers. He looks up at her, catching her straight in the eye, and she starts back, embarrassed. He is younger than she first thought: despite the gray hairs, his skin is smooth, and there is a liveliness to his expression that makes her want to smile—as if all this northern exploration could be . . . *fun.*

"That would be most interesting."

There is a creaking from beyond the partition. Both of them look around.

"In terms of geology and meteorological observations, these are the areas we covered . . ."

He outlines areas on the map and adds notes. His handwriting is small and neat.

"It's a pity Mr. Dixon isn't here. I could explain the main points to him more . . . with him being a geologist, I mean." He gives her an apologetic smile, an anxious look in his brown eyes. His smile, like his laugh, has an infectious quality.

"And the northern journey?" she asks, wondering if Armitage is working at all, or is simply sitting behind the packing cases, listening. De Beyn takes out a packet of cigarettes and offers her one, which she declines.

"Do you mind?"

"Not at all."

"Mr. Armitage? Would you like to talk to Mrs. Athlone about the northern journey?"

They both look at the drawn curtain.

"No. You can explain the salient points."

"Well, briefly . . . Mr. Armitage and Dr. Urbino established insularity." He bends over the map again, putting his pencil on the north coast, where the previously established coastline peters out, and draws a curve that wiggles southeast. He pencils a line from Neqi across the ice cap and back again.

"I congratulate you all," says Flora, loudly enough to be heard behind the curtain. "Two most successful trips. Thank you for telling me."

De Beyn gives her a quick smile and looks back at the map. "There is so much more to be done."

At dinner, they drink a rather bad wine. The Americans unearth some delicacies to accompany the fried seal—canned peas and potatoes, chocolate pudding, candied fruit, and raisins. The atmosphere thaws. Even Armitage, on Flora's left, seems to have relaxed a little. De Beyn and Urbino keep up the flow of conversation, and Flora finds herself warming to them. She is not surprised to learn that they have been friends since college. They are served by Meqro and a girl called Tilly, whom Flora does not know, but she notices she pays a lot of attention to de Beyn. She is disappointed that the beautiful Mr. Shull will not return before they leave.

The talk is general, with both sides avoiding anything that could sound like interrogative questioning. Dr. Urbino turns to Flora.

"Mrs. Athlone, I gather you spent much time here as a child. That must have been an unusual education."

"I suppose it was, though it didn't seem unusual to me, since my father came here every year. I discovered a great love for the place."

"What did your mother have to say about it?"

"She died when I was young. My father could have sent me away, but he chose instead to bring me with him."

"Did you not miss female company?" Urbino asks.

"Well, here I had female company, of course—like Meqro and Simiak. And on board ship, it never occurred to me to miss it. There were boys my age among the crew. Perhaps I was brought up more like a boy than a girl, in that respect."

"How remarkable," says Armitage in his clipped voice.

"And you learned the language then?" says de Beyn.

"Yes. My first friends here were Aniguin and Tateraq. In fact, when I first came, they thought I was a boy."

Silence, then de Beyn bursts out laughing, followed by Urbino. Erdinger, Seddon, and Armitage have near-identical frozen expressions on their faces. She says, "I don't know why Maurice looks surprised. He already knows."

Maurice forces a smile. Flora is pleased to have caused a stir. She rarely makes people laugh.

"If you think about it, it's not surprising. In winter, everyone is bundled up almost all the time, and boys have long hair too."

"So how did they find out the truth?" asks de Beyn, eyes wide and apparently innocent.

"They would talk about me as my father's '*erneq*.' He thought '*erneq*' was the word for *child*. As you probably know, the word for *brother* and *sister* is the same. Then he heard someone refer to their daughter as '*panik*' and their son as '*erneq*.' So, then he . . . told them."

"Mrs. Athlone's fluency means we can dispense with an interpreter," says Seddon.

"What is the word for brother and sister?" asks de Beyn.

"*Qatannguh*."

De Beyn attempts to repeat it in the same half-swallowed, glottal fashion, and laughs at his failure.

"*Qatannguh*. Yes."

He tries again with more success. Armitage clears his throat with a sudden rumble. It has the effect of dampening the atmosphere. They fall silent. Armitage dabs his mouth with a napkin.

"This has been a pleasure, Mrs. Athlone. But I have work to do. And I'm sure you want to start back early in the morning."

Flora has brought her own tent. Maurice bids her his usual, formal good night and crawls into his tent, pitched at a discreet distance. It will be light all night. Flora gets her diary and leans against a rock, her back to the low sun. She starts to write, but has not been there more than a minute before she is joined by Ivalu and Aniguin, then Meqro and Ehré.

Aniguin fills his pipe. He looks at her notebook and says, "Why are you writing?"

"My memory is not as good as yours. I need to remember things when I get back to England, so that I can write them down, and it will be made into a book for people to read about this place."

"You write about us, Fellora?"

"I write about everything, Aniguin. For people who have never been here, they can't picture it. So, to make them see, I write about the ice, the snow, and the seal hunting, and you, and the Americans . . . and the darkness in winter and the light in summer."

"To make a picture?"

"Yes. In Britain, no one knows it can get so cold it freezes the water in your eyes."

"But here is Te Peyn . . . He makes pictures with his box. If you can have pictures, why do you need to write as well?"

Footsteps crunch on the gravel behind them. De Beyn is carrying a pasteboard folder.

"Te Peyn," calls Aniguin, "she is writing about you."

De Beyn smiles uncertainly. "Oh? Is Dr. Seddon here?"

"Dr. Seddon has retired."

"Ah. I brought some of my photographs. He said he was interested in seeing some examples, but, no matter."

"Please wait; he won't be asleep yet. I'm sure he'll be interested, as would I."

She goes to his tent.

"Maurice? Mr. de Beyn has brought some photographs to show you."

There is a mumble from inside the tent. De Beyn says to her, "Thank you. I didn't mean to disturb you."

"You haven't. If you don't mind showing all of us, I'd like very much to see them too."

* * *

De Beyn opens his folder and takes out some prints. His attempts to explain each one soon break down as they are passed back and forth and exclaimed over.

"This is remarkable." Seddon is holding a picture of an iceberg. "The detail is superb."

"That one . . ." de Beyn glances at the back. "I've been experimenting with colored glass in front of the lens. That one was red. This one, here, is taken through yellow glass . . ."

Ivalu finds a picture of herself. She holds the photograph upside down.

Flora leans toward her and turns the photograph around. "Like this!"

Ivalu is unconvinced. "It is the same. Same Ivalu."

"Yes, but that way"—Flora turns the picture upside down again—"your head is down here, and your feet are up here . . . and the sky is below the earth! The sky is above the earth, like this."

Ivalu laughs. "I know where is the sky, Fellora."

Ehré is peering at a photo of the bay at Neqi. He holds it sideways and points out the place where he recently butchered a seal. Meqro stares at a picture of the Americans.

"Here is Ferank, and you, Te Peyn!"

Flora is handed a photograph of a glacier, in an unfamiliar landscape.

"Where was this, Mr. de Beyn?"

"Ellesmere Land, on the west coast."

"One of your discoveries?"

"Yes. We called it the Kampfer Glacier."

"It's beautiful."

He smiles at her. "Kampfer is a railway baron. One of our main sponsors."

"Ah."

"You know . . ." de Beyn looks around him. The midnight sun is low on the horizon. "The light is good now. If I get my camera, may I take your picture? And Mr. Seddon?"

"Well . . . if you wish."

When de Beyn starts taking pictures of the villagers, there is much laughter. Seddon, uncharacteristically animated, goes to get *his* camera, and, as the hilarity rises, more villagers come out of their *tupiks* to watch, to pose for the photographers, to make jokes and, most of all, to laugh. Dr. Urbino joins them and has his photograph taken with Meqro perched on his knee. Seddon, finding himself the center of attention, is almost skittish, blushing as the women surround him, jostling for position.

Someone lights a fire and sets up a cooking pot. Smoke rises off the beach, straight up into the pale sky. Someone else produces *kiviak*—slimy, rotten auk meat—to growls of appreciation. Pipes are lit. De Beyn and Seddon promise to take a picture of every person there.

De Beyn turns to Flora and says, with a searching look at her face, "Perhaps if you were to face this way, like that . . . yes."

Flora is aware that she has not looked in a mirror since the day before yesterday. She touches her hair and says something conventional.

De Beyn looks at her and says, "You have nothing to worry about. Trust me."

Horribly self-conscious, she assumes a serious expression. He peers into the camera, winds on the film and presses the shutter release, then looks up.

"The exposure is very quick; you don't have to keep your face still. It can capture the expression of an instant, or an action."

He smiles, to encourage her. But, to Flora, the prospect of having her mood snatched and caught forever is alarming, and she gazes sternly into the middle distance. De Beyn takes one or two more pictures and inclines his head to her—a semi-serious salute.

"Thank you."

She nods, obscurely disappointed. She says, "These aren't for your expedition records?"

De Beyn looks startled.

"No, of course not. Now, Meqro . . ."

Meqro wants a picture of her with Flora. They stand stiffly, side by side, but Meqro, whose glossy head just comes to Flora's chin, murmurs something up at Flora, and makes her smile, and Flora is rather afraid that he has captured it.

Flora wishes, as she often does when she feels uncertain, that Freddie were here. Social gatherings are his field of expertise, not hers. She feels a sudden flood of gratitude, and a prickling at the back of her eyes. Freddie was in terrible pain when they left, but he insisted she continue without him. Ordered it. She feels a twinge of guilt to be smiling—possibly, even, enjoying herself. She wishes that he were well, that he were with her to share this, of course . . .

But. Would she be held in such account, if he were? Would Armitage have spoken to her (even unwillingly)? Isn't she, in some way, glad to be here without him? This is her place. These are her friends. And now that the ordeal of being photographed is over, she begins to unbend. Simiak, Aniguin's mother, pushes in next to her, and puts a hard, brown hand on her arm.

"*Aja*, Fellora, do you remember the first time you came? When we sat on the big boat? You were so shy, so quiet; you were like this!" She stretches her eyes wide, and laughs.

"Yes, I remember." Flora smiles.

"I'm so happy to see you, Fellora—such a fine woman you are! You're like my own child."

"I'm happy to be here, Simiak. Many times I thought of you all and longed to come back, but it's hard."

Simiak laughs, but has tears in her eyes. Flora finds herself holding both of Simiak's hands in hers, and has to swallow the lump in her throat.

She so nearly didn't make it. So many things stood in her way.

Something happens. From the cliffs behind them, disturbed by who knows what, an immense quantity of auks suddenly takes flight. The mass that detaches from the cliffs is so vast, so solid, it's as though a part of the cliff sheers away and, instead of falling, lifts heavily into the air. The sky grows dark as more and more birds flood out in a living cloud, squawking and screaming, wings whirring and clacking, deafening them. The people on the beach look up in wonder; the boys run for their nets, and the photographers spin around, laughing, lifting up their cameras, like nets, in hope of capture.

At times, the land can seem sullen and lifeless. It gives nothing. It wants nothing, except to be left alone. And then there are times like this, when it is overwhelmingly rich—glorious and unnecessary, as though the birds are the land's laughter.

Like the others, Flora gazes in awe as the exodus goes on and on: an impossible number of birds; a million, two million . . . An endless shower of black sparks, bursting from a beaten fire.

Chapter 19

Neqi, 77°52' N, 71°37' W
July 1892

Jakob wakes early, feeling the aftereffects of the wine. He hadn't thought he was drunk—had he behaved like it? Not in his memory, but he feels bilious, his head pulsates. Pulling his clothes on, he lets himself out as quietly as possible and wanders away from camp to relieve himself. Normally, they are not especially delicate about bodily functions—the Eskimos, men and women alike, squat a few feet away from their tents and the dogs remove all traces. The Americans have learned to do likewise—but normally there are no white female guests in the vicinity. He walks much farther than usual, heading for a sheltering fall of rocks.

A dog trots after him: one of the team from his Ellesmere trip—a piebald bitch named Curly. She is one of the friendlier sled dogs—meaning that she is likely to bite only half the time—and he became fond of her, although the fondness was tempered when he saw her eat one of her puppies. The dogs inspire equal measures of affection and revulsion: they run their hearts out to transport the men wherever they want to go—they will pull until they literally drop in their traces—but then they do something appalling, like devouring their own offspring, or killing a weakened colleague. He has heard the Eskimos tell the story of a boy who became lost in a blizzard. When the family found him, all that remained were his bones. Jakob sometimes wonders if the terrible stories they hear are true, but, having seen what the dogs are capable of, he thinks that one probably is.

"Go away, you horrible, shit-eating cannibal," he says, attempting to shove the bitch away from his bare, shivering hindquarters, to no avail.

By the time he is finished—and Curly has done her unspeakable business—the sun has emerged from a bank of cloud, and he is rather appalled to see Mrs. Athlone standing outside the British tents as he walks back, although she cannot possibly have seen . . .

He finds her hard to fathom: there were times on the beach last night when she seemed to lose her guardedness; at others, moments later, she was again withdrawn and serious. He saw her face transform as she gazed, laughing, at the storm cloud of birds—he wanted to snatch another picture, but didn't dare.

"Good morning! Did you sleep well?"

"Good morning, Mr. de Beyn. Well, but little. After you and Dr. Urbino retired, I was half the night with Apilah's family. They will sleep till after lunch." She smothers a yawn.

"It's been a long time since you saw them?"

"Four years."

She smiles at something behind him, and Jakob is horrified to see Curly trot toward them wagging her tail, as if hoping for more tasty morsels.

"I'm sure I recognize that dog . . . A bitch, isn't it?"

"I . . . I'm not sure. Do you have to leave immediately, because . . ."

He loses his thread as Curly goes straight to Mrs. Athlone and rubs her head on her trousers, tongue lolling out of her mouth. He watches in horror as Mrs. Athlone stretches her hand to the dog and Jakob is appalled to find himself aiming his boot at Curly's ribs.

"Get away!" he shouts over the dog's pained yelp. Mrs. Athlone recoils, astonished and repelled. Jakob realizes that he has, to all appearances, launched an unprovoked attack on an innocent, friendly animal. Curly looks at him with reproach, Mrs. Athlone with icy disdain.

"Excuse me. I'm very sorry, but"—he can't think of a single excuse that doesn't point to the truth—"but that's a very reprehensible animal, and you don't want to . . . to go anywhere near her," he finishes, lamely.

Mrs. Athlone draws herself upright, any warmth in her eyes quite gone.

"You're right. I should know better."

"She's a notorious biter," he says warmly, feeling the sweat springing out of his pores. "She nearly took Erdinger's hand off, and it got infected. You know, what with—with what they eat." He laughs abruptly, not wanting to pursue it further.

"Well, I'd better . . ."

She turns away. Clearly her opinion of him is very low, and this distresses him more than he can account for. The sweat under his arms now chills him.

"Please don't think I normally go around kicking animals. Not without very good reason."

Mrs. Athlone looks at him with one eyebrow slightly raised.

"I'm glad to hear it."

Sure that she is laughing at him now, Jakob feels his face hot.

"Well . . ." He starts to back away. "I meant to say, last night: the photographs . . . I'll try to develop them before we leave, but if I can't, I'll send you prints—if you give me an address."

"It's not necessary." She seems to find this unacceptably forward.

"I thought you seemed uncomfortable, last night, and I don't want you to feel that I was . . ." Unsure how this sentence is going to finish, he abandons it and tries another. "Some people think a photograph steals their soul, and I understand. But if you have the results yourself, then you . . . you have it back, don't you?" He laughs again, unsure why he is talking such rubbish.

"If I thought that, it would make my role as leader of an expedition difficult in this day and age."

"I don't talk of a rational feeling, but a photograph does carry an essence of its subject. It brings someone closer. That's why I keep my mother's portrait, to keep her in some way alive to me. I'm sure you know what I mean . . ."

Jakob wonders how on earth he got onto this topic, which seems enormously inappropriate. He has begun to apologize when she smiles, quite kindly.

"I think I understand, Mr. de Beyn. Anyway . . ."

She turns back to her tent.

"Yes. You have much to do. Stay away from that dog." He aims this at her retreating back.

She turns around. "I'll try to."

She smiles then, a proper smile, at him. It is like glimpsing another person who lives inside her skin. There is something both reckless and intimate in her smile that makes the raw morning seem warm.

Lester has woken in a good mood, and invites the British for breakfast. They eat porridge and scrambled auks' eggs and drink the last of the coffee, and it is possible to tell from the atmosphere that Lester has decided the British expedition, under their unlikely leader, poses no serious competition.

Jakob does not get the chance to speak to Mrs. Athlone again, but, in the course of swallowing a mouthful of coffee, he becomes conscious that something has changed. It is a sudden and precise conviction (before the mouthful, it didn't exist; after, it irrefutably *is*), and it is this: that Mrs. Athlone is thinking about him. The certainty of it shocks him. He glances toward her. Was something said? Is everyone looking at him, aware of this momentous change? Her eyes are on Frank as he speaks, or on Lester; she speaks little; she says nothing at all to him.

Jakob and Seddon continue to discuss the difficulties of glare, the preponderance of blue light; he listens to Seddon's views on ice photography and responds as though everything is normal, but all the time he knows that she is intimately aware of everything he says and does, that she is surrounding him with her heartfelt attention, and . . .

In answer to her question, Armitage says, "It depends on the ice, when we leave. We are hopeful of seeing the ship before long. Then you will have a clear field."

There will be no "and." He will leave shortly and never see her again. He looks at the crumbs on his plate. They hardly know each other. Still, the conviction remains: a heady certainty. When the parties make their farewells on the beach, it is as real as the rocks and the wind. Standing with the others, Jakob shakes Mrs. Athlone by the hand and wishes her a safe and successful stay, and she thanks him, holding his gaze for a moment—not long enough for anyone else to guess what has happened, but long enough.

It has not happened to him before. He imagines it to be what grace feels like: something undeserved, bestowed. A precious nugget he chooses to keep, in the face of all likelihood and common sense.

Chapter 20

Unnamed cape, 76°14' N, 69°51' W
August 1892

The sea is white; the sky, the same gray as the land. A freezing wind hurts their eyes, sticks sharp fingers under hoods, through gaps in clothes. It picks up snow crystals and flings them in their faces, and sprays them over the hillside where Pualana and Ayakou toil with shovels. On the slope that faces the sea, they have dug a pit eight feet in diameter and a yard deep, and have uncovered what Lester was so determined to find. The snow puts up a fight: it tries to harry them into submission, tries to fill the hole they have made, to cover what it contains, but the thing is visible under a carapace of ice.

Armitage and Shull saw it a month earlier. Armitage set off, ostensibly to secure the promise of dogs for "next time." But that was not all they did. Last winter, Johannes had told them about the meteorite that had for a long time been the Eskimos' only source of iron. He called it the sky stone. Lester persuaded some locals to show him its location, and on finding that it lay near the coast—perched on a hillside above a rocky inlet—he formed a plan to pry it from its resting place and take it home.

They have little time. It is August and the water is shrinking in the sound. The *Sachem* is moored at the end of the fjord, its captain on the verge of abandoning them. Somehow—no one is sure how—they are to dig this huge rock out of its bed, lever and roll it down the slope, and convey it to a point on the shore where the ship can approach. Then lift it onto the ship. Erdinger has calculated that it weighs at least six tons, but, like an iceberg or a molar, it could extend far beyond sight.

Armitage has commandeered the *Sachem*'s spare mast timber for rollers, and brace beams to use as levers, themselves almost too heavy to lift. Frank and Erdinger have evolved a plan; like any mechanical problem, there is a solution. Erdinger says the seven of them should be able to do it. Taking turns, they chop out the frozen ground around the stone, enough to insert the beams, and then all throw their weight on the uphill levers, until it starts, minutely, to shift.

Jakob, the smallest and lightest member of the expedition, steps back to hammer the shorter beams into the new space, and thus, little by little, the giant is cajoled up out of the hillside. It takes hours and all their strength, but at last they flip the stone onto its back, like a giant beetle. The underside is rounded, implying that, when it fell to earth, snow cushioned its fall. That same snow inched it toward the coast, until there was no ice left to convey it further, and it settled here. On the upper side are marks where the Eskimos hammered and chipped off flakes of iron; mounds of trap stones testify to the years of use. Strangely, to Jakob's mind, neither Pualana nor Ayakou seem unhappy at the thought of the iron stone being taken away from them. Ayakou says no one has used it for years. After a century of whalers have come and gone, trading iron tools for ivory, every hunter has nails and a file, every woman has needles and a scraping knife with a blade that hails from Dundee or Hull. Lester is rewarding the two men with a gun each.

Lester releases Jakob so that he can sketch the hillside and take samples. He works at frantic speed: a find of such importance; he imagines the papers he will write about it; after all, no one is in a better position than he. It could bring him modest fame, perhaps a book . . . He scrambles around taking photographs, measuring dip and incline and plotting the site as accurately as he can. He turns his back to the wind to take another photograph, waiting for a lull in the blowing snow. He tastes the ambition in his mouth, and grins.

The shrieks make him turn around. The camera is instinctively held to his eye, but for long moments he does not understand what he sees: forty yards down the slope, the meteorite has sheered away from its path; a body lies beside it, distinct from it, the others swarming around, but not enough . . . not enough of them. A wail pierces the white air. Jakob plunges down the hillside toward them.

There was nothing they could have done. A beam cracked under the enormous weight, the meteorite rolled—just as it was planned that it would roll, but more to one side than they planned—and one of the men was a shade slow jumping out of its path. It caught a foot, he fell—downhill—and somehow, slowly, cruelly, the stone sucked him under its alien gravity. It came to rest on his trapped body.

Frank lies face down in the snow, his head pointing toward the sea and home. He is invisible from the chest down, the lower half of his body crushed under six tons of metal that has no business here. He is alive, conscious, calm with shock, completely aware that this is the end.

Jakob is on his knees by his head, screaming at the others to get the beams in place to lift it off him, and they struggle to do so, frantically shouting, straining, working. Ayakou has also been injured; Pualana kneels by his son. Lester yells at him to help them. He does so. The men roar at the stone in their rage. Jakob jumps up to join in. Shull and Erdinger and Lester are hammering beams in either side of Frank to lever it up.

"Go to him," Erdinger says shortly.

Frank, belching blood, gasps at Jakob, who kneels and takes his hands—spread-eagled on the ground—in his. He struggles for breath, but can only speak in a funny, crushed voice.

"Jake . . . have to hear my confession."

"I can't . . ." Appalled, Jakob watches the blood ooze between his teeth.

"You can. Allowed . . . Say sorry . . . to Marion."

"There's no need." Jakob shakes his head, denying it through freezing tears, but Frank begins to confess. Jakob has to bend until their heads are touching to hear him, but after a few sentences, he can no longer make out words. Frank has so few sins to confess. He still breathes, and Jakob mutters soothing things—hopeful, meaningless rubbish he doesn't believe: that he is going to be all right, that they will free him, that they are going home.

Frank's eyes are closed now, his face relaxed, the lips no longer pulled back in that terrible snarl. The snow has drunk his blood; the red stain spreads around his head like a halo. Jakob prays that he is unconscious. He goes on talking to him, holding his hands in his.

At some later point—he doesn't know how much time has passed or what the others have been doing, but his feet and hands are frozen, and Shull is tugging at his shoulder, repeating his name—he realizes that he is talking to no one.

The wail he heard came not from Frank, but from Ayakou, who was relatively lucky—the stone caught him but rolled over his right leg and moved on, leaving it broken and bloody. Grimly, Lester issues orders; Shull, Jakob, and Pualana are to take Ayakou to the British base, several miles up the coast. Erdinger is to go to the ship for reinforcements, who will move the stone and deal with Frank's body. Jakob hates to leave him; there is something awful—pathetic—about the stump of his friend poking out from under a stone, but he knows Lester is right. Lester is immaculate in a crisis—decisive, calm, thorough. He is terribly upset, Jakob can tell, although his face barely changes. Ayakou, after that first cry, makes no sound. Even as they half lift, half drag him down to the sled—clumsily, without Frank to tell them how best to do it—he does not moan.

The journey around the bay is long and difficult. They try to keep the sled on a smooth course, but it is impossible. At some point, to their relief, Ayakou passes out. The weather gets worse, until the wind is screaming. They are forced to stop and wait out the blizzard under a cliff that offers little shelter.

Forty hours until they make it to Siorapaluk in the middle of the night. The British are woken by the howl of dogs. They know before anyone speaks that something terrible has happened.

Dr. Seddon and some villagers carry Ayakou into the house. Jakob's hands are like blocks of wood, incapable of gripping anything, incapable even of removing his own mittens. Shull takes them off for him, and, when he pulls off the left one, a portion of his little finger remains in the glove. Jakob stares in dull shock. Shull swears, shakes out the piece of frozen flesh, which falls to the floor.

"What is it?" Mrs. Athlone has come over. Embarrassed, Jakob bends down and tries to pick up the fragment of his body—it being his responsibility, after all—but his hands are too numb to grasp the damn thing.

"I'm so sorry, I can't . . ."

"Oh, heavens, you poor thing!" she cries. She bends down and, incredibly, picks up his finger, and takes it to Dr. Seddon.

Afterward, he is sat at the table with a bowl of tepid water and told to soak his frozen hands. Shull alternately eats and pushes spoonfuls of food into Jakob's mouth. At one point, a mug of brandy is lifted to his lips and he drinks, which makes him cough.

Seddon is operating on Ayakou's leg. The blizzard has returned, and howls around the house, thumping the walls with angry, thwarted blows. Mrs. Athlone is busy, boiling water, going to and fro from the makeshift operating theater at one end of the hut. Shull and Jakob sit at the table, mute with misery and exhaustion.

Jakob must have slept, as he wakes to find Seddon pulling off his socks.

"Shull said I should have a look at you. I'm afraid there's nothing I can do about the finger."

"It's all right," croaks Jakob.

Seddon examines his feet—they are white and burning with pain. As he points out, the fact they hurt is a good sign.

"You're lucky; you'll lose some skin, but it's not too severe. Let's see the hands . . . Were you not wearing gloves?"

"I don't . . . I think . . . I was using the camera when it happened."

"It's been how long? More than forty hours?"

Jakob nods. Seddon fetches his surgical bag and, with a tool that looks like a pair of pliers, neatens up the stump, and sews fresh skin over the wound. Now he has nine and a half fingers. Jakob watches dispassionately, only wishing it would hurt more; he would have given up his hand—his arm—if it meant that Frank could be here. In answer to his question, Seddon tells him that Ayakou will keep his leg and should survive, more or less whole. Seddon beckons Mrs. Athlone to hold the bandage in place as he binds it up. She does so efficiently, without squeamishness.

"I'm sorry to have taken off more tissue, but I don't want to take risks with gangrene. You'll need to be careful of it for a while. And, er, try to stay out of the cold."

Jakob nods, unable to raise a smile.

At last, Seddon rolls his shoulders and slumps into a chair. Mrs. Athlone pours mugs of brandy and tea, and brings one to Jakob.

"Shall I hold it? You can manage?"

He nods and takes it between bandaged palms. Her look seems to acknowledge what he felt at their last meeting, but he does not know what to do with it.

"I'm so very sorry about your friend. Mr. Shull told me how close you were."

Jakob nods. He is disgusted with himself. While Frank's future hurtled to its end, he was enjoying thoughts of his future success. He titillated himself with the boons the damned rock would bring him, while it had gone about killing his friend.

When there is no more to be done, she makes them go to bed. Jakob rolls into a bunk with his clothes on. He thinks about Frank's sisters, and how he will have to tell them what happened. Marion, too. They don't know the calamity that has just befallen them. For weeks, they will go on thinking of Frank, thinking that he is alive. Frank was loved by a lot of people. Far more than love or would mourn Jakob. He cannot avoid the conclusion that it would have been better for the sum of the world's happiness if he had died in Frank's place, but the world does not appear to take such calculations into account.

Before he sinks into oblivion, he becomes once more aware of her, quietly moving around behind him and then settling with a sigh into a chair. There are creaks and sighs all around him, but even with eyes closed he seems to see her every move; he hears her breathing, feels her weight turning in the chair, and the conviction returns with greater force than before—he is bathed in the warmth of her attention, and is glad. And he knows that she is aware of his regard. There is nothing to be done about it, but the knowledge gives him comfort; it is a distant lighthouse seen from his small craft: a faint, still point of light across dark, treacherous seas.

PART FOUR

ARCTURUS IN BOÖTES

The constellation Boötes represents a herdsman driving the bear
of Ursa Major. The name of Arcturus, which lies on the hem of his
garment, derives from the Greek for "guardian of the bear." It is of the
first magnitude: the brightest star in the northern sky.

Chapter 21

Gander, Newfoundland, 48°57' N, 54°36' W
April 1948

Doubtless, to some of the creatures on earth, the stars in the sky are as undifferentiated as so many grains of sand. To those who use their lights to guide them, they are distinct in brightness and meaning—old friends whose testimony can be relied on. To those who have lived with them through an Arctic winter, using them as landmarks and seamarks, a constant through the long dark, the stars have not only meaning, but characters, like people. Some, like Spica, are shy and gentle, others strident: Sirius, for example, or Arcturus—an insistent, boastful fellow. Some are steadfast: Polaris and Betelgeuse; some, like Aldebaran, with its shadowy cohorts, untrustworthy. Others are dear as family: Vega, of course, and Pollux. Some tug at the heart, like loves lost.

All fancy, but in the last few years Flora has become increasingly fanciful. Her younger self would have derided such feelings, although it must have been her younger self that gave rise to them. Now, different stages of her life—her childhood; the last love affair (ah, Mr. Choudhury, teller of tales)—seem equally distant, equally near.

She knows that, to the others at the air base, like the boy with the teeth, she is merely old. How would he react if he knew (for example) that she had been a septuagenarian adulteress? If she told him of the things she had done in the Arctic? With disgust, probably. Embarrassment and disbelief. He would find it easier if she were dead, when both her youth and her old age would be beyond reach. But as the old woman who is here now, she is expected to have erased certain sections of her past, to have become a harmless concoction of . . . what? Memories, eccentricity, and knitting. But only five years ago (or is it seven?), she shared a bed with Ravi Choudhury, Labor counselor in the Gorbals. Her third and last husband, Bill Cochrane, dear man that he was, had lost interest in her in that way, by then, and didn't care. Dead, both of them, now, of course.

Recently, cajoled by her favorite stepdaughter, Flora saw an American movie, which, silly piece of nonsense though it was, has stayed with her. Increasing evidence of brain decay, she supposes, or of the way humans grasp after comfort in the face of the unknown. The film was a piece of fluff about a young widow who falls in love with the ghost of a sea captain. She agreed to see it purely because the title, *The Ghost and Mrs. Muir*, suggested Scottishness (it wasn't, of course). Realizing that their love could never be, the ghost nobly gave her up and pushed her into the arms of the living man who was pursuing her, which worked out badly. On the widow's deathbed, after a lifetime of implied chastity, the ghost popped up again and off they walked, hand in hand, she restored to youth and beauty. (There was no mention of the ghost of her husband, or what he thought about this.) The moral of the story seemed to be that sacrifice is pointless—a sentiment Flora heartily agrees with. Ridiculous as it was, the story moved her. In more fanciful moments, she muses, Would any of them come back for her? Who would it be?

Increasingly, Flora seems to have acquired her own private, involuntary movie theater. Whereas, once, her mind moved along sane, predictable paths (as befitted a scientist), now it lies in wait to spring at her. Great blocks of memory drop without warning into her consciousness, vivid and all-consuming. She has grown wary, as she never knows what may ambush her and hold her in thrall: a face; the taste of blubber; the sound of dogs; the voluptuous dream from the plane.

The memories, most often, come from long ago; she is immersed in sights and feelings from her childhood in Greenland: being carried on a dogsled, snow crystals stinging her face, the air burning her throat . . .

Or, the dear *Vega*: the slosh of waves against the hull, the eager motion; catching the thread of Ian Sellar's voice in the weft of noise . . . how it plucks at her, makes her body resonate like a harp . . . Oh, what if Ian were to come back for her, fulfill her vague, adolescent yearnings? Only a few years after that voyage, he was dead: drowned in a cold sea. All that wasted beauty . . .

Or, again . . . crawling down the entrance of an *illu*, she collides, head on, with Simiak, who laughs at Flora's horror and consternation. (Simiak rubs her head and strokes her hair, and twelve-year-old Flora bursts into tears, though not with pain.)

No, she wants none of those. In a hotel in Liverpool, it is simply the green, glossy texture of bathroom tiles under her hands, beaded and sweating with condensation, accompanied by unspeakable joy . . .

"Mrs. Cochrane, did you have a nice rest?"

Flora glares at the young man. Youth is no excuse for rudeness. But he is smiling that engaging smile, galloping down the corridor behind her like a dog that has spied a ball.

"Hello, Mr. Crane." (Since she remembers his name, she is damn well going to use it.) "Thank you, yes. Did you?"

"Erm . . . yes—well, I was working—making some notes, you know, for the article. Could I get you a drink before dinner?"

Flora supposes that he could. It is a long time since an attractive young man offered to buy her a drink (although *fetch* is probably the operative word, rather than *buy*), and she is not so discomfited by the surroundings, or her memories, or even his ulterior motives, whatever they are, that she will not enjoy the attention. He is so young—midtwenties, at most. The same age she was when she was exploring. How *ridiculously* young she had been, and thrust into leading a group of men, all older than herself . . . How had she dared? He is just a boy: cocky enough on the surface, but surely, underneath, wondering when he will be found out.

Outside the uncurtained window, it is still twilight; it will not be truly dark for hours. Every time she looks up, more stars have appeared, quietly emerging from the depths of space, populating the empty quarters of the cyan heaven. Once, the place they are going to was designated "Unexplored Regions"—a white blank on the maps. Now, the only unexplored regions left are up there.

Not so strange, really, to have had that dream, since it is associated with where they are going. She sees the glossy, dark eyes of the fox that used to visit them in the valley. It would sit, fearlessly, and stare at their strange, human behavior. She had named it *Imaqa*, the Eskimo word for "maybe." Im-mah-ka . . .

"Excuse me?"

Sometimes the memory-theater coexists with the person present, as though she stands amid a crowd of ghosts.

"Oh . . . nothing." Flora smiles. "I must warn you, Mr. Crane, that you begin to talk to yourself as you get older."

Randall Crane grins back at her. A conspiratorial smile, a kind one.

"I think I do that already."

They are in the cheerless lounge bar of Gander airbase. A large, square room with a low ceiling, filled with uncomfortably low chairs. He asks her about Lester Armitage, what she remembers of him. Flora gathers her thoughts. Of course, he wants something from her. Armitage . . . Increasingly difficult to keep things in the order in which they happened. They come instead in fragments, or in avalanches.

"Mr. Armitage? Well . . . of course, I met him in '92. On my first expedition."

"Ah! I don't remember that from his book."

"I don't think he mentioned it."

"So, what happened?"

"Shortly after we arrived in Greenland—that is, I, Dr. Seddon, Mr. Dixon, and Mr. Daneforth—we went to visit the American party. They were on the point of leaving. We wanted to pay our respects, of course, and see what we could find out—where they had been, what they had done and so on."

Flora remembers—but finds it hard to believe—how nervous she had been at the prospect of meeting Armitage. He did nothing to allay her discomfort.

"Etiquette demands that you do not ask such questions too directly. Separate expeditions are, on the face of it, colleagues; but, of course, you're also rivals."

"Ah . . . yes." Young Crane looks interested, leaning forward in his chair. "What were your impressions of Armitage?"

Flora recalls a large, gingery mustache and disconcerting eyes. Forbidding: that is the word she associates with Armitage. She had disliked him from the start.

"He was a determined man. Very serious. Very . . . ambitious."

"Did he help you, with what you wanted to know?"

"Oh, they were quite frank—up to a point. Of course, they were a year ahead of us, and had done very well. We stayed the night; we'd walked twenty miles to see them. They gave us dinner and breakfast."

"So you talked about the work they had done?"

"Yes."

"Which was?"

"I'm sure you've read Armitage's book . . . They told us about the two journeys they made, as detailed there. There was no conflict of interest—our focus was on scientific work; theirs was to explore."

"Did you like him?"

Flora pauses. "People have asked me many things over the years, but I don't think anyone has ever asked me if I *liked* Lester Armitage."

"Oh." Randall Crane seems unabashed. "Well, did you?"

"I respected him. He was driven and organized. Rather standoff-ish. But then, we were the competition."

"So he was competitive?"

"We were all competitive, Mr. Crane. Explorers may dress their ambitions in patriotic or scientific garb, but in the end, it tends to come down to personal glory. Well . . . or escape. Glory, or escape."

"You think Armitage was for glory?"

"If you're interested in him, you must have read his book."

Randall laughs. "Yes. I suppose that comes across. And Jakob de Beyn—which was it for him?"

Flora takes a sip of her gimlet. The color reminds her of an ice cave—*the* ice cave: the high, light chamber at the glacier's inmost heart. The sun glared off the ice on the surface, and the cavern ceiling glowed with an exquisite green light. She closes her eyes, feeling dizzy. She imagines the vitamin C (whatever that is) coursing through her veins and in some way, she hopes, fortifying them.

"A Scottish invention, Rose's Lime Juice—did you know that?"

"I didn't. I would've thought . . . the Caribbean, somewhere like that."

"It was invented for the Royal Navy. To reduce dependence on rum, I imagine."

"Ah?" He waits.

"I'm sorry, you'll have to forgive me."

"Of course . . . Was that the only time you met Armitage?"

"They were on the point of leaving Greenland. In the north, you know, one time seems much like another. It isn't like London or New York, where they put up a new building, or tear an old one down. It doesn't change. Or it didn't use to. Now, I think, even there, modern life has caught up with them. Mr. Armitage didn't like me. I think my presence in the north was, to him, a kind of insult."

"Oh. Why an insult?"

She wonders if he is really dense, or whether this is just the way with journalists.

"Because my presence in Greenland made being there seem easy. If a woman could explore, could do those things, he could no longer feel himself to be remarkable."

Randall shrugs. "Could it not be that you too were remarkable?"

"Thank you, Mr. Crane. But all we were doing was living and traveling in a place where men and women passed their whole lives. Children grew up there. We were simply unused to it. Our being there was not remarkable. Getting there, for any of us—that was the remarkable part."

"You mean, the journey, at that time?"

"No. Heavens! The voyage was a few weeks. No, I mean raising an expedition. Finding the money, organizing it. The credit for that, in my case, was due entirely to my then husband, Mr. Athlone. As we used to say, any fool can put on warm clothes and eat and walk."

"Your husband was supposed to accompany you on that first expedition, I believe. May I ask what happened?"

"You have done your research. Yes, he was. There was bad weather on the journey out, and he had a fall. He broke his pelvis. He never fully recovered."

"Ah. I'm sorry. That must have been very difficult."

Flora pictures Maurice Seddon's face in the governor's house at Godthåb. Freddie, cocooned by morphine, urged them to go on. She was supposed to disagree. Maurice stared at her as though she had become a monster, when she should have been a nurse.

"Abandoning the expedition was out of the question. One goes into such debt, you understand. It was felt that we should continue, with myself as leader. Without that accident, things would have been very different. Circumstances conspired to thrust me into that role."

"So, the men on the expedition—you had no difficulties with them?"

"They behaved very well. They felt they owed it to Freddie, I think . . . to Mr. Athlone."

She looks to see if he believes this. He nods sympathetically.

"To you too, I'm sure. You went back again, with some of the same men. So you clearly succeeded. Not all your contemporaries can have felt as Mr. Armitage did—about your being there, I mean."

"Well, they didn't all give that impression. Perhaps they hid it better."

Randall laughs, then looks at her coyly.

"De Beyn and Armitage were colleagues on that expedition. Did you meet him at the same time?"

"Dr. Seddon and I met all the Americans; there was Mr. de Beyn, Mr. Erdinger, the physicist, of course, who became so well known, and Dr. Urbino. And Mr. . . . Shull? If I remember rightly."

"What was your impression of de Beyn?"

"De Beyn? He was interested in photography. Dr. Seddon shared that interest. I remember them talking about the problems of photographing ice. He was an old friend of Dr. Urbino. He was greatly affected by his death. You know about that, I'm sure."

"I read the account in Armitage's book. But what were your impressions of him as a man?"

Flora looks at the ceiling, as though searching her memory. What can she say?

"De Beyn? Well, the most striking thing about him was his hair, which was quite gray—prematurely, of course. He called it his winter plumage. But you mean, in character, I suppose? He was friendly . . . spirited. He and Dr. Urbino were the most welcoming."

"It sounds as though you liked him."

Why is he so interested in de Beyn? As opposed to any of the others?

"I did. He didn't condescend, like Armitage . . . But these were superficial impressions, remember, from fifty years ago."

"Oh, sure. I don't suppose . . . did you form any sense of how the two of them got along?"

"Heavens, I hardly . . . You have to understand that there is no privacy there. That's how the Eskimos live—in public. One always wears a public face. Do you know what I mean?"

"I think so. Isn't that how we all live, though, wherever we are?"

"Yes, but up there it is total. If you're in a hut, or an *illu*, you are with ten or twelve other people, all piled on top of each other. You are never alone. It's hardly conducive to confidences."

"You make it sound oppressive."

"People think the north is all wide open spaces and pure white snow; solitude . . . freedom, but, in some ways, it's quite the opposite. There's certainly no clean white snow anywhere near a village!"

"But you must have liked it; you spent so much time there."

"Yes. But it's not some primitive Utopia—noble savages living in harmony, that sort of thing. You see those stars there—go left from Orion's belt—one above the other?"

She points at the window; Canis Minor is clear beyond.

"The Eskimos call that constellation '*sikuliaqsuijuittuq*.' They have a story about a hunter who took more than his fair share of meat. That's not a joke to them. They drove him out onto the summer ice; he was too heavy and fell through and drowned. That's him up there—the Murdered Man. A reminder of their justice."

Crane smiles politely. Flora wonders if she is trying to frighten him.

"So Armitage and de Beyn—"

Flora sighs. "What is your interest, Mr. Crane? Do you plan to write about them? Are you going to quote me?"

Randall smiles, and looks down at his drink. "I don't exactly know what my plan is. It rather depends."

"On what? Do you expect me to provide solutions to old mysteries?"

"I don't hope for that much! Of course, I wouldn't use anything you said unless you agreed to it."

The bar doors swing open with a burst of male voices, and a number of uniforms come in, winking with braid and medals. Their commander comes over and greets Flora with effusive courtesy.

"Good evening, Commander Soames. I'm fine, thank you. Mr. Crane was asking me how I survived as a woman in the Arctic among all those male explorers."

"I'm sure that a lady such as Mrs. Cochrane would have had nothing to fear."

Flora checks herself. Gallantry often takes the guise of obtuseness—and vice versa.

"I was about to tell him that I never experienced any great difficulty—I think because the Arctic is a very practical place. The Eskimos taught us that. Survival is the beginning and the end of everything. It makes things very clear, very simple. Isn't that so, Commander?"

"Very true," he says. "Shall we go in? Is everybody here? Have we lost Dr. Metcalfe?"

It is not true, and never could be. Things were not simple, either at that time, or later. Randall Crane sticks near to her as someone goes to find the missing oceanographer, and, leaning close, murmurs in her ear, "Which was it for you, Mrs. Cochrane—escape or glory?"

Flora purses her lips. Some people don't know when to stop.

"Mr. Crane, can you imagine a society that makes it almost impossible for you to gain an education, or have a career, or travel alone without being abused, or keep the money you earn, or behave as you want without risking disgrace? Or do anything other than follow the most restrictive, silly, demeaning rules? And, if you lived in such a society, wouldn't you want to escape it?"

The young man looks startled. Perhaps he was expecting an answer as flippant as his question.

"But in the Arctic you were with your colleagues still—men from home. And you said that you could never be alone. So did you really escape it, even there?"

The missing scientist arrives, making a joke of his lateness. The commander turns to Flora and proffers his elbow, to lead her into the mess.

For dinner, they are served broiled reindeer, accompanied by a Californian wine (the alternative being Coca-Cola). Flora tries to forget the young man's troubling persistence—she weathered it, and tomorrow there will be no time for talk. But she is nagged by his final question; cannot decide what her answer would be.

Chapter 22

New York, 40°42' N, 74°00' W
Spring 1893

My companions and I battled icy winds, plodding over the rough surface. Our feet were in agony from frostbite, and our clothes were frozen stiff, but the warmth of our bodies melted the frost as we toiled, rendering them heavy, wet, and cold. Ice formed in balls on our beards and on the fur linings of our hoods, making it even harder to see. The dogs—those few that remained after illness and treachery—were near the limits of their endurance, as were we men. But the ground was gradually sloping downward and I dared to dream that my goal was within my grasp. We had walked five hundred miles through the most inhospitable land on earth, and at last we came to the summit of a mighty precipice. I was in the lead, and felt my dogs come to a halt of their own accord. Hardly able to believe my eyes, I shouted to the others. My voice was hoarse with lack of use. They came stumbling up to join me. And there—far below us, and stretching away in an unbroken plain to the horizon—was the flat, crumpled ice of the Arctic Ocean. We had come to the end of the world!

I turned to the doctor and we shook hands, too overcome with exhaustion and emotion to speak. We had established beyond any doubt that Greenland was an island—an island whose north coast faced that elusive prize—the North Pole.

But the best and most extraordinary was yet to come. We pitched camp and boiled up some pemmican and biscuit, and then the thick weather began, imperceptibly, to lift. At this latitude, in May, the sun never sets. I stood on the summit of the cliff I had christened Cape Flagler—over a thousand feet in height—and watched as the horizon cleared. And then, to my astonishment and joy, away to the northwest, my eyes perceived something that no human eyes had ever seen before—a new land! I called to my companions, Dr. Urbino and the hunter, Metek, who quite literally danced with joy, and we stood and stared at that undiscovered land as long as the fog permitted us.

Battling the Ice; An Expedition to Northwest Greenland, 1891–2
Lester Armitage (New York, 1893)

By the time he finishes the latest chapter, Jakob is trembling with shock and rage. He grinds out his cigarette, mashing it on his plate far longer than is necessary. The diner is not far from where he and Frank used to eat lunch when they were students. He stares at the book, wondering if he has made a mistake. No, there it is on the cover—Lester B. Armitage. His own name appears in the first few pages. His own journey on Ellesmere is—albeit sketchily—recounted. But this, in the chapter he has just read, is the first whisper of the discovery of new land, and he is convinced it is a lie.

On their return from the north, Armitage had announced that they had established insularity, but that was all. He seemed dissatisfied. Would he not have been overjoyed at having discovered new land, rather than in the sullen mood that had persisted for the rest of their stay? In contradiction to the printed passage, Frank denied they had seen *anything* from their furthest north. He said—Jakob can hear his voice saying it—the fog was so thick they could not even be sure it *was* the north coast. But here, in black and white, Lester states that Frank was with him, that Frank saw this new land and knew it for what it was. Here, in black and white, are the coordinates of his discovery: "Dupree Land."

Could Lester keep such a discovery to himself? He is, above all, a man who likes to be in control. Could he have sworn Frank to secrecy—and would Frank have obeyed? Frank was never one to hide his feelings—had always been incapable of doing so. That day on the beach, his confidences had been all the other way—that they could not affirm it was the north coast, that they had discovered nothing; that they had not even known where they were.

Armitage has made a claim that will advance his ambitions, and the only man who can confirm or deny its truth is dead. What if (he can't be thinking this, surely?)—what if Frank's death wasn't an accident? No, that's crazy. He is not a monster . . . Jakob lights another cigarette, becomes aware that his hands are shaking.

The youth behind the counter takes away his cup of cold coffee, saying, with a smile, that he is not supposed to do this, but they won't tell anyone. Jakob picks up the fresh one, grateful for the small kindness.

"It is a good book?"

"I beg your pardon?"

The youth gestures to the volume. The lunch crowd has dwindled and the diner is almost empty.

"I ask, it is a good book? You have read for one hour without pause."

Jakob looks down at the book, at a loss for words.

Two days later, he is on his way to the Urbinos'. He has a standing invitation to spend Sundays at their house, and Frank's parents claim that his presence is a comfort, so he goes. He thought about making an excuse this time, because they will want to talk about Lester's book, and he doesn't know what to say.

While he is knocking the rain from his hat in the porch, Clara opens the door. She lives downtown, sharing an apartment with Lucille Becker, but spends weekends with her parents. Johnny comes when he can, but now that he has joined a law firm, his work often prevents it. Anna has never moved away.

Jakob follows Clara into the sitting room. Anna glides toward him. She holds out both hands to him—a faintly disturbing habit she has developed. Her eyes glitter with tears and her face has an unhealthy pallor. He wonders if she sleeps. Frank's death hit them all a terrible blow, but it seems to have affected Anna most of all. She dresses in mourning from head to foot, whereas Clara has gone back to her regular wardrobe. It has been nine months since Frank's death—eight since they learned of it in the letter Armitage wrote from Nova Scotia. But every time Jakob comes to their house, her grief feels as fresh as the first day he came.

"Jake . . ." Anna allows him to take her hands briefly. "So good to see you."

He presses her hands firmly and then, just as firmly, lets them go. "And you. How are you?"

"Oh, well . . ." She gives him a brave smile. "We carry on as best we can."

Jakob has begun to wonder if Anna will ever give up her role as chief mourner. She has embraced it with such fervor, he sometimes thinks she enjoys it.

Marion Rutherford and Mrs. Urbino greet Jakob and ask after his brother and family. Both women wear black. Marion carries a familiar volume.

"Mr. Armitage's book! Have you read it, Mr. de Beyn?"

"No . . . not yet."

"Oh!" Marion's eyes gleam. "I read it through in one sitting. I simply couldn't stop before I'd finished it. It's wonderful, isn't it, Sophia?" She turns to Mrs. Urbino and touches her on the arm.

"Yes, wonderful," murmurs Mrs. Urbino, whose look of pleasant bewilderment has only intensified since her son's death.

"Such a fitting tribute to dear Frank. He was a hero . . . A hero," she repeats in a hollow whisper.

"Yes," says Jacob.

That is not at all the impression he formed. As Lester recounts it, on the northern journey, Frank forever stumbles in Lester's wake, gasping for breath. Lester forges ahead; Frank follows—is trusty, loyal, submissive. Occasionally he is allowed to display a particular skill, as when he removed an abscessed tooth from Jakob's upper jaw during a gale. This last, Lester made into a little comedic episode ("The geologist is relieved"), which, for him (he remembers nearly crying with pain), it wasn't.

"Have you all read it?" he asks.

"I haven't been able to finish it. It made me too upset." Anna's voice dwindles to a choked whisper.

Marion glares: as the deceased's fiancée, she clearly believes she should not be upstaged in the matter of grief.

In the garden, Clara faces him.

"You have read it, haven't you?"

"Was it obvious?"

Clara shrugs. "No. They know you're busy. What's wrong with it?"

"Marion doesn't think there's anything wrong with it."

"But . . ."

"I don't know . . . It's fine."

"*Fine?*" She looks at him derisively.

Jakob shrugs. "Some of the events"—he hesitates—"are not exactly as I remember them."

Clara stares. "That wasn't what I was expecting. Are you saying that Mr. Armitage is lying?"

Jakob lowers his voice. "It's mostly a matter of bias, or . . . I suppose it's a temptation, if you're writing a book, to paint yourself in a good light, sometimes to the detriment of your companions."

"He is detrimental to the rest of you—to Frank?"

"Yes, I think he's detrimental to Frank. He undervalues his contribution. Sometimes he makes him seem . . . almost like a buffoon. And that's unfair and wrong."

Clara looks upset. Jakob wishes he hadn't come.

"That's my opinion. You'll have to read it yourself. There's no point talking about it till then."

"I will," she says. "But I'm just one of the women who wait at home and then listen to the men's wonderful stories. You were there."

Over lunch, Marion does something she has never done before: she astonishes everyone. She announces, with a sly glance at Anna, that she has found someone who is helping her in her sorrow. Everyone looks at her. There is a strange fervor about Marion, all the odder as she has never, to Jakob's knowledge, displayed excitement of any kind.

"What do you mean, Marion?" asks Anna, with a hint of asperity.

"I mean," Marion lowers her eyes, "I've been introduced to a remarkable woman—Mrs. Jupp. She has a beautiful gift; the most wonderful thing. I ask you not to judge right away. I know . . ." She laughs, a little nervously. "I know you may be skeptical, but she has . . . enabled me to talk to Frank. Actually talk to him!"

In the silence that follows, she looks at Mrs. Urbino. Her eyes are bright, but she looks as though she might weep. The sisters stare at Marion: Clara stern, Anna aghast. Lucille looks down at her plate—in embarrassment, Jakob feels, which he shares. Mr. Urbino looks grave. A man of few words, he puts his knife and fork together and clears his throat.

"Marion, dear, I know you are as grief-stricken as we all are, but in times of sorrow, the best way to find comfort is surely in prayer."

"Of course, but—"

"This person . . . I'm sure she means well, but this sort of thing is against the teaching of our church."

Marion's lips harden. "I only tell you because, of course, others may like to join me at Mrs. Jupp's." She looks defiant. "I *know* it was

Frank who spoke to me, Mr. Urbino. I know it. He said things . . . things she couldn't possibly have known. It was his spirit!"

She is trembling in her conviction. Her pale cheeks have a faint flush. Jakob finds himself, for the first time, almost admiring her—the girl actually has some guts, even if she is quite mad.

"And what," Clara asks, "did Frank have to say?"

Marion lifts her chin. "He had a message that was just for me, a beautiful message. But he also wanted to tell us—everyone—that he's happy—yes!—and he doesn't want us to grieve too much."

She stares around the table. After his first glance at her, Jakob drops his eyes. He wonders what Marion would say if he kept his promise and apologized for Frank's infidelity.

"Incredible," says Clara. "That certainly sounds like my brother."

Mr. Urbino frowns. Mrs. Urbino is looking at Marion and patting her on the arm. There is a violent scraping noise as a chair is shoved backward.

"Excuse me," Anna says in a choked voice, and rushes from the room.

By tacit agreement, the subject is dropped. Marion maintains a wounded and dignified silence. Lucille asks Jakob about the geological treatise on Ellesmere that he is writing, and he answers dully. They then discuss the meteorite, which Lester is donating to the Museum of Natural History in Frank's memory. It is, the family has heard, going to be known as the Urbino meteorite. They find this an honor.

Over the next few days, Jakob tries to reread Lester's book with greater detachment, but his suspicions only grow stronger. He is irritated that, although Lester has used several of his photographs, he has not credited him as the photographer. Not one photograph graces the brief account of the Ellesmere trip (the best work Jakob has ever done), and their achievement in mapping so much coastline is mentioned in passing. He knows that these are petty and self-regarding concerns, by and large—after all, it was Lester's expedition and it is Lester's book—but they serve to underscore his (everyone's, surely?) impression that Lester considers every achievement of the expedition his own personal triumph. He paints himself as a lonely figure, accompanied by shadowy ciphers of scientists more interested in counting rocks than in the patriotic work of exploration. Adding to his sense of injustice is that, in the account of Frank's death, he does not so much as mention the Eskimo hunter who was injured. Ayakou, a cheerful and willing worker, liked by all, has been omitted from the record.

"How is your book coming?"

Bettina asks this regularly—usually on Fridays when Jakob comes down to breakfast. Today he is late—he has not been sleeping well. He shrugs.

"It's fine."

"You're working too hard. You look tired. *Komm schon.*"

She places a cup of coffee in front of him and puts a hand on his shoulder.

He smiles at his sister-in-law, but is astonished to feel a treacherous heat prickle his eyelids and throat. No one else wonders how he is, or tells him when he looks tired. Bettina sometimes has that effect on him—she behaves, still, as though he is one of her children and not really capable of looking after himself.

"I'm not working hard enough. That's the problem."

"I thought you had nearly finished."

Jakob sighs. He is finding it difficult to fulfill his brief: he has received a very small sum from a scientific publisher to produce a treatise on Ellesmere, illustrated with his own photographs. That should be easy enough. What is difficult is avoiding the feeling that this is a trivial affair when there are so many other things on his mind. And what is unique about the place is not its rocks, but the ice that covers them. That is what he wants to write about. He wants to recount their journey, in a way that will likely not please Lester Armitage. Under the terms of Jakob's expedition contract, he cannot publish anything until the anniversary of their return, which is August 29, but even then, he has been given to understand that expedition narratives are the sole preserve of its leader.

"Jake?"

"Sorry?"

Bettina shakes her head.

"It's as I keep saying: you need a wife. Someone to look after you."

Jakob grins. "What would Vera say?"

Bettina and Hendrik's daughter—now eight—has assured him that she intends to marry him when she grows up, and he has promised to wait.

"Tch. You know the Mullers, from our old block? I saw Mrs. Muller with the daughter yesterday. Maria . . . no? Well, she's younger than you. My word, she has grown up pretty! So well dressed! And she works—very modern, although she's *very* respectable. She works in a ladies' clothing store. They were *so* interested when I told them about you. 'How marvelous,' they kept saying. I must invite them to tea. They'd love to see you."

Jakob rolls his eyes and forks bacon into his mouth.

"Mrs. Muller told me something . . ." She stops and seems to lose her thread. She looks down at the shelf of the dresser.

"Told you what?"

"Oh, you probably won't remember them. They moved away before we did. The Gertlers. Cora Gertler was a friend of mine. Do you remember them? He was a taxidermist. Well, it's so sad . . . She passed away—last Christmas. Cancer." She clicks her tongue. "She wasn't much older than me."

Jakob's food has turned to ash in his mouth. He has to force the mouthful down, and takes a swig of coffee.

"But anyway . . ." Bettina turns her back to him and busies herself stacking plates. "These things happen. Only God knows how long we're granted."

"Yes," Jakob manages to say after an age. And then, some time after that: "I remember her."

Bettina puts the stack of plates on the shelf and lines up the edges. She half turns around, but doesn't quite look at him.

"I thought you might. That's why I told you."

Jefferson Shull seems to have grown even more handsome in the months since Jakob last saw him. He is wearing a new coat and has cultivated a golden mustache. His boots gleam with the mirror brightness that speaks of twice-daily polishing. He greets Jakob with a show of bonhomie, but is not quite as friendly as he was in the north. Social and financial differences count for little in the Arctic; here, on Fifth Avenue, especially in the hushed surroundings of Shull's club, it seems a different matter.

After some idle talk, the subject of Lester's book comes up.

"It's rather good, isn't it?" says Shull. "He was saying that it should help raise money for his next trip."

"You've seen him?" Jakob had thought Lester was on a constant round of lectures and engagements, too busy and important to talk to any of them.

"Yes. The other day. In fact"—Shull gives a light laugh—"he's asked me to go with him again."

"Well, that's great. Do you want to go?"

"I may go. He might give you a call, too. . . . He did say, though, that he wants to concentrate on the exploring next time, rather than scientific studies. 'Science takes too long,' he says!"

Jakob laughs angrily. "They aren't always compatible."

After another drink, Jakob feels Shull getting restless.

"Shull, there's something I wanted to talk to you about."

"Oh?"

"Dupree Land . . . That chapter in the book was the first I'd heard of it. Armitage didn't say anything about seeing new land after the northern trip; nor did Frank. Don't you find that odd?"

"Oh, well, Armitage said something about that. He wanted to keep Dupree Land to himself precisely because it was so important. He didn't want any hint leaking out before he announced it."

"But what about Frank? He was there. He would have told me."

Shull glances at the door. As he speaks, his eyes stray constantly to the hand holding his cigar.

"Ah, well . . . apparently Urbino was so done in when they reached the coast, he just went to sleep. Armitage saw the land when the fog lifted, but Urbino never did. And Armitage didn't tell him."

"But in the book he says Frank was with him! He uses him to corroborate the sighting."

"I was about to say . . ." Shull's face assumes a respectful expression. "After Urbino passed away, Armitage thought it would be a nice gesture for the family if they thought he'd shared in the discovery."

"Did he say all this the other day?"

Shull shrugs. "I guess he knew it might raise a few questions."

"Well, I guess that answers mine," says Jakob.

"You won't tell Urbino's family? You do know them, don't you?"

"I'm not going to do anything that would hurt them—or Frank's name."

"No. Of course not." Shull mashes out his cigar on the copper plate that has been brought for the purpose.

Some hours later, Jakob is in a beer cellar in his old neighborhood. He came here to get drunk, which he has achieved, but somehow it hasn't helped as much as he thought. His fury is undimmed, but he is unable to think what he can do about it, other than go to Greenland to see for himself the mythical Dupree Land, or lack of it . . . Well, then that is what he must do. Once that becomes inevitable, there is nothing to stop the news of Cora's death from overwhelming him.

Since yesterday, he has pushed it to the back of his mind. Now he allows it to engulf him, although it has been more than eight years since he saw her, and he has rarely thought of her.

He should have seen the end coming. He was in his second year at City, and their liaison had been going on for many months. Jakob was just as happy as at the outset, but, once or twice, after Christmas, when the apartment's customary odors were masked by oranges and cloves, Cora had seemed distracted, almost irritated on his arrival, turning away in silence at the door, leaving him to close it and follow her into the bedroom, wondering if he had done something wrong. If he asked her what was the matter, she would say, "Nothing's the matter. I'm just tired." Eventually, she would consent to be taken in his arms, and things would take their usual course.

Until, that is, the evening in February, when Jakob arrived, as usual, just after seven. Cora pulled the door open and swept him inside, her tongue inside his mouth before the latch clicked home. She barely said a word, or let him speak; they knocked over a copper jardinière on the way to the bedroom. Jakob was hardly going to complain about an excess of passion, although it struck him, even at the time, as odd.

At half past nine, she rolled away from him and got up.

"Where are you going?" asked Jakob, who knew without having to look at the clock that they had another half hour.

"Get dressed," she said, pulling on her clothes.

"It's only half past."

"I need to say something."

He began to dress, miserably aware that something was wrong. Before he had buttoned up his shirt, she started: "We're leaving New York. My husband and I are moving to St. Louis. I'm sorry, *Liebling*, but this is the last time."

It sounded rehearsed.

"No," he said. "Why?"

She frowned impatiently. "Because he has a job there."

Jakob either couldn't understand the words, or didn't believe them.

"Is there someone else?"

Cora had an effective technique for arguing, which was to refuse to take part.

"You don't have to go, Cora. You don't love him!"

"Jake . . ." She shook her head. "I don't expect you to understand now, but one day you will."

He realized with horror that he was going to cry in front of her. He became angry. He begged.

"Why didn't you tell me before?"

"Listen, my dear boy, I didn't tell you before because we would both have been sad. We've had a good time, no? Now it's over. Sooner or later, you will fall in love with a girl your own age. That will happen, whether I'm here or not. I would rather not see it."

"No! I won't . . . Cora, don't . . . please . . ."

He knew nothing he said would make a difference. He had never had any influence over the course of things. As he left, his dignity in tatters, she said, "Nothing lasts forever, *Liebling*. Nothing good; nothing bad. You'll see."

Thinking the St. Louis story might be false, he spied on her apartment for the next two weeks, but never caught a glimpse. Clumsily casual inquiries proved that they had, in fact, moved to St. Louis. The simple, horrible truth was that he hadn't mattered that much to her. He stewed in misery for nights on end, convinced that no one had ever felt as wretched as he. Hendrik and Bettina would hold discussions in hushed tones that broke off whenever he entered the kitchen. They couldn't know the reason; he had never told anyone, other than Frank, and even Frank did not know her name.

Cora was right: as spring galloped into the city, he began to recover. He would fall asleep even as he was admiring the depth and nobility of his suffering, and surprised himself one day by walking past her street without a qualm. He allowed himself to

believe that, since the affair with Cora had come to him so easily, the same thing would happen again before too long, and his
life would contain (maybe!) a whole succession of Coras: accom-
modating, seductive women, undemanding yet passionate.
He waited. But the time that healed his hurts proved this hope
erroneous.

The respectable young women he did meet, like Frank's sisters,
were quite out of reach—unattainable, except through marriage,
for which he had not yet the inclination, or the money, and he
would not stoop to deception to get what he wanted. There had
been other women, eventually—even a couple, like Swedish Kate,
of whom he had been really fond—but no one has ever been as
good to him, as forthright, as sensual, as Cora Gertler—and now
she is dead.

By ten o'clock, the beer cellar is crammed with people in various
stages of dishevelment, night has fallen, and he is maudlin, allowing himself the indulgence of remembering Cora in the most sentimental way possible. Some time later, he is astonished to hear his
own name spoken. The astonishment doesn't extend to responding
in any way, but he is surprised to feel his shoulder being shaken, not
gently.

"Mr. de Beyn . . . Mr. de Beyn . . . Jake! Good heavens, are you all
right? What sort of a state is this?"

He looks up to see a vaguely familiar face.

"It's Lucille. Lucille Becker."

"I know," he says with dignity. "Hello, Miss Becker." His voice
sounds sepulchral, as though he is speaking from the bottom of a
well.

She shakes her head in exasperated concern.

"Don't you think it might be time you went home?"

"What are you doing?"

"Here? I'm buying beer. Does that shock you?"

Jakob shakes his head, and then stops, as it makes him dizzy.

"Will you go home now? Are you all right to walk?"

Jakob is sure he said yes, but the next minute she is pulling him to his feet, her arm, thin and surprisingly strong, around his back.

"No, no . . ." he protests mildly. Standing up, he has discovered, is a bad idea.

"Come on. You need some coffee. We only live around the corner. And it's always better to talk to other people, I find, rather than yourself."

Somehow they make their way out—accompanied by humorous comments on all sides—into the cool night.

Jakob lets Lucille steer him around the corner, insisting he can walk on his own, that he is all right, really, not that drunk. But when she lets his shoulder go, he falls over his feet, and she seizes his arm again in a vice-like grip.

"Here we are," she says at last, letting them into an apartment building. Vinegary smells waft down the stairwell—disturbingly similar to the Gertlers' building. For a terrible second, he thinks he is there, before noticing that the stairwell winds the other way.

"Don't mind the smell," Lucille says. "It doesn't make it into the apartment." She rattles keys and pushes him inside, calling out, "Clara? We have a visitor!"

There is no sign of anyone in the apartment. Lucille leads him into a tiny kitchen with a tiny table, where she makes him sit. He sinks into a chair with relief while she boils a pan of water. When she has made coffee, she pours two cups and places one in front of Jakob, who has to concentrate to stop himself slumping forward and resting his head on the table.

"Drink that."

"Where's Clara?"

"I don't know. She may have gone to her parents'."

"Is she coming back?"

"Well, if she *has* gone to her parents', I shouldn't think so, now."

As if aware of what she has said, and feeling the shadow of impropriety descend, she grips her coffee in both hands and leans against the stove.

"I probably shouldn't have spoken to you at all, the state you're in, but you seemed so upset. Do you want to talk about it?"

"Oh . . . it's just . . ." Jakob considers brushing it off, but the prospect of feminine sympathy is too tempting. And there is something so straightforward and intelligent about Miss Becker that he finds himself telling her . . . well, almost everything. She is a modern, sensible girl—she doesn't seem shocked to hear of the death of his former lover; indeed, she is sympathetic. Encouraged, he finds himself rambling incoherently about Frank and Lester and his suspicions, although he thinks she struggles to follow his reasoning.

"You should talk to Clara about this."

"Yes. I know."

He stares up at her. She now has her arms folded in a protective—or defensive—gesture. He has previously thought of her as amiable and jolly, but rather simian in appearance: one of those women one assigns, almost without thinking, to the category of lifelong spinster. But now, as if a veil has been torn from his eyes (dissolved in beer, perhaps), he notices the honey-colored skin of her neck where it vanishes into her dress, the spirals of dark hair escaping from her bun. The way her bodice molds itself over little, pointed breasts. His throat constricts with lust. He focuses on his coffee, horrified, embarrassed—he has never found her alluring before, but then he never before noticed, well, certain things about her.

"More coffee? Is it helping?" Without waiting for an answer, she refills his cup. It is strong and bitter, and is having the effect, if not of sobering him, then of taking the edge off his sottishness. "You can probably go home soon, if you're feeling better. I have to work tomorrow."

"You're very kind," he blurts out. "To listen to me like this, I mean."

"Oh, well. I'm sorry about your . . . finding out like that. It must have been a shock."

Both her hands are holding her coffee cup: pretty hands, delicate and slender.

If he had been either less drunk or more drunk than he is at this moment, Jakob would not have done it. He reaches out and touches one of Lucille's hands. She freezes, but doesn't move it away. He looks up into her face, which is turned to one side, as if she doesn't dare look at him. Her lips are parted; her throat moves as she swallows. Emboldened, with his other hand he takes her cup and puts it on the table. More than anything, he longs to put his arms around a warm, female body and to feel arms around him in return. As he stands up—swaying—he pulls her toward him, and then he is conscious of her head against his shoulder, his hands stroking her thin back, and her arms close around him. She is so slender and little, the top of her head barely reaches his chin.

"Lucille . . ." he begins, trying to think of some appropriate words, and she tilts her head up toward him, and her mouth brushes softly, primly against his. Electrified, he opens his mouth against hers, parts her lips with his tongue and, completely inflamed, presses her body against his, throwing restraint, caution, manners to the winds, swept along by a hot flood of desire . . . It is too much; almost instantly, he is aware of her twisting away from him, pushing fiercely at his chest.

"Stop!" she hisses.

"Please . . . You're so . . ."

As he becomes aware of the noises in the hall, Lucille shoves him in the chest, which, on a drunken man, has the effect of overbalancing him and pushing him back into the chair. His elbow meets the wall with a sharp rap. He bends over the table, his heart racing. Lucille picks up her cup, wipes her mouth, assumes the position of someone leaning casually against a stove, and manages to look calm as Clara walks into the kitchen.

"You're still up . . . My goodness! Jake!"

Clara peels off her gloves, looking at him with a mixture of puzzlement and—he is sure—suspicion. He blinks at her, realizing with despair just how drunk he is. He speaks very carefully to make up for it.

"Hello, Clara. I must apologize to you both. Miss Becker found me in a rather sorry state, and was kind enough to bring me here to, well, sober me up." He smiles at her. "I'm afraid I've bored her sadly with my troubles."

Clara looks at them both. Jakob is cold with horror. His elbow hums with pain, which he can't account for. He also seems to have bitten his tongue.

"I'm sorry, Miss Becker. I'm ashamed of myself. I'm fine now."

"You don't look fine." Clara's gaze flicks from his face to Lucille's and back, like the spike of a metronome. "Does he, Lucy? You can't walk home in this state. You'll fall in the river or end up in an alley with your throat cut. We have a trundle bed. You can sleep in my room, and I'll go in with Lucy. No, it's fine. We've done it before."

"But the neighbors . . ." Jakob says weakly, as he now desires nothing more than to lie down—even on the floor; the corner of the kitchen would do, or the hall outside . . .

"Oh, I think the damage is done there," says Clara.

Lying in Clara's bed, in the dark, head spinning, he despairs of sleep. His mind is a mess of thoughts, mostly sad and unpleasant, but his body is full of the impression of holding Lucille in his arms, and he seizes on it as a way of blocking out the rest. How slender she was, how meagerly fleshed (not really his type at all); she felt like a fragile, sharp-boned bird, but full of warmth . . . And she *had* kissed him—seemed, at first, to welcome his effrontery. In his blurred, drifting state, his hand closes around his warm, tumescent penis (more for comfort than anything else), but then he imagines Lucille unbuttoning in the next room, just the other side of the partition wall, Lucille welcoming him, revealing her hot, secret places . . . It is only when he is breathing quickly and his heart is racing that the consciousness of what he is doing breaks upon him—and that he is doing it in Clara's bed. Sickened, but past the point of no return, he finishes with a strangled gasp, a half-spoiled climax and a wave of self-disgust, holding the bedclothes away from himself in an attempt not to defile them. Panting, he reaches for his jacket; his handkerchief has mysteriously (and yet unsurprisingly) vanished. He finds his shirt in the darkness and wipes himself with the shirt tail, wondering if the loss of self-respect now afflicting him will be temporary, or fatal.

He awakes to a weak, dreary light. Not knowing if Clara and Lucille are still in the apartment, he dresses quickly, feeling ill and ashamed. He peels back the bed covers to inspect them: as far as he can tell, there is no trace of his misdemeanor. He can't quite believe he did *that* last night; perhaps he only dreamt it—yet the shirt tail convicts him. He feels wretched.

He puts his ear to the door, wondering if he should slip away unannounced, but that seems too cowardly and low, even for him. Then quick footsteps and a rap on the door make him leap away to the middle of the room.

"Jake?"

It is Clara's voice.

"Yes! I'm up." He smooths down his hair, panics for a moment, and opens the door. Clara stands in the hall. She looks smart and fresh: as groomed as always.

"I've made coffee."

"Thank you. I don't want to put you to any more trouble. I'm terribly sorry about last night."

Clara regards him levelly, nods.

"Lucille told me what you said to her last night. You shouted a name in your sleep. 'Flora!' Was that the name of your friend?"

"Um . . . Cora."

"Perhaps that was it."

In the kitchen, they light cigarettes and Clara pours coffee. Lucille has left for work. Clara has the day off; she is due to go to her parents'. Jakob can't tell how much she knows about last night.

"Please pass on my apologies to Miss Becker. I'm afraid I made an awful fool of myself."

"You did, rather. Don't look so miserable; I'm not angry. I'm worried about my parents, and about Anna. Can you believe, she's been dragged into this awful spiritualist thing with Marion. She's become quite evangelical. It's . . . unhealthy. I could always talk to Frank about things like this. God, I miss him."

"I do too."

"I know. I'm sorry about your bad news—Lucille told me. Was she your mistress?"

She says this carelessly, as she would ask if she was fair-haired. Jakob gapes in astonishment. "W . . . er . . . yes. I mean, it was long ago . . . at college. But it was a shock."

"Frank used to tell us what a reprobate you were, that you had a mistress in the city. We didn't know if he was serious. I thought perhaps he was warning us against you. Of course, he was wildly jealous." She smiles, although her voice has become tremulous.

Frank's presence is suddenly a palpable thing, as though he were just out in the hall. There is something else, as well; it never occurred to Jakob that Clara might have needed warning against him.

He looks at the clock with a show of surprise. "Goodness, I'd better be going. I've bothered you quite long enough."

"Yes. I have to go if I'm to be there for lunch."

"Should I wait, or . . . ? I'll be discreet as I go out."

"It doesn't matter. All sorts of things go on in this building. That's why we can afford it."

Chapter 23

New York, 40°42' N, 74°00' W
May 1893

In the course of the following week, Jakob receives three letters. The least troubling is from Anna Urbino. She describes in breathless terms a visit to Mrs. Jupp's, and the wonderful experience of being "in the comforting presence of dear Frank's spirit."

Jakob wonders why she is bothering to write to him, until he gets to the final page, where he is surprised to be invited to accompany her to Mrs. Jupp's; apparently, Frank's spirit (in the person of Mrs. Jupp) announced that he has a message for him. Anna knew immediately that it was for Jakob because Mrs. Jupp—"who knows nothing of Frank's life!" (other than what she gleans from the papers, Jakob presumes)—described him in detail, even down to his gray hairs, and said it was his friend in the icy north. The message is for him alone, and will only be disclosed in his presence, so Anna fervently hopes that he can lay his skepticism aside in order to hear it.

The second letter is in an unfamiliar handwriting, but postmarked locally. He opens it to find a single page:

Dear Mr. de Beyn,

I hesitate to be so forward as to write to you after what passed between us the other night, yet I fear I will find no peace until I do. I have been thinking of all you said and did ever since, and I want to tell you that, although our actions were, of course, improper in the extreme, I bear you no ill will. In fact, on the contrary, I have long held you in high regard, and was—I dare to admit it!—happy to be the recipient of your impetuous declaration. Sometimes I think that under the loosening influence of alcohol we are most ourselves, and if it has enabled you to express sentiments that you previously hid for the sake of propriety, I welcome it. Please don't regret what you did. I don't.

Affectionately yours,
Lucille (Becker)

For some minutes after reading this, Jakob sits slumped in his chair, cursing. His hope that the shameful episode would be decently forgotten is dashed. What an idiot he is. He hates the idea of hurting Lucille. He likes her, has always enjoyed talking to her, but . . . does he like her more than he thought? Thinking about her now, even making himself think of her in a sensual way, he feels no trace of the desire that ambushed him in their kitchen.

The third letter, which arrives the same day, is also in an unfamiliar hand, but he guesses instantly, from the Nova Scotia postmark, what it is, and tears it open with a mixture of excitement and trepidation.

Siorapaluk, April

Dear Mr. de Beyn,

I write partly in response to your request, last autumn, to be informed of Ayakou's progress after the meteorite accident. As you know, Dr. Seddon set the broken leg, and after some weeks we became hopeful that he would recover the use of it. He is walking again, but Dr. Seddon is of the opinion that he will always be lame and troubled by pain. I enclose a summary of his prospects from Dr. Seddon, for the attention of Mr. Armitage, in the hope that he might see his way to providing some compensation, since the injury was sustained in his service. That would be a very small thing to Mr. Armitage or his backers, but could make Ayakou's life much less of a hardship. I regret to tell you that his wife has left him for another, since Ayakou is not able to hunt. The nature of life here is such that I cannot blame her—and last winter has been exceptionally hard.

Now for other, perhaps more important, news. In March, Meqro gave birth to a daughter. As you know, Meqro was the faithful companion of Dr. Urbino while he was in the north, and, as the child was conceived last July, it is undoubtably his—it has pale skin and rather Caucasian features. Her name is Aamma. The position of widowed mothers can be perilous, but her father and mother have kept her with them, and Meqro is determined to raise her child. Shall I tell you how dangerous the child's position could be? If a hunter dies and his wife has a child young enough to be carried in the hood, she is expected to smother it. This will not happen to Dr. Urbino's daughter. There is our presence, and I hope, once we are gone, the thought of "kallunat" interest will keep her safe. I have told everyone that the Americans are coming back—and that they expect to see the girl. I wonder whether Mr. Armitage would consider her another case deserving of compensation?

Forgive me—this is beginning to seem like a begging letter. I should perhaps address this to Mr. Armitage, but I know you and Dr. Urbino were great friends, and I would rather pass to you the choice whether or not to tell his family of Aamma's existence. I apologize if it is a difficult one. These things are not always simple.

I will not detain you with all that we have been doing since last year, but work has been progressing. I have made some interesting observations of the aurora in relation to earth's magnetic field, and long desperately for a magic camera that could make a proper visual record of it. Will that ever be possible? Next time, perhaps! (This is our constant refrain here.)

I hope that you are well and that your finger gives you no trouble.
I think of you whenever I see a particularly fine arrangement of ice,
light, and shade—the photographs of yours I saw at Neqi seemed to
me very fine.

Respectfully yours,
Flora Athlone

Once he has read the letter through several times, Jakob simply sits
with it in his hand, looking at the abstract shapes made by her writing. Out of all the difficulties and ramifications that arise from its
contents, and from the other letters, he finds he has fixed on that last
sentence. She thinks of him.

Chapter 24

Philadelphia, 39°57' N, 75°9' W
May 1893

Erdinger says, "Haven't you heard?"

"Heard what?"

Jakob arrived in Philadelphia yesterday evening, having left New York, Lucille's letter still unanswered, with a guilty feeling of relief.

"About the meteorite? I thought that was why you'd come."

"No. What about it? Has he donated it, then? I haven't read a paper for a couple of days."

"Donated it? Hell, no—he *sold* it to them."

"To ... the Museum of Natural History?"

"No! To the Academy of Natural Sciences, here. It's quite a coup for Philly. I guess they outbid the others."

"But Armitage was going to donate it in Frank's name! He said ..."

Erdinger shrugs. They are sitting in a small park near Erdinger's university. It is hot in Philadelphia, hotter than New York, and Jakob is sweating in his coat. Erdinger is sweating too; he has put on weight since they returned.

"I guess, if you're fund-raising for another expedition, every dollar counts. They only said they bought it for 'an undisclosed sum.'"

"He was going to name it the 'Urbino meteorite.' Has he?"

"I don't know about that. The paper I read said it had an Eskimo name—'*Uttukalualuk*.'"

"That means, 'the old man.' What am I going to tell his family?"

"It's not your fault. I'm with you. I think, if you say you're gonna do a thing, you should do it."

Jakob sighs. "Actually, I came to talk to you about the book. Armitage's book. Have you read it?"

Erdinger hesitates. "Parts."

"Did you read the part about discovering Dupree Land?"

"Yeah, I read that."

"And? What did you think? 'There's a surprise'?"

"I suppose so. I wasn't there. Maybe they saw something and didn't tell us."

"Come on, Erdinger. Is that the way people behave? Frank told me they didn't see a thing. The fog never lifted. He was there, and he wasn't asleep. Armitage didn't even know where they were. He took two longitude sightings the whole trip."

Erdinger looks across the park.

"Have you thought maybe Urbino made a mistake? Or maybe he was embarrassed to admit he fell asleep."

"He was talking to *me*, Erdinger! If he'd fallen asleep, he would have said so, but that's not what happened. You saw what Armitage was like afterward; depressed, almost desperate. Does that fit with discovering a new land?"

"I don't know. I don't claim to understand him. I know that, if he wants to raise funds for another trip, he's got to have something to show from the last one."

"He's using Frank's death to do it! He's profiting . . ." Jakob bites off the rest of the sentence.

Erdinger picks at a piece of fluff on his trouser leg. "I don't know. Does it matter? Urbino doesn't care, where he is. Armitage wants to go north again. Say you come to the coast, and the fog's so thick you can't see anything . . . Who's to say there *isn't* a new land there?"

"Come on. Is that how you do physics?"

"Well, this way, Frank shares the credit for discovering a new land. Isn't his family happier for thinking that?"

"And when the truth is discovered and Frank looks like a fool—or a liar?"

Erdinger shrugs. "I guess Armitage knows what he saw better than anyone else."

"I'm going back," Jakob says at length. "Next year."

Erdinger nods. "Thought you would. I've done my bit for geography. I have two years left to make history. Although . . . did I tell you, I'm getting married?"

"No!" Jakob is astonished. "Congratulations."

Erdinger makes a face. "I know: probably a mistake. I have to concentrate on my work while I still can, and women can be distracting. But she has money, so it seems too good an opportunity to miss. That's what it comes down to, right? That's why Armitage is making a fuss about some so-called island that's never going to be any use to anyone."

"So you *do* think he's lying?"

Erdinger shrugs and smiles—a disconcerting sight, especially as he has a fragment of greenery lodged in his upper incisors.

"I don't know. Neither do you."

New York, 40°42' N, 74°00' W

Back in New York, he finally writes to Lucille. He rewrites the letter several times, but even then it does him no credit. Well, she may rail to Clara about him, or (if he's lucky) she may keep her humiliation to herself.

He also writes to Clara, saying there is something important he needs to speak to her about, regarding Frank; could they meet? He names a rendezvous and arrives at the café early, with a trepidation induced by guilt.

As soon as he sees her face, he realizes that Lucille has told her everything. She sits opposite him without speaking, and plucks savagely at her gloves.

"I have absolutely no desire to speak to you."

"I'm terribly sorry, Clara . . ."

"It isn't me you need to apologize to."

"I tried to say how sorry I was to Miss Becker. I know it was unforgivable. I'm truly sorry to have been the cause of upset or embarrassment."

"You took advantage of her kindness in the most disgusting way, and then humiliated her!"

"Yes . . . and I'm—"

"Perhaps you don't know, perhaps you can't imagine, but Lucille has had little admiration in her life, and any attention of that sort is apt to be overwhelming to her. And she's always admired you—God knows why. So to be told that making love to her was a . . . horrible, drunken mistake—can you see how cruel that is?"

Jakob shrinks in his chair. "All I can say is that it *was* a mistake. I didn't mean to be cruel. I was in a sad state. It was night, and—"

"Don't make out that it was her fault! She said you were *crying* when she found you! What was she supposed to do?"

"Of course it wasn't her fault; it was all mine. I'm ashamed of myself. Other than apologize, what am I supposed to do? Propose marriage? Nothing happened, really. I know that doesn't . . ."

Clara glares at him with contempt.

"You have made my dear friend terribly unhappy."

"Nothing you say could make me feel worse than I already do."

This is not true. He wasn't proud of himself, but had managed to classify his behavior as an understandable lapse under the circumstances. Now she is ruining that. He tries to quell his irritation—surely, having apologized, she should let him be?

"We think you're so harmless and easy to talk to. But you're not harmless. You're a brute. A brute in disguise, which is worse."

"All right. We've established beyond doubt that I'm a brute. My faults aside, can I tell you what I came to tell you?"

"Go on."

"I've had a letter. Perhaps it would be best if you read it."

He takes Mrs. Athlone's envelope out of his pocket. Clara looks alarmed.

"Who is it from?"

"It's from the leader of the British expedition in Greenland. They arrived before we left. They're still there."

She seems to have some premonition of the import of it; her hands are unsteady as she takes the pages and starts to read. Jakob gets out his cigarettes and offers one to her.

Clara reads, without reaction, to the end. Then, as he had done, she reads it again. Then she folds the letter carefully, puts it back in the envelope, and holds it out for him to take. He waits for her to speak. She smokes her cigarette down and stubs it out. Her eyes are big and bright with tears.

"I wish you hadn't shown me that."

"I couldn't keep it from you. I realize that you can't tell Marion, but your parents perhaps would—"

"My parents would be devastated!" She looks down and says, in a voice that vibrates with feeling, "God, I hate men! What is the matter with you all?"

"Hate me, but don't hate Frank. He was the most pure-hearted man I've ever known. He was afraid he wouldn't come back from the northern journey. When death is that close . . . things are very simple . . . stark."

"He was engaged to Marion! He loved the stupid little idiot!"

"Yes. He did." Jakob is unable to hold back a smile. "He begged for her forgiveness with his dying breaths."

Jakob has never seen Clara cry, not even when the news of Frank's death was fresh. Always so composed and polished, to see her undone is awful. She sobs loudly, drawing censorious looks and mutters from the other customers. Jakob supposes that, to the people around them, they look like actors in a familiar, sordid drama. He holds out his handkerchief—fresh this morning, thank heavens.

"I don't know what to do!"

Her wail is so loud that people stare. Well, let them. He waits for the storm to subside, and she carefully dabs her face until the worst traces are gone.

"I must look a fright."

He shakes his head. "I had no idea about this. Frank didn't know. You need time to think it over. If you want me to break the news to anyone, I will. Otherwise I won't say a word."

Clara sniffs. "Can I have another cigarette, please?"

She pulls on the cigarette and visibly steadies herself.

"Please don't judge Frank harshly. He wasn't the only one."

She gives a sharp sigh, and speaks without looking at him: "Did you all do it—have . . . *companions*?"

It is the question he has been dreading, but supposes he can't sink any lower in her estimation than he already has.

"All of us except Shull."

She lets out a half laugh. "Why not him?"

"I don't know."

"So it's possible to resist."

"I can't speak for anyone else. I'm only trying to speak for Frank because—"

"You surely don't include Mr. Armitage—he's married . . . His wife was at school with Angie!"

Jakob is provoked into glancing around him, and lowering his voice. "For that matter, some of the women were married. Armitage's, er, companion was, and her husband knew of it. They don't think of these things in the way we do."

"They're true, then, the rumors of wife swapping?"

"Perhaps, when you know death is so close, such things are less important."

"What was she like, this girl?"

"Meqro wasn't married. She was a nice girl, very quiet and loyal. And truly fond of Frank. He didn't . . . for months, he resisted all approaches. It was only when he knew he was going on the northern journey, and realized what it involved; he became frightened. He got the idea in his head that he wouldn't return. When you're afraid, you take comfort where you can find it."

"Does comfort have to be . . . *that*?" She spits the words out.

"I'm trying to explain how it is—perhaps not very well. To be somewhere so remote, so harsh; to live for months in darkness. To feel that cold. You walk outside in a blizzard and, within five yards, you're lost. To not know whether the hunt will be successful, but to know that, if it isn't, you will starve."

Clara folds her pasteboard coaster in half, then in half again, then unfolds it and starts again.

"You said it wouldn't be dangerous."

"I didn't know what I was talking about."

"Can I see it again?"

Jakob hands her the letter.

"May I keep it, for the time being?"

"Of course."

He must have hesitated a fraction too long.

"Mrs. Athlone's Christian name is Flora."

"Yes."

Clara puts the letter away.

"I'll return it. I'm sure she will think of you whether the letter is in your possession or not."

Then, seeing the look on his face, she says, with a gentleness he has done nothing to deserve, "I'm sorry. That was uncalled for."

Jakob walks home, glad to eat up a couple of hours in movement, letting the clamor of the city wash over him and drown his thoughts. In the middle of the Brooklyn Bridge, he stops to look down at the boats heading out to sea. Far below, the surface of the water is a wrinkled gray-green, arrowed with wakes that all seem to point the same way: to the north.

Chapter 25

Siorapaluk, 77°47' N, 70°38' W
Summer 1893

At the end of June, the British expedition has been in the north for almost a year. Two months remain before Captain Traill and the *Resolve* will return to take them home, but Flora is convinced she has failed. The program of exploration they planned has not come about. The Americans' achievement in mapping new ground means that to reach areas on the map that are still blank they need more time, but the weather throughout the spring sledging season has been appalling—worse than anything Flora can remember. Gales blow without cease. Smith Sound is a mass of grinding floes—there is never either clear water or safe ice for more than two days on end, making travel to Ellesmere all but impossible. Not a single whale ship is seen. Siorapaluk, known for being an oasis in summer, with its sandy beach and grassy meadows, is never free of snow. Though neither weather nor Americans are Flora's fault, she fears that neither will be seen as sufficient excuse.

If the season is bad for them, it is worse for the Eskimos. Though the presence of the British and their supplies means that no one starves, hunting is poor, and three young men drown during a walrus hunt. Bad news comes without ceasing. The bones in Ayakou's leg fail to knit, and Seddon says he will be permanently lame. Ayakou's wife takes their children to live with a man whose wife has died. In February, they heard of an elderly couple who had frozen to death.

They do what they can: Flora has her data on the aurora, although the equinoxes have not produced their usual spectacular show. Magnetic readings reveal unusually low levels of activity—but she cannot say which caused the other. She has kept a full year's meteorological record, with stations on the shore and on the ice cap, but it is frustrating; she accumulates the data but cannot explain it. Are the poor auroras and the bad weather interrelated? Could they have been predicted? Even knowing the value of observation, it is disheartening to realize how tiny and insignificant her one year's results are.

Ralph Dixon and Edwin Daneforth spend the summer making magnetic and geological observations around Melville Bay, and map a portion of its coast. Maurice Seddon collects an elegant set of data on Eskimo physiology. Flora spends the rest of her time writing a dictionary of their language, and has begun a compilation of their myths.

She hopes to expand this into an entire mythic cosmogony—a description of Eskimo religion—but knows it is scrappy and incomplete. Sometimes she has the feeling that people do not want her to know their stories, despite her telling them that, if the white man knows they have a religion, they will be taken more seriously. The elders look at her in puzzlement. Many of them say, "Why do you want to know this? They are only silly stories, only for the Inuit, not for *kallunat*." They also ask her, continually, "Where is Mackie? Where are the *upernallit*?"

The whalers were predictable: they arrived in spring, they hunted and traded, took meat and ivory, left tools and nice things, and went away. Sometimes they left behind a child: Ivalu is one such—her biological father was a Scottish sailor whose name no one can remember. (And there are rumors—rumors Flora ignores, as she has no way or intention of knowing if they are true—that there is, some-where, a boy whose father is Mackie.)

Flora encourages Ayakou to tell her stories. He sits around the house, mending things occasionally, but mainly moping. Meqro brings her baby and keeps Flora company. Despite her bereavement, Meqro is cheerful. Perhaps she had never expected to see Frank Urbino again. Flora cherishes the hope that Ayakou and Meqro might find solace in each other, but when she brings up the idea, in a lighthearted way, Meqro bursts out laughing.

"Fellora, no! Ayakou does not like me. He likes you!"

Flora shakes her head, smiling, expecting that, as usual, she is being teased.

"Yes, Fellora. He asks me, do I think she wants another husband?"

"I have a husband, Meqro. I don't want another."

Meqro looks down at her sleeping daughter as she sews the pieces of a shirt together.

"But your husband does not give you children. Ayakou can give you children. He may have bad leg, but he has good *usuk*!"

She collapses with laughter. Flora blushes, but tries to cover it with a smile.

"Well . . . please tell Ayakou, I'm not looking for another husband, thank you. I love Freddie."

Meqro smirks and sews for a minute, and then says, "Do you not miss *kujappok*?"

"Ah . . ."

Kujappok is their everyday term for sex, which is much discussed, without embarrassment, by men and women alike.

"I don't really think about it, here. You know, Meqro, people don't talk about *kujappok* in Britain."

"No? But still . . ."

Flora shakes her head, smiling, meaning: please stop.

She does think about it. She thought about it particularly after an incident in December. Ralph had accompanied Maurice to visit a sick woman along the coast, and she was alone in the hut with Edwin Daneforth. They had had an enjoyable morning, poking through their stores and discussing preparations for Ralph's forthcoming birthday.

"We can use the raisins. I'll make a suet pudding. That's his favorite," said Edwin.

"*I* will make the pudding, Edwin. After last time . . ."

The last time, Edwin's pudding had exploded. Subsequent investigations revealed he had used bicarbonate of soda instead of flour.

"You mean, when I invented the patent Daneforth suet-weapon? Ha ha! It would be festive—you have to agree."

Flora shook her head. "Still . . ." She laughed at the memory. "I think it wiser . . ."

They smiled at each other. In the ensuing silence, the fire in the stove popped suddenly, making her jump, and Edwin suddenly seized her by both hands.

"Flora, I can't stay silent any longer. I have long wanted to speak to you alone."

The look on his face was shocking; familiar, although she had not felt that peculiar, visceral thrill since her student days, with Mark Levinson. Freddie never looked at her like that: that was her first thought. She froze.

"You must have noticed. I know that we . . ."

Flora came to her senses, wrenched her hand away, and walked blindly to the door, calling for Ivalu. She did not look around, was waiting for him to seize her from behind, but he did not follow. She walked outside, into the freezing darkness of the day, where an aurora was crackling audibly, sending white streamers writhing across the sea. The dogs were barking—their infernal din, worse when they were inactive. Flora realized she was not wearing gloves. Her heart pounded. She was afraid and did not know what she was afraid of. She waited for him to come after her, but nothing happened. Eventually, Simiak came out of her *illu*, shouting at the dogs, and Flora went over to her, with a feeling she assumed was relief.

* * *

That evening, Edwin was his usual self, chatting to the others when they came in. He did not look at Flora, but did not entirely ignore her. Still, she was disturbed. Feeling it was her duty, as leader, to clear up the matter, she took the earliest opportunity to speak to him alone.

"I want you to know that, the other day . . . I attach no importance to it whatsoever. Of course, I have not and will not mention it to anyone."

Edwin turned to her, a pleasant smile on his face.

"I'm sorry, Mrs. Athlone, I don't know to what you refer."

Annoyingly, Flora blushed.

"I refer to the day before yesterday, when you . . . when you took my hand. I'm sure it was just a passing moment, and meant nothing. I regard it as of no importance. It's quite forgotten."

Edwin raised his eyebrows, his smile turning puzzled.

"I'm afraid I don't know what you mean."

He looked at her quizzically. Flora felt a chill—one not entirely explained by the minus-ten-degree breeze off the sea-ice.

"Oh. Yes. Then there's nothing more to say."

"Of course, Mrs. Athlone."

Edwin laughed pleasantly, yet his laugh somehow managed to insinuate that she herself had said something strange and extraordinary.

Incredulous, Flora tramped off to the weather station alone.

In the dark of winter, people do strange things. The Eskimos talk of winter madness, *perlerorneq*, which manifests itself in an out-burst of violent mania that can last for hours. Years before, Flora watched Aniguin's mother, Simiak, tear off her clothes and run out in the snow, screaming obscenities and eating the excrement of dogs. Flora was terrified: Simiak was almost like a mother to her. Restrained from attacking another woman by a handful of men, she at length fell into a sleep that lasted a day and a night, then awoke with no memory of what had happened, once again her normal, cheerful self.

Flora tried to behave as though nothing had happened between her and Edwin, but she could not forget it. The way he had seized her hand, the look in his eyes, awoke something inside her. He was personable, handsome even, but . . . unthinkable, of course—let alone his caddishness in denying what he had done. He was, anyway, having a relationship with a local woman. The men did not talk about such things with her, but she knew.

In February, the sun returned. The lengthening light and increasing warmth made everyone's blood run quicker. Flora wondered whether her colleagues had any idea what was in her head. She observed as shy, quiet Ralph began a relationship with the widow, Ainineq. She tried to imagine what would happen if she did the same with (for the sake of argument) Ayakou. It was unthinkable—well, not unthinkable, since she was thinking it—but absolutely, utterly beyond possibility.

Increasingly, as the depressing summer wears on, she leans on Aniguin. It is he who tells her most of the myths in her collection and explains any words she doesn't understand. He has become—as he told her he would—an *angekok*: a shaman. The former orphan is respected—not exactly popular, but people come to him, ask his advice. He married Ivalu, the most beautiful girl on the coast. Flora is glad for him, thankful that their friendship has survived.

Yet it was Aniguin who told Armitage about the meteorite. She had assumed that he would help her, and not the Americans. Flora knew about it, but it had not occurred to her that anyone would want to take it away. She assumed that would be impossible. It was another sign of her failure as a leader—she lacked vision, drive, the ability to make the seemingly impossible happen.

As their plans for exploration come to nothing, she looks at the tally of achievements—notebooks of tables, facts, and measurements; cases of rocks, plants, skins; stories, sketches, photographs—but nothing to match de Beyn's glaciers; Edwin turns out to have little aptitude for photographing the subtle light here. His attempts to capture the aurora are hopeless. She quietly asks Maurice for his help, and is refused, on the grounds that he had been relieved of that responsibility against his will. Perhaps he would have done no better.

Before they left him behind in Godthåb, Freddie impressed on her the need for the spectacular. Something the papers could get their teeth into. She didn't think, in this extraordinary place, the spectacular would be so elusive.

In July, with their time in Greenland running out, Flora, Ralph, and Maurice make a journey along the coast, and Pualana, the hunter who knows the land like no one else, leads them to a tiny, secluded bay—really a cleft in the mountainside that runs down to the sea. They leave their packs on the beach and climb for an hour. For once, there is sun and a faint warmth, but they quickly leave it behind, climbing into shade. Despite that, they sweat into their furs.

They reach a spot where the slope becomes even steeper, and Pualana stops. There is what looks like a fall of rocks filling a hollow in one side of the cleft. An overhanging rock-face keeps rain and snow off the site, and it faces north, so is never touched by the sun. Ralph turns to her.

"You may as well wait here. It will take a while to lift the stones."

Ralph is unhappy about the whole thing. He will not defy her, nor will he hide his disapproval.

She sits down, glad of her fur parka now, and the men set to work. After half an hour, Pualana climbs out of the hollow and fills his pipe, refusing to look at them.

"Mrs. Athlone." Maurice beckons to her.

The men stand in silence. Flora feels a throb of disquiet. Ralph holds out his hand so that she can steady herself, and she looks at what they have uncovered.

Upside down, a face—empty-eyed, bone-white, the lips drawn back in what looks like a scream—gazes back. A thrill of horror passes through her, but she forces herself to look at the woman—she knows it is a woman because the head is covered by a sealskin hood of a similar pattern to those of her friends. The uncanniness of it is that the whiteness of the face is not bone, but flesh—mummified, but intact. The blackened lips have shrunk, baring the teeth in that alarming way.

Ralph is upset. "Are you sure about this? Are we really going to take them from their resting place?"

Flora moistens her lips. "Pualana, how old are they?"

Without looking around, Pualana says, "Very old. Many, many years."

"I don't want to move them if they are anyone's ancestors. We respect your feelings in this."

Pualana, who is being handsomely rewarded for his services, says, "They are no one's ancestors. We don't know who they are."

"All right then."

She nods at Maurice and Ralph. Maurice is unmoved by the sight of the mummy, but he has presumably seen worse things in his career.

They uncover the whole body—the woman lies in the cleft as if she were pressed into it, her arms huddled to her chest, knees bent, feet neatly together. She was buried in her furs, is dressed just as Meqro or Ivalu would be in life: pointed hood, long sealskin jacket, short fox-skin trousers, bear-fur *kamiks*. Maurice supervises the lifting of it out of its resting place and wraps it in a length of canvas, like a winding sheet. It is rigid, but light. He and Ralph carry it down to the sled without difficulty. Pualana refuses to touch it.

There are four bodies in all, one lying on top of another. There are no signs of violence. Maurice thinks they probably died together, in an epidemic or of hunger. But someone took the trouble to carry them all the way up here and bury them where animals would not disturb them. Flora insists they take all of them. She tells herself—and the others—that, if they do not take them, another expedition—there is bound to be one sooner or later—will do so. She is demonstrating vision. Maurice concurs. Ralph complies with a face of studied blankness. When she repeats to him that they are not the relatives of anyone living—are so old as to be without an identity, like the Egyptians—he frowns and says that they are still someone's ancestors.

"Don't be ridiculous," she says. "If Pualana doesn't know, no one will. They are remarkable. It is our duty to preserve them."

Despite her words, there *is* something frightening and awe-inspiring about the mummified bodies, with their noiseless, gaping mouths and stiffly poised, grasping fingers; perhaps that makes her speak more sharply than she might otherwise have done.

The most striking of the four are the first they found—the woman whose face is so whole and ghastly—and the last. This is the body of a small child dressed in immaculate furs, its face perfect, even the lips and eyelids intact, slowly dried into an empty mask of innocence. It could be a doll. Flora can picture the stir the infant mummy will make on display in London. She supervises their packing in chests stuffed with hay and ice, and knows she has something unique. She tells herself how pleased Freddie will be.

Chapter 26

London, 51°31' N, 0°7' W
September 1893

Months later, in London, seeing the mummies' faces uncovered no longer bothers her. She has grown accustomed to them. Under the disappearing white bloom, the skin is a leathery ocher. But the flesh has retained its shape and the furs show no sign of disintegration. She lightly strokes the fur hood of the screaming woman with her fingertip. She doesn't touch the skin itself, or the abundant black hair.

"I'm sure I don't need to reiterate," says Flora, reiterating, "just how important it is to preserve their appearance exactly as it is."

"Of course," says Dr. Murray. He is curator of Northern European Antiquities at the British Museum and is fascinated by the mummies. They have agreed on a long-term loan, with a forthcoming exhibition. "You understand that the white mold will disappear, as it is merely the result of surface dampness. The method of preservation is different to those of ancient Egypt, being natural, but the results are similar. I don't think that the cold is particularly important now, as long as they are kept in a state of desiccation."

"Are you sure?" Flora is anxious. Since they arrived in London, she has housed them, at enormous expense, at a brewer's premises that has a compression refrigeration unit.

"Oh, yes. I think so," says Murray. He sounds confident, but he cannot be sure, because he has never seen anything like this before.

After she concludes her meeting at the museum, Flora goes home to Kensington. It is two weeks since she returned from Greenland. Even now, she feels a nervous flutter on going to the flat where Freddie lives. Where she lives, she means . . . Where they live.

She opens the front door. She pauses for a moment, as she always does, then calls out, cheerfully, to her husband. In the short period between their marriage and their departure for the north, this flat never felt like home to her, and now, even less.

Freddie left Godthåb the previous September. Governor Carlsen arranged his passage on the last Danish ship of the season. He spent some time in a Copenhagen hospital before going on to a spa in Bavaria to recuperate. He arrived back in London only a few weeks before she did.

Having had only one letter from him—brought by Captain Traill on the *Resolve* in August—Flora did not know what to expect. Her first sight of him was when the ship docked at the Pool of London, and Freddie was there to greet her. He was impeccably dressed, but moved with painful slowness, leaning on a cane. Startled by the presence of photographers, confused as to what to expect, annoyed by the pimple that had that morning erupted on her chin, Flora was wary and almost silent. They posed together for the *Northern Chronicle* before they had exchanged a word in private. When they arrived home, she burst into tears, and felt fraudulent as Freddie comforted her, instead of the other way around.

"I'm sorry; I'm just tired, and . . . you must tell me how you've been . . . What do the doctors say?"

Freddie spoke calmly, but she wept again at the tale he told. His lower vertebrae gave him constant pain; the pelvic fracture was incompletely fused. The poor healing was due to his underlying illness, and so—he said with a grimace that was meant to be a smile—his exploring days were over.

"You will have to do it on your own now, Flora. Or rather—continue on your own. Perhaps it was always meant to be this way."

"Freddie, it's far too soon to say that . . ."

She was sitting beside him, holding his hand. He had not attempted to touch her since they met, apart from putting his hand on her arm, for the cameras. But Flora, who almost never touched him after their failed intimacies, could do so now.

"Dr. Seddon stressed how long such injuries take to heal."

Freddie shook his head. "I have been told not to expect too much. The doctor in Bavaria has made a study of such injuries in syphilitics. He is the foremost expert in Europe. Steady degeneration, that's the prognosis. No point beating about the bush."

"There are other doctors, Freddie. We will see someone here. Or in America."

"Yes, yes. Of course. But in any case, I have made my peace with it . . . really, I have. You should know what to expect. I know it sounds bad, but there are many worse off than I—that is one of the things I learned in Bavaria. I saw many poor wretches. I've learned to be thankful."

Flora had anticipated distance, resentment—even anger. She was unnerved by this humble acceptance. He had changed. She was suspicious, and then resentful. She did not want to be married to a saint.

"There is something else I want to put to you, Flora. We've been apart for more than a year—longer than we were together. I'm telling you of my prospects for another reason. You may feel that you no longer wish to be married to me, and, if so, I won't stand in your way. You could annul the marriage, if you so wished."

Because this thought had crossed her mind in the past year, and for many other reasons, Flora felt tears spill over again.

"Do you no longer wish to be married to me?"

Freddie caressed her hand. "My dear girl, I don't pretend that we were the romance of the age, but I do love and honor you, and I will do my utmost to ensure that your career will flourish."

"Freddie, please, don't. I can't bear it . . ."

"If I can bear it, surely you can?"

"I don't understand. Why did you marry me?"

Freddie smiled, rather sadly.

"I thought we could do something wonderful together. Perhaps my reasons were selfish. But I really thought we could be happy."

Flora looked at him and thought that he seemed a perfect stranger, a person she had never met before.

"As man and wife are supposed to be happy?"

Freddie licked his lips nervously. Flora had the sense that she was suspended over an abyss of unknown depth. Just then, footsteps sounded on the landing and the door opened without a knock.

From Bavaria, Freddie brought back a private nurse. Somehow he had managed to find an Irishwoman, Eileen Capron. She is a rectangular, hard-faced woman of middle years, with black hair parted to reveal a pink scalp, and oyster-colored eyes. She is experienced in cases like his, he says, and therefore invaluable. Despite this—and the glowing letters of recommendation from German doctors—from the start, Flora took a dislike to her.

She interrupted their conversation with a dry cough.

"Mr. Athlone, it is time for your dose."

Such a soft, melodic voice should by rights have belonged to someone else. She stood by the door, looking down at her shelf-like bosom, a black pillar with a white capitol; she wore a kind of starched headdress that made Flora think of nuns, although she was not a nun.

"All right, nurse," said Freddie. "Flora, dear, you will have to excuse me."

To Flora's surprise, she is also nervous the first time she sees Iris again. Having encountered criticism since her return, she is afraid that Iris too will judge her for leaving her injured husband to the mercy of strangers. But, as soon as she enters the familiar drawing room, awash with autumn sunlight, Iris's welcome is profuse and warm.

"Oh, Iris. It's so good to see you. Sometimes I feel that everyone hates me."

"Don't be silly. They don't hate you—to many modern women, you are a heroine. Anyway, what if they do? They talk about you."

"Well, for one thing, they might not buy my book."

"You're wrong. The more controversy there is, the better. I read about your terrifying mummies. They sound frightful."

"They aren't. They are pathetic, in a way, but strangely dignified. They're so old, and so still. I did feel a ghoul carrying them away. Ralph Dixon—you know, the geologist—he was terribly against it. I didn't know he was so religious. He said it was ungodly, even though they weren't Christians."

"But people are fascinated. The paper I read said there is a little child?"

"Yes. It's extraordinary—like an ancient doll. Actually, there is something awful about them. Sometimes I lie awake and I can't get their faces out of my head, wondering if their souls are . . . roaming around unhappily, not knowing what's happened to them, or where they are. I say to them that it's all right, they're only in East London."

"That doesn't sound like you. Have you acquired spiritualism in the north?"

Flora laughs. "When you see them, you'll know what I mean. Next time I go to visit Dr. Murray, I'll tell you."

Iris pours more tea and regards her critically.

"I'm reminded of the first day you came here."

"You all but inspected my back teeth."

"You were so green. Terribly unsure, but defensive. Ready to lash out at a moment's notice."

"I was not. You terrified me."

"You look different. You have grown up. More, even, than I thought you would. How were the men, after Freddie's accident? They accepted you?"

"They behaved well. But Iris, I spent almost every moment of every day wondering if I was making the right decision, or if I had done the right thing or said something in the right tone of voice . . . and whether one of them—Seddon, probably—would turn around and say, 'You really aren't fit to do this, you know.'"

"But they didn't."

"They restrained themselves."

"I suspect all leaders have those doubts. The good ones. How is Freddie now?"

Flora sighs. She has never spoken to Iris of the problems in their marriage, but thinks that Iris has had her suspicions.

"He's in constant pain. He is brave. But they don't think his prognosis is good."

"God, as bad as that? I thought it was broken bones!"

"It was . . . but they haven't healed. There was a . . . an underlying condition."

Iris frowns. "You don't have to tell me."

"He has syphilis."

Iris draws in a sharp breath.

"Oh, my dear . . . Are *you* all right?"

"Oh, yes. He . . ." She shakes her head.

"Flora, I'm so sorry. But when did this . . . ? When did you know?"

"He told me when we married. He didn't want to put me at risk."

"My dear girl. You know what that means? If he knew when he married you, you could annul—"

Flora shakes her head firmly.

"I can't leave him—not now. He's done so much for me; I'll always be grateful. We've reached an accommodation that suits us—or suits me. I just wish he didn't suffer."

Iris looks suddenly weary; the muscles in her face sag without her normal vivacity to animate them.

"Poor Freddie. But how could he . . . ? I encouraged you; I feel it's my fault."

"Of course it isn't! I chose . . . I *choose* to stay."

"Yes, but—"

"I'm fine. We are . . . fine."

"Well." Iris looks at her for a moment. "I suppose you know best. What will you do? Stay at home and take care of him? Is it all up with the Arctic?"

"Well, I have to finish the book; that takes up most of my time at the moment. But Freddie doesn't want me to stop; he already talks about the next expedition. And he's found a marvelous nurse. I don't have to look after him, in that way."

"Thank heavens for Freddie's money. How old is this nurse?"

"Oh, old—at least forty."

"Darling . . . have a heart!"

"She's much older than you! And not . . . in any way attractive."

Iris pats her on the arm. "Please tell him that I—" she begins, and then the front door bangs, followed by running footsteps on the stairs. Iris stiffens.

Flora turns to Iris in surprise. "I'm sorry, should I go?"

"No. That'll just be Helen. I didn't tell you I have acquired a secretary, did I?"

As quickly as Iris lost her vivacity, it returns. She stands up and glances in the overmantel mirror with a small smile, pats the curls on her forehead.

Flora has just time to wonder what Iris needs a secretary for, when the door bursts open and a young woman comes into the drawing room. She is fashionably dressed in dark gray, which emphasizes a graceful figure. She has a face of singular and striking beauty, dark hair and large, dramatic eyes. The newcomer regards Flora with raised eyebrows. Flora looks questioningly at Iris, whose momentary look of intense feeling speaks volumes, and thinks . . . Oh.

"Helen, this is my great friend, Mrs. Flora Athlone; you've often heard me talk of her. Flora, this is Miss Helen Tomlinson, my secretary."

Flora holds out her hand to the newcomer, who touches it briefly with gloved fingertips.

"Lord, the bus was so crowded," says Miss Tomlinson, as though picking up the thread of a previous conversation, "There was an awful fellow on it, wouldn't leave me alone. I had to change seats twice." Then she looks at Flora properly, having made her wait, a sly smile flickering over her lovely face. "Hello there."

"Flora has just come back from a year in the Arctic. She's the explorer, you remember?"

"Well!" says the girl. "I bet you're glad to be back. Must be horrible an' cold down there."

Iris smiles at Flora with a look of helpless, proud apology. "Helen is from Stepney. Geography isn't her strong point, is it, Helen? I'm not sure what is."

Chapter 27

London, 51°31' N, 0°7' W
Winter 1893–4

Brooklyn, October

Dear Mrs. Athlone,

I hope this letter finds you well, and that you are now settled back at home. I trust that your husband is restored to health.

Since you were kind enough to write with news of Ayakou and Meqro, you might be interested to hear of recent developments over here. Having sent Dr. Seddon's note to Mr. Armitage some time ago, I have finally heard that he intends to do something for the man. He has been busy raising the backing for another expedition, but since the Panic earlier this year, money for such endeavors is scarce and I do not know when (or indeed, if) it will take place. I will keep pestering him.

As regards the question of Dr. Urbino, his sister has not told the rest of the family yet, but in time, may do so. The problem (if I can clumsily put it that way) is that Dr. Urbino was engaged to be married, and we do not want to add to his fiancée's grief. I hope to go back north soon, and when I do, I will have the child's welfare very much in mind. Frank was the best friend I ever had, and his daughter deserves a fair deal.

I should perhaps say that I will not return with Mr. Armitage (not that he has asked me). I do not know whether you have read his book, but there are things in it that do not accord with my memory of events, or my knowledge of the people involved. The publishers may be to blame for this, of course. It may be wrong of me to tell you this, but I feel as though I can trust you with my opinion.

If it is not an imposition, I would like to present to you the book I have been working on. It is a short geological treatise on Ellesmere. Let me say immediately that I would understand if it is not of overwhelming interest to you! But perhaps it would be to your colleague, Mr. Dixon. I am quite pleased with the photographs, and you were kind enough to say something about them in your previous letter. On that note, I am also taking the liberty of sending copies of the photographs I took in Neqi. I never did have time to print them there; there was always so much to do.

[Here, words are crossed out and illegible]

I often remember meeting with you and Dr. Seddon in Neqi. It is one of my happiest memories of the place.

I look forward to reading your account of your experiences in Greenland. I wish you the best of luck with your writing, and assure you that I remain,

Your friend,
Jakob de Beyn

There is the small, clothbound volume, indifferently printed. She flicks through it and puts it to one side. A second, smaller envelope was inside the first—she opens it and a few photographs slither out. She is disturbed, in a way she does not quite understand, to see herself like this. In the first picture, she stares into the middle distance, severe and self-conscious, a strand of hair blowing across her cheek; in another, she and Meqro stand together, smiling at each other. She was right: he had caught her off-guard, their fleeting expressions frozen forever. But it makes her smile, remembering that evening on the beach. It is one of her happiest memories, too. There is a third picture, which shocks her, because she was unaware he had taken it: it shows her sitting on the ground, holding hands with Simiak, and captures a moment of intense feeling between them. It makes her feel strange, the thought that he has looked at her face, and her face so full of emotion, when she didn't know.

There is a picture of Meqro sitting on Dr. Urbino's knee; Dr. Urbino grins sheepishly at the camera, but his arm is tight around her waist, and Meqro looks at him with every sign of adoration. All the time, he had a fiancée in America (well, nothing should surprise her) . . . and now he is dead. There is Aniguin, who, alone among the Eskimos, is unsmiling. There is Maurice Seddon with his camera, laughing, and, though she searches her memory, she cannot remember seeing him so carefree. There is the great cloud of dovekies, staining the sky dark. And there is a photograph of Seddon and de Beyn together. Seddon has his familiar dogged expression; de Beyn is smiling at the camera (held by Urbino, perhaps?), his eyes dark, his hair a white flare in the sunlight. She had forgotten how gray his hair was; she has not forgotten that smile. She wonders why he sent that picture: because it shows Seddon? Or because it shows himself?

She thinks it a strange letter—rather gauche and indiscreet, but he seems genuinely concerned with the fates of those left behind. She looks at the photographs again, and is reminded of his words the morning after: that a photograph carries some essence of the person depicted; that they bring closer those who are far away.

The grand opening is at the British Museum in November, when Dr. Murray deems the mummies safe to exhibit. An invited audience is the first to view them. Freddie is there, propped and pumped by Nurse Capron into a state of apparently reasonable health. Having seen what he was like earlier in the day, Flora has to admit that she can work miracles.

The mummies are arranged in a lecture theater, in glass cases, shrouded by sheets. Dr. Murray begins with a short talk. Then Flora gives her lecture, and, at its climax, she walks to each case and, with a flick of her wrist (carefully rehearsed), uncovers the mummies, one by one. She saves the infant until last. There are gasps, moans, murmurs as she reveals each one. When, at the end of the lecture, she reveals the baby, there is a breathless silence. And then a woman says, "Oh," in a breakingly tender voice, and the murmurs start up again, louder and louder. People are overwhelmed, amazed, shocked. It is an astonishing success.

When the mummies go on general display, there are accounts of women fainting and people being overcome with terror. But the more it goes on, and the more attention there is in the press, the less Flora likes to think of them. One day, she reads an editorial in the *Manchester Review* that calls the exhibition, "depraved, unchristian, vile, and polluting, not fit for women or children—hardly fit for men of the sternest stuff . . ." She herself is castigated as "immoral and unwomanly." She should be used to it, but she throws the paper aside in anger. She never wanted to be part of a "puppet show" (she has not forgiven her father for that); all she wanted was to go back north.

At a dinner the following evening, she is surrounded by people in high spirits, so she smiles, even as she wonders how many of them have been reading the public censure. On one side is Lionel Fortescue, the actor with meretricious chestnut hair, telling everyone of his forthcoming Iago; on the other, Jessie Biddenden, who knows what it is to be vilified—in her case, for licentious writings. She has never seemed in the least worried by criticism.

Flora is not the only one who is quiet. Her attention is drawn to Iris, whose eyes are on Helen, opposite her, deep in conversation with a handsome young actor. They are laughing, their heads almost touching. To Flora, it looks very much like a flirtation. She does not like Helen, who seems to treat Iris with a casual disrespect that borders on contempt. Jessie says she is a gold digger.

She turns to Jessie, and finds herself complaining about the editorial. Jessie listens with a knowing smile on her face.

"I heard a rumor about that piece—do you know who wrote it?"

"It was anonymous."

"A little bird told me it was your old friend, Mr. Whitfield."

"R. G. Whitfield? You can't mean it."

"The very same. Apparently he's furious that you abandoned him."

Flora is nonplussed. "I hadn't heard from him for years before I left. What was I supposed to do?"

"Well, journalists, you know . . . he obviously felt he had discovered you for the world, and deserved some credit. And by 'credit,' of course, I mean money."

Flora is sobered. Once upon a time, he was so complimentary. The tone of this piece was vicious. She remembers that she had meant to write to him, ages ago, to express her gratitude, but he had slipped her mind.

Dundee, December 5

Dear Flora,

Thank you for your letter of Wednesday last. I trust you continue in good health. My knees are a little better. I am afraid that I will not be able to join you and Freddie over Christmas, so must regretfully decline your invitation. I have much to do here—there is a dispute between the shipyard and the owners regarding the latest refit, and I trust no one else to keep them all up to the mark.

I suspect that the exhibition of the Greenland mummies would, in any case, not be "my cup of tea," so there is no hurry to visit. We will see where we stand in a few weeks. My best wishes to your husband, and, of course, to yourself.

Your loving father,
William Mackie

London, January 1, 1894

Dear Mr. de Beyn,

Let me take advantage of the date to wish you a very happy new year, and hope that it is the one in which your plans come to fruition. Thank you for your latest letter; I am happy to hear you are making progress. I must say, I agree that to make a big fanfare around an expedition is unnecessary, and in some ways unwise. We both know how plans in the north can be forced to change—drastically and at short notice—and the fewer people to whom you are answerable for such changes, the better.

I am intrigued that the mummies have made the papers in America; they seem hardly important enough for that. You don't say what American opinion of them is; here, there has been much criticism; people have been quite outraged. I suppose that is only what one might have expected. I have learned to turn a blind eye and a deaf ear to the worst of it, but sometimes I find myself agreeing with them. One can argue that they are of great scientific import, but the impact on the public is not due to that, rather to their uncanny appearance and the ghoulish associations of dead bodies. I regret that they have become theater (and a particular sort of theater), rather than science.

I lent your Ellesmere book to Mr. Dixon (you were wrong: I was very interested in it!) and he has now returned it with many compliments. I believe he is going to write to you independently. When we discussed

it, I felt sorry that he had so little opportunity to do work of that kind.
Really, the only answer to the unpredictability of the climate is to go
for two or three years on end, and then, if one season is a bust, you
have another chance.

I had hoped to have my manuscript ready by the end of the year,
but I am afraid I have gotten rather behind. The new year's resolution
is to finish it in the next two months. And then what? I too want to
return, but it seems an uphill struggle . . .

Flora pauses. The temptation has grown to treat her letters to
Mr. de Beyn as if they were a diary that no one will ever see. Inocu-
lated by three thousand miles of ocean, it has become easy to consider him—a near stranger, really—a confidant. And yet, where is
the harm?

Perhaps the weather is affecting my mood. It is gray, drizzly, and
damp. Everyone complains of the cold, but of course, it is not cold! In
a strange way, I miss the north even more in winter than in summer.
I miss the constant darkness, and I long for snow . . .

PART FIVE

POLARIS

The navigator's benchmark for centuries, the current pole star appears to be the only fixed point in the sky, and all other stars wheel around it. This is an illusion.

Chapter 28

RMS Etruria, at sea
April 1895

Mr. Lester Armitage, whose book, *Battling the Ice*, enthralled readers last year, is once more setting off for the icy north. With the backing of many of New York's most prominent businessmen, he will set sail in June, and this time, it is "the Pole or nothing." He has learned much from his previous trip, when he discovered Dupree Land, a new island at the northern limit of Greenland, and means to harness all energies and manpower to the achievement of his goal. Previously, he explained, objectives were divided, and consequently they could not achieve much in the way of exploration. Science, he says, is "for other men. Valuable though it is, you cannot carry out a full program of research while also seeking to explore and discover in such a difficult environment. This time, we will concentrate on the Pole and, God willing, bring it back for the United States of America!"

Manhattan Chronicle, April 3, 1895

Jakob decided against a cabin with a porthole. There are advantages to this: he saves money, and he doesn't have to look at the ocean.

After three years on dry land, he had forgotten how much he disliked sailing, and, for crossing the Atlantic, he seems to have picked the week of the worst storm in years.

On the third day out, the ship wallows somewhere in mid-ocean, engines laboring, the massive screw threshing air as the ship is tossed like a cork. Few passengers can eat in the heaving dining rooms, fewer still can sleep, unless one can call the miserable stupor they fall into "sleep." A grim camaraderie prevails in the corridors and in the thinly populated saloons. Those still walking greet each other with respect, as survivors of a particularly sordid battle. Groans of distress are heard from behind closed doors; occasionally, screams.

Coming back to his cabin after a meal of crackers and water, Jakob congratulates himself on negotiating the corridors and stairs without losing his footing. Then, just as he opens his cabin door, two gigantic waves slam against the ship in short succession. He loses his balance, and a combination of malevolent forces propels the edge of the door and his forehead against each other with great force. Some time later, he finds himself lying on the floor of his cabin. When he puts his hand to his throbbing forehead, he finds a lump that feels like a hen's egg. He hopes that he has been unconscious for a long time—it would be the best way to spend this journey—but, when he looks at his watch, it has only been a couple of minutes.

He drags himself into his bunk, vowing to stay there for as long as possible, and wonders if he is being punished for his sins.

About a year ago, to his surprise, he fell into a romance of sorts with Lucille Becker. They met in the street (it always amazed him to bump into anyone he knew in New York, but it happened with surprising regularity), and he found himself begging to see her again. Perhaps there was an element of making atonement, perhaps a desire to redeem himself, but, at first, he thought he had stumbled on the right, happy thing: she was a good companion, amusing and independent. But, after he persuaded her into bed, instead of intensifying, things deteriorated.

"What do you want me to do?" he asked, in some desperation, and not for the first time, after his best efforts had again failed to procure the desired result.

"Nothing," she assured him, but a worry line creased her forehead. "I don't know what you want me to say."

"I want you to say what will give you pleasure."

"It does . . . I mean, you do."

"Well, but, not . . . enough."

She sighed. "I don't know what you mean."

When he explained what he meant, that only made things worse. Beforehand, she said bitterly, she hadn't realized there was anything wrong with her. Her previous lover (he was surprised but relieved to discover there was one) had not noticed anything amiss.

"There's nothing wrong with you," he said, unconvincingly. "It might be me. Perhaps I'm just not doing it right . . . for you."

"But for other women . . . ?"

"Well . . ." He thought, miserably, of Kate, and then, to cheer himself up, of Cora. "Sometimes, um, it doesn't happen, and sometimes the woman pretends to . . . enjoy it, but usually . . ." He shrugged.

"How do you know if she's pretending?"

"Well, you don't always. But . . ."

Lucille made herself very small—a coil of ribs and hip bones, crossed shins.

"I just want you to be happy."

"I'm fine."

He put his arm around her shoulders. "It's all right. It doesn't matter."

"Clearly it does."

She shrugged his arm off. He felt as though he were torturing her for information she didn't have.

"Please don't worry about it."

"How can I not worry about it?"

"I forbid you to worry about it," he said, hopefully.

"Ha!"

Trying to be funny didn't always work with Lucille. She brooded. She couldn't leave things alone.

"How do you know they weren't all pretending?"

This went beyond his ability to be reasonable. Jakob jumped out of bed. "Yes! You're right! They were *all* pretending."

He stormed out of the bedroom, stark naked, and slammed the door. Clara was staying at her parents' house for the weekend.

"All?" yelled Lucille, after him. "*All?*"

Jakob began to dread their nights together. He tried to tell himself that it didn't matter, but she was too honest for that; she accused him of being distant and dissatisfied, said that he was secretive, that she never knew what he was thinking. She said—she was embarrassed to admit it—that she wanted marriage, and when he went quiet, she accused him of having no desire to settle down, or, what was worse, that he didn't want to settle down with her. He knew her accusations were justified, but did not feel they were genuine cause for complaint (apart from the last). She had known him long enough, he thought, to understand him.

"I can't share everything that's in my head, Lucille. I don't need to know what you're thinking every minute."

"No." She laughed bitterly. "You don't care. I'm not saying I always want to know. But you're so often . . . unreachable. I can't help but think that you would rather be somewhere else—or . . . or with someone else."

"I don't want to be with anyone else. I like being with you, as you are. God knows, I'm not perfect. Can't we be imperfect, together?"

There was another thing on his mind that caused him to be distracted and distant: he had started visiting his father. For years, he had found excuses not to join Hendrik on his trips to Blackwell's Island. Usually his work saved him the bother of having to make an excuse at all. Many weeks after that original letter, and shortly after his final exams, the brothers had taken the ferry over to the asylum. They waited in their Sunday best, surrounded by slow-moving, murmuring visitors; the strained smiles on relatives' faces, the brusque platitudes of the staff. It did not seem an altogether bad place, although they lowered their voices, moderated their movements, so as not to startle an inmate. But meeting Arent de Beyn was a shock—how could it have been otherwise?

The man they said was their father looked physically vigorous—he was tall, ruddy, with a fine head of hair that sprang off his forehead—and he greeted them distantly, but with coherence. He looked like Hendrik would look in the future. Jakob was violently glad he did not take after him. An attendant had assured them that he knew who they were. They walked in the gardens, and Arent pointed out the view of the East River and the trees of Manhattan in the distance. He was unemotional. He listened politely as Hendrik told him about Bettina and the baby and his business—and Hendrik goaded Jakob into discussing his studies—but it was hard to know if he took any of it in. At a certain point, he turned to them and hissed, "Have you seen my sons? You will tell me if you see them? They're trying to kill me."

Appalled, Jakob looked at Hendrik for a cue; he hadn't wanted to come in the first place.

"Of course we will," said Hendrik, finding his voice at last.

Shortly afterward, Jakob left on his first survey in the west.

After Frank's death, he resolved to do better. He began to visit regularly when he was home. At least, after that initial letter, there was no further talk of releasing him. Arent was harmless but unpredictable; he had developed an obsessive fear of starvation, and was now very fat. Jakob had learned not to try to lead the conversation; he let Arent meander through his favorite topics: food, fishing, his thieving neighbors. Sometimes they managed to have a coherent chat about fly tying, which Arent enjoyed. That was how Jakob thought of him: not as his father, because he didn't know what that would be like, but as Arent, a peculiar old Dutchman for whom he felt a sticky, irritated obligation. Sometimes, disconcertingly, sanity would come leaping out of the old man like a visitation of angels. Leaning forward, with his hand on Jakob's knee, he said, "You look just like Annette . . . remarkable." Jakob's blood would stop in his veins, and his mind would be clogged with questions—scrabbling frantically for the most important, the thing above all others that he needed to know—but before he could marshal it, Arent would have drifted away, would be looking around him: "Have you seen her? She was over there, a minute ago . . ."

Lucille was one of the few people who knew about his mad father. She offered to go with him to Blackwell's Island. Jakob was touched by her offer, but declined. He did not want her to see that, to associate that with him.

Then, every couple of months, he would receive a letter from England, which pulled his thoughts away from his messy, flawed surroundings and sent them winging northward. Mrs. Athlone's letters were innocent of anything more than friendliness. But he experienced a tremor of pleasure whenever he saw her handwriting, an echo of the connection that sparked into being in Neqi. He no longer knew if it was because of an attraction—what could that mean, after all this time?—or because she connected him to something that he loved: she was a link to his time in the north, his greatest adventure, his future aspiration. He told himself that it meant nothing. But their correspondence was something he guarded jealously, one of the secret parts that Lucille complained of, and, wisely perhaps, feared.

Before he left for a six-month survey in Arizona last autumn, he had ended it, with dignity on her side and a gathering depression on his. In the desert, he wondered if he had made a mistake and should instead have proposed to her; after all, weren't all marriages a compromise? People—his brother, for example—said you had to work at it, that companionship and comfort were the main boons, that attraction was an unstable basis for a lifelong union, that you could not expect passion to last more than a few months . . . (In which case, Jakob would conclude, although only to himself, why marry at all?)

On his return to New York, weeks ago, he had visited the Urbinos, hoping to see Clara. But she was not there, and her parents seemed reluctant to give him news of her. He was saddened. She seemed to forgive him his initial indiscretion with Lucille, but when they started an actual romance, she had withdrawn from both of them, been elusive, distant, in some way or other always unavailable.

Now, braced in his bunk in his cheap cabin, he is at leisure to contemplate his selfish and irresponsible existence. Such dark moods have come on him more frequently since Frank died. He has never lost the feeling that he has an obligation to retrace his northern journey, but he is as far as ever from being in a position to do so. What is he, really? What has he achieved? He is an itinerant geologist, with no home of his own, no family, no permanent income or position. He has more than once (to the dismay of Hendrik and Bettina) turned down an academic post that threatened to keep him in one place. He has avoided lasting emotional ties. He has been living in a state of rootless readiness to go back to the north, but he has not gone back. On his last birthday, he was thirty years old. He cannot hold up youth as an excuse.

Then, on his return from Arizona, he read in the newspaper that Lester Armitage was shortly to leave for an attempt on the Pole. *He has managed to raise the funds he wanted*—has bought and outfitted a ship, the *Polar Star*, apparently capable of forcing its way through the heaviest pack ice to the north coast of Greenland. As long as he was not in the north, Jakob was consoled by the thought that the man he has come to regard as Frank's tormentor, and his enemy, was equally thwarted. A foolish consolation.

Beneath him, in the bowels of the *Etruria*, the deep grinding of the screw falters and changes note. In his cabin, the humming electric light flickers and goes out. Complete blackness. Jakob waits, listening: all is weirdly silent. The engines have stopped. He finds—he observes it with a curious detachment—that his muscles are locked rigid. Surely the ship is listing more than before? He thinks about climbing out of his bunk, but lacks the ability, or the will. There is a lurch as another gigantic weight of water slams into the ship's hull. His bunk is on the "downhill" side of the cabin, and he seems pressed into it by some enormous force.

He thinks, This is it. Sweat has broken out in armpits and groin. He is catapulted back to the shared bedroom at the Koppels, where he awoke from nightmares of drowning. The water, the freezing cold, the darkness that pulls him down to the bottom . . . The ship is foundering. But this is no nightmare, and there will be no waking. The joke is, the nightmares were not an echo of his father's mythical death: they were a premonition of his own.

Needle-like screams come from down the corridor. Irregular thuds of running, stumbling feet. Shouts of alarm, orders, questions. After those seconds of being paralyzed (a curious sensation, but short-lived), he hauls himself out of the bunk and gropes his way out of the cabin. As he does so, the corridor levels itself and begins to tilt the other way—in other words, is normal. The electric lights buzz and flicker back to life. He sees a steward pacifying a couple and, through the glazed door at the top of the stairs, there is daylight.

"All right, sir?" asks the English steward, in a harsh, flat accent. He sounds cheery. "Nothing to worry about. The storm's dropping. We'll be out of it soon."

"What happened to the lights?"

"The generator has a little hiccup sometimes—it gets overloaded if everybody keeps their lights on all the time. But they've come on again. Everything all right now!"

"Thank you. But the engines—they stopped?"

The steward cocks his head.

"No; perfectly normal, sir."

"Oh . . . right. Thank you."

"Sir? Sir . . . what happened to your head?"

On deck, he has to grab the railing to keep his feet. The sea is chaotic; flint-dark hills of water rear up in all directions. The horizon still swings wildly, but a gash of pale blue lights up the eastern sky. Perhaps he is not fated to drown, after all. Gripping the rail with one hand, Jakob touches the tender lump on his forehead with his fingertips. His head throbs like the engines underneath his feet. The doctor has given him "something for the pain." He has the bottle in his pocket, but decides not to take it. A little pain feels salutary.

Chapter 29

Liverpool, 53°24' N, 2°58' W
April 1895

Rain has smeared the windows of the train since leaving Marylebone Station. Hard to believe it is spring: few of the trees are showing leaf; the fields are mud, innocent of new growth. Heavy cloud presses down on the land, halfway between drizzle and fog. A gray land, hardly worth looking at, yet Flora cannot concentrate on her book, or on her work, and stares out of the window.

She has arranged to visit some firms that manufacture canned goods, dangling the possibility of switching allegiance from Kemp's if they offer to supply the expedition free of charge. She has many such trips to make, now that Freddie is virtually housebound. He has given her his blessing to travel and negotiate on her own. For much of the time, their lives run on contiguous but separate paths; Freddie keeps up a wide correspondence—his ability to inspire and persuade is unimpaired, and his devotion to her career seems undimmed. They meet every evening around six to exchange news on sponsors, backers, the state of their budget. She used to wonder why he did it, when his own ambitions were so cruelly curtailed, but he said that, if he did not, what he lost would be for nothing. She thinks of him with great fondness. She did not see him this morning; she kissed him on the forehead last night, and said she would write. She has many firms to see. If some of them are in Liverpool that is not her fault.

A hansom takes her from the station to the Adelphi Hotel through streets dark with recent rain, a yellowish fog creeping inside the carriage. The air feels colder than in London, grimy and damp, as if it clings to her skin. Even in her hotel room, with the fire lit, there is a pervasive hint of soot, the sea, and drains. She unpacks her case, hanging up the new peignoir she bought last Saturday—a Chinese pattern in soft blues. She washes her face and hands, then unbuttons her jacket and blouse to wipe a cloth over her armpits. Still, she feels unclean. She tugs the blankets loose on the bed to let the mattress air (the sheets feel damp, or perhaps it is just the chill). Suddenly she feels faint. She sits down at the desk in the window. If she goes over her lists of figures for the provisions required, perhaps that will help. The list of provisions floats unread in front of her eyes: jam, potted beef, carrots. Lime juice. Cocoa.

She has another piece of paper in an inner pocket, and now takes it out to look at, as she has done countless times. It is a letter, written in January, from the improbably named Flagstaff, Arizona. It tells of plans to travel to Switzerland for the summer. And gives details of a ship, the *Etruria*, which is due to dock, in Liverpool, tomorrow. He writes that he plans to stay at the Victoria Hotel in Liverpool for a few days. Given that he also says he hopes to call on her in London, it seemed significant that he would give details of his accommodation in Liverpool. Now that she is here, it seems less significant. On the surface, it is a neutral letter. Is it really possible to see it as anything more? In her reply, she cordially looked forward to seeing him in London. Since then, there has been no further correspondence.

She lies awake that night, telling herself that, even if she is foolish, it hardly matters. She has done nothing wrong. She has done nothing at all. (From the wardrobe, the silk peignoir reproaches her.) She still has the choice to do nothing, and no one will ever know.

The next morning is the seventeenth, when the *Etruria* is due to dock. Flora writes a note and addresses it to Mr. de Beyn at the Victoria Hotel. After handing the letter to the clerk at reception, she walks out of the Adelphi nearly blind with panic, heedless of the cab that almost knocks her over as she crosses the street, and of the shouts that follow. What has she done? Suggested a meeting, over tea, in the Palm Court.

The day crawls by, seeming full of judgmental glances from strangers. She feels too inexperienced in intrigue to know what to do with herself. (Clearly, despite her sophistry, she feels guilty of something.) She tells herself over and over that she isn't doing anything untoward. Tea with a friend. An acquaintance. In any case, he won't come.

After lunch, she wanders around a department store, sightlessly gazing at hats and gloves. Invited to look at some new combination undergarments, just imported from America, she buys a pair, impulsively, as a sort of talisman. The girl says they will suit madam's coloring. She seems to Flora to have a knowing look in her eye as she says this. Outside, she stops to watch an organ grinder and his monkey—a sad-eyed, wise-looking creature. She drops a half-guinea into the man's upturned bowler, for luck, and is shamed by the gratitude on his face.

At three, she is back in her room at the Adelphi, undressing, washing, and putting on the *combinaisons*. They are defiantly expensive, of pale green silk. I look like an actress, she thinks. She takes them off and throws them on the floor of the closet. She dresses in the same clothes as before. They are barely friends; they have corresponded on topics of mutual interest. What she felt in Greenland—a feeling she could not put into words—was three years ago. It has never been acknowledged in their letters. Half past three. Time has slowed, and yet she wishes it slower. At four o'clock, she is still in the room, waiting for the minute hand to creep away from the vertical. She will be a little late. In fact, there is little point in going, since no one will be there to care whether she arrives or not.

At quarter past four, she is sitting in the Palm Court, alone. So this is how it is to be. She tries not to look at the clock, tries not to torture herself with each passing minute, ticked off with an agonizing flatness that mocks her presumption. An ache has swollen to fill her whole body. At half past four, she assumes a purposeful air, dragging it on like armor, and leaves, as though she has somewhere to go.

In the evening paper, she reads that the *Etruria*'s arrival has been delayed due to bad weather. Initially, she is swept with a wave of relief; then, as quickly, it drains away. This is hardly the consolation that it might be. Can she live through another day like this? Schooled in endurance, and because the unendurable does not disappear simply because we wish it to, she climbs the stairs to her room.

The next day, she is still enduring, still conscious of impending wickedness or humiliation or, perhaps, happiness—is that possible? Shortly after four, she decides she must go to the Palm Court, because not to do so would be cowardly, an admission of defeat, an admission that she cared enough to mind.

From the lobby, she looks around the tables, divided by potted plants. She sees a gray-haired figure, a youngish man, who sits alone, as far away from the piano as possible. Her first thought is: Oh, that isn't . . . It can't be him . . . And then: Have I really been tortured with nerves because of *that*? And then: What have I done?

He looks up at a waiter bringing a tray. He speaks to the man, smiles, and the waiter smiles in return. She remembers how disarming his smile is. Then he looks around and sees her. He stands up. She makes herself walk across the room, and he takes a step toward her. He has stopped smiling, and this gives her courage. If he didn't care, she tells herself, he would smile at me as he smiled at the waiter.

They say each other's names. They shake hands. His hand feels cold through her glove. "How nice to see you again," they say.

"I owe you an apology, Mrs. Athlone; I realized only an hour ago that your note was written yesterday. Stupid of me."

"I read about the *Etruria*'s delay. It didn't matter. I have tea here, in any case."

"Am I inconveniencing you, now? Perhaps you have other plans?"

"No. By no means."

She manages to smile at last, and sits down in the chair he holds out for her. He looks older, she thinks—or is it thinner? Perhaps it is the hair, which is grayer than she remembers. His face is the same, really, and it is a nice-looking face: expressive and changeable. Is it the fact that he is clean-shaven that makes his demeanor seem less guarded than that of most men? They hide their uncertainties behind mustaches and whiskers, but his face is bare and capable of doubt. There are shadows beneath his eyes—no, bruises—and his forehead looks . . .

"What happened to your head? You are bruised."

"Oh." He touches his forehead and smiles. "I'm afraid I look rather disreputable. The door of my cabin attacked me. There was a storm that lasted the whole voyage. It's the reason we were delayed. I should have written this morning—"

"It's no—"

They both stop, having spoken over each other.

"I was so pleased to get your letter . . ."

At his shoulder, the waiter coughs discreetly.

As he tells her about the crossing, Flora glances at his left hand and its shortened little finger. He notices and closes his hand.

"I never properly thanked Dr. Seddon—and you—for treating me that day. God knows what would have happened had you not been there."

"I'm glad we could be of some help. I was sorry we couldn't do more."

She sees the memory saddens him. But it also affirms the link between them. There is a pause.

"I don't think I told you: I read Mr. Armitage's book."

"Oh?"

She does not say that she read and reread the sections where he is mentioned. She seems, without consciously trying, to have committed whole passages to memory.

"What did you think of it?"

"I thought he seemed rather eager to seize all credit for himself."

"Well, it is his book."

"Yes, but no expedition succeeds entirely on the basis of one man. He writes sometimes as though he were alone there."

"I think, in his mind, he was."

Flora senses the tension in him at the mention of Armitage's name.

"So, you're going to Switzerland?" she says, to change the subject.

"Yes. I've been corresponding with a Professor Birkel there, who has done much good work on Alpine glaciers. He's been kind enough to invite me to join him for three months—that's brave of him, is it not?"

"Brave? Why?" Flora asks, distracted.

"Well, because my company is untried . . . I may get on his nerves." He gives her an amused look.

Aghast at her own dullness, Flora cannot manage a reply. She is cast down. Do they have nothing in common outside of their interest in the north? Is he disappointed to see her again?

He asks her how long she is staying in Liverpool. She hesitates. "A few days. It depends . . ."

"Depends . . . on what?" He leans forward. His eyes are serious.

"On . . . I have to see one or two potential sponsors."

"Oh, of course." There is another uncomfortable pause. "How are your plans progressing?"

"Slowly. I don't think we will be leaving next summer. It may depend on the outcome of Armitage's latest endeavor. Everyone seems to have the idea of the Pole in their heads now. Anything else is somehow . . . less."

"Yes. Indeed."

A definite coldness in his voice. Flora is distressed to realize that he harbors a profound dislike of Lester Armitage. It seems proof of a pettiness in his character. He is flawed—and she wants him to be entirely admirable . . .

"And yours?"

"I'm sorry?" He has been looking down at his teacup.

"Your plans—to return to the north? I thought you had found a sponsor in this Mr. Welbourne."

"Oh, yes. Like you, I'm not sure. This year, Mr. Welbourne has gone to Africa to shoot big game. The world is his hunting ground. Perhaps next year, but nothing is certain."

His gaze rests on the table, as does hers. The tablecloth is damask, patterned with roses and some round fruit: cherries perhaps, or plums.

They could be strangers meeting for the first time. They make small talk. Flora can see them, when the teapot is empty, shaking hands, saying their good-byes, walking away with a dull relief. They weren't like this in the north, were they? Or in their letters? He notices her glance toward the door; is he hurt, or bored? She thinks, I must say something to acknowledge what happened in Neqi, although nothing happened. But we are here; we are—both of us—*here*.

"Mrs. Athlone . . ."

"Yes?"

"Flora . . ."

The use of her name shocks her like a jolt of electric current. Their eyes meet and she has the sense of being scalded. His voice is low and he speaks rapidly.

"May I call you that? It is how I have come to think of you. I have to ask: Is your being here, in Liverpool, now . . . is it just a coincidence?"

Despite everything, she is panicked by the question. Her mind forms the words of demurral, a deflecting laugh. She focuses on his hands—sinewy, tanned, the nails broken off short—and says, closing her eyes, "No."

He lets out a pent-up breath.

"I hoped not. I've often thought of that time in Neqi. You may not agree—you will tell me if I am presumptuous—but I felt when we met that there was a . . . an affinity. Is that presumptuous?"

She feels him looking at her, but doesn't dare meet his eyes. "No. I felt it too."

"But..." She hears him smile; an attempt at levity. "I'm aware that much time has passed since then, and if you regret coming here, it is no matter."

Looking up, Flora experiences another shock. She reads appeal and doubt, the possibility of rejection.

"Do you regret it?" Flora asks, in a whisper. At that instant, all her doubts and cavils vanish and are replaced by a single, anguished fear.

"No, I don't regret it at all."

She feels something like a blush steal over her whole body. She is unaware that, at this moment, she is smiling.

"Nor I."

He smiles, looks delighted, and his face becomes familiar. The look in his eyes warms her. The way his cheeks crease when he smiles—she could never forget that.

"I was afraid you would be disappointed when you saw me again, that you would think, What a poor, meager creature he is, with his old-man's hair."

"No."

She moves her fingers until they rest lightly against his hand on the table. Even the clock holds its breath. Flora draws her hand away, and they both sit back, looking around at the new world they are in.

"Do you have any engagements for this evening?"

"No," she says, terrified, her eyes on the tablecloth. She will remember its pattern as long as she lives.

"Would you do me the honor of dining with me, then?" he asks, with such comically exaggerated politeness that she laughs.

In her room, she is thankful for the time alone. She has no doubt that they understand each other, but the knowledge only creates a different anxiety. She is crossing a border into a new and danger-ous country whose customs are unknown to her. She confronts her reflection, looks for signs of wickedness, a burning mark that must have sprung up, but sees only the imperfections in the mirror, as if her face has less substance than the glass. She lifts her chin; her face looks dim and unreal. She has the sensation of falling.

"Shall we walk a little?" Jakob says, when they emerge from the restaurant into the night. He glances at the fog, which has thickened while they were eating. "I would say we could have some fresh air, but I'm not sure that is available."

He offers her his arm, and she takes it, aware of the firmness of his bicep through her glove and his sleeve, but taking care not to walk too close to him. Both walk more slowly than they would like, but then, they don't know where they are going. The fog confounds them, making streets they passed through earlier unfamiliar and disorienting.

"This way, I think . . . Fog in Greenland was never like this, was it? Sometimes it was violet, or yellow, but I don't recall it being brown."

He is trying to set her at ease. Flora could hardly bring herself to eat, has no idea what was on her plate, or what they talked about, and drank too much wine. She could only meet his eyes for the briefest of moments, as if his gaze would shrivel her. Her heart is thumping so hard she is sure it must be visible through her coat.

"I think the main street is just down here. Flora, are you all right?"

"Yes. I'm just . . ."

She looks at him and presses a hand to her breastbone. Breathing is a struggle. He stops and looks at her with concern, one hand lightly holding her arm.

"I'm sure we're only a few minutes from your hotel. I will walk you there. Tomorrow, if you wish, we could . . ."

Like a sleepwalker, she floats toward him—she has no memory of taking steps—and kisses him, bumping into his jaw, jerking back as he turns to her, and then his mouth finds hers. She has not anticipated this moment—not exactly—but is aware of his lips being first cold and then warm, dry and then wet, like butter in her mouth, and she thinks, Yes.

A passerby, from nowhere, mutters an indistinct, though clearly coarse, remark.

Flora pulls back, again can't meet his eye. "I feel as though everyone knows," she whispers.

"They don't. Anyway, they don't care."

"But is it really possible?"

"Anything is possible. Anything you want."

She lifts her eyes at last.

"Flora, you look as though you're being tortured, and I don't want to torture you. Come, I will walk you back to your hotel."

Flora fixes her eyes on his fog-bedewed shoulder. "Can we go to your room?"

Jakob looks positively alarmed. "Now? Are you sure?"

She almost wants to laugh at his expression. She nods. "If you want to, that is."

His face changes and he grins. "I want to. I just wish you didn't look as though you were being led to your doom."

Up to this point, she has not thought, specifically, whether she desires him or not. But at this moment she knows. She wants to make him happy . . . and hopefully, herself, although she isn't confident about that. They kiss again, for longer, and she opens her mouth against his. His tongue stirs her, engendering a restless ache. His hands are on her back, chastely still; there is an uncomfortable space between them. Flora wants to wind her arms around his waist; she wants to feel his body against hers and, as she steps inside his coat, his arms tighten around her. With a shock that is also a thrill, she feels his erection against her belly, and presses against it. Her own boldness excites her. It makes her think, Yes, this is possible.

When they finally pull apart, he looks into her face, his eyes slightly dazed and soft, faintly embarrassed by the evidence of his desire.

In complicit silence, they turn toward the Victoria, her arm in his. At least, that is the intention, but after a couple of turnings, they realize they are lost. The buildings are meaner, the streetlamps fewer and dimmer. There is a pungency of drains.

"Perhaps this way . . . I will ask someone." Jakob sets off confidently. But the streets are empty of people, and the windows of the houses lightless. A huge, shapeless cat with sulfurous eyes crouches on a sill, regarding them with spite.

"I think we should be heading over there." She points to their left.

Jakob smiles a rather sickly smile. "Perhaps. We should be able to manage this—we are, after all, explorers."

Flora hiccups with laughter, and because she is nervous and they are lost, and, because a hiccup is not a dignified form of expression, she giggles and can't stop. He joins in. The cat turns its back, tail twitching.

"We may starve . . ."

". . . in the back streets of . . . Where are we? Liverpool."

"They will find our bones in years to come, picked clean by"—a string of young men in bowlers appears at the end of the street—"swells."

Jakob lowers his voice as they pass the nearest man, whose eyes, from a pallid slab of a face, rake Flora with a hungry glance. "I think you have lured me here on purpose, and now your confederates are going to set upon me, an innocent tourist, and rob me . . . Well, they will be disappointed."

"I have no confederates." She smiles at him. "And I don't think you are an innocent tourist."

As they reach the end of the next street, they both recognize the thoroughfare. More lights and hansoms; a gas man mending a street-light; people. And there, in the distance, is the Victoria Hotel, ablaze with light like a beacon of sin. The bubble of laughter in Flora's throat disappears.

Jakob tells her to go in first. She walks past the desk with a thumping heartbeat, but no one looks up as she passes. Jakob joins her on the landing. He takes her by the elbow and they walk along the corridor, in silence, like any couple who have something or nothing on their minds.

Jakob stirs up the fire and insists she take the armchair in front of it. She holds her hands out to the flames. He opens the wardrobe and takes out a bottle of wine and two glasses, and proffers them with an ironic flourish.

"Oh, thank you."

She accepts a glass of wine. She doesn't really want it, but holding the glass gives her something to do. He sits on the rug close to her chair. She thinks, He has done this before.

They touch their glasses, self-consciously, though neither can or will name their toast. They have gone beyond small talk without arriving at anywhere else. Flora looks to the window. The curtains are drawn; the stars are not visible, and would be no help if they were. She, who is sure of herself at sea, without landmarks, is lost here. She takes a sip of wine, which turns out to be a mouthful. She prays: Help me; make me less afraid.

At length, though it is possible only a minute has passed, Jakob takes her glass and puts it down; he kneels, facing her, and takes her hand in both of his. She is aware of his geologist's callouses, the difference between her hand and his.

"If you've changed your mind, it's all right."

Flora shakes her head. She presses his knuckles to her lips, feeling the ridges and calloused skin. He turns his hand to cup her cheek, and rough pads of skin graze her face. She brings her face closer to his, aware of the smells of soap and tobacco and some scented lotion that barbers use. And then his mouth is against hers.

Flora slides into the heat in his mouth, tastes the bitterness of the wine, feels his tongue against hers, and feels her limbs loosening. It is not one kiss followed by another, but a slow, deliberate process of dissolution, and it undoes her. She touches the softness of his hair, feels the bones of his skull, the movements of his jaw. His hand goes from her arm to her waist, and heat flares from the epicenter of his touch. She presses toward him. His hand creeps up to cup her breast and a moan escapes him.

She is subject to a sudden and complex restructuring: finite to formless, solid to liquid . . . She gasps and turns her head away.

"What is it?"

She pushes him away and leaps to her feet.

"Flora? I'm sorry . . . Are you all right?"

Flora sees the washstand on one hand, the bedroom door on the other, wavers, then rushes to the washstand and is unstoppably, unbelievably sick into the bowl.

Paralyzed with horror, she hunches over the stand. The smell of vomit assaults her nostrils, from inside and out. The monogrammed *V* in the bottom of the bowl is obscured by a stew of wine and undigested cutlet. She coughs, her throat burning. Jakob is next to her.

"You poor darling, here . . ." He pours a glass of water and holds it out. He doesn't touch her. She keeps her eyes on the glass, rinses her mouth.

His voice sharp with distress, he says, "Flora, I'm so sorry. Are you ill? Tell me, please."

She shakes her head, hot tears in her eyes. She brushes away a strand of hair that is sticking to her lip.

"I'm sorry—I don't know . . . I'm sorry."

"Are you finished?" Jakob takes her arm and he leads her back to the armchair.

"Sit down." He is almost comically solicitous. "Are you hot?"

She nods, and he opens the window, after a brief struggle and an oath. The smells of soot and fog mingle with the smell of vomit. It is not altogether an improvement.

"Shall I send for a doctor?" He crouches beside her, looking into her face, although she can't bring herself to look at him.

"I'm not ill. I'm . . . in a tumult."

Hesitantly, he strokes her hand, very lightly. As though his touch is the last straw, a tear spills out of each eye. He puts his arms round her hunched shoulders. Her tears are blotted by his jacket.

"I'm sorry . . . I . . . I can't."

He says, "It's all right, it's all right," then relinquishes her. She feels abandoned, suddenly chilled to the bone. Is this what her morality is made of? The inability to go through with flouting it?

Jakob takes the bowl into the corridor. She hears his voice as he calls to a member of staff: "Excuse me, I'm afraid my wife was taken ill . . ." His voice is crisp and commanding: he lies convincingly, a part of her registers. The voices fade to a murmur. She slumps back in the armchair, a hand over her eyes. The door opens and closes softly.

"They're coming back with another bowl." He hovers inside the door. "Flora, tell me what you would like. I can send for a doctor . . . If you want to be alone here, I can leave you . . . Or I'll call a cab to take you to your hotel. Please say what you would rather."

When she dares look at him, his face is strained. The bruise on his forehead seems more livid in gaslight. How ridiculous we are, she thinks. And we think we choose the course of our lives.

"I'm sorry, this is horrible. Me, I mean, not you." Another tear slips down her cheek and she wipes it away. "Please know that I don't regret anything . . . but perhaps you do, now."

Jakob comes over to her. "I regret that you are suffering, that's all. I'll do anything I can to alleviate it."

A knock at the door. Jakob takes the clean bowl and returns it to the washstand. She thinks of how he called her his wife, how impersonal it sounded.

"Well . . ." He waits for her to say what she wants, but she doesn't know. "Perhaps the best thing is for me to take another room here. If you write a note, I will fetch some of your things."

When he has gone, she exhales with relief. Every nerve and sinew in her body seems to have been strung tight for hours—days. She is lightheaded with exhaustion. She shuts the window against the fog. She washes the strands of hair that still reek. She opens the closet and trails a hand across his clothes. They are workaday, well worn. The only new clothes are the ones he is wearing.

She undoes her hair and dries it in front of the fire. Then, as quickly as she can, she undresses, terrified that he will return while she is doing so. She takes off her jacket and blouse, fumbling with the buttons, her skirt and petticoats, her shoes and stockings. She rinses her mouth again. She takes off her camisole, and is left in her chemise and drawers. The bed seems to have been made so tightly as to defy anybody's attempts to get into it. Perhaps they know, she thinks to herself, with a hysterical giggle. At last, she hauls back the bed-clothes enough to get in, shuddering at the cold sheets. Finally, she lies down and pulls the blankets up to her chin. Her heart is going like a piston. Clasping her arms, she is revolted by her gooseflesh. She thinks of paintings of seductresses lolling naked and smooth on cotton sheets—clearly in different, warmer climates. If she ever believed in the reality of such depictions, she now knows them to be false. She is shivering, clammy, afraid. She wonders if this is what it feels like to be sinful: mainly, it transpires, that is cold and rather ill. She thought it would be easier.

Jakob's despondency on leaving the Victoria has quite lifted by the time he reaches the Adelphi. He is even, in some measure (pathetic to admit—probably a sign of advancing age), relieved. He has not slept more than two hours together for the past week and is more tired than he can remember. In the hushed warmth of the Adelphi lounge, as he waits for Flora's overnight case to be brought downstairs, he pretends to read a newspaper, and allows his eyes to close. The ordeal of the voyage—he had joked about it, but it took its toll—steals up on him. The gorgeous luxury of solid ground—which even now he doesn't quite trust . . . He could fall asleep right here.

But now that he is alone with his thoughts, he feels an upwell-ing of delight and . . . what? Hopefulness? Perhaps he is not entirely without merit, because she came here to be with him. Since reading her note this morning, he had been in a fever of excitement that drove him to take a bath, then to the barber's shop; an excitement seasoned with anxiety that he had misunderstood, or that she would take one look at him and change her mind. But she had kissed him; she had thrillingly, deliberately pressed her body against his . . . There was a touching candor in her actions, a sense that she was offering her entire self. Behind the *Evening Mercury*, he relives the exquisite sensation of nestling against her soft, unstayed body, and his hand involuntarily hollows, as if it still cups her breast . . . His fluctuating tumescence, nagging for the past several hours, quickens again.

Carrying her case and some food bought from a stall, he knocks gently on the door. There is no answer. Opening the door, he sees with a shock—a deep, galvanizing thrill—that she is in his bed, then realizes that she is asleep. Her breath is loud in her throat. She has turned out all the lamps but one, which picks out bright highlights in her hair. He puts the case on the dressing table, and is collecting his things when her breathing changes. He jumps like a startled thief.

"Hello. I'm just taking my things to the other room. It's on the floor above: number twenty. I've brought you something to eat, if you would like. You didn't eat much earlier."

"Thank you. Please don't go yet."

She raises herself on one elbow. Her cheeks have a hint of color. Her eyes glitter in the lamplight. Weariness and want tear him in different directions.

"You're very kind; I am causing you a great deal of trouble."

"No . . ." He smiles, because it is patently untrue. "In any case, I am causing you more trouble, I think."

"I don't want you to think that this is . . . I'm here because I want to be with you."

She draws herself up to a sitting position, causing the bedding to fall down to her waist, and holds out her hand. Jakob comes over, his eyes drinking her in; a thin chemise is all that covers her nakedness. He takes her hand, aware of her heat, his coldness.

"Are you feeling better?"

"Yes. Is it cold, outside?"

"Not very."

She pulls on his hand to make him sit on the edge of the bed. "I haven't done this before, so it is . . ." She closes her eyes and takes a deep breath. "I am afraid, but it's only fear. Tell me you are not repelled."

He smiles and shakes his head, places his free hand on her hair. It feels heavy and slippery and cool; underneath it, her skin burns.

"No, and no. I'm sorry, my hands are freezing."

Flora kneels up on the bed, takes his hands in hers and chafes them. Then she takes one of his hands and places it on her breast. He gasps and squeezes the delicious, poised weight, feels the nipple stiffen under his palm. She sighs against his cheek.

His face, his lips, even his clothes retain the night's chill. The rough cloth against her bare arms sends peculiar shivers through her.

He shucks off the coat, unbuttons his waistcoat, and pulls off his necktie. She cups her hand around the nape of his neck, feeling cords of tendon, the base of his skull under soft, cold hair. She wants to warm every part of him.

They smile shyly at each other. How many clothes they wear! He has to struggle out of his shoes, socks, trousers. He takes her in his arms. The rasp of his undershirt against her skin is as exciting as the fact of his arousal.

"Flora . . ." He kisses her hair, her cheekbone, her ear, her mouth.

She puts her hands on his neck and slides them down to his waist, and pulls his undershirt up until he lifts his arms over his head. His hair stands on end. In the lamplight, his eyes are black, his torso gleaming white. She grazes the nipples with her palms, strokes the sides of his chest, feeling ribs under soft skin. This is happening. He kneads her breasts, watching his hands as if performing an operation of rare importance. She pushes into him. She wants his hands on her, everywhere. He pulls the chemise down off her shoulders and kisses each inch of skin as it is revealed. No, this, now: his lips, his tongue; he tastes her and sucks her, his tongue as insistent as a question. Her breathing replies. Now she lies back on the pillow; now she lifts her hips to let him peel off her drawers. His face presses into the soft, sprung flesh of her belly and he mutters something, but she doesn't catch it. Does it matter? Should she ask him to repeat it?

Before she can decide, he pulls himself up to lie full length on top of her. He says her name. She wonders what she is supposed to do, or say, and slides her hands over the sharp ridges of shoulder blades and hot saddle of lower back as his tongue explores her mouth. The weight and heat of him are strange and wonderful. She is aware of what he is made of: bones, muscles, tendons, flesh. Skin, hot and slightly damp, pressed to skin to the waist, rough flannel below it. And through that his erection feels hard and unyielding against her thighs, unlike flesh and unlike bone—something else. And now this is what she wants. Is she still drunk? She feels reckless, irresponsibly single-minded. His eyes, closed, open as she pushes the flannel down over his buttocks. This is happening.

"Wait a minute . . ."

He leaves her—how cold it is when he has moved away—only to dive over the side of the bed, fumble for something and sit back, concentrating as he unrolls a sheath over his penis; he gives it a tug, to make sure. She wonders if it is wrong to watch. Then he kneels over her, lightly stroking her belly, down her thighs, up the inside of her thighs, until his hand brushes against her hair. Her thighs open greedily. His fingers slide inside her wet softness, and make her gasp. She looks up and is astonished by this silhouetted, angular incubus, prick heavy with intent, pointing at her, hooded, and then he lowers himself onto her, guiding himself one-handed. Despite her molten warmth, it's difficult; the breath catches low in her throat. She feels a burning sensation, and she prays: Do not let me fail at this. His eyes are shut; he is concentrating, perhaps; it hurts; then, with an excruciating push, he is through, and sliding smoothly up to the hilt. Her breath catches again, in a different place, and she says, "Oh," in a strange tone of voice, one she has never heard in her mouth. She can feel the length of him inside her, which is not like anything else, but part of her thinks, Yes, *this* is what I thought . . . When she opens her eyes, she finds his are open too, very close to hers. She can't move.

He is still for a long moment, as if he is waiting for a signal, but what it might be she doesn't know. Then, just when she fears that something is amiss, that she is supposed to react in some way that she does not know, or that he has encountered something wrong inside her—has found out her terrible flaw (something, anyway, that is her fault)—he kisses her again, slowly, his tongue deep in her mouth, and she has the feeling of being . . . joined up. He starts to move, very slowly, easing himself in and out, stroking her from the inside. It burns, but not in the way that Freddie burned her. She raises her knees—ah, better—nestles him deeper and yet more comfortably inside her and her hands grasp for his buttocks, feeling cool, slightly rough skin, the deep play of muscle and bone at the base of his spine.

The first flush of pain has changed into something else. Her throat is as hollow as a cave. She can feel the friction working; she is anointing him. He starts to move faster. And, from his breath catching and hissing next to her ear, she thinks that he is nearing the end. Finally, he gasps and clutches at her breast, as if it might save him, and she is filled with feral triumph as he shudders and moans in her ear. She can feel a pulsing inside her, and then, when he is still again, panting, lying heavy on her, his heart beats wildly against her ribcage, next to hers. He presses his lips to her cheek, and she wraps her arms around him.

This is happening.

When their hearts have slowed, and their skin dried, and they have exchanged soft, smiling kisses, he withdraws from her, peels away the rubber sheath and stares at it for a moment, and then, lying down beside her again, he says mildly, and with a touch of awkwardness, "Darling, I'm sorry, I feel like a brute. You should have said."

Flora feels a stab of alarm. "Said what?"

"That, um . . ." he is embarrassed, "it was your course. It doesn't matter. I mean . . ."

She sits up and shifts to one side to look at the sheet. It is smeared with blood, and there is blood on her thighs.

"It isn't."

"Then . . . I hurt you. God, Flora, I'm sorry."

"No. You didn't."

She shakes her head, but he is gazing at her with something like shock.

"Um"—he rubs his hand over his face—"when you said you hadn't done this before, I thought you meant . . . Is this the first time?"

She looks down, and her hair almost hides her face. "Not exactly. Yes."

"You . . . Your marriage . . . ?"

She looks away. Her voice is almost inaudible. "Please, I can't talk about it."

"No, of course. It doesn't matter. Sweetheart . . ." He draws her down to lie in the crook of his chest and upper arm, and smooths the rope of her hair in his hand. "Are you all right?"

"Yes. It's not important, is it?"

"No. Not at all."

But he lies; he is thrilled, however ignobly . . . He tightens his arms around her.

"I'm just sorry I hurt you. I would have taken more care. I want you to like it too."

She blushes. He thinks he can actually feel heat flow into her face. "I did."

"But . . . not quite all the way? You know what I mean?"

She hides her face against his shoulder, and nods. He is enormously relieved.

"Well, then . . . I do believe you're blushing." He smiles and kisses her cheek.

"To talk of such things . . . it's . . ." She stammers, can't say more. She turns to hide her face in the pillow.

"If we do them, why can't we talk about them? Otherwise, how will you tell me what you like?"

"Ah . . ." She looks panicked. "I don't know."

"All right, if you don't like something, then say . . . no, just poke me on the shoulder."

He kneels again and kisses her all over: her throat, her breasts, her ribcage, her stomach. He is so slow and gentle, she sighs with a demented, impatient pleasure. He lifts and moves her knees and wriggles into the space between. Before she realizes what he is about, he has begun to lap at the soft, complicated flesh between her legs. She feels a panicked, pleasurable anxiety. What if it doesn't work? But his tongue is soft, teasing, unhurried, sometimes barely moving, but undeniably there; and with an almost conscious effort, she gives herself up.

By herself, she never made a sound. Not when she was young, on board ship, for fear of discovery; not in her bed at home, out of long habit. She became adept at keeping her limbs anchored, still, so the secret wave would break over her body and no one would know. Now, she wants him to know. At some point, she forgets to be anxious. She is adrift, cast loose, rocking easily. Her breaths are tattered gasps. She does not have to choose. Sooner than thought, it comes for her, engulfs her gloriously, and her back arches, she is lifted, her fists clutch at air, there are little vixen cries, calling out, sharp, ah, ah, ah.

He wipes his mouth on the inside of her thighs. She is panting, her heart going like mad—a wild, rebellious beating. She slowly comes back from wherever she has been, grateful, delighted. Relieved. She thinks, Maybe there is nothing wrong with me, after all. He clambers back up the bed and she pulls him to her, her skin rosy and slick with sweat. He smiles at her, a question in his eyes. She kisses him with even more abandon than before, tastes her briny tang, hopes he wants to do it again; she thinks it—she—will be better this time. She reaches for him, but she can already feel his penis against her thigh, reassuringly hard. That he too wants this seems a miracle.

She whispers, "It's safe."

"Yes?"

He guides himself to her. She is breached, defenseless, her boundaries given way. He slides inside her more easily, though it still causes her to moan. He begins to move in her with a slow, weary tenderness. It burns, being licked by a gentle flame, but he fits, as though they have been cast from opposite sides of the same mold. She watches the uneven flicker of lamplight; she is burning too, stirred, lit. His eyes are closed; his forehead rests against hers as if he is overcome with exhaustion. He quickens suddenly, shudders, with a modest gasp, and stays in that position, his weight resting on her. He gently kisses her cheekbone, before sliding off her to lie by her side. Their eyes meet across the pillow. She breathes his air, and he hers.

Hunger drives them out of bed after midnight. Flora has put on her blue silk peignoir out of vanity; it isn't really warm enough. Jakob wears his shirt and wraps a blanket around his torso. They sit on the floor, as close to the fire as possible, their knees touching, eating ravenously. He has poured the last fragments of coal on to the embers.

"I should have gotten more." He peers into the basket. "They had apples, but they looked old . . ."

She shakes her head and drinks the milk, which is on the turn. She feels his hand touch her hair and her neck. She closes her eyes, to savor it.

"Can I take it from your appetite that you are recovered?"

"Yes. I think so."

He peers at her face, making her laugh. He can turn the simplest action into a comedy.

"You're still pale."

"So are you."

"That is due to seven days' appalling seasickness. I was tanned and healthy when I left New York. You won't believe me, but my sister-in-law said I looked handsome. She is German and not prone to giving compliments."

"You see, I was merely sick in sympathy with you."

"Thank you. But, though pale, you are beautiful, and I'm not prone to giving compliments either."

She smothers the lurch of happiness, thinks, You are more beautiful, but says nothing, merely reaches out and brushes her fingertips over his bruised forehead.

"Your poor head."

"That ship was a beast. When we docked, some of the passengers swore they would never go home. They said, no matter how old-fashioned Europe is, they would make the best of it."

"I haven't told you about the *Vega*."

"The *Vega?*"

Jakob is first amused and then touched by the way her face brightens when she talks about her father's ship.

"What happened to her?"

"She's still there."

"Could you charter her for your next trip?"

"I don't know. I've thought about it, of course, but . . . You're falling asleep!"

"I'm listening with my eyes closed. It sounds as though you loved her."

"She was my family. As much as my father is my father . . . the *Vega* was like a sister . . . or a mother."

Jakob smiles sleepily at her. "Half woman, half . . . whaleboat. That didn't sound right." He bursts out laughing, and Flora, after a second's hesitation, joins in. He has the intuition that she does not often laugh.

"I beg your pardon. In fifth grade, my teacher said, 'Jakob is not a poet.' I'm afraid he was right."

"Who can trust a poet? Fine words are neither here nor there."

"Certainly not here."

She pulls him up off the floor and captures him in her arms. They stand for a moment, he swaying with tiredness. She tightens her arms around him, not daring words to convey what she feels. They get into bed, where he wraps his limbs around her and plummets into heavy sleep, like falling off a cliff.

Flora lies awake. These things are shockingly new: the shared nakedness, the weight and press of another body, the feel of another's heart, the sound of his breathing, the bewitching heat and softness of his skin.

She trails fingertips down his arm: his skin is white down to the elbow, then the forearms are sunburnt and brown, rougher to touch, almost polished. Then over his chest: white, sprinkled with wiry dark hairs, his life's motor beating right under her hand. Down over his white belly . . . He sighs. She cannot believe how tender this hidden skin is. She can feel his ribs, which moves her with an intense, visceral protectiveness. Now, she worries for him. Such thin ribs; such delicate bones can break. Such soft skin can be damaged. But he is strong too; even in sleep, his forearm is dense with muscle under the skin.

She is pinned by the weight of the arm that lies on her ribs, the leg bent across her thighs. She does not want to push him away. She does not want to sleep—wants to think about the astonishing new thing her life has become—but she does, dreamlessly.

Chapter 30

Liverpool, 53°25' N, 3°0' W
April 1895

In the end, they stay in the room at the Victoria for five days and nights. It is possible to believe, in a city neither of them knows, that there are no consequences to their actions. Flora visits suppliers of canned foods and listens to their proposals with a sense of hilarious unreality: their medal-winning corned beef; their improved recipe for pemmican; their immortal jams. What is real are jangled nerves and unstrung limbs, her unguarded heart. She thanks them for their time, thinks of the hollows at the base of his spine.

After the second meeting, she walks back to the hotel under a weak sun. She could take a cab, but prefers to walk. The ache it arouses affirms this new intimacy. It is early yet, and the morning seems enchanted, the fog gone, the air brilliantly clear. She is happy to be briefly alone, hugging the thought of him, the repeated proofs of his desire for her. She pictures him lying in bed, naked and drowsily warm, awaiting her return . . . She has lost nothing she valued.

She finds him writing letters, wrapped in her blue silk peignoir. She is disappointed, and taken aback by the peignoir.

"I'm nearly finished," he says, holding a cigarette in his left hand. The room reeks of tobacco smoke, sweat, and sex. (The state of the bed appalls her; she can't let a maid see that; heavens . . .) Crossly, Flora opens the window a hand's breadth and grimaces.

"How was their canned beef?"

"It won a gold medal at the Bremen exhibition."

"Oh, good."

He writes a sentence. His writing is surprisingly neat. She loves the care he takes. Now she stands behind him and places her hands on his shoulders.

"Why are you wearing this?"

"Do you mind it?"

"No . . ."

"It feels nice; although, I have to say, it's not exactly warm. I'm writing to Professor Collee."

Collee is the eminent geologist he has been hoping to meet. The day after his arrival, he wrote to apologize for being detained by a severe head cold. This reminder of his departure makes her bend and brush her lips over the skin of his neck.

"Damn. I've made a blot."

"I'm sorry . . ." She straightens up, instantly contrite. Perhaps there are consequences, after all.

"It's all right." He presses blotting paper onto the letter and turns to her, slides his hands around her waist and nuzzles his face into her bosom with a groan of contentment.

She cradles his head, rakes her hands through his hair. "You look like a dandelion."

"What? I can't hear, here."

"Your hair—it's like a dandelion."

"It's not yellow."

"A dandelion clock."

"Hmm . . ." His eyes narrow. "Well, *your* hair is like the beach at Coney Island."

"I have never seen the beach at Coney Island, so I've no idea if that is a compliment, or the reverse."

"When the tide goes out, and you get those ripples on wet sand—that's what your hair is like, the color and the ripples. You said I look like a weed."

He pulls the pins out of her hair, a determined look in his eye, and she does not protest. She kisses him and feels his hand, which has invaded her skirts, smooth the skin of her inner thigh. She pushes the material away from his shoulders so that she can look at his naked body: something she cannot seem to get enough of. When they are on the bed and he thrusts into her, it burns and makes her gasp. A word she has never used pops into her head with a jolt of dark pleasure: This is *fucking*, she thinks. It is short, sharp, and it takes her breath away . . . (But, says a voice somewhere, it is *morning* . . . the door is *unlocked*!) He finishes with a series of anguished grunts and kisses her, panting.

"I could have sworn I was writing a letter . . ."

Flora catches her breath, exhilarated, but wondering whether she actually liked it. After the last couple of days, she is sore, which was all very well when she was alone, smugly congratulating herself, but now . . .

"You insult me and debauch me . . ."

Jakob slides off her and his fingers stray over her belly to the dark, raw place between her thighs. She stays his hand.

"Darling? Are you all right? What is it?"

"Ah . . ." She allows her eyes to unfocus to the point where she can believe she isn't saying this. "It just . . . stings a little."

"Sweetheart, I'm so sorry. Will you forgive me? Forgive me . . . Oh, God!"

She has to laugh. "I forgive you. Can we just . . . ?"

"Of course, darling. Actually, I hurt too." He laughs, seemingly at himself, and lies back on the bed, grinning at the ceiling.

"You don't have to look so pleased with yourself."

"I don't look pleased with myself!" he protests, trying not to grin. "I look happy."

Flora learns that she can feel unalloyed joy for whole minutes before it gives way to worry, fear, guilt, or irritation. On waking in the middle of the night, she is convinced that the man sleeping beside her wishes her ill. What if his desire is not for her, but would be the same for any woman, and she is just the one who has thrown herself in his path? He must be a prolific seducer; his skill, his frankness surely attest to it. In fact, he is only pretending to sleep; he is plotting his disentanglement as he lies there. Or he will strangle her and steal her underclothes . . . When she wakes again, to daylight and relative sanity, and finds herself fitted so gently into the crook of his body, sees the look in his eyes, and his smile, she no longer believes that, but . . . still! What does she really know about him?

And when they make a rare excursion, to an art gallery, she is tense and fearful lest—no matter how unlikely—she is seen by someone who knows her. She stares fiercely at the paintings, trying to commit titles and names to memory, so that she can put them in a letter to Freddie and enflesh her alibi for staying longer in Liverpool than a few meetings about canned meat could justify.

Jakob, not realizing that she is undertaking a task of such importance, mutters irreverent comments about the paintings, or points out a foible of a visitor's demeanor. When she doesn't respond, and ceases even to look at him, he falls silent. She glares at the posturing allegories and drooping maidens, chestnut-hued and unbelievable. She does not even like them.

They drift in silence toward a painting that is quite different. A chill, monochrome landscape with areas of darkness and ragged white mountains, it reminds Flora of the landscape near Godthåb, after autumn snowfall, looking across the fjord of black water. Close to, she sees tortured birches, and eerily beautiful figures of young women floating above the ground, hair spiraling around them as though drowning in air, tangled in sheets that reveal their nubile bodies. The title of the painting is *The Punishment of Lust*.

Jakob reads it. "Well," he murmurs, "it doesn't look so bad."

Jolted with shame and embarrassment, Flora turns and walks away.

"Did you really think I would be here?" she asks.

Flora has pulled him into the crook of her shoulder. With a finger, he traces a contour around her right breast.

They have weathered their first disagreement. As a result, she feels they have reached a deeper, sweeter understanding.

"Here? No. I hoped I *might* see you in London, but beyond that, I had no idea . . ."

"I didn't know if you would even reply to my note. I thought perhaps I'd misconstrued what happened in Neqi."

"You didn't misconstrue."

Flora pulls herself away so that she can look into his face.

"It was the strangest thing. Even with the others there, I felt as though a light had come on—and it shone only on us. And I was sure that you knew . . . It sounds silly."

"No, it doesn't. I felt the same thing. I knew you were thinking of me in the same way I was thinking of you."

"Oh? What way was that?"

He grins. "I don't mean like that. Of course, ever since I met you in Siorapaluk, I knew, but that was different."

"Knew what?"

He lowers his face so that only his eyes are visible over her breast.

"That I wanted to be your lover."

The word shocks her; she is unused to hearing such words. They are as inflammatory as his touch.

"I don't suppose I was the only one. Everyone talked about you. To see a young woman, so competent and experienced . . . it was astonishing. We couldn't believe it."

He rubs his upper lip across her nipple until it stiffens, takes it delicately in his mouth. Flora is suddenly appalled by his energy, his competence. His experience. Experience with whom? One of a thousand things she doesn't know.

"Well, you've got what you wanted," she says.

"Flora?" He lifts his head and looks at her, but her face is turned to the window.

She doesn't speak, because she doesn't know what to say.

"What is it? Flora, tell me."

She shakes her head, and feels with fury the heat of tears just behind her eyelids. "Nothing."

"Clearly it isn't nothing. Tell me, I would not hurt your feelings for the world."

Flora pulls herself into the far corner of the bed, draws her knees up, and wraps her arms around them. She looks at the window.

"That is the trouble with . . . sex."

He looks away from her and doesn't speak for a minute.

"I don't know what you mean."

"It doesn't *listen*. Your body goes on behaving one way, when . . . when you have feelings that . . ."

She takes a ragged breath. Jakob pulls himself up to sit beside her, without touching her.

"Feelings that what?" His voice is flat.

"I know . . . I knew . . . It doesn't matter, but . . ."

He sighs. "You knew what? Wait a minute, I'm going to smoke."

He gets out of bed and pads across the room to where his jacket was cast on to the floor. She can't help but look at his bare back with the dimples above his pelvis, his buttocks with their lovely, shadowed hollows, the dark pouch between his legs—he seems unconcerned by his nakedness. The bedsprings creak as he sits back on the mattress.

"What did you know?"

"Just . . . I knew you must have . . . done this sort of thing before, and when you said about the others, about being my lover . . ."

She can't quite put the shameful thoughts into words. Jakob expels a stream of smoke at the ceiling.

"'This sort of thing'? Do you think that I'm going to boast of my conquest of you? Before moving on to the next one—is that it?"

She moves her head sharply. It sounds so ugly.

"No. But . . ."

"But what? You seem to have a very low opinion of me."

"No! I'm trying to explain. I've never done this before, and you . . . have. They always say it's different for men. You . . . know what to do. When you touch me, I can't think. But I hardly know you. How do I know what your life is?"

"I will tell you. What do you want to know?"

"I don't know how you live! You could be married, or engaged . . . I wouldn't know!"

"Of course I'm not married! Nor am I engaged. In New York, I live with my brother—you know that. Haven't we corresponded for the last three years? I have been to bed with women before; I'm thirty years old and I'm not a monk. But there is no one at home. And you *are* married, Flora . . ."

"You know what my marriage is. And I'm afraid."

"Afraid of what?"

"I'm afraid that, after this, I won't be able to go back to what my life was. And that you will."

Jakob picks a stray piece of tobacco from his tongue. It is the thought that neither has yet dared speak aloud. He throws his cigarette (minor, auspicious victory) into the fireplace. "Why do you assume I want to go back to what my life was? Do you think I'm just a . . . a libertine?"

She shakes her head. "I don't know. Are you?" She tries to look lighthearted.

Jakob is annoyed. "If I say no, will you believe me?"

"I have no experience of this!"

"Are you afraid because I have experience?"

She nods.

"But experience is just the past. It is past. You are the present, Flora . . . and I would like you to be the future."

Flora absorbs this. But her face shows nothing.

"Why don't you come and meet me in Switzerland?"

She smiles her slow, reluctant smile. He loves to watch it; from tiny beginnings, it rises up to possess her.

"Before I catch the train, I'll be in London for one or two nights. Will you meet me there?"

"Don't say that because you feel you ought to."

"I don't say anything because I feel I ought to! I say it because I want to see you. I want to go on seeing you."

"I want to go on seeing you, too."

He puts his hands on her shoulders and turns her toward him.

"Shall I tell you the things I have not done before? I have never felt what I felt in Neqi—that connection that seemed to bind me to you. I've never crossed an ocean hoping to see a woman I barely know, but who has been in my head for three years . . . like a light."

He strokes her hair and traces a finger down the side of her face. "When you touch me, *I* can't think. And I don't want to be without you."

Her face has softened, but she has stopped smiling. "I don't want to be without you. I don't know what that might mean."

Neither of them can think, or will say, at this moment, what it might mean. But Flora kisses him, with the longing for reassurance, with relief; and with relief Jakob responds, and they begin to make love, even though neither really wants to, because doing so means they can forget and procrastinate, because, in the end, no matter how passionate or accomplished or tender, it is a sequence of repetitive and simple actions, and difficult decisions are not required.

When they walk out in the sunshine of that afternoon, Flora wears a blue dress that makes her skin glow. The knowledge of their lovemaking surrounds her like a cloak. They find a restaurant that looks suitably grand to appeal to their fancy. There are white tablecloths that crumple onto the oxblood carpet, shoals of silver cutlery, clusters of crystal. The menu is in French. They choose a corner away from the window. There are not many other diners at this hour, but perhaps there were not many earlier; it is expensive. Flora picks up the menu and studies it as though she were rehearsing a part. Her lips are pressed together in that look she adopts; to the outside world, it appears either that she disapproves of something, or that she is trying not to laugh. Even now, he cannot decide which it is.

"I don't understand most of it," she says with a smile (in London, she would have been too embarrassed to admit this). "What do I want, dear? Do I want *rognons* or *merlan*?"

"I don't know about *merlan*. *Rognons* are kidneys."

"Hmm. Then . . . I will have the tournedos. That is steak, isn't it? Very rare."

Jakob does something he has never done before and orders oysters and champagne. The napkins are enormous and stiffly starched—like snowy mountains. They eat oysters and she tells him that she left school when she was twelve; the university only accepted her because of her notoriety. He tells her about the Koppels. Although the account is grim, he is cheerful and funny. Flora longs to put her arms around him, but since she can't, she presses her leg against his under the table. The beef arrives and she saws into it, blood running onto the plate. She picks up a chunk on her fork.

"It makes me think of Greenland."

"I'd like to go there with you."

She looks up, moved.

"If I could come to Switzerland . . . would you really like it? I wouldn't want to be in your way."

She watches him, to gauge his reaction. He puts down his fork and takes her hand.

"I would like that more than anything." He doesn't smile. "Do you believe me?"

She nods.

They order dessert—Jakob orders lemon tart; Flora, *îles flottantes*. She has had it once before, and it seemed to her—a confection without flour, fruit, or even a good, honest flavor—to embody Continental decadence in the highest degree. When it arrives, she looks down at the smooth white mounds emerging from a yellow sea and wants to laugh; they seem ludicrously, erotically suggestive.

"Is it all right?" he asks.

The slippery soft stuff melts in her mouth, tasting of nothing, but suggesting much. On an impulse, she eases one foot out of her shoe, then, concentrating on her plate, works her foot onto Jakob's chair and between his thighs. He sits up with a jerk at first touch—she looks up questioningly—then looks sternly at his plate. She pushes her foot into his groin, finds it already half hard, and tries not to smile.

"How is your tart?" she asks.

"Good," he says thickly, and adjusts the napkin over his lap.

She puts another spoon of meringue into her mouth and squeezes it to nothing against her palate. She pushes against his hardening prick, feels it throb against her sole, and a wave of heat washes through her. He takes another mouthful, looks as though he is thinking of something far away. She feels faintly hysterical.

In the room at the Victoria, he unwraps her like a longed-for present, peeling off layer after layer of clothing. He undoes each ribbon, each button, with measured care. They don't speak; they are heavy and languorous with food and champagne. He moves around her, touching her so lightly his hands feel like lace. She shivers, but not with cold. His touch is so restrained and precise, she can hardly bear it; she feels something hot run down her thigh. He lays her on the bed like a precious garment. She watches him strip off his clothes and climb over her. He kneels, spreads her, looking down at her gravely for a long moment, then he lifts her hips and enters her with a rush that makes her cry out in surprise. It hurts less now, but the initial thrusts are still uncomfortable. Looking down, he watches himself withdraw, very slowly, right to the tip, then plunge in again with a groan. She looks down her body to see this take place; this masculine sleight, a magic trick: he appears and disappears. She shifts and her legs wind around his body. It is no longer uncomfortable. Encompassing him, taking him inside her body to keep, she digs her nails into his buttocks and he moves more urgently, stirring her in great circles, and she feels as though she is coming apart. He quickens, quickens, and his body clenches above her like a fist. It looks as though it hurts him. When he collapses on her, his skin glazed with sweat, his heart thumps so hard against her breastbone she is afraid he will have a heart attack. Or it is her heart. He rolls off her at last, panting like a runner.

She feels wetness in her eyelashes, in the hair at her temples. When they have breath enough to speak, they whisper words to each other across the damp pillow: promises they have no idea if they can keep.

Chapter 31

Zermatt, 46°1' N, 7°45' E
May–July 1895

You enter a porch, pillared by icicles, and look into a cavern in the very body of the glacier, encumbered with vast frozen bosses which are fringed all round with dependent icicles. At the peril of your life you may enter these caverns and find yourself steeped in the blue illumination of the place. Their beauty is beyond description, but you cannot deliver yourself up, heart and soul, to its enjoyment. There is a strangeness about the place which repels you, and not without anxiety do you look from your ledge into the darkness below.

—Monsignor Rendu, *Memoirs* (1841)

What effort of the imagination could transcend the realities here presented to us?

—John Tyndall, *The Glaciers of the Alps* (1860)

Jakob stands on the edge of the Gornergletscher in the predawn gloom of a May morning. It is overcast, and the world is softly monochrome. He adjusts the screws of the theodolite until satisfied that the lines are exact, then holds up his arm. Out on the glacier, the little figure that is Otto pushes a stake into the snow and hammers it in with great blows of a mallet, which echo in the still air. Otto makes the signal that confirms it is done, then strides an agreed number of paces to position the next stake. On the other side of the glacier is a vertical slab of rock. Yesterday, he and Otto clambered up the rock to paint a line on it. Theodor stood at the bottom, shouting excitedly up at them. There is a similarly distinct marker behind Jakob. He bends over the eyepiece, readjusts it, makes hand signals.

He enjoys this work; it is soothingly precise and repetitive. And the surroundings are peerless. The clouds are moving now. Dry snow squeaks under his boots. The gray of the dawn is slowly lifting; a blush of color and light pulls their eyes upward, to the mountaintops. The ice is deep and calm beneath them, creaking and grumbling like a sleeping animal.

Otto hammers in the last stake as the sun climbs over the shoulder of a mountain—which one is it? The Strahlhorn? Or the Rimpfischhorn? Jakob can't remember, but just turning over the names in his mind makes him grin. Otto waves again. Although he is so far away, Jakob thinks he can see his huge smile. In the east, the sky ignites. Buttery light crowns the great crumpled obelisk of the Matterhorn.

He wishes he could photograph these colors. He tries to describe this sunrise to himself, to fix the memory in his head as he would fix a photograph: nacreous pinks and blues, tender lilacs, soft golds; above the ridge a palest turquoise . . . But words will not do. The colors are elusive, ever-changing, compelling you to look until your eyes water.

Footsteps crunch the snow nearby. Theodor calls up to him, "See, *mein Herr*, today is not just a morning, no—today is the *ur*-morning!" And Jakob grins his agreement.

Jakob arrived in Zermatt two weeks ago, in the first week of May, and met Professor Theodor Birkel at the Monterosa Hotel. Professor Birkel turned out to be a handsome, saturnine man of forty, with a dark, neat beard and romantic mustache. From their first meeting, he treated Jakob as though, instead of merely exchanging letters and opinions on glaciology, they had known each other intimately for years.

"My dear chap"—Birkel liked to show off his rococo English—"how excessively pleasant it is to see you after so much time and letters!"

Jakob found himself laughing, and Birkel laughed too. "Ha! Do you speak German, my fellow?"

"*Ein bisschen*," said Jakob.

"Capital! *Herrlich!* Then I can introduce you to my stupid assistant."

"Delighted to meet you," said Jakob, in Lower East Side German, as Birkel dragged forward a blond, youthful giant with a toothy smile, who was hovering, round-shouldered, behind Birkel. His name was Otto Lichti. Birkel dealt him a great blow on the shoulder.

"Otto speaks no English whatsoever—he is a brainless peasant!"

Jakob gathered from the laughter that Otto was accustomed to this sort of teasing. The youth pumped Jakob by the hand, as though meeting him had been his lifelong ambition.

"But the boy knows how to climb; he is a mountain goat, a chamois; he is a marmot! Tomorrow we will show you where we are working, but now, come, we will eat . . ."

Birkel led them to a restaurant where he knew the landlady, and they were treated like royalty. They sat on the terrace, watching the sunset paint the Rothorn, though its ruddiness was swallowed up early—because behind them was the great dagger of the Matterhorn. It was astonishing: mountains that had only been names and photographs to him, infamous silhouettes, sprang to life, were more breathtaking even than he imagined.

Birkel outlined the work they would be starting in the morning ("if, my sir, you are not too fatigued after your journeyings?"), while Otto sat and smiled with his big white teeth. After his fatiguing journeyings, Jakob was moved by this simple, straightforward friendliness.

The week in Snowdonia with Professor Collee was not quite the success he had hoped for. As they peered at examples of the Caledonian orogeny through curtains of rain, the older man raked through Jakob's knowledge of the northern Laurentian Shield and, his manner implied, found it a poor storehouse. He had a habit of waiting until Jakob was scrambling over a wet rock, or slithering down a muddy path before springing questions on him: a technique perfected on generations of hapless students. Greenland was irrelevant, he concluded. It added nothing to his theories—and he certainly did not want to hear anything that might detract from his theories. Collee only came to life when describing his own work and its importance. He was an old windbag who had seen better days, but an old windbag who was spending his retirement writing a definitive textbook on the geological history of the world, and he could be helpful to Jakob, if he felt so inclined.

Jakob had arrived in Wales in high spirits, ready to be charmed by everything, even an irascible old professor, but the weather was atrocious, the sun—and usually the mountains—invisible, and the old man's querulousness tested his good humor. The farmhouse where they stayed was dark and damp, and the legs of his bed stood in saucers of vinegar—a precaution against what, he didn't even like to ask. He was tired, he feared he was really getting the cold he had claimed as an excuse, and he missed Flora.

"Young fellows these days—no stamina," barked Collee on the last day. "When I was your age, I surveyed Connemara, in the rain, for a month. Slept in a tent!"

The cold duly arrived as his train pulled into Paddington Station. Feeling ill and repulsive, the prospect of seeing Flora again made Jakob nervous. It was a week since their parting in Liverpool; a week in which the solitary bed he had looked forward to had felt increasingly lonely. He longed to see her, but, at the same time, what had taken place between them seemed almost unreal. Could that really have happened?

Flora came to his hotel, tense and distracted. He feared the worst. But his illness disarmed her; she relaxed when she saw how unwell he was; she even laughed, and apologized for laughing. She ordered him to bed, went out to buy supplies, made him beef tea with brandy in a spirit kettle. He lamented his state of health. She stroked the hair off his forehead.

"Don't be sorry. I was almost afraid of seeing you, but now I'm not afraid."

"Why were you afraid?"

She dropped her eyes. "Because, here, I feel more . . . wicked, I suppose. I didn't know if I could carry on. But when I saw you, I knew I couldn't not carry on. I feel torn in two . . ."

"Darling, you shouldn't feel guilty. You know, with a . . . a situation like yours, it's possible that he wouldn't mind. It's not as if you're depriving him . . ." He gave in to a timely spasm of coughing, aware this was gimcrack reasoning. In his mind, her husband was an ancient cripple—a barely human figure. He didn't want to know if this were not the case.

"I'm sorry, I'm just glad you've come. It's wonderful to see you." Talking made him out of breath.

"Shh. I'm glad I came as well."

"Would you rather I leave you?" she asked, when he had finished the tea.

"No. Only if you find me intolerably disgusting. I wouldn't blame you."

Flora shakes her head. "No, never."

"It's all right. I find myself intolerable, sometimes."

She bent and kissed his temple, his cheekbone, his jaw. The skin under his ear. The side of his mouth. Her breath fluttered against his neck.

"I want so much to kiss you, Flora, but I can't breathe."

"You don't have to do anything." She spoke close to his ear. "I want to get in next to you. Would that be nice, or . . . ?"

"It would be nice."

She half turned away as she took off and folded her clothes with self-conscious care. He half watched, telling himself that they weren't going to make love, but it was impossible not to look; she was uncovering her beautiful body just for him. She looked around and caught his eye, and he smiled in embarrassment, unsure why he was embarrassed. He was urgently excited, despite feeling, a minute earlier, at death's door.

Flora got into bed beside him, making the springs complain. It was a railway hotel and the mattress had known better days. Doubtless it had known other irregular liaisons.

"Oh, you're cold," she murmured. She made him take off his underwear, as if they were in Greenland, as if they were Eskimos. She pressed her bare flesh against his, putting her arm around him. He turned his back to her, so that she could curl herself around him and infuse him with her heat.

"Is that all right?" she whispered. She rubbed his arm and chest, and stroked his goose-bumped flank where it was tucked against her body. "Is that better?"

"Much better," he said, with a sigh. Her breasts pushed softly against his back, her skin was velvety and hot, felt as necessary as sleep. Something more than warmth flowed into him, below the level of thought. It made him feel safe. He thought of the last night in Siorapaluk, when she slept in a chair behind him, the conviction that she tended him and cherished him, no matter how little he deserved it. He was about to speak of it when she whispered, against his shoulder, "Sometimes I think there's something wrong with me."

"Why?"

"All week, I couldn't stop thinking about you . . . like this."

"I couldn't stop thinking about you either. I took you to bed with me every night—my narrow, lumpy, uncomfortable bed. The legs stood in bowls of vinegar. What was that for?"

"Oh, goodness . . . Rats? Cockroaches? I don't know." She brushed her lips over his skin. "What did we do there, despite them?"

"Mm . . . everything."

"Tell me if you want me to stop . . ."

Her hand went on stroking and caressing, circled nearer his groin—he said nothing—and finally brushed over his stiff and throbbing cock. Although he had resolved not to, told himself he didn't want to, he turned onto his back, breathing heavily. His body felt as if it were in two distantly related halves: the part near his head, depleted, useless, and feverish; his loins, a bursting mass of energy that she took hold of with a delicious purpose. He came with alarming speed and violence, gasping for air, and collapsed into a fit of coughing. She rummaged for a handkerchief and used it to wipe the semen off his belly; she was so tender and fastidious, it made him laugh—and then cough again. She folded the handkerchief, curled herself around him, and put her hand on his heaving chest, feeling for his foot with hers.

"Thank you," he said, and laughed at himself. "God . . ."

She laughed too. "You're warmer now."

"Mm. You're an angel."

"I am not."

"You're a lovely, warm angel and you're very kind to me."

"Kind?" She sounded almost angry. "I am not kind. Kindness is universal."

"Then I'm glad you're not kind. But you are an angel, and I'm sorry; I'm a poor sort of lover for you."

"No. I want no other."

Jakob released her hair from its coiled braid and laid it across his chest like a sash. He loved the feel of it: thick and strong: a rope on which you could climb to safety. He wound the ends around his hand.

"I have you," he said. "I'm not going to let you go."

"Do I have you too?"

"Yes, you have me. There's nothing you can do."

Her arm tightened around his chest.

"My train doesn't leave until ten, tomorrow evening. Will you come back?"

"Yes. In the afternoon."

"I'll be better then. Promise me you'll come to Switzerland."

Had there been a tiny pause?

"Yes, but you must write once you're there, and tell me if you still want me to come. You don't know what it'll be like; I don't want to be in your way."

"Of course I will write. But you couldn't possibly be in the way."

He thought about saying something sentimental. The words were in his head. He cleared his throat in readiness.

"You'll come back to London on your way home?"

"Yes. But you have to come to Switzerland. I will show you the most beautiful glacier."

"I'd like that."

He felt dizzy, and decided the words could wait until tomorrow.

The next morning he felt no better, and dragged himself to a chemist's shop, where he confided the gist of his problem to the young man behind the counter (Why not? He would never see him again). The chemist tapped the side of his nose and sold him a bottle of tonic wine, swearing it would cure any cold or other malady and marvelously enhance the vital forces, "temporarily, you understand"—this was accompanied by a wink.

The bottle featured a picture of the Pope, and the results were miraculous. Within half an hour of drinking a couple of glasses, his symptoms had all but vanished, and he felt exultant, brimming with energy and optimism. When Flora arrived, she was astonished (even amused) by the extent of his recovery. Jakob wanted to imprint on her an experience of pleasure that she would be unable to forget, that would wipe away his poor showing of the day before. It started well enough—he buried his face between her thighs and used his tongue to bring her to an unmistakable ecstasy. He reveled in the juices that ran out of her, swallowed what he could, then kissed her with lips still wet so that she tasted her own nectar.

But when he was inside her, deliciously held in the warm, wet embrace he had been dreaming of, he could not come to the finish, no matter how exquisite the sensations. This was unprecedented. He ended up—not part of his plan—threshing for an unconscionably long time, while his heart raced at unnatural speed, wondering if he were about to have a seizure, or if Flora were starting to hate him. At last, he gave it up as a bad job and rolled off her, panting, the temporary enhancement of his vital forces clearly (with one exception) over.

"Is something wrong? What should I do?"

She worried it was her fault. Jakob shook his head, which was throbbing again. He was exhausted; his stubborn, aching cock no longer felt part of him, but a separate, possibly malevolent, entity. He was downcast, their last embrace, for who knew how long, spoiled.

"Nothing. I'm sorry; I don't know . . ."

"It doesn't matter—not for me. I'm worried about you."

"It's all right. It must be the cold . . . or that tonic."

She picked up the bottle and read the label. "'Vin Mariani, strengthens and stimulates . . .'" She raised her eyebrows.

"Well, the Pope swears by it!"

They looked at each other and started laughing, and then couldn't stop. She folded him in her arms and kissed him, and told him to stop apologizing. The conviction that he had ruined everything abated. Nestled against her warmth, he felt an overwhelming peace. The afternoon was saved, one or other of them continually bubbling up with laughter; one look at the pontiff's goblin face was enough to send them into fits of undignified silliness. But the clock raced at unnatural speed, the minutes slipped away. They stopped laughing. She had to go home. He had to catch the boat train. When there was no more time, they got up and dressed in silence, without catching each other's eye. She helped him pack, then tied his muffler carefully around his throat, her eyes unusually large and dark. Dressed, Jakob felt they were both further apart and more bound than ever. They stood in the middle of the room with their arms around each other.

"I hate this—saying good-bye to you," he said; the tightness in his throat nothing to do with his cold.

Her lips by his ear, she murmured, "I know. I do too."

"You'll come? You must. I can't be without you now."

"Yes . . . My beloved."

The ticking from the mantelpiece clock was like an impatient hand, tugging insistently at his sleeve—not now . . . not now . . . *not now . . .*

But then it was now.

Chapter 32

For their first climb, Theodor and Jakob start up the Monte Rosa long before dawn ("Easy—an Englishwoman has climbed it!" says Theodor, scornfully). Jakob is entranced by the views unveiling in the waxing light. He has not climbed with such an experienced alpinist before, never attempted such faces, and, anyway, these mountains are different from those he has known: sharper, steeper, dizzier, in air that is, as the sun climbs with them, so warm and full of light that it feels like a tonic wine. By ten o'clock, they have reached the western ridge, and turn to look down at the vast whiteness of the Gornergletscher. Its dirt bands are sharply defined, sinuously graceful, and, from up here, perfect—the giant, coiling power of it winding away toward the Dent Blanche, the Obergabelhorn, the still scarcely believable Matterhorn.

"Jakob—over here!" Theodor calls to him from a hundred yards away. Jakob tramps over, keeping to the exact center of the precipitous ridge. He finds the height and airiness alarming, but he is all right as long as he doesn't look straight down.

Theodor, careless of the dizzying drop on both sides, takes his friend by the arm and extends his other arm in a lordly sweep. "I present you—Italia!"

To the south, the land falls away in a layered, violet haze. He feels as though he can see for hundreds of miles, over the curvature of the earth: there is Vesuvius . . . Sicily . . . Africa! In every other direction, white peaks and blue shadows dazzle them, stretching away beyond sight. Above, the sky darkens to ultramarine. His chest heaves with the thinness of the air. He takes off his pack and unstraps his camera, grinning with delight.

To be near their work on the glacier, they live in a mountain hut perched on an alp studded with tiny, gem-like flowers. The three of them sleep on wooden bunks that are little more than shelves. Every morning, a young shepherdess walks up the mountain with a basket of food—milk, cheese, bread, and onions and soft, wizened apples that have been maturing in a cellar since autumn. For the evenings, the girl's mother makes them meat stews, packed at red heat in a basket stuffed with hay. The girl climbs all the way back up with the heated basket at the end of the day. She doesn't mind this toil; she has fallen in love with Otto, and his smile grows even bigger. He accompanies her down the mountain after dinner, "to protect her from beasts," and comes back, surefooted, long after dark. ("We should not too much envy him," says Theodor wistfully, as they watch them go down the path, hand in hand. "He insists to me, she is a girl devout.")

Jakob and Theodor spend evenings in the hut huddled near the stove, reading, writing letters, and talking. Despite their short acquaintance, Jakob has come to regard him as a close friend. It is the closest he has felt to a man since Frank died. But Theodor is wiser and more worldly than Frank—different, in fact, from any American Jakob has known. He has been married for fifteen years, and a professor for nine. His wife and children live in Freiburg, where he has the chair in geology. He also has a mistress, who lives handily close to the university. He writes to the two women in rotation. He is very fond of them, he says, but prefers climbing to both. "Yes, my friend—just as exhilarating, and mountains do not argue with you, or demand new clothes, or sulk."

If Theodor is alarmingly pragmatic, he is never gross. He seems to be that rare thing: an intelligent, cultured man who is happy. When Jakob accuses him of this, he replies that he is always happy in the mountains. His enjoyment is infectious. When Theodor hints about the recipient of the serial letter Jakob is writing, he does it so gracefully that Jakob hardly feels annoyed.

"It is someone most dear to you? I thought so. It is in your face when you write." He smiles with modest triumph when Jakob assents, and turns to Otto, who looks at them, not understanding.

"*Ich hatte recht, Otto. Er ist verliebt, genauso wie du!*"

Otto grins sympathetically at him.

Jakob looks down, feeling the vertigo he holds at bay on the mountains rush forward: that same mix of exhilaration and fear.

The crowning achievement of their work for the summer is to study the Gornersee. This is a phenomenon Jakob has never seen before: in spring, meltwater pools into a lake at the crux of the Gorner glacier and its tributary, the Grenz. When Jakob first sees the lake, it is little more than a pool choked with ice. He cannot resist boasting to Theodor about Melville Bay and its palatial bergs.

"One day, my friend, we will go there," says Theodor. "But, for now—if you stay long enough—you will see something wonderful."

Over the following weeks, the lake grows. The water takes on a milky, turquoise hue. It is so sheltered that it forms a perfect mirror to the mountains and the sky. It is their intention to study what happens when the lake, as it must, drains away. It might be gradual, seeping and tunneling under the ice, or sudden. The glacier must move differently when such a weight of water is released. Their measurements will, for the first time, reveal how it changes. But the truly marvelous thing is what might be left behind: tunnels and caverns carved by the passage of water. Jakob cannot wait; at last, he may get right inside a glacier.

In the evenings, he writes a serial letter to Flora, partly because he cannot get to the post office in Zermatt often, and partly because they agreed not to write too frequently, which might raise suspicion. The disadvantage to this style of communication is that he reads over what he has written day to day, and has second thoughts. It is easy enough to write about his work and the grandeur of their sur-roundings; less easy to describe how he feels, without using hack-neyed phrases that make him uncomfortable. He is averse to cliché, but he can no more pin down his feelings in his own words than he can capture the colors of the morning.

It doesn't help that sometimes he feels ashamed. Looking back, it seems to him that they hardly got out of bed, and he thinks about her body so much that he worries he has done her a wrong. When dawn tips the mountains with its rosy light, he finds himself thinking of her breasts. In fact, almost any aspect of the Alpine landscape—dark wedges of pine tucked into the hillside; little pink, pea-like flowers; bergschrunds—turns out to have undreamt-of erotic potential. He is afraid she might think herself used.

As a result of this uneasiness, his letters are stiff and awkward. He wants to express feelings that are on a higher, more ethereal plane, but words are not his strong suit. He throws many attempts into the stove. And he cannot write about the nights when he gives free rein to his memories and fantasies. He doesn't want her to think that the pleasures of the bedroom are all he thinks about, even though, when he goes to bed (or rather, climbs onto the shelf near his snoring companions) they are almost all he thinks about.

His most cherished, oft-repeated memory begins with the sea-green tiles of the Victoria's bathroom, which lay at the end of the corridor. He can picture their exact, rather bilious color, their gloss. Flora wanted to wash her hair, and he begged her to let him watch, which he thought pleased her. As she washed, and steam from the noisy plumbing swirled around them, bedewing his clothes, he encouraged her to talk about her childhood on the *Vega*, a topic of never-ending fascination to him. She felt a little awkward to have him there, to be naked while he was dressed, but he knew she did not find it unpleasant. He made himself useful by sitting on a stool and trickling water from a jug to rinse her hair as she held her hands over her eyes. She glanced up at him from time to time, noting his eyes on her body as the water found pathways over shoulders and breasts. Then, when her hair was clean, he soaped his hands, leaned over, and slid them over her breasts. She lay back in the bath and sighed, watching him with a sleepy, amused look in her eyes.

"I thought you wanted to talk to me."

"I can do both," he said, as he caressed her, although, as it turned out, he couldn't. He became mesmerized by the slippery plumpness and heft of her breasts, the nipples instantly hard and teasing to his touch. Sometimes she seemed almost maddeningly alluring: flushed with heat, each line of her body a lovely convexity, as if she had been filled and plumped with water. His fingers dived under the surface and he watched her face, with closed eyes and uneven breathing, as he concentrated on rousing the red bud of her clitoris until she whimpered and threshed, unable to prevent, delightfully, water slopping over the sides of the bath. He was sure he could feel the waves clenching and rolling down her body as she struggled to stay still. Panting, she let the water in the bath grow calm again, and then stood up into his waiting arms, wet skin silvered in the light from the window. He helped her out and they kissed—he could feel her mouth smiling against his, her tongue growing abandoned, reaching for the inside of his skull. She was his shining, silver catch, soaking the front of his shirt and trousers with her hot wetness. She pressed herself against his erection; he was extremely hard, already close to bursting point. He grasped the damp flesh of her buttocks, bent at the knees until he could push his fingers up inside her and felt her breath, her moans, her tongue squirming in his ear. He took each provoking nipple in his mouth, rubbery with water and tasting of soap. Her breasts smothered him. One of her hands was rubbing his bursting groin, while the other plucked at his trouser fastening. She moaned as he turned her to face the tiled wall, but reached behind in encouragement as he wrenched open the last buttons of his fly and pushed his trousers down over his thighs. She bent forward, her back a white road in front of him, hair snaking darkly over her skin. Round white hips framed swollen flesh, made for him a triumphal arch. His cock ached, the skin tight and sore with use, but was inexorable; he found his way into her wet, welcoming cunt with a burst of delight; she was his homecoming, his hot, sweet harbor. He looked down, holding her hips just so, pulled out almost to the tip of his glans, and slid inside her again, for the pleasure of watching himself disappear, appear, disappear. Watching, feeling the heat inside her body, the way the walls of her vagina clung to him as he withdrew, the storm that seized him was violent and unstoppable. He thrust into her as hard as he could, heard her cry out, saw her clenched fists, didn't know what they meant, was unable to stop had he wanted to. He gave himself up, was hurled upon her shore; he was shipwrecked and silent and safe.

There were tears streaking her face, he found, when at last he could see and realize something outside his own body. Worried, he stroked her hair and kissed her.

"Darling, what is the matter?"

She looked around at him, seemed dazed and far away. She shook her head, sniffled, and smiled through the tangles of wet hair. "Nothing . . ."

Later, she said, when he asked her again, "It was as though I had left my body behind. I had no end . . . It was . . ." Again, she shook her head.

"Was it good?" he asked.

"Yes, it was good," she whispered, shy, smiling in that embarrassed, provocative way he loved.

Back in their room, they did not speak, but lay in each other's arms on the rug in front of the fire, covered only with her peignoir. Jakob grew cold and uncomfortable, and the arm that pillowed her head was dead to the world, but he did not want to be the one to break the spell.

Burnished with repetition, the memory is more than exquisite; it has the power to move him like the act itself. It leaves him shuddering and emptied in the darkness of the hut. Sometimes he questions himself: Had it really been like that? An experience so seismically intense it seemed not to take place on the level of his individual body, but must, surely, have thrown up a mountain range, torn a continental plate in two . . . He felt shifted, on some profound, subterranean level. And, hard to be sure, but he thinks she was similarly moved; such a violent, rapturous collision. Perhaps his memory exaggerates a little, but, in the end, does it matter? Each separate event that afternoon happened, each caress is burned into his mind. Like Theodor's indescribable, perfect sunrise; it happened, and nothing can ever take it away. An *ur*-morning. An *ur*-fuck. He has sometimes thought that there is one, in every relationship. Perhaps in every lifetime. Is that his?

He writes, *I so look forward to seeing you again, my darling. I hope everything is going to plan, and that your next letter will bring me news of your arrival.*

True, accurate, polite . . . bloodless, insipid, dull. Words (his words, at least) are hopeless. When he sees her, then she will know how he feels. He wants to write something vital, something that will take her breath away. He wants to say something about the future, their future, but does not know what it could be. The future only exists in words, and they have never talked about it, so there is none.

It is a warm summer, and, in late July, the Gornersee empties. It happens overnight, but they are there, having noted the gradually dropping strandline around the lake's rim for days. On the fourth night of their vigil, while they take it in turns to watch by lantern light, it begins to sink more rapidly. Otto wakes the others and they stare, realizing with excitement that the level is dropping visibly. There is, to begin with, little sound: just a muffled murmuring. They leave the lanterns burning on the ice and clamber higher up the scree slope above the lake, wedging themselves in next to large, deep-rooted boulders. Jakob stares at the points of light in the vast darkness, straining to make out the water. Then there is a low, growing growl. Then a rumbling. Without stopping, the rumble grows into a roar that goes on and on; then, in the space of a blink, the lanterns all go out together. Jakob blasphemes as, in the darkness, the roaring becomes tumultuous and they feel the deep shuddering in the mountain. They can no longer see anything—because the lanterns have fallen into the lake, because the lake has fallen into a chasm, and great blocks of ice tumble after it. Rocks and stones hurtle down the slope around them. The mountain is moving.

"*Halten Sie sich fest!*" yells Theodor, and Jakob clings to his boulder.

He wants to shout out—something, anything—and then he hears Otto yelling: a wordless scream of exhilaration. Or exhilaration mixed with fear, because the world is tumbling and roaring around them, and they cannot see what is happening. Then they are all screaming, making noise, giving out whoops of joy and terror because something as beautiful and perfect as the lake is destroying itself.

In the morning, gray light creeps slowly back into the valley, as though ashamed of what it reveals. A chaos of ice: sugar-white blocks the size of houses, riven with blue veins and fissures, giant spoil heaps of dirty rubble ice, boulders and scree ripped from the mountainside where they had clung—all this choking a deep ravine that yesterday did not exist. Where once was a turquoise looking-glass reflecting the still majesty of the mountains, now there is nothing but destruction.

"There may be floods, downriver," says Theodor, as they pick a cautious way down to what was the shore of the lake. Jakob sets up his camera and starts to photograph the chaos—no one has ever photographed this before. He tries to stand in the exact places from where he previously photographed the lake, but the landscape is so changed it is nearly impossible. He lines up the skyline, the peaks as he remembers them. Exulting in the back of his mind is the thought, I will show her this: I will show her caverns of ice.

They work slowly and thoughtfully. They had shouted with glee as the glacier ripped itself apart in the night, but now there is an atmosphere of melancholy. A cold wind pours down from the Lyskamm as they plod about, measuring and recording, pausing to stamp their feet and clap their hands to ward off the cold. The change in the glacier is extraordinary: below the collapse, their numbered markers have been ripped up and thrown about, but, by plotting their positions, they can piece together the short history of the convulsion. Their experiment is a resounding success. But what was yesterday beautiful, serene, lovely, is now smashed and spoiled.

A couple of days later, as bad weather prevents them from working or climbing, Jakob and Theodor walk down to Zermatt in pouring rain. At the Monterosa Hotel, Jakob finds a letter from Flora awaiting him. Heart beating hard with joy and anticipation, he tears it open as he walks into the residents' lounge to read it in the light of the window.

Theodor collects his own letters and exchanges pleasantries with the desk clerk. He is in no rush. He envies Jakob; he remembers the days when he would have been as excited to receive his sweetheart's letters. A long time ago, alas.

After a minute or two, Jakob folds up the letter and puts it back in the envelope, staring fixedly out of the window at the drumming rain, while water drips from his trousers to form a puddle on the carpet.

"*Alles gut?*" says Theodor absently, because this is what he always says.

"Ah . . . yes." Jakob's voice is distant and unconvincing.

Theodor looks up from his own correspondence—a tale of minor domestic dramas, childish ailments, a social slight suffered—notices the stiffness of his colleague's back, and realizes that something is wrong. He knows Jakob was hoping his inamorata would visit him in Switzerland (a prospect Theodor privately deplored; he does not mix women and mountains, himself), but perhaps not, now. She has been false to him, he thinks, and a small, jealous part of him rejoices. But when he sees Jakob's face—that of a man paralyzed by vertigo, his smile a rictus—his better nature reasserts itself. My poor young friend, Theodor reflects (women cannot help it; their nature is essentially perfidious), he is not as worldly as he thinks.

Flora's letter is short and to the point. She writes that she is very sorry, but her husband is very ill and she cannot leave him. She will not be able to see Jakob again. Under the circumstances, it is impossible. She hopes he will understand.

PART SIX

THE CONCRETE SEA

In the fourth century BC, the Greek navigator, Pytheas, wrote about his voyage to Thule, furthest of all; the "land under the pivot of stars," where he experienced the sun that never set and the "*pepeguia thalatta*"—the hardened ocean. At the time of writing, there was no North Star. The celestial pole was empty.

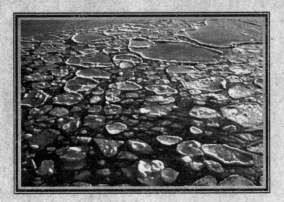

Chapter 33

Washington Land, 80°45' N, 65°09' W
1895–6

The most expensive ship in the history of Arctic exploration sinks in Kennedy Channel on August 17. Not a life is lost, but Lester Armitage wishes he were dead. The *Polar Star*, the ship in which he has invested so much—his time and ideas and energy, not to mention his own and other people's money—has failed, and he has failed, and that is all that anyone will remember of him. The last of the crushed and mangled hull takes forever to disappear—the bowsprit remains stubbornly visible for days, poking skywards, a memorial to his ambition, and a rebuke.

His plan and his hope of the last four years—and the success of his ambitions rested precariously upon it—was to force a ship through the pack ice to the north coast of Greenland before wintering on the shore of the Arctic Ocean itself. This would enable him to begin his polar quest from significantly closer to the goal. And, in the summer, they had gotten so far, through Kane Basin, past Hall Basin and Thank God Harbor, right up Robeson Channel, reaching farther north than any ship since the British Navy's *Alert* nearly twenty years ago, all in a difficult season of heavy ice and relentless gales, and then they were nipped fast in tremendous crushing ice. Arguments raged between Lester, the head of the expedition, and the captain of the ship, Newfoundlander Thomas Chafe. At this point, they were being carried north by the winds—well, north was the way Lester wanted to go, whereas Chafe wanted to burn all the coal in his lockers trying to ram their way out of their moving prison and find a safe harbor. When they were within a biscuit toss of the Arctic Ocean, the winds changed, and they were swept back to the south, without coming close either to freeing themselves or finding safety. They stopped arguing when they realized their arguments were moot; the ice that held them didn't let up for a second. The ship had been doomed from the start.

Wooden splinters, empty barrels, discarded belongings, foodstuffs, filth, and the general detritus of a steam ship—all those are still there. They are scattered mockingly over the pack ice, and the crew and Eskimo passengers set off over the floes to the nearest land—the Greenland coast, north of any native settlement, but far south of the Arctic Ocean.

Like any explorer, especially any Arctic explorer, Lester has to make the best of things. They build their hut on a sliver of shore under the iron-clad cliffs of Washington Land, but it is uncomfortably crowded—designed to take only the members of the expedition and some Eskimo helpers, it has to accommodate the shipwrecked crew as well. Forty-five people now live in a building meant for twenty. As winter draws in—or, rather, falls on them, like a hammer blow—resentments bubble up.

Captain Chafe—no longer captain of anything—unable to control his sailors, and unsure what to do with himself, manages daily to achieve what should, by Lester's calculations, be impossible: he is almost continuously drunk. One of the sailors deserts to live with an Eskimo woman in the south; the others, deprived of routine and authority, grumble and whine: this is not what they signed up for. Why can't they wander off by themselves? (Because they will get lost and die.) Will they be paid, despite the loss of the ship? (Yes.) Will they be paid extra for the hardship? (No.) What is the point in getting up at seven when it is always dark and there is, anyway, nothing to do? (A hard question to answer.) Lester worries about them, but most of his concern is focused on John Hyland, the expedition doctor.

Hyland is a narrow, intense man with thin, chiseled features and a wispy blond beard, vigorous and seemingly immune to cold. Initially, Lester had liked this intensity; he reminded him a little of his younger self. Now he realizes his mistake. His other recruits are more biddable: George Shattuck and Philip Royce are young men from good families who sat in his office and demonstrated a flattering respect for Lester's achievements. Shattuck is the expedition's biologist, and Royce is another of those keen, well-connected young men—Lester met so many—who was looking around for something to do, but whose sheer willingness to please (and family's generous donation) made him an irresistible choice.

Lester learned lessons from his first expedition, and avoided more experienced scientists with ideas and ambitions of their own which conflicted with his drive to explore. But it is a fine balancing act between choosing men who can lead others when necessary (that is, when he deputizes them to carry out a task vital to his overall success) and those who thirst to be a leader on their own account.

They are now only days away from his long-planned departure for the Pole. It is early in the season—the sun is just a dull glow on the southern horizon—but, because they are further south, they have further to travel, and must make both outward and return journeys before the warming sun makes travel over the sea-ice too hazardous. It is a daring attempt. Lester almost believes they could do it. But Hyland has a way of puncturing noble ideals.

"How are your bowels?"

They are standing behind the wall of wooden cases that separates Lester's bunk from the rest of the hut, and (usually) lends him a fragile, much-needed privacy. It has been temporarily co-opted as Hyland's consulting room.

"Oh, you know," says Lester. "All right."

"Sluggish?"

"Well, sometimes. Whose aren't?" He forces a smile.

"Mine are fine," says Hyland. He has no sense of humor. Lester has no sense of humor either, but does not realize that they have this in common.

In the darkness of the February afternoon, Hyland carries out the latest of his fortnightly checks on the health of the expedition's members. Although just twenty-five, he is a strong character who has gained in stature over the winter. Lester has tried to get on with his plans, but he has—to be frank—not been entirely well for several weeks. He finds his usually formidable powers of concentration drifting, and his thoughts dwelling on all the things that have gone wrong. He suffers from stomach cramps (not unusual with their unbalanced diet, but still). Worse, he has become uncharacteristically clumsy. This morning, he stood up to leave the breakfast table and somehow knocked over the jug of coffee. What frightens him about this trivial incident is that, even replaying his actions in his mind, he cannot understand how it happened. He has never done such a ham-handed thing in his life. To make it worse, he swore in front of the others, and saw from their expressions that he had lost face. He wonders, for the first time, if they see him as an old man.

"I don't like the look of your tongue," says Hyland. "And you're pale. How are you sleeping?"

The doctor peers into his eyes under the hanging lantern. Lester almost recoils. Hyland's skin is unpleasantly smooth and tight. The eyes seem merciless, as though he senses weakness and is homing in for the kill.

"I sleep fine. Damn it, Hyland. It's February! We're all pale. We're all sluggish. That's what happens in winter. You haven't been here before, but the winter night is simply to be got through. I've been doing a lot of work that you probably don't appreciate—writing and planning for the spring. I have hundreds of calculations to make, thousands of decisions to weigh! When you all retire for the night, my work is only half done. I have the well-being of the Eskimos and the sailors to consider as well! I have . . . I'm wasting time with you now. I need to get on. Perhaps you could continue with the others in the main hut."

Hyland has taken a step back, and his eyes widen.

"I mean no disrespect, chief. I'm simply trying to carry out my duties. If you are overburdened, could you not delegate some of your tasks to the rest of us? We are often underemployed, and—"

"I am not overburdened! And my decisions cannot be delegated. When you have more experience, you will appreciate these things."

Hyland swallows. "Of course."

He nods, blinking, and goes out, grappling with the red blanket that serves as a door. A minute later, Lester hears him talking in a low voice to someone in the main room—yes, Shattuck. Undoubtedly talking about him. Annoyingly, he was thinking of delegating some of the calculations. But if he does it now, Hyland will think that he is taking his advice . . . Will that weaken him in their eyes? He reflects that he would, anyway, have to check over somebody else's work. Taking responsibility, doing what needs to be done—that is what a leader does.

He doesn't remember having these doubts on the last expedition. Has he changed over that time, or does the fault lie in the men he has chosen? He never thought that he would feel nostalgia for the uncouth Erdinger or de Beyn's irritating levity. And he positively misses Frank Urbino. The doctor was such a good companion: strong, helpful, practical. Most of all, loyal—an incalculable virtue. What a pity things came out the way they did . . .

Two days later, preparations for the polar journey are finished. Calculations have been completed and checked, rations packed into sledging cases. Lester and Philip Royce, along with two Eskimo drivers and forty-eight dogs, are due to leave.

After breakfast, Hyland hands Lester a letter. In it, he states that he has diagnosed the leader with the early stages of pernicious anemia, and possibly scurvy, and, in his opinion, he is not fit for the journey to the Pole. Lester takes him aside and relieves him of his duties as his doctor.

"You cannot!" cries Hyland, aghast. "I am the medical officer and I have to tell you what I find. I have a duty!"

"It is not your duty to interfere with the expedition's goals. In any case, I dispute your diagnosis. I feel fine!"

Hyland shakes his head. "What if your condition leads some of the men into peril?" His face is even whiter than usual under his fur hood, and he appears to be trembling with emotion. "That would be on my shoulders."

"My condition? I have no condition! You are not God, Hyland! You are a very young man, with very little experience of this part of the world. With little experience of medicine, I might add. We are all here to serve a greater purpose for our country—that is *my* duty, and I must fulfill it. All other duties are secondary."

There is a pause.

"Will you please clarify my position, sir?"

Lester bares his teeth. "Of course. You will carry out your medical duties to the best of your ability, but if anything appears to threaten the plans of the expedition, you will inform me, in confidence, before you do or say anything else."

Hyland draws himself up, becoming even taller and narrower. They are both shivering, having stood outside for the last five minutes in temperatures of minus twenty.

"Very well. I strongly suggest that you increase your intake of raw liver. It may help with your symptoms—"

Lester tries to smile through his anger. "Thank you, that will be all, Dr. Hyland."

"One more thing—Royce's toe is refusing to heal. I cannot recommend that he . . ."

By the end of April, Lester has to concede that his polar attempt has failed. Perhaps it was always going to fail, because the Pole was too far from their starting point. But he was not helped by Philip Royce being too lame to walk, or by the Eskimo dogs falling prey to a mysterious illness that halved their numbers in the first two weeks of the journey. The final blow came when he, with Shattuck (a poor replacement for Royce, it turned out—by turns vacillating and stubborn) and the two sled teams, driven by Metek and Sadloq, after struggling for days across a wilderness of crumpled sea-ice, came to a stretch of open water that cut right across their path. They explored the shores of this huge lead, but it stretched out of sight for miles east to west, and was more than three hundred yards wide. Shattuck had the temerity to say what a pity it was they had not brought the collapsible boat. There was one in the hut, but it had been sacrificed (he really had no choice) in the complex calculations of weight, food, and distance. Lester ordered them to make camp and they waited to see if the lead would close up or freeze over—the sea-ice was always moving, and their position shifted even as they sat there, the icepack drifting them to the southeast. But the open water remained, and more dogs died.

Lester wondered if the lead was a permanent feature of the polar pack. Three of their remaining dogs were lost when a piece of ice broke off their shore and floated away in a gale. They never saw them again. Metek and Sadloq were restive and sullen, muttering to each other and falling silent when he approached. After a week of waiting, while Lester calculated their dwindling food supply, dividing it into the miles between them and their destination, and the Eskimos threatened to leave them, he gave the order to return. Only he knew that, with their painfully slow rate of travel, their food had never been sufficient in the first place.

After his bedraggled return to base, he has to think up ways of salvaging something from the wreckage of his expedition. Well, he has been farther north than anyone else—although by a paltry twenty-two miles, which is almost humiliating. He wonders whether to stick it out until next season, but doubts he could carry the men with him. It is all due to the infernal bad luck of the sinking of the ship—without it, the crew are a dead weight, on the verge of mutiny. All they want is to go home. With just a few good men, the right men, he could do it, but not with a hut full of whining, idle sailors. Was ever an explorer so beleaguered as he?

Lester often works out his plans by writing letters to his wife. Dearest Emma, to whom he can write anything. Anything that reflects his best self, and thus recalls him to his duty, his honor, and his destiny. She is a good wife: loyal, patient, and proud. Before he left on this latest venture, she had crushed him to her (she is a robust woman) and said to him, "I know you are a hero, my dear. I always knew, ever since we first met. I knew that my children would have a hero for a father. No matter what happens, I will be behind you."

He weighs up his success, or otherwise, in her eyes. It makes for a chilling appraisal. Newly discovered land—none. Sponsors' names immortalized on map of same—none. Meteorites—none. Mummies or similar sensational artifacts—none, and no chance of them. Miles northing—a few. A paltry, ignominious few. Simply to get home, they will have to sled south to the Eskimo villages and hope to get picked up by a whaler.

He can spin a story of disaster and shipwreck and survival, but he needs something else—something unprecedented and newsworthy. Otherwise, his career as an explorer will be over before he has had the chance to really achieve anything. He thinks of his forebears in impossible endeavor, of Hannibal and his battle cry: "Find a way, or make one." So be it.

Chapter 34

London, 51°31' N, 0°7' W
Summer–Winter 1895

At the supper party to celebrate the publication of her new book, Jessie Biddenden was taken aback when Flora Athlone congratulated her with a hug; although possibly not more taken aback than Flora herself—this was, after all, Jessie, by whom she had always been intimidated. Iris, who could see Jessie's face over Flora's shoulder, smiled knowingly to herself. Anyone for whom Flora had any tenderness noticed a change in her: she touched them more often; leaned toward them, laid a hand on their arm. Some put this new warmth down to maturity; some, when the news about Freddie's illness became widely known, to her assuming a more maternal role toward her husband. It took Flora some time to realize what she was doing; her body was bereft, it cried out for contact of any sort. She drew her friends to her, because they were all she had.

Iris was the only one who knew what had happened in Liverpool, and Flora made her swear never to talk about it again—this on the evening Flora told her that Freddie had suffered a paralytic seizure, and that she would not be going to Switzerland, after all. A terrible blow, a double blow, but it was not, Iris thought, like the day she had found out about Mark Levinson's marriage. Flora had grown up since then. Iris felt sorry for her—the romance had been such an adventure, and Iris felt that, after four years of presumably thrill-less marriage to Freddie, she deserved some adventure. But, as Flora herself said, it was not as though she and the man in question had been intimate for very long. It was really just a . . .

Here, Flora paused in front of the open window and allowed herself to be dazzled by the sunlight that poured into Iris's drawing room.

"Just . . . an experiment. To see what it would be like. After all, even without all this, there could be no future to it, could there?"

"I suppose not—living so far apart," said Iris.

Flora had not turned around from the window, and Iris wondered if she should go to her, offer a condolence. She thought her friend looked unwell, and her eyes were puffy, as though she had been crying. Otherwise, she did not *seem* particularly upset—she was dry-eyed and frowning in apparent concentration at the trees in the park opposite. Children's cries, laughter—the sounds of an English park on a summer evening—wafted in through the window. Perhaps she was just preoccupied with Freddie's illness—that was quite enough to worry about. Flora let out a sigh and turned away from the blazing sunlight.

"I'd better go back. The doctor is coming again later."

Iris quelled her Presbyterian distaste for scenes and took Flora's hands in hers.

"I'm so sorry about this, Flora. Please give my love to Freddie. Let me know when I can come and see him. And, of course, if there is anything at all I can do . . ."

Flora held on to her hands in a way that was uncharacteristic of her. The look in her eyes gave Iris a tremor of concern.

"Actually, there might be something . . ."

At that moment, there was a noise on the stairs that meant Helen had returned. Automatically, Iris withdrew her hands and turned to check her reflection in the mirror, biting her lips, wondering (as she always wondered) if Helen would be in a good mood.

"Why don't you come here on Thursday? Around two. Can you do that?"

Iris stepped away from her as footsteps mounted the stairs. Flora nodded. The door burst open (Helen never just opened a door) and she marched in, unbuttoning her gloves and throwing them on the sofa. Everyone agreed she was more dazzling than ever. There was something almost horrible about her vitality, like that of a carnivore whose existence is predicated on many small deaths.

"Lord! It's that hot . . . Hello, Flora."

"Hello, Helen. I'm sorry, but I'm just on my way out. My husband is not at all well."

"Oh. Sorry to hear it."

Flora almost admired the way Helen flaunted her insouciance while mouthing platitudes. Then Helen smiled, and glanced from Flora to Iris with a look that was so bold, Flora caught her breath. When she looked at Iris again, she knew that Iris had shared her deepest secret with her lover. She found it difficult to forgive her.

Flora went back to Iris's house that Thursday, not because she wanted to, but because she did not feel she had a choice. She had never liked Helen—had given up trying to disguise it—and particularly did not like the fact that Iris was so in thrall to her. Helen seemed to her the most self-centered person she had ever met. Iris never denied it.

They sat in her drawing room, full of a reflected green light from the plane trees outside. Flora did not know how to begin.

"I'm sorry, my dear, but I don't have all day. What is it?"

"What I'm going to say, Iris, I don't want you to tell Helen. Will you promise, please?"

"Yes, all right," said Iris, frowning.

But after Flora had explained her difficulty—it did not take long; a humdrum, depressing tale—Iris was silent for a minute.

"My dear, I'm afraid that Helen is precisely the person I must tell. I don't think I know anyone else who could be of help. She herself has been in this situation. She went somewhere in Pimlico, I think, and it was no problem at all, over in a flash, apparently, so . . ."

"Oh. Well, if you think there's no other course . . . I can pay. That, at least, isn't a problem." She kept her eyes on the floor and said, in an exhausted voice, "Lord, Iris, it's such a mess."

Iris reached over and took her hand.

"Come, come. It is an unfortunate set of coincidences, to be sure, but one thing at a time. Do I take it that your gentleman friend doesn't know about this?"

Flora shook her head. "No. There's no point. Especially now."

For the first weeks after Liverpool, Flora existed in a state of feverish, sometimes dream-like excitement. With Freddie, little by little, she sounded out the idea of a summer trip to the mountains. She wanted to try alpinism, she said; it would be good practice for the next northern trip. She thought first of Austria, then seemed seized by the idea of Chamonix and the Mer de Glace . . . Cunningly, she wove a web of half-truths and misdirection. She told Freddie she had decided on Switzerland because, there, she could meet an industrialist and his wife: potential sponsors who would be spending the season in Zermatt. The whole fabrication sounded fantastic to her, but Freddie made no adverse comment, nor did he press her for details. The very fact that he displayed so little interest made her wonder whether, in fact, he suspected the truth; in which case, did that mean he understood? Even condoned it? For a time, she allowed herself this thought, and was comforted by it. They were getting on well—better than they had for a long time. One evening, they were talking, when Freddie stopped, almost mid-sentence, and smiled at her.

"What? Have I said something to amuse you?"

"I'm just glad to see you like this—you seem happier than in a long while. I know I'm dull company, Flora. I worry sometimes that you're living a life unsuited to one of your age."

"Oh! Heavens . . . No," said Flora.

In truth, the prospect of going to meet Jakob was a kind of torment. She longed to be with him, ached for it, but the idea of going with the sure intention of adultery was somehow odious. She lived to see his handwriting on an envelope; even her address, written in his hand, affected her as though he were tracing the letters on her skin. In her bed, she relived their intimacies, touching herself as he had touched her. In her mind, she re-created every detail of the room at the Victoria, and all they had done there. Sometimes she couldn't believe it had been real. She wondered if this violent craving was indeed love, or a sort of illness. She did not want to recover. She pored over his letters, which alternated between rambling and enthusiastic accounts of his work and climbing in the mountains, and sweet, stilted avowals of his longing to see her. But the more she reread them, the more she was nagged by doubt. Did he really care for her? The letters said that he did, but she thought she detected a certain distance. Was she imagining it? And even though she knew they were only letters, and letters can never be entirely secure, she was disappointed, even hurt by their lack of passion. He did not refer to any of the things they had done, the things that obsessed her. Did that mean (as he had warned her) that he was not a good letter writer? Or had his passion waned—was he drawing away from her, having second thoughts? Had he met someone else?

Then she began to feel unwell. As spring turned to summer, she could not ignore the growing suspicion, the accumulation of evidence, the feeling of dread. She, who thought she had been so careful—even she could be caught. Her own body was a snare, it had lain in wait, and it had trapped her.

Possessed by a slow-burning anger (but it was her fault—she had believed she was safe), she tried the handful of remedies for "obstructions" that were advertised in certain magazines. Patent they may have been—unpleasant, certainly—but they did not work. She was frightened and furious—with him, with her own body—most of all, with her lack of sense.

One day in July, after the most recent failure, Flora was in her study. She reread Jakob's latest letter, wondering whether she could or should share the problem with him. Trying to guess his reaction to her pregnancy, she could not imagine any response but horror and blame, or, worse, suspicion that she had done it on purpose. Instinct warned her against it; what could he say or do that would change the situation for the better? What if he had indeed changed his mind? In anticipation of this hypothetical rejection, she felt rage, and was already in a temper when the housemaid committed the sin of bursting into the study without knocking. Flora turned around, ready to tear a strip off the girl.

"Mam, sorry mam, it's Mr. Athlone . . . He's . . . he's . . ."

The girl's face was gray. The words Flora had been about to utter were never spoken. She shoved the letter into a pile of papers and knocked her chair to the floor in her haste to follow the girl out of the room. She found Nurse Capron kneeling over Freddie on the floor of his sitting room. He lay in a twisted huddle, his left arm slack, his face appearing, horrifically, *melted* and his eyes . . . his eyes, when they saw her bending over him, beseeched her in terror.

Flora knew that God was punishing her—for, now, how could she leave?

It was more than a week after the stroke that she wrote to Jakob to say that she could not come to Switzerland, and that, under the circumstances, to see him again was impossible. The reason she gave was her husband's illness, but the business in Pimlico was at least as much a reason—she had been terrified, angry, and alone. That might not have been Jakob's fault, but *he* had not had to go to the dismal street leading down to the river, wearing a ridiculous veil for fear of being recognized. *He* had not had to endure the indignity and squalor, the smoothly insinuating doctor and his oddly cheerful female assistant. (Actually, they were perfectly decent and respectful, and tea and biscuits were included, but her temper was thoroughly sour.) He had not had to go through the painful, bloody aftermath. At least it had worked.

In the end, things did not go as badly with Freddie as they first threatened. The seizure left him partially paralyzed. His left side was useless, his speech a mangled drone, so that at first she feared his mind was affected, although it was not. It was terrifying to see; he seemed to have aged years that morning, and he was not yet forty. Full of a burning pity that seemed stronger than anything else she felt, Flora sat with him every day, determined to be cheerful and kind, to show her real affection for him, to devote herself to his recovery; the doctors were guardedly hopeful. If she felt neither guilt nor repentance for her infidelity, she *was* ashamed—for all her horror at seeing him struck down, her first thought had been for herself. She wanted to make up for her selfishness, and, in some incoherent, unscientific way, she felt that sacrificing what she most wanted would help Freddie, would go some way toward . . . She never knew how this thought would finish.

As summer flared briefly, waned, and turned to autumn, Freddie's recovery was steady—remarkable, even, the doctors said. Everyone was impressed by his courage, and by Flora's devotion. After several weeks, he began to regain the use of his left arm, and, over time, the slurring in his speech was much reduced. By Christmas, he was able to resume letter writing, and he encouraged Flora to pick up the plans for her next expedition.

Never, at any point, did he remark on the canceled trip to the Alps.

Chapter 35

London, 51°31' N, 0°7' W
Spring 1896

It is a bitter April, especially in the museum's basement. The boy—he can be no more than fifteen—levers up the lid with a shriek of iron on wood. Flora peers into the crate that sits in a corner of the freezing cellar—not actually frozen, unfortunately: moisture is running down the walls. The lamp he holds gutters in the foul air. Flora hopes the smell is only drains.

She pokes a hole in the straw and uncovers a terrible grimace. The boy jerks the lantern back with a gasp, making shadows dance wildly over them both.

A shock, the first time you see it again. But it is not quite as it was before. The skin is dark. Flora dabs her fingertip to the mummy's forehead and holds it up: a smear of black mold.

Dr. Murray did not know the mummies were in the basement. He is overwhelmed with treasures from all corners of the Empire.

"I'm sorry, Mrs. Athlone, but we have so many things to look after here. All equally important."

"They are covered in mold! I entrusted them to you. They are unique. No museum in the world has anything like this!"

"I know. I will . . . I'll see that they are moved."

"That's not enough. You can't let them rot! These are . . . They're *people*! They had names, and souls, and . . ."

To her horror, she finds herself choked with tears. Murray stands patiently by. Flora fishes a handkerchief out of her pocket and blots her eyes, breathes deeply for a moment, recovers herself.

"I apologize, Dr. Murray, but it distresses me to think that, after all the effort and care we spent to bring them back for the . . . the edification of the people, they are being neglected like this."

"I understand. I assure you, we will see to it. We have a consultant chap who helps us out when we have something unusual. I'll write to him."

"Today?"

Murray brightens. "Right away. In fact, I think I saw him earlier. He may still be in the building."

"Then we could go and find him now . . ."

Flora is embarrassed by her outburst. She did not feel sentimental about taking the bodies from their grave, is not superstitious about gaping mouths and empty eyes, and shares none of Ralph's religious scruples. What is the human body, after all, but an envelope: a vehicle, perhaps not for the soul, as she claimed, but for the mind?

This morning, she woke to the knowledge that it is April 18, a whole year since she met Jakob in the Adelphi. She has tried to put the memories out of her mind, but in Murray's office they overwhelmed her. She had a powerful sense of him. The feel of him. Impossible to think of him as separate or apart from his body. Not just impossible—a nonsense. The mummies were once as particular as he, as warm to touch. Their names and flaws and loves are secreted in the past, but none the less real. Their bodies are themselves.

She follows Murray down corridors and staircases, and into a low-ceilinged room full of stuffed animal carcasses. Two men are bent over a table under the high window.

"Ah, Mr. Carruthers? Could I borrow Mr. Levinson for a moment?"

Flora is rooted to the spot. Mark turns around from the table and stares in shock. Neither of the museum men seems to notice. They are introduced. Flora finds her tongue at last and says, with a suspicion that she is blushing, "Mr. Levinson and I have met before. We were both students at the University of London."

"Were you? Well . . . capital! Shall we take a look at the beggars now?"

After the mummies are put into their new, temporary home in an unheated gallery, Flora contrives to leave the museum at the same time as Mark. From his silence, she is aware that he would rather not be alone with her.

"Mark, please wait a moment." She glances behind her. "I know we didn't part on good terms, but that was long ago. It doesn't matter now. And if we're going to be working together . . ."

Mark grimaces. She is struck by how much the same he is—energetic, prickly, his hair a wiry halo. His glasses could be the same pair . . . even the jacket—it is not the same lovat tweed jacket she grew to love, but a close cousin.

"You haven't changed at all," he says, accusingly, to her surprise. She almost laughs.

"Oh . . . I have. I have."

"Not to look at. Of course, you're even more famous now. 'The Snow Queen' for good and all! I read about you, you know, in the papers—what you're doing."

Nonplussed, Flora jabs the ground with her umbrella. "Now you've seen the mummies, I hope you can do something."

Mark looks away from her. "I think probably they'll be all right. I've worked on Egyptian mummies. The principles must be similar."

"I'm relieved to hear you say it. How did you . . . ?" She shrugs and gestures to the building behind them.

"End up doing this? Because, when I . . . left the university"—he pronounces the words with a delicate savagery—"I had to get a job, and I started working for a taxidermist. He was a good man; he saw I was wasted, and he persuaded me to go back and finish my degree. Now I teach chemistry at the Regent Street Polytechnic and, um, do this on the side. A brilliant scientific career!"

"Oh."

Flora would, if it were anyone other than Mark, venture congratulations, but she can imagine how these would be received.

"How is your family?"

Mark snorts. "They're all right, if you really want to know. And you—you married the rich man. I knew you would."

"*I* didn't . . . know, I mean. But—yes."

"So, everything has worked out for the best, then! Well, Mrs. Athlone, it's been exceedingly nice to meet you again, but I have to go."

He raises his hand in a mocking half-salute. She lets him walk away, since that is what he seems to want: to have had the last word.

Over the next few weeks, several things fall into place. Ralph Dixon writes from Cape Town, saying that he has married the daughter of a South African lawyer, but will nevertheless be delighted to join Flora's second expedition as its geologist. A young Cambridge doctor called Henry Haddo applies to join them. He has a special interest in scurvy, and is not only keen, he is highly thought of. There is a sizable cash donation from an industrialist she has never met. She entertains, briefly, the idea of offering a place on the expedition to Mark, just to see the look on his face.

Strange how stubbornly life goes on, when all had seemed hopeless. The expedition is coming together. News has emerged from the north that Lester Armitage's expensive ship has sunk, and he has failed to do more than extend the furthest north by a few miles, which gives her a secret satisfaction. People are starting to believe that she will go north again.

But, sometimes, when she goes home, she walks through the front door and wants to scream. She goes in to see her husband and asks how he has been, and is humbled by his suffering. Freddie is not given to complaining, but most of his energy is absorbed by his failing body. Nurse Capron puts him through a program of exercises every day, and there is hope that he will be able to do more than limp for short distances. But, because it is hard to distinguish the effects of the pelvic injury from the stroke damage and his underlying syphilis, the prognosis is unclear. When she asks him, he rarely says anything other than that there is slow progress.

"At least," he says, "I'm not getting any worse."

She doesn't know if this is true. Recently, he has been having trouble with one of his eyes. This, she eventually finds out from the doctor, is a symptom of tertiary syphilis. Neither Freddie nor Nurse Capron would tell her. The two of them have a peculiar relationship: they bicker constantly, but she hears them laughing too. They never laugh when she is there. They have shouting matches, but Freddie never raises his voice to Flora. Irrationally, she feels excluded.

He apologizes for being helpless, for not doing more for the expedition, which makes her feel selfish and unworthy. The more selfish and unworthy she feels, the angrier she becomes. She is twenty-five. She thinks, From this point on, I will only lose what allure I have. I am dying here, unloved and untouched. She reminds herself of all she has to be thankful for. At times, she finds herself wiping tears from her eyes, over supper, but only if she is eating alone.

After she wrote to Jakob breaking it off, he replied once more. This letter was less stiff and formal than the others. He begged her to change her mind, said he would be in London in a few weeks; perhaps she would feel differently then. If she would just write and say she allowed him to write again . . . The letter struck her as sincere, but she did not know how to answer. The abortion had soured her memories of their affair, and of him. She was angry with him for being ignorant of it, but imagined his anger, if he knew. She wanted to be with him, longed to be in his arms again, but she was scared.

She would never be careless again. Such joy, such happiness, she had learned, comes at a price.

The stroke left her, in different ways, as paralyzed as her husband. Some part of her thought that Jakob must understand how she felt; she knew that he would come back through London on his way home, and by then, perhaps, she would know what to do. But September passed, then October, and, as the nights drew in and Freddie grew stronger, she realized, with leaden certainty, that Jakob had already gone.

Chapter 36

New York, 40°42' N, 74°00' W
August 1896

Exotic visitors at the museum!
Mr. Armitage brings People of the North to Manhattan!
ESKIMO Men, Women, Dogs!!
Remarkable spectacle . . .

Headlines in the *Brooklyn Advertiser*, August 1896

The visitors make all the papers. Jakob is not surprised to find that
Lester Armitage has done such a thing, but he is surprised when
he reads the names of the Eskimos currently residing in the Natural History Museum, even put through the editorial mangle of the
Brooklyn Advertiser: "Anick" and "Ivalo" are surely the *angekok* and
his wife (Lester's former mistress—can he really have brought her
back to America?), then "Ajax" and "Patla," which puzzled him until
he realized they sounded like the injured Ayakou, and his wife, Padloq (but hadn't she left him?). They are to go on tour. They will give
demonstrations of dog-driving, igloo-building, and hunting. They
can be viewed for a price.

He is sitting at the breakfast table with Hendrik and his niece, Vera, when the headlines catch his eye. He experiences the familiar jolt of discomfort (he refuses to call it envy) that the sight of Lester's name causes him. Indeed, who could envy Lester his last expedition? Jakob's potential sponsor, Scotty Welbourne, cabled him after the news of the *Polar Star*'s demise got out: *Ha! We will beat him yet!*

"Vera, look, there are Eskimos here in New York."

His niece seizes the paper. At ten, all too conscious of her lameness, she has grown quiet, serious, and solitary.

"Uncle Jake, can we go and see them?"

"That's a good idea; why don't you take her?" says Hendrik, finishing his coffee and wiping his mustache. "That is, if you have time."

"Of course. I wouldn't miss it. I think I know these people. Ajax is really, I think, Ayakou—the hunter whose leg was broken when . . . when Frank died. I have to visit the engravers this morning, but this afternoon—if you're free, madam?"

Hendrik stands up. "While you're at your engravers, I must shout at people about the new refrigeration facilities—totally inadequate. Meat cannot be trifled with."

"No, indeed. Your father is quite the tycoon, Vera. A regular meat baron; a peddler of flesh."

"I know he is," says Vera proudly.

Hendrik glares at Jakob, and kisses his daughter on the head.

"Don't believe everything your silly uncle tells you, honey pie. And, for heaven's sake, don't repeat it in front of . . . anyone."

He was going to say "in front of your friends," but stopped himself in time.

Hendrik worries about his brother and his daughter; they share a quality he distrusts: he thinks of them both as having their eyes fixed on something beyond the horizon, longing for something that cannot be seen and might not be there at all. It is a bad card in the deck, an unlucky hand. He and Bettina have nothing of the sort, and their son, Willem, has escaped too, but he sees it in Vera.

It has taken Jakob to far-flung and no doubt interesting places, but, last fall, when he came back from Europe, Hendrik had never seen him so withdrawn and unhappy. He claimed to have had a productive time, but Hendrik and Bettina agreed that he seemed to have lost something: a part of his bright spirit, that mercurial quickness that had always been his most attractive quality. Perhaps it is only the inevitable consequence of growing older, and yet . . . As for Vera, who is not only a girl, but a cripple—what sweets can life hold for her? If she does not marry (and she is not even pretty, so who will have her?), what can she do with that lively mind? Jakob doesn't help matters; he inflames her imagination with his pictures and stories, fills her head with wild, unlikely ideas.

Only a week ago, Hendrik took her aside and said, "You know when Uncle Jake tells you about the places he's been to? I know he sometimes says he'll take you there, but, really, he won't be able to do that." He forced a laugh. "Girls don't go to such places."

"Uncle Jake's friend does—Mrs. Athlone. She's been to Greenland. She had her own expedition."

Hendrik sighed. He has wondered about this Mrs. Athlone, privately deciding she sounds no end of trouble.

"What you mean is, I can't go because I'm lame. I know that." And she looked at him with her clear, level gaze.

Hendrik felt his heart turn over, painfully. "Little treasure . . . I just don't want you to dream of things that are impossible, and then be disappointed."

"I know. It's all right." She smiled and patted his hand. He thought how it was supposed to be the other way around.

Jakob and Vera walk up to the museum in ninety-degree heat, fanning themselves with playbills. Jakob wonders how the Eskimos are coping. Inside the museum, he makes inquiries of an attendant, who says they are not on display at the current time. When he persists, he is passed on to an official, who says that the Eskimos are "away."

"They're not going on tour until September," says Jakob, as pleasantly as he can manage.

The official frowns. "No, but there are other engagements. They are important visitors."

"Of course. When will they be here again? I brought my niece especially to see them."

Vera tugs his hand in embarrassment, hisses, "Come *on*, it doesn't matter!"

The official's eyes dart all over the place. "I can't say for sure."

"Never mind, Uncle Jake." Vera is used to disappointment. "We can come another time."

"Let's visit the basement while we're here. That's where they're supposed to be." He hustles her toward some stairs. "I'm not sure that man was telling the truth."

"Why wouldn't he?"

"Because I think something's wrong. Shall we find out what it is?"

He smells them before he sees them. There is a mephitic dankness in the air this summer, but in the basement corridor he smells something he has not smelled since Greenland—rancid seal fat, sweat, and urine. Vera gasps but keeps silent, and, as they approach a closed door at the end of the corridor, it bursts open and a man walks out.

"This corridor is out of bounds. Get her away from here!" he shouts, slamming the door.

Through the open door, he briefly sees bodies lying on the floor. Jakob takes Vera back upstairs and puts her in a cab.

"I'm sorry, Vera. You'll have to go home. I have to see them. They're my friends and they're in trouble. Do you understand?"

Vera nods solemnly.

Things are worse than he thought. Jakob pushes open the door and stems the doctor's objections with the explanation that he is a friend of the Eskimos. The doctor, who has never encountered people like this before, welcomes him.

"Thank God. I thought you were never coming! When I saw the girl, I didn't realize . . . I can't understand them, even when they claim to speak English! It's impossible to keep them clean."

"You're expecting someone?"

"Of course . . . For days I've been expecting you!" He registers Jakob's puzzled expression. "You are Mr. Armitage?"

"No. I'm Jakob de Beyn. I was the geologist on Mr. Armitage's first expedition—that's how I know these people. But I am here in a private capacity."

Jakob turns to Aniguin, standing patiently beside them. He wears Western clothes, and his hair has been cut short—the effect is very odd—but he smiles his gap-toothed smile, seemingly delighted to see him.

"Te Peyn, you have come! Are you well? Is Armitage here?"

"No, Aniguin. I haven't seen Armitage in a long time. I'm not here on his behalf."

"He told us to come to New York, that we would see wonderful things. He told us it would be good for the Inuit. But Ivalu is ill—look. And he has not come to see us."

"I'm sorry to hear it, but I'm happy to see you all. *Qooviannikumut.*"

He greets each of them. Ivalu and Ayakou are lying on makeshift beds of dirty furs, breathing with difficulty. Ayakou grips his hand and smiles, but seems unable to speak. His brow is beaded with sweat. Padloq, the wife Jakob remembers, sits beside him, mending a boot. Their daughter, Aviaq, a girl about Vera's age, gives him a solemn stare. He turns to the doctor.

"What's wrong with them?"

"What's his name? Ayakou? He has pneumonia in both lungs. And his leg pains him. It was badly broken. This woman"—he indicates Ivalu—"has pneumonia too. The other females have head colds, but I fear a turn for the worse. I've tried to throw away those furs, but they made such an unholy fuss—they seem to prefer them to clean beds."

"I expect they're all they have with them from home. Who is responsible for them?"

"I was asked to come by Mr. White, the assistant curator."

Jakob looks around at the close, airless room. The only daylight—and air—comes from a grating near the ceiling.

"They should be in a hospital. Where do I find Mr. White?"

"His office is on the second floor."

Jakob turns to Aniguin. "We'll find somewhere better than this place. Somewhere they will make you well."

"Can you do that, Te Peyn?" Aniguin looks at him. "Will you speak to Armitage?"

"I'll do better than that. If necessary, I will speak to the press."

"Who is the press? I do not think I have met him."

In the end, he has no need to go to the press; at the threat of a genuine Arctic explorer telling the papers of the sad state of the Eskimos, Mr. White—a youngish, heavy-set man with a pink face and plump, hairless jowls—panics and, within days, the Greenlanders are moved to Mount Olivet Hospital.

Jakob writes to Armitage, saying that he is sure he has no knowledge of their conditions and that he will personally see to their well-being. He asks about plans for taking the Eskimos home. His indignation is unfeigned; he is filled with an energy he has not felt for a long time.

A few days later, he visits Mount Olivet to find them in a worse state than before. Ayakou is asleep, but his breath struggles in his throat. The young girl, Aviaq, has become ill with pneumonia-like symptoms.

"You hear from Armitage?" Aniguin asks.

"No. He may be away."

It could be that Lester is away, or that he is busy. Or it could be that he has seized on Jakob's intervention as an opportunity to wash his hands of the whole embarrassing affair.

"Did you want to come to America?"

They walk up a slope to a stand of trees, and pause in the shade. Flies and gnats buzz around them. Jakob takes out a handkerchief and blots his forehead. Aniguin lets the sweat run down his face, unheeded.

"Yes. Armitage says I can talk to important people—perhaps then there will be more trade. We need tools. You need furs and ivory. Few whalers come now. I don't know why. There are whales still."

"Ayakou? Did he want to come?"

"No." Aniguin's voice holds a tinge of contempt. "He was afraid to come, but he is a poor man at home, since he cannot hunt. Padloq said she would return to his house if he came to America. He will be rich if he comes, and brings back many things, you see."

Jakob nods.

"Te Peyn, why did you not come back with Armitage?"

"There are things we did not agree on, Aniguin. I'm a scientist, and he is an explorer above all else. He wants the Pole."

"Ah, yes. He wants to go to the Big Nail." Aniguin shrugs at the pointlessness of such an idea. "Where is Fellora? Why has she not come back?"

Jakob hesitates. The sound of that name causes an unpleasant pressure in his chest.

"I don't know. She lives far across the sea, in Britain."

"I would like to send her a letter. Can you write it? Perhaps she will take us back."

"No one can take you north before next spring. If Armitage does not promise to take you back, then I will take you."

It is a bold claim, but as he says it, he feels the resolution crystallize.

"It will be winter soon. There will be snow here. In spring, I'll take you back."

Aniguin shrugs.

"Spring is far way. What if we die? I want to send a letter to Fellora. Now I am in America, I act like the *kallunat*. You see, Te Peyn, I cannot be *inuk* here. There are no spirits in America. I cannot make my people well, not even my wife."

Chapter 37

"I worry about him. He suffers with his knees—he was very lame when I was there, although he tries to hide it."

Flora has just returned from visiting her father in Dundee.

Iris sharpens the ash of her cigarette to a point. Helen has gone to see her mother in Stepney, and they are alone—something that is rare these days.

"He's not young. These things happen."

"That's what he says. I wish he weren't alone."

"So his sailing days are over?"

"I don't know. I hate to think, if he can't, what he will do. He's not yet sixty."

"Would you have him to live with you?"

"Oh, I don't think there is any danger of that!"

The thought makes Flora laugh. Her father's opinion of London has not improved since she moved here, and, although he doesn't say so, he finds her intention to return north, leaving her husband (in short, behaving like him), unnatural and unbecoming.

"He keeps reminding me of my wifely duties! Of course, he doesn't know . . ."

Iris smiles. "I've been meaning to ask . . . Is there anyone . . . ?"

"Is there anyone . . . ? No! No . . . heavens." She shakes her head. "I can't imagine . . . You know, I still think about him."

"The American? I thought that was water under the bridge."

"It is. Still, I can't seem to . . . Stupid, isn't it?"

Stupid thoughts; pointless. When she gives in to them, she pores over his letters, the face in the photograph, just to remind herself that it was real. Some of her memories are vividly intense: the softness of his skin, the way he felt inside her. (But would not—this is the kind of thought her mind proposes—would not any man have left those impressions?) Other things—both less and more intimate—are slipping out of her grasp. Although she has his likeness, she finds it hard to remember the way he looked at her, his peculiarly sweet morning smile. Every time she looks at the picture, it threatens to make them again into the strangers they were on the beach at Neqi.

"When Freddie fell ill . . . I was so afraid for him, I told myself I was doing good by being there. I thought if I gave up what I most wanted, it might help. Isn't that ridiculous? He would have recovered anyway."

"I think he would have suffered greatly if you'd left him."

"I wasn't going to . . ."

Iris looks at her, as if assessing the truth of this.

"The last year has been a trial. But things are looking up, aren't they? Freddie's doing well."

"Yes, considering."

"Have you heard from *him* again?"

"No. He wrote, after I broke it off, asking me to reconsider; he said he would come to London on his way home and . . . It just seemed too awful to make an assignation when Freddie was so ill—different, somehow, from before. And . . . you know. I didn't know how to reply. I'm sure he's forgotten all about me. Perhaps it never meant much to him in the first place."

"You thought he was quite attached. As you were to him?"

Flora looks to the window. "I felt so. But I have little experience. How would I know?"

"Oh, stuff—you're not an idiot. It seems to me that you have two choices: either forget about him—and, believe me or not, eventually you will—or write to him again. Either he won't write back, and then you will know, or he will—and then you would have a problem. Either way, you will have eliminated uncertainty. I recommend the first course."

"You make it sound simple!"

"Well, it is simple . . . and quite mundane, to be honest."

Flora laughs. "I'm sorry to bore you!"

"Oh, *you* don't bore me. Other people's loves—Lionel Fortescue, for example, falls in love every third Tuesday, and each time it's the greatest romance since what's-their-names'—but not you."

"Shall I tell you something that may not bore you?" Flora gives a strained laugh. It is something that has been on her mind, a nagging devil of a question that won't go away.

"Do you want another drink?"

"No, thank you."

Iris helps herself to brandy and soda water, her back to Flora. Even so, Flora can speak only by focusing on the floor and the patterns of leaf shadows.

"You see, I don't know . . . I think, if I could think of him . . . without desire, then I would know if what I felt was love, rather than just . . . But I can't separate them, so I don't know."

Iris comes back and sits beside her. Flora wonders if she is laughing at her, but, when she dares to look up, Iris appears to be considering the matter seriously.

Flora continues, "Sometimes I wonder if what we call love is just . . . a kind of selfishness. If you take pleasure from another person, and their presence makes you happy, then . . . well, that is *you* taking pleasure, and wanting to be with them is *you* wanting to be happy . . . Is that not self-interest? Isn't 'love' just the word we use to dress up our desires? I wonder if I'm just . . . selfish."

Iris is looking at her with the beginnings of amusement.

"Goodness, Flora, what a creature you are! Of course love is self-ish! But so what? Marriage is just the social sanction for arrange-ments of financial and physical benefits . . . You are no more selfish than anyone else. Less, in some ways: you have stayed with Freddie."

"There is nothing unselfish in that. He's done far more for me—"

"But, forgive the vulgar question: Are you happy?"

Flora laughs. "As happy as anyone is, I imagine. As my father likes to say, 'Life is not a pleasure garden.'"

"Mm. Well . . . But if I understand you correctly, you aren't sure whether it's the man himself that you're missing, or, shall we say, the intimacy, in which case, your course seems obvious."

Flora sits back in her chair, regretting her outburst. "That's not what I said!"

"Isn't it? As you are forever telling me, you're a scientist. Well, as a scientist, undertake an experiment."

"What experiment?"

"The man . . . or the act? You cannot have the man, at the moment, but . . ." She raises her eyebrows.

Flora bursts out laughing.

"It's logical, is it not?"

"No! It's not logical! It's . . . appalling. You're an appalling woman."

"I merely observe that, firstly, his feelings are even more of a mys-tery than your own. More pertinently, you are here, and he is in New York. A great mass of water separates the two—or so it appears to my limited understanding."

Flora studies her empty glass. "Perhaps I would like another . . . No, I'll get it."

"Nonsense, give . . ." Iris sweeps to the end of the room. "Have you seen Mr. Levinson again?"

"He's working on the conservation of the mummies, so I see him at the museum, of course. What is this apropos of?"

"Apropos of nothing, my dear."

Iris hands Flora the fresh glass. As she does, the lace cuff on her sleeve falls back, revealing a bony, white wrist marred with dark marks.

"A minute ago, you were complaining that you lack experience. Experience is there to be had. I can make suggestions, if you really have no ideas of your own. Lionel, for instance, has always shown a marked predilection for you."

"Oh, God!" Flora nearly chokes. "How old is he?"

"He's thirty-nine—which, let me tell you, is not that—"

"He *says* he is thirty-nine," says Flora. "And he wears rouge."

Iris raises her eyebrows, as if she is at the end of her very long tether.

"It was merely a suggestion, and I'm told, on good authority, that he gives great satisfaction. You don't want some young boy who doesn't know one end of a woman from the other. I observe that you can be unkind, sometimes, Flora. It is a fault of youth."

Flora stares at her in frustration.

"Well, I observe that you have bruises on your wrist again, Iris, and that is apropos of nothing, also."

Chapter 38

New York, 40°42' N, 74°00' W
October 1896

"You've found a sense of purpose? You seem different. More serious."

Clara leans back in her chair, squinting through wisps of smoke. They sit in a booth of a restaurant, and the light above their table casts unforgiving shadows. Jakob has not seen her for two years.

"I've been drifting about for too long. I meant to do this sooner—for Frank, as well as myself. Now others are relying on me."

"You still feel you need to avenge Frank in some way?"

"I wouldn't say 'avenge.' But Armitage used Frank's death to bolster his false claim, and I don't want his name to be associated with a lie he would have had nothing to do with, had he lived."

"You admit that is just your belief."

"That's why I have to prove it beyond doubt. Sooner or later, the truth will come out. More people will go there—eventually, everything will be discovered."

"What if Mr. Armitage was telling the truth?"

"Then Frank really is the discoverer of a new island. That too will be beyond doubt."

"And what do you want for yourself—rather than for Frank or Aniguin and the others?"

Jakob smiles. "I want to do some exploring, it's true. I want to work on the glaciers there, the sort of work I did in Switzerland. No one has studied glaciers at such latitudes."

Clara squashes out her cigarette.

"I hope you manage it. Now, do you want to hear my gossip?"

"Of course," he says, with a small sinking feeling.

"Well, to begin with"—she smiles—"Anna is engaged to be married."

"Really?" He's glad to find that he feels genuine pleasure. "Who to?"

"To a very respectable gentleman she met at the spiritualist's meetings. Mrs. Jupp—you remember? Anna went on going after Marion decided it was not seemly to make contact with the spirit of one's former fiancé when one is engaged to someone else. But she had the temerity to tell us that Frank's spirit gave her his blessing! Can you believe it? Anyway, that is where Anna met Mr. Nathaniel Stafford. He's a widower; terribly ancient—over fifty—but they seem well suited. He's artistic, has a great long beard, that sort of thing. He was trying to contact his dead wife."

"Goodness . . ." Jakob laughs. "Did she give her blessing too?"

"I'm sure she did. He has the grace to have a sense of humor, so I'm cautiously optimistic."

"I'm delighted to hear it. Your parents must be so pleased."

"You cannot imagine. He's even well off, so that's a great load off their minds. She's done better than any of us."

"So, with Marion engaged, have you told your parents about Frank's daughter?"

Clara is silent for a moment. "Somehow I've never found the right time. I was afraid they'd be angry with me for not telling them earlier. I realize that's a poor excuse. I'm ashamed."

"Don't be. I could tell them. I could say that I've just found out, from Aniguin. You need not have known. I should not have given you that dilemma."

Clara makes an impatient movement. "No. God. It was my decision. Wrong decision."

"Now there's no impediment, I think they should know. I'll see the girl—next year, I hope—so they should have the chance to . . . send her a message, or whatever they want—don't you think?"

Clara nods. "She must be three years old. I can't pretend I didn't know. Perhaps—if you were willing—we could tell them together?"

Jakob is touched by this sign of trust. "Yes, if that's what you would like."

"I think I would. You can explain it far better than I."

"Will you invite me to lunch, then?"

"I will, but I haven't finished the social circular." She pauses and gives him a beady look. "Lucille is married."

"Oh! I am glad."

"Surprised?"

"No; why should I be?"

"It was rather sudden. She'd only known him a few weeks. They've moved to Buffalo, where he practices law."

"Well . . . You've met him?"

"No. For some time past, we weren't as close as we once were."

She smiles, lifting her chin and her eyebrows—an expression of finality.

"I'd like to offer her my sincere congratulations," he says, after a somewhat awkward pause.

"I don't know if that's a good idea."

Jakob swallows, looks away from her. "I was, and am, very sorry for the distress I caused. Perhaps I understand now what I did . . . better than before."

"Oh? You have been wounded in the heart, at last? About time."

He laughs. "Thank you for your sympathy."

"Was this when you were in Switzerland?"

He hesitates. "In part. I thought she felt the same as I did—was certain of it—but . . . apparently not. There were complications. She was married."

"Oh."

Clara cannot suppress the flicker of intelligence in her eyes, and he thinks, She knows.

"Did she make you think she would leave her husband?"

"I don't know that we thought that far."

He cannot begin to describe his affair with Flora. Planning hardly entered into it. To stave off further questions, he leans back and smiles.

"What about you? You've always been so mysterious."

"Ha!"

"It's not impertinent to ask, is it? We've known each other for years. I can't believe you haven't had offers."

"Oh, I was born to be an old maid."

Jakob looks at her skeptically. Clara lights another cigarette and sucks in the smoke. She looks around her, smooths the hair under her jauntily angled hat.

"Are you going to stare until I answer? Well, I did meet someone, of whom I thought, I have arrived. I've come home, because you're my home." She smiles, but he can tell she is strongly moved. "Do you know what I mean?"

He nods. "I think I do. What happened?"

"Well, clearly"—she spreads her hands, taking refuge in sarcasm—"they preferred somebody else."

Jakob leans forward and touches her on the hand. "Then he was a fool. May I be impertinent now and ask who it was?"

Clara takes a deep breath and lets it out in a jerky sigh. "Oh, I don't think I can tell you."

He bows his head, then something extraordinary occurs to him, and he looks at her, wonderingly. She reads the look on his face.

"It's not you! God! Men are so vain."

Her tone is so outraged that, even in his mortification, Jakob has to laugh.

"I . . . Sorry. Of course . . . Ha! It's just that I always wondered, myself, what might have happened if, instead of Lucille finding me in the beer cellar that night, it had been you."

Clara stares at him, her eyes very large and brilliant. "Did you? But you see . . . it was Lucille."

"I know, but if it hadn't been . . . if you'd been there—"

"No, I mean, it was Lucille. The person who was my home: it was Lucille."

Jakob is struck dumb. He remembers—cringing—incidents from the past, trying to fit them into this extraordinary new pattern. He is deeply embarrassed, not so much out of shock, although he *is* shocked, but because the revelation makes his actions appear, in retrospect, so idiotic.

"I've shocked you."

Clara looks at him with an expression he cannot judge.

"No . . . I mean, I'm surprised. I had no idea."

"No one was meant to have any idea."

"No, but I don't quite understand. In that case, why was she so upset by what I did?"

"Lucille never agreed that she was really like me. She wanted things I couldn't give her: family; a kind of respectability." She shrugs. "I hope she finds that now."

"Lord, you must have hated me." He laughs nervously, but thinks back to his blind, priapic blundering. What a conceited fool he'd been . . .

Clara shakes her head. "I didn't hate you. What you did was not so unreasonable . . . It was just too hard to see you together. I thought you might marry; it was horrible. I would have lost you both. You're part of Frank—the only part I have left. That sounds wrong . . . I don't mean that I don't value you for yourself, because I do. I do."

"I'm sorry that, well . . . for everything. Most of all, I'm sorry you didn't get what you wanted."

Clara takes the hand he holds out to her. He feels he has passed some kind of test.

"I always thought I could tell you, and you'd be nice." She puts her other hand over his. "I, too, am sorry you did not get what you wanted."

At her parents' house, they break the news of Frank's daughter to Mr. Urbino. Jakob is at pains to explain (once Clara is out of the room) that Frank was far more chaste than the rest of them, was overcome with feelings of foreboding, feared he might not return, etc. Mr. Urbino listens with apparent calm.

When he congratulates Anna on her forthcoming marriage, he thinks she seems a different person from the tragic mourner of two years ago: more mature, clearly happy. There is a lunch, with much laughter. Looking around the table, Jakob thinks, They have survived. They prosper. They have come to terms with Frank's death—far better than I.

When Jakob returns to Brooklyn that evening, with the satisfaction that one thing, at least, has been resolved, he finds a letter waiting for him. It is in an unknown hand, from Mount Olivet Hospital. It tells him that, early this morning, a little before dawn, Ayakou fell into a state of unconsciousness. By ten o'clock, he was dead.

Chapter 39

London, 51°31' N, 0°7' W
October 1896

"Isobel Kirkpatrick, with the fair hair? A lecturer?"

"That surprises you?"

Mark leans back in his chair, assessing whether Flora is teasing him.

They are sitting in a café near the museum. It is a habit they have fallen into, after discussing the progress he is making with the mummies. They can talk about their university past now, without rancor. Flora enjoys these meetings; she realizes she has missed this—the easy rapport with someone her own age, in front of whom she does not have to act.

"In Manchester. She's one of the youngest female lecturers in the country."

"I thought she didn't have to earn a living! Don't look at me like that! I say, 'Good for her.' Do you still see her?"

"Rarely. We write. Poppy, too, but she's a doctor's wife in the country, and he doesn't find me a respectable friend, I don't think. I miss them."

"Hmm. I don't miss those fellows. Certainly not Herbert and Oliver. Tom Outram was the only one who was worth anything. He wrote to my father, you know, trying to find out why I left—offering to help. You and he were the only ones who bothered. I wonder what he's doing now."

"He went to South Africa, I believe. He wanted to go into the law, but was discouraged, because of the stammer."

"Pity. He was clever. But it was hard to tell, since he could hardly get a word out." He smiles sympathetically. "Few of us have fulfilled our promise, then. I except you, of course."

"You're a lecturer, Mark!"

"At the polytechnic."

"How many lecturers there come from the East End?"

"That's what you mean: I've done well *for someone like me*."

Flora doesn't bother to reply. He is still morbidly sensitive, but she is no longer afraid of his moods.

"The pay is terrible. It's hardly enough to maintain a family on, let alone . . ."

He falls silent. He discourages mention of his family. She has assumed it is not a happy home, or is that wishful thinking?

Then, over the pot of tea, he makes an impassioned declaration: his marriage is over; they live apart, each blaming and resenting the other.

"Seeing you brings it all back. How different things could have been. The worst part is I know it was all my fault."

For a terrible moment, she thinks he might cry.

"Mark, please . . ."

"You were the best part of my life."

"What about your children?" she says, after a pause.

He snorts. "It's only Samuel I care about, not the twins. I wanted to do the right thing—but I ended up hating her for it. And she will poison him against me."

"He will make up his own mind."

But Mark has decided not to be consoled—a mood she remembers without regret. She thinks, Thank God; if we had married, it would have been a disaster, for both of us.

"Being with you was a glimpse of a better life, but I knew, even then, it wasn't for the likes of me."

"For heaven's sake, that is morbid self-pity. If you don't stop, I'm leaving."

"Go! Back to Kensington. 'Twas ever thus, was it not?"

"'*It*' is what you choose it to be! I chose my life, and it's far from perfect, but I'm not going to moan about it."

"Yes, I know . . . You're right."

His mood switches with alarming suddenness. He smiles at her with what looks like tender affection.

"I'm sorry, Flora, to be such a bore. We shouldn't have met again; despite the mess with Edie, I was bumping along all right, until then."

"I'm glad we did."

"Are you, really?"

He looks at her so beseechingly that Flora puts her hand on his arm and nods. He puts his hand over hers, crushing it in his grip.

He says, in a different voice—low, passionate, "You must know I've always loved you, Flora. Even when I left . . . when I could only read about you, I always loved you."

Flora does not really believe this. She thinks it the sort of wild declamation to which he has always been prone. She imagines, for a moment, believing him. The truth is, she wants to believe him, because there are times when even a counterfeit passion is better than none.

She finds that it is easier to commit adultery a second time. She is no longer shocked by her depravity; that is a given. And she can tell herself that, because she did not plan this, it is not really her responsibility. Perhaps it is also easier because she is not in love. What she feels for Mark is a mixture of nostalgia, pity, affection—and she is attracted to him; she always had been.

A few days after the scene in the café, she goes to his rooms—he has moved out of his marital home and taken lodgings in Bloomsbury. A dingy semi-basement, but, with entrances both front and back, it has the advantage of being discreet.

The first time they are in his bed, she has to hold him back and ask, in an embarrassed whisper, whether he "has anything." He mutters that he doesn't. (Why not, since we arranged this the day before yesterday? she thinks, with prophetic irritation.) He is so downcast that she agrees to his withdrawing. But he pulls out almost as soon as he has come in. He apologizes, saying it has been a long time . . . He has not, despite everything, had much experience! She reassures him that it doesn't matter. He seems overwhelmingly happy to be with her. And it is so sweet to be lying next to a warm, naked body, to be caressed and kissed, and told she is beautiful, that, at first, she believes she is happy too.

Their meetings settle into a pattern. Once a week, she goes to his lodgings. She has to revise her unconscious assumption that all men (Freddie excepted) would touch her in more or less the same way. Mark may labor earnestly (and properly armored, which helps prolong matters), but no matter how long he goes on, she does not approach the finish. It is not unpleasant—far from it; it is very nice, but . . .

Mark does not seem to be aware of this. When she hints at her lack of fulfillment ("Perhaps . . ." she says, taking his hand and guiding it between her legs), he is at first puzzled, then sulky.

"Why do you not come to it in the natural way?" he asks. "To resist, as you do . . . it's unwomanly. If you were just less willful . . ."

Flora is momentarily speechless. "I'm not resisting! It just . . . It doesn't . . ."

She remembers Freddie, with a terrible coldness. Is there something wrong with her? Jakob didn't think so, she thinks, with a surge of despairing longing.

"Perhaps it's the, er, the preservative?" Mark says, looking at it anxiously. "It isn't healthy, really, for man or woman. It impedes a true union."

Flora does not think it is the preservative—and is certainly not prepared to try without—but does not know what else to say. He has changed more than she realized. Where did their empirical experiments go? Where his curiosity, his thirst for truth?

"Or maybe you don't love me enough."

"Oh, Mark . . ." She strokes his face and kisses him.

She kisses him because she cannot tell him that he is right. She feels affection for him, but she remembers what it was like to love him, and that is not what she feels now. And she remembers what she felt with Jakob, and that is different again. Once the truth is dead, how can it hurt to bury it again and again? The next time they meet, she allows herself to demonstrate more pleasure than she in fact feels, and this gives him so much happiness that she wonders why she didn't do it sooner. Her feeling is one of relief, and pleasure at giving him pleasure. What harm can such a small falsehood do?

True, she is still dissatisfied, and she despises herself, a little, for the deception, and despises him for being so easily—willingly!—deceived. Undoubtedly (she argues with herself), it is a function of experience, and Jakob's greater experience was the thing she feared and distrusted. (But if Mark were more acute, or more open-minded, the voice argues, he would *know* that it was a lie . . .) Her mind can drive her to distraction.

And worse. As they lie together on his single bed, she caresses his arm as it rests on her body. His skin is soft and white, the hairs on his arm dark. She finds herself thinking, with a detachment that alarms her: Mark and Jakob have a similar build, even similar coloring. Both are of medium height, slender, dark-eyed. Mark has the finer profile, Jakob the more beautiful mouth. Beyond that, they are quite different, physically and mentally. Jakob was calm and easy to be with. Mark is touchy and unpredictable. The flesh on Mark's arms is flaccid, the muscles those of a man who wields chalk and test tubes. She recalls in precise detail (now, of all times) Jakob's forearms, with sun-burnished skin and dense muscle. The way he would walk around the room naked, quite unembarrassed (he told her, a fact she treasured, that they would sometimes go naked in Greenland, in summer), whereas Mark snatches up the first thing that comes to hand to cover himself. And, then . . . well, Mark is circumcised; Jakob is not. Jakob's penis is browner, is slightly curved, thicker; he felt different inside her. She blushes to think it—she shocks herself by thinking it—but it is true.

She turns the memory away; it doesn't help. There is nothing wrong with chalk or test tubes. She reminds herself that Mark is the cleverest person she has ever met. And he wants her. And he is here.

Chapter 40

New York, 40°42' N, 74°00' W
Winter 1896–7

"What do I say? Dear . . . ? Dear Fellora . . ."

Jakob writes, *Dear Mrs. Athlone,*

"This is the correct thing to put in a letter, Aniguin. Even if you call a person something else in person. It's polite."

As you see, I am here in New York. Do I surprise you? Mr. de Beyn . . .
[Jakob adds the "Mr." himself] *. . . writes this letter for me. He is my friend here.*

Jakob pauses, but writes it down. If she knows he is there, it will be awkward not to add some brief note from himself. An omission would say more than any words. (Like her omission to write to him.) He summarizes Aniguin's description of the situation: Armitage bringing the Eskimos to New York; Ayakou dead, buried in the garden of the museum; Ivalu, Padloq, and Aviaq ill with pneumonia; Aniguin healthy but unhappy. Armitage has not been to see them since August.

I wish you to know this. De Beyn says he will take us back in spring—if we still live. I hope so. I do not know what we would do if he were not here. The spirits told me to come to America—I do not yet know what their purpose is, but there must be one. When are you coming back? When is Mackie? I hope he is well. We would like to see him again. I hope to see you there, in the land of the north. I wish you good health.

I am always your friend . . .

Aniguin looks at him, anxious. "Is that a good letter, Te Peyn?"

"It's a very good letter, Aniguin."

He reads it back, and thinks, After all, what have I got to say to her?

Sealing it in an envelope, he finds he can address it from memory.

London, 51°31' N, 0°7' W

When Flora comes in after being with Mark—another rendezvous where she wondered why she is doing this, but the energy required to end it seems more than she can muster—a letter is waiting on the hall table for all to see: the New York postmark; the—to her—utterly distinctive hand. She walks into her study and stands for some moments in total confusion. It's been over a year since she saw his handwriting, longer since their last parting, yet something makes her tremble. She goes over to her desk and leans on it.

Opening the letter, she reads with piercing disappointment the sentence written across the top of the page: *Dictated by Aniguin to J. de Beyn.* She scans the letter, and her feeling changes to horror and grief. It is short—Jakob added nothing to Aniguin's bleak words. Perhaps he didn't think it appropriate. Perhaps she is less than nothing to him.

Composing herself, Flora reads through her other correspondence and places it on her desk in order of priority for the morning.

Then she puts her face in her hands and rests her elbows on the desk.

In a minute, she will go to see her husband and ask him how he is.

Kensington, November 1896

My Dear Aniguin,

How pleased I was to hear from you—but how terribly saddened to read your letter. I am so sorry to learn of Ayakou's passing. He was a good man. I hope that by now there has been some improvement in the health of Ivalu, Padloq, and Aviaq, and that you continue well. I am glad that Mr. de Beyn is being a good friend to you. He is right: the quickest way for you to go back home is to sail from New York with him next spring.

You ask when I will come north again. It has been difficult to arrange things because my husband has been very ill for more than a year. You may remember that, on the last trip to Greenland, he had an accident which left him crippled. Last summer, he suffered a seizure, which led to a paralysis. For a time, we thought he might die, but now, at last, he is somewhat recovered. His illness meant that I could not think of leaving London to see my friends, no matter how much I longed to do so. Believe me when I say, I have thought of you very often, wondering how you are, and if you are well and happy.

At present, I am planning to go north next year also, arriving at Siorapaluk as soon as the ice allows, so we will meet again before too long, all being well. I look forward to that day more than I can say, dear friend.

Very few whaling ships go to your country now, because they cannot sell the oil and bone for much money. My father, Captain Mackie, has not been to Davis Strait for two years. He also has not been well, with inflammation of the knees, but is much better now. He hopes to go back soon, but I do not know when.

I will see you soon, Aniguin, I'm sure. Please give my best wishes for health and happiness to your wife and all your friends, including Mr. de Beyn.

> *Please believe that I remain your very good friend,*
>
> *Flora Mackie Athlone*

New York, 40°42' N, 74°00' W

Jakob is too busy to dwell on Flora's letter. When he does think of it, he is irritated; it seems to him a clumsy attempt to make excuses for her silence toward him—a silence that made him wretched. He had stayed in Zermatt long after Theodor went home, waiting for a word from her, trying to decide whether to go to London despite everything, and then concluding, with anger and self-disgust, that she was the sort of woman who burned bridges with ruthless efficiency. He changed his passage home to one leaving from Rotterdam, so as not to set foot in a country that had become vile to him.

But, wrapped in a cloth, at the back of a drawer, he has kept her letters, along with an envelope of photographs. He does not explain to himself why he keeps them, except that to go to the trouble of destroying them would accord them too much importance. After reading her letter to Aniguin, he finds himself, a couple of days later, opening the envelope and emptying it onto his desk.

There are the pictures from the beach at Neqi, where she looks self-conscious and absurdly young. The photograph of her with Simiak, when she did not know she was being looked at. The one of Flora and Meqro (their expressions make him smile, despite himself). And then there is the one that he really should not have kept, or even taken in the first place, but all things seemed possible and right in that hotel room. It is a picture of Flora sitting in an armchair by the window in that room, hair loose around her shoulders, her eyes directly on him, her half-smile a mixture of embarrassment and intimacy that stirs him still, while light from the window falls on those delectable bare breasts . . . It is quite a good photograph—light and shade nicely balanced. When he'd asked her if she would sit for him naked, expecting her to refuse, she had demurred, then laughed; he had the sense that she liked the idea of him having such a picture, that she knew her power over him and wanted him to bear a token of it.

If he wanted to test himself against that power, he is failing miserably. He stares at the pattern of dark curves and light, which is all it is, then puts his thumb over her face, wanting to erase her, annoyed that the image still has the power to arouse. It could be any well-made young woman; any cheap, erotic image would have the same effect . . . He tells himself that *if* they meet, and that is not at all certain in such a vast country, she will be changed, uninterested, and he will feel nothing, nothing . . . This, as he unbuttons his fly and rummages within, cock stupidly engorged (ashamed, but really it is the fastest way of dealing with it). She had desired him (the memories are as brilliant as ever, an eternal present of the senses just below the surface, like warm, rich groundwater), she may even have cared for him, for a while, but she had not chosen him, and that was the end of it. He was not important enough. Her letter to Aniguin demonstrates her weakness: as with most people who inflict pain, she still wants to be liked.

He finishes abruptly—an urgent, unsatisfying release—wipes his hands with an expression of distaste, and tidies his clothing. He is barely out of breath. He picks up the Liverpool photograph again—having, so to speak, neutralized its effect—intending, as he has intended before, to cast it on the fire. And then, as he has done before, he tucks it back in the envelope, underneath the others.

It is not important enough.

Lang's Farm, Pocumtuk Point, Lake Champlain, December

Dear Mrs. Athlone,

I deeply regret to tell you this, but last week saw the deaths of Padloq, Aviaq, and finally of Ivalu, who died late on Saturday night. Aniguin has been ill with influenza and bronchitis, but seems to have recovered—physically, at least. The others sank very quickly, despite everything that could be done. The staff at the hospital were upset and many shed genuine tears; I think they were truly fond of their unusual patients. It is a terrible thing.

At Mount Olivet, the hospital in Brooklyn where they were being cared for, the governors allowed Aniguin to bury his wife and friends in the grounds and to observe mourning in the way he wanted, as far as possible. Mr. White, of the museum, the doctors and nurses at Mount Olivet, as well as my brother's family and myself were there to pay the final respects. I have written to Mr. Armitage to tell him the sad news, but he is currently away.

I have brought Aniguin to stay at a farm in the mountains north of New York. I hope that it will help him to be away from the scene of so much tragedy. The first snows have fallen, so it is a little more like home. He is outwardly stoic, but I suspect he is very low. He says, over and again, Ayornamut, which I believe means something like, "It cannot be otherwise" or, "It is fated"—but you will know better than I.

The farm people are kind, and I will come up regularly to see him. I thought it would be better for him than staying in New York all winter, and he agreed. I'm sure it would cheer him greatly to hear from you. You can write to him here, care of Mrs. Lang (from now on I will be traveling, so correspondence will reach him more quickly that way). I hope this is the end of his misfortunes.

With best regards,

J. de Beyn

What a terrible letter. I am so sorry.

Chapter 41

London, 51°31' N, 0°7' W
February 1897

"My backers are interested in finding new lands—that is their sole interest." He smiles, revealing small, widely spaced teeth. His accent is impeccable, as are his manners.

Opposite, Ralph Dixon shifts in his chair, which creaks under his weight. Gilbert Ashbee, the biologist they are interviewing—although perhaps he is interviewing them—pauses for a moment. A thickset man of medium height, in his mid-thirties, with blond hair and mustache on a short upper lip, he radiates confidence and a certain brutish charm.

"Have you experience of Arctic travel?" asks Flora.

"I have climbed extensively in Austria and Norway, and I spent two winters in Iceland. I know that's not the Arctic, but I hope my experience in the cold will count for something."

"We cannot compromise the scientific program, so exploration efforts would have to fit around completing that body of work."

"Of course, but I understood from Professor Dixon"—he nods to Ralph, who fidgets, as though the designation of "professor" is an awkward fit—"that you're thinking of carrying out map work on Ellesmere, where there may be as yet undiscovered islands."

Flora looks at Ralph, who maintains a look of studied blankness.

"That's a possibility. But we have to be flexible and adapt to conditions as we find them. What is the interest your sponsors have in new land?"

"There is a serious and idealistic purpose to their interest—an interest, I might add, that reaches the highest levels of government. There are very highly placed individuals concerned with this matter."

"Oh?" Flora allows a silence to develop. "I'm puzzled, Mr. Ashbee. If they are so highly placed, why do they not mount a government-sponsored expedition?"

"Perhaps I can put it like this: at this early stage in the discussions, discretion is of the utmost importance. The parties involved would rather make inquiries first, study the feasibility of their purpose, before alerting the press and general public to their intentions."

"Which are?"

"Here, you embarrass me. I very much regret, Mrs. Athlone, that I'm not at liberty to say."

Flora sits back in her surprise.

"Then I'm afraid I cannot help you, Mr. Ashbee. I cannot be a party to something that I know nothing about."

His mouth tightens a little, but he bows his head.

"I can only assure you that the motives are admirable; the project would lead to nothing less than a general amelioration in the human condition."

"But you can't allow me to make up my own mind."

Ashbee inclines his head again. "I regret. If it was solely up to me, I would. My hands are tied in this."

"Then perhaps I should meet with someone whose hands are not tied."

She speaks a little waspishly, and Ashbee's face stiffens.

"I will report your concerns, Mrs. Athlone." He shoots a glance at Ralph before getting up.

Afterward, Flora shrugs at Ralph crossly. The initial introduction to Ashbee had come through him.

"Do you really not know what he's talking about?"

"I'm sorry. I have no idea. I only know that they have money, so I thought it worth a meeting."

"Yes, of course."

They walk out onto the pavement—a side street, near Whitehall.

"How are the finances?"

"We could always do with more," she says. In fact, she has been worrying nonstop. Since the last, awful letter from America, she has been plagued by the fear that Aniguin too will die before she sees him again. They *have* to go this summer. Her father has helped broker a ship passage, on a Dundee sealer called the *Clansman*. But unless they find a significant sum of money in the next few weeks, they will not be going.

When she asked her father about chartering the *Vega*, more than a year ago, he was suffering from an inflammation in both knees that kept him housebound, and his temper had not improved. He had glared at her.

"I cannot rearrange Dundee's shipping for your convenience, Flora. This is an industry. Men's livelihoods depend on it."

"I'm not begging favors, Daddy—we're going to pay for the charter. And you're part-owner. You surely have some say?"

There was a pause. Her father sighed.

"I have not been part-owner of the *Vega* for quite some time, Flora."

She gaped at him then, as though he had slapped her. He was talking about the *Vega*—her sister in wood and water.

"When did this happen?" She found her throat clenching. "Why did you not tell me?"

Her father gave her a severe look.

"I sold my shares in the *Vega* to give you the money for your first expedition. Where did you think it came from?"

"I didn't know," she whispered. "I thought . . ."

In truth, she had not thought about it at all. She had been too wrapped up in her own plans to wonder where such help came from, had taken it as no more than her due.

A few days after the meeting with Ashbee, she comes home and walks up to Freddie's sitting room. As usual, she knocks, saying, "It's me," before going in without waiting for an answer.

She sees the peculiar look on Nurse Capron's face before she withdraws. Flora looks at Freddie. His face is whiter than usual.

"Are you all right? Has something happened?"

"I think that is for you to say."

"What do you mean?"

Freddie picks up a cheap-looking envelope.

"This is not the first time I've had a letter like this. I thought at first that I would not worry you with what it alleges. But it makes some very unpleasant accusations. Against you."

"What accusations?"

Of course, she knows. Freddie gives a mirthless smile. "The usual sort. As I said, I was not even going to ask you about it, only, it is very detailed, and I'm concerned for your reputation, if it is known."

"You believe them, then?"

"The previous letters were anonymous, so I ignored them. This one is signed. By a Mrs. E. Levinson."

Flora feels a slither of shock.

"Mr. Levinson is in charge of conserving the mummies. You know I see him."

"I don't imagine you were conserving mummies at fifty-seven Calthorpe Street. Last Friday."

Flora is silent.

"Do you have nothing to say?"

Flora drifts over to the window. She has thought of this moment, but it is nothing like she imagined.

"No."

She had been almost sure that he suspected her affair with Jakob, and chose not to confront her. It seems bizarre to be found out now for something that matters so little.

"I know there was a connection between you at university. Perhaps you've always loved him? Has it . . . gone on ever since?"

"I hadn't seen him for years, until we met at the museum."

"Are you in love with him?"

"No."

"I suppose what I mean is, do you want a divorce?"

"Oh, Freddie . . ." She passes her hand over her eyes, an immense wave of tiredness threatening to engulf her. "I'm sorry. It doesn't matter in the least. It's not important."

"You don't love him?" He sounds incredulous.

"What is it that matters to you, Freddie? I have no idea! I've taken advantage of . . . of you, I suppose. I've often wondered why you went on with the work on my behalf. It's not as though you love me—it was never that, was it?"

"Of course I do! Since the accident, I know I've not been a husband to you—with this wretched body . . ." He gestures at himself, grimacing with disgust.

Flora stares. "No, not 'since the accident'! You were never a husband to me. You never wanted me!"

Freddie stares at her with a terrible sincerity.

"It was you who never wanted me, Flora. Have you forgotten?"

Flora feels her head spin.

"Not . . . like *that*."

"So Mr. Levinson gives you whatever it is you want?"

Flora stares past him, shaking her head. "For God's sake . . ."

"After the accident, when my own hopes were destroyed, I was comforted because I still had you. You carried my hopes with you. I told myself we had something finer than a mere animal connection—affection, a purpose . . ."

"If it is finer, then we still have it. If not, then . . ." Flora takes a deep breath. "You can divorce me, of course. But I'll be gone in a few weeks, anyway."

They stare at each other; Flora is frightened by what she has just said. Despite everything—*everything*—they are used to each other. Being his wife is the only adult existence she knows.

"That's not what I meant," he says at last.

"Then what do you mean? What is it you want?" It comes out as a cry. And, for a moment, she thinks he is going to tell her.

"As you say, you are shortly to leave. That is my priority. As it must be yours." He looks at the letter, as if surprised it is still in his hand. He drops it on the table. "I'm sorry. It upset me."

"Don't be sorry! Whatever she alleges, it's true."

"But you don't love him?"

"No."

"Yet he makes you happy."

"Actually, I was about to end it."

"Then we don't need to speak of this again."

Flora makes an inarticulate noise, but cannot bring herself to go on. Indeed, does not know how.

The following week, Gilbert Ashbee signs on as a member of the expedition. The final argument—to which she has no answer—is the five thousand pounds contingent on his participation. Without it, she will not see Aniguin, and she will not (perhaps) see Jakob de Beyn—although she believes this last plays no part in her calculations. And London has become intolerable. Pride and integrity are luxuries she cannot afford.

Money is the crux of it. Sacrifices have to be made—exploration demands them of everyone involved, and of some who are not involved and will not even benefit, like Ralph's unborn child, who will not meet its father until it has spoken its first words, and may never meet him at all.

Flora writes her final letter to Mark. She finds herself weeping over it, recognizing a truth she has been avoiding: her tenderness was all for the brilliant youth he was, and that youth is gone, just as the girl she was has gone. Had she assumed that his intimacy with her would be a healing balm? That she could wipe away bitterness, self-pity, time? If so, she overestimated her charms.

Chapter 42

New York, 40°42' N, 74°00' W
April 1897

Jakob has not set foot in the Natural History Museum since Ayakou's funeral in its grounds. Inside the porticoed entrance, he pauses to breathe in the atmosphere. It acts on him like a salve. With the endless worry of expedition planning, he has no time to himself, but as a student he used to spend hours in the mineral halls, sketching and making notes. He would lose himself in the almost sanctified air of the place; a hushed antidote to the teeming city.

Finding himself early for his appointment with the assistant curator, he takes a roundabout route to White's office, where he is due to talk about fossils, wandering past familiar displays and through the Choate Hall of Mankind. In the domed space with its cathedral echoes, there are signs of change: his eye is drawn to a new case, the card of which is snowy-white, and, before he has read it, a cold finger of unease runs down his spine. On the card is typed: *Eskimo male, around thirty-five years old. Northwest Greenland. Acd. 1896.*

He knows that Armitage is only the latest in a line of explorers to bring back remains of the dead, but the cold feeling deepens. The bones are not an ocherous brown, like those of the ancient hominids;

they have not been unearthed. Then he realizes what his brain registered before he consciously noticed it: the damage to the bones of the right leg, which had, in life, been badly broken and poorly knitted together. Jakob is sure of one thing: that he was there when the damage was done, and he was there when the bones were splinted, in Siorapaluk, four years ago. He looks at the grinning skull, and cannot discern the face that covered the bone. But he looks at the leg, and he knows—he *knows*—that he is looking at the skeleton of his friend Ayakou.

A father with two young sons drifts over to stand close by.

"It's so short," says one of the boys. "It's a midget!"

They all laugh.

"Savages are always small," says the father. "They're primitive, like that Neanderthal man, there."

Blood rushes loudly in Jakob's head.

"His name was Ayakou."

"Excuse me?" The man's voice is hostile.

Jakob looks at him. "His name was Ayakou. This man, here. He wasn't a savage, and he died only a few months ago, right here in New York."

The man lifts his lip in a snarl, puts his hands on his sons' shoulders and hustles them away, muttering, "Crazy . . . Shouldn't let people like that in here . . ."

Outside, he locates Ayakou's unmarked grave. It looks undisturbed; a thin haze of new grass covers the earth. Does this mean his fears are unfounded? He was there himself, for God's sake! Or had they . . . (surely unthinkable) dug him up immediately? Then, as he stands, surrounded by impudently blooming daffodils, an even more terrible possibility strikes him: Was it even Ayakou's body they had buried in the first place?

In White's office, Jakob is excited and distracted and cannot remember what he came here to say. He finds himself interrupting the initial small talk with an abrupt laugh, and says, "I wonder if you could set my mind at rest . . . It may be the craziest thing, but I noticed, as I was coming here, a new exhibit in Choate Hall . . . Eskimo male, from northwest Greenland. Acquired last year. Where did it come from?"

White glances down at his desk, in which moment, Jakob knows he is right, and that White is going to lie.

"I'd have to look at the paperwork. Can't remember every exhibit offhand, I'm afraid! I'm pretty sure it came with Mr. Armitage's last consignment."

Across the desk, backlit against the arched window, White's outline seems to sparkle.

"Now, ah, the fossils you mentioned . . . We would be interested in some examples of—"

"Because I was with Ayakou when the meteorite was taken, Mr. White," Jakob interrupts, a hot energy coursing through him. "When his leg was broken in two places. I was there. And that skeleton has the right leg broken in the exact same two places. That skeleton is Ayakou's, isn't it?"

White gapes at him, managing somehow to look shocked, ignorant, and uninterested, all at the same time.

"You and I were there, along with his wife Padloq, when we buried him in the garden. Can you explain that, Mr. White?"

White gives him a tight smile. "I cannot comment on individual exhibits, Mr. de Beyn. But the museum has the perfect right to mount its specimens in the way that best educates and informs—"

"He's not a specimen! He's a man you knew! His name is Ayakou. You knew his wife! You can't just stick him in a case for people to gawk at! I thought you had a conscience—"

"You're excited, Mr. de Beyn. The tragic case of the Eskimos has been upsetting for everyone involved, myself included, and—"

Jakob finds himself on his feet, clenching his hands. "If your wife died tomorrow, would you send her body upstate, boil it in a vat until the flesh fell off her bones, then stick them in a case for everyone to look at?"

"Mr. de Beyn, that is . . . a . . . an outrageous . . . ! How *dare* you mention—"

"How dare I? How dare you do it! Apparently, things like respect and consideration don't matter to you! As long as it *educates and informs!*"

White's jowls quiver with rage. But he keeps to the shelter of his desk, as though Jakob is a dangerous prospect.

"You don't deny it."

"I think . . . I think you should leave, Mr. de Beyn."

Jakob turns to go and has his hand on the door when he remembers he carries a note from Aniguin in his breast pocket.

"Aniguin gave me a letter for you. He wanted to tell you that he doesn't blame you for anything. But then he doesn't know what you did to his friend. Shall I tell him? According to you, it shouldn't matter in the slightest."

White makes a whinnying noise. Jakob throws the envelope onto the man's desk. Only then does another thought occur to him.

"I'm going to Mount Olivet now. If I find that any attempt has been made to remove the bodies that are buried there, I will take it to the press."

As he walks down the corridor, he hears Mr. White calling after him, "You have no proof! I admitted nothing, d'you hear?"

Jakob walks at high speed away from the museum. He cannot imagine setting foot in the place again. After a few minutes, he slows down, still trembling with the aftermath of his outburst. The streets are gray with old slush. A keen wind blows off the East River. Once the heat of his anger subsides, he finds that he is freezing. In the course of his melodramatic departure, he has left his overcoat in White's office.

Cursing and shivering, he turns and walks back to the museum, passing red-nosed New Yorkers—pinch-faced, mean-eyed, squalid, self-centered, importunate city-dwellers—the sort of people who stand in front of a man's mortal remains, consuming the spectacle without knowing or caring where he came from, or what was his name. He hates them all. He, Jakob, (now climbing the steps of the building he just vowed never to enter again) is as squalid, as ridiculous, as any of them.

Suddenly, the urge to leave is overwhelming. He has to stop and put his hand on the banister. He shuts his eyes and pictures the hillside on the coast of Ellesmere—the austere, endless light, the uncomplicated joy he knew there. Only a few weeks until he sails away from this place, these people, the worst parts of himself.

He straightens, and continues on up the stairs.

PART SEVEN

THULE

Thule, lying icebound under the pole star.
—Claudian

Chapter 43

Gander, Newfoundland, 48°57' N, 54°36' W
April 1948

"I'm sorry folks, but we've just had the weather report."

Commander Soames holds up the offending piece of paper and glances around at the gathering in the dining room. (Why do scientists have to be so scruffy? Straightening a tie and polishing a belt can hardly be beyond their capabilities.)

"There are high winds across Baffin and Ellesmere, and I'm afraid we're going to have to wait until they die down. We need the best possible conditions if we are to land. We should get another report in around four hours, and then we'll make a decision. So, until then, if you could be patient with us . . ."

His smile has a certain perfunctory quality. It's not as though anyone has a choice. Randall Crane is disappointed. Then, as he often does, he sees the upside.

He has been watching the Snow Queen this morning. She did not seem inclined to meet his eye at breakfast. She was lively at the dinner last night, smiling—flattered and charmed by the men's attentions. The flattery—or the wine (or both)—made her seem younger, warmer. Perhaps she was, as he had been, invigorated by the sense of occasion. There had been an air of something exciting and momentous—history, perhaps—in the dining room. They were going to be the first people to stand—*incontrovertibly* stand, that is—at the North Pole. The previous claimants, whose accounts are clouded by various densities of fog—uncorroborated reports, dubious navigational sightings, unfeasible speeds, the sheer impossibility of *proof*—all can be swept aside. No one here is pretending to be an explorer, but they are the chosen ones, chosen because they deserve it. This morning, that exhilaration is hard to recapture. It is cold, cloudy, and beginning to drizzle.

Flora, who told her father she was going to the North Pole when it was the center of white space on the map, now feels little excitement at the prospect. Instead, she merely experiences some curiosity, some fear that the headache she developed overnight will intensify and spoil things. This morning, she is tired. Being questioned by the young man, being here—it brings memories of the north close, and all that went with it.

Randall runs her to earth in the lounge, where she sits with a cup of coffee and a newspaper. She looks up at his greeting, without warmth.

"Mrs. Cochrane, good morning. I have a confession to make."

"Really? I'm sure it's of no great consequence, Mr. Crane."

"I think it might be. I'm afraid that I rather annoyed you with my questions yesterday. You asked the nature of my interest in Armitage and de Beyn, and I wasn't entirely frank with you. I apologize for that."

She folds the paper and puts it on the table. He sits down beside her and takes a deep breath.

"Before she married, my mother's name was Vera de Beyn. Jakob de Beyn was her uncle."

The Snow Queen stares at him. Her mouth is a frozen O of surprise. Her eyes are wide; she seems to be scrutinizing him in minute detail. Then she says, "I see. And you didn't you tell me this yesterday because . . ."

Randall laughs, embarrassed. "I suppose, because I'm here in a professional capacity and I have a job to do. It so happens that I also have this family connection. It's why I became interested in the Arctic in the first place . . . I wanted you to take me seriously. And I didn't know how you would . . ." He shakes his head and smiles, hopeful. "Anyway, I'm sorry."

"His niece, Vera, is your mother?"

"Yes, that's right."

There is a long pause.

"I can understand your interest in what happened to him. But it doesn't mean that I can tell you any more than I could yesterday."

"You do believe me?"

She looks cunning. "His niece was crippled. He was afraid she would never marry."

Randall nods.

"She had polio as a baby. She's always been lame. She married late—she met my father after the first war. He was discharged in 1919, with wounds, and she was working in the hospital. She was quite a bit older than him. He says his recovery was all down to her."

Her face changes; the suspicion is melting away, he thinks.

"I'm sure Mr. de Beyn would have been happy to know that. I think he was very fond of her."

"Mom adored him. She always said that, when she was a little girl, she wanted to marry him."

He watches her, but has no idea what is going on behind that impassive face.

"Mrs. Cochrane, I hope you'll forgive me for saying this, but we have so little time." He looks around him to check that no one else has come within earshot. "After Jakob's death, my grandfather—that is, his brother, Hendrik—went through his things. He found your letters."

She blinks rapidly. "Oh."

There is a long pause. Randall waits.

"I'm sorry, I'm not sure I remember . . . What letters were these?"

Randall takes a deep breath. "You corresponded with him after the first Greenland expedition in 1892, and then I believe you met again, when he went to Europe in '95."

He doesn't know how to go on. He has read the letters. In fact, he has them with him. At first, the letters from Flora Athlone to his great-uncle are formal, friendly. The first one deals with a child that a friend, Frank Urbino, fathered in Greenland, and an Eskimo man who was hurt in the accident that killed Urbino. It is the passing on of news—careful, concerned. Over the next two years, the correspondence becomes increasingly easy and familiar, until, in the spring of 1895, it suddenly changes: from a letter every few months, there is a spate, and the tone has become passionate, intense. They have met again, in Europe, and the relationship—it is fairly clear—has been consummated. There is mention of her joining him in Switzerland. There is passion and longing. There are doubts, delicately expressed, about his feelings for her, although not about her own for him. Letters from a woman in love, you would say.

Then, three months later, she ends it; her husband is seriously ill. This is the first time she has mentioned him, although Jakob seems to have known she was married. Perhaps she has thought better of the affair. Perhaps she has been found out. Perhaps her passion was passing and shallow. She does not explain.

In the envelope with the letters were a handful of photographs. A few were snaps of Flora Athlone (as she was then) in Greenland, on a beach. One particularly engaging photograph shows a very young Flora with an Eskimo girl, whose head only reaches her chin. They are looking at each other and laughing, mischief lighting up both faces. And there was another photograph—the one his mother only showed him a few days before he left. In this last picture, the same young Flora is sitting in an armchair in a dark interior, smiling shyly at the camera. Only, here, she is naked, her skin glowing like a pearl in the light from a window. When Randall saw it, he laughed with embarrassment.

"This is her—the girl on the beach? The old devil!"

His mother sighed. "Really, Randy. I know I'm your mother, but I expect you've seen pictures of naked women before."

"Well, you didn't show me *this* before," he said. "You know, she's not bad."

"I hope you're not going to smirk like that when you meet her."

"Mom, for heaven's sake!"

He was amused more than anything (and titillated)—which now makes him feel hot with shame, although he really cannot connect that soft-fleshed girl with the old woman before him. His embarrassment was less to do with the girl's nudity than with the expression on her face. It is such an intimate picture—so clearly that of a woman looking at her lover—that he cannot mention it.

Now the Snow Queen breaks the silence with a sigh.

"Do you plan to write about that?"

"No! Please don't think that. I wouldn't dream of it. My family—especially my mother—would love to know . . . well, anything you could tell us about him. The north was such an important part of his life. Whenever he came back to New York, he lived with Mom's family, but she said that he was always itching to leave again. No one in the family could really understand it. But you must know what that was like. And, of course, we would love to know what happened to him, in the end. If there's anything to know . . ."

"Oh," she says again. "It was all so long ago."

"I understand it might be difficult to talk about."

Randall looks at her, feeling the resistance in her. He could almost shake her. Of course she has the right to her privacy—but he and his mother have the right to know, don't they?

"We may never get another chance to find out. I . . . Please . . ."

The woman is gazing out of the window.

"I realize he was only a small part of your life. But he was greatly loved and missed by my family." He pauses, hoping for a sign. "I'm named after him."

She looks at him accusingly. "I thought your name was Randall."

"It is: Jakob Randall Crane. When I was at school, I decided 'Jakob' was old-fashioned." He grimaces in apology.

She examines him again. "Your eyes have a look of him."

He smiles. "That's what Mom says."

She seems to be meditating. She looks at her watch. Randall finds himself praying that the bad weather will continue.

"Shall we go for a walk? We have time."

Randall grins. "It would be a pleasure. Thank you."

"Don't thank me. I don't know what I can tell you that will be of any use."

Wrapped in coats and scarves—it is only a little above freezing—they walk away from the box-like buildings into the gray morning.

"If we go southeast," she says, "we will come to the lake." And before he can agree or otherwise, she sets off briskly.

"This is southeast?" he asks. When she nods, he says, "How can you tell? There's no sun."

She looks at him. "I just know."

Across the empty highway, a low rise is covered in spruce. It is not a picturesque country, in Randall's opinion: the landscape is flat and scrubbed-looking, with nothing but monotonous dark trees to cover its bareness.

Randall takes out his Luckies and offers her the packet.

"No, thank you. I've never smoked. He smoked, of course. They all did."

"They?"

"All the men, up there. All the time. And the Eskimos. Tobacco was a big part of trade with them. They couldn't get enough of it."

Randall laughs. "Very convenient, to get your trading partners addicted to something that only you can supply."

"Oh, it started long before we were there." She looks at him rather sharply. "But you're right. There were so many things that only we could supply."

She walks quickly. Randall almost has to hurry to keep up.

"We met again, your great-uncle and I, on my second expedition, in '98. Did you know that?"

"No. You mean in Greenland?"

"Yes."

He waits for her to go on. She continues walking, looking straight ahead into the trees.

She says, "He wasn't a small part. Not at all."

They climb over a bank of shattered clinker that has been left by the road menders. Randall holds out his hand to her. She doesn't take it.

She says, "He was greatly loved by me, too."

Chapter 44

At sea, North Atlantic
May 1897

Self-righteousness is the most disgusting of human traits, intensifying other faults and curdling virtue; Jakob fought it on one hand, but
(he has to admit) enjoyed it on the other. It enhanced the energy
with which he swept away difficulties; it gilded his tongue when
talking to sponsors; it made him more serious and more passionate.
He was rather appalled to discover this capacity in himself, but then
he has never before felt himself entitled to it.

Now, the *Micmac* plows through heavy swells over the Grand
Banks and, for the first time in months, there is nothing he can do to
help. Fog accompanies them, and vast clouds of seabirds, swirling
noisily over the gray water, dipping into the rich broth below the
surface. Despite the cold, Welbourne and he spend much time on
deck—Welbourne with a rifle slung over his arm, looking for things
to shoot, Jakob staring at the horizon in an attempt to quell his seasickness. They see seals and dolphins and, one day, a pod of right
whales just off their bows. Aniguin spends most of his time in his
bunk, asleep.

The week before they left, Jakob and Hendrik took the ferry to Blackwell's Island to visit their father, and Jakob explained that he was going away again. As usual, Arent de Beyn was largely silent, although whether this expressed disappointment, disapproval, or indifference was hard to say.

Aniguin received another letter from Flora Athlone, telling him of her plans to arrive in Siorapaluk in a few weeks' time, and he found that he could read it aloud with a notable absence of feeling. Then he took Aniguin to visit the graves at Mount Olivet. Ivalu, Padloq, and Aviaq were buried in a corner of the hospital grounds, under a grove of chestnuts. The graves were marked with simple white crosses, each inscribed with a name and date. Brilliant grass grew over them.

"I was thinking, Aniguin, there should be a plaque, explaining who they are," said Jakob, as they stood and looked at the three mounds. Aniguin didn't seem to know what to do there, but he took off his bowler when Jakob doffed his, and stood with it in his hands.

"What is a plaque?"

"A notice. A marker, so that people remember them."

Aniguin sniffed. "I will not forget," he said.

"No. I know. I also wanted to ask you, I should have done so before, but . . . it might be possible to take their bodies back to Greenland. Not now, but in the future. Would the families—would you—like that?"

"Why?"

"You could bury them near your home." He did not know if it was customary for Eskimos to visit their dead.

Aniguin turns away. "No."

"Right. Yes . . . I just wanted to ask."

Throughout the visit, Aniguin seemed uncomfortable; he had acquiesced to the suggestion that he visit the graves, but Jakob suspected he hadn't wanted to come at all. After all, the dead were taboo. Thinking about it now, he realizes Aniguin never disagreed with any of his suggestions, until the one about the bodies. His way was to agree politely, to smile; he expressed gratitude and appreciation in his soft voice. He laughed easily. Jakob wonders whether his whole experience of America was an unmitigated horror.

Now, when Aniguin comes on deck, inhaling the sharp air, he smiles with what Jakob hopes is genuine pleasure. He can smell ice, he says, long before they see any. The *Micmac*'s captain claims that icebergs smell of cucumbers. When the first berg hoves into view—a great bolster of ice, striped like a humbug—they stand at the rail, sniffing. Jakob cannot detect cucumbers, just a raw, faintly acrid tang that does not smell like anything else in his experience.

The thing that gave him most pleasure in the last weeks before sailing was his rekindled friendship with Clara Urbino. They met frequently, lunching in a restaurant near her department store. Jakob had the irrational sense that, by talking to her, he was indirectly including Frank in his plans. He found it comforting to be with someone who knew the most discreditable things about him (there was very little she didn't know) and yet still seemed to feel genuine affection for him. There was no coquetry in their friendship, no expectation; it was undoubtedly that which made it so easy.

A few days before they sailed, he met her for the last time. He was unnerved by the proximity of his departure.

"Is something wrong, Jake?"

"If I've made mistakes, it's too late to correct them, but I think about everything I've ordered, and checked, and"—he shook his head—"even if I find nothing wrong, I can't stop."

"As you said before you went north with Frank, people live there all year round, making do with what the country provides."

"True, but that doesn't stop me from worrying."

"Jake, from what I know of you, I'm sure it will be all right. Not that my opinion carries much weight in these matters."

"You're wrong. Your opinion means a great deal to me." He hesitated. "There's something I wanted to say to you. You'll probably think I'm crazy."

Clara looked at him in astonishment. "Yes?"

"Please don't dismiss it out of hand."

Clara looked wary.

"We . . . um, understand quite a lot about each other, wouldn't you say? We have a great deal in common. And we . . . that is, I've never had such a good friend as you, Clara. I'll be thinking of you, while I'm away, and there is no one I will look forward to seeing again, as much as you."

He thought of the words he had rehearsed, but now they seemed silly, so he simply said, "Will you marry me?"

Clara burst out laughing, then stopped and looked at him. "You're not serious." She was smiling.

"Yes, I am. I don't mean right now . . ."

She looked down at her plate. "I'm . . . startled."

Jakob smiled, rather wanly. "I know this is very sudden and that it must seem strange."

He leaned over the table and lowered his voice further: "I know about Lucille. I don't expect you to change. But there's no one I care about more than you. I want you to be safe . . . safer than you could be on your own, perhaps."

"You don't pretend to be in love with me, then?" She smiled, as though this were a relief.

He shrugs. "Whatever that means. If two people care for each other as much as I believe we do . . . isn't that worth a great deal?"

She sighed, but there was a warmth in her eyes, a flush in her cheeks.

"I don't know what to say, Jake. You've astonished me."

"May I leave you with the idea?"

"What has brought this about? You've never struck me as a man who wanted to settle down."

"I suppose not. I always wanted to be free, and I have been. I've led a selfish life. But I've thought a lot, recently, about what's important, and affection and companionship seem to me the greatest things in life."

Clara looked at him, and the last traces of her smile left her.

"When you explained about Frank and his Eskimo girl, you described it as the need for comfort—the need to cling to someone before you leave for unknown dangers. Isn't this the same thing?"

Jakob bit back the denial. He thought of Swedish Kate, of how she had accused him, rightly, of wanting to save her. With her, he had been swept away; but, with Clara, it was a sober decision, he believed, born out of sincere affection.

"Perhaps, partly. But I do love you, Clara; when we are to meet, I so look forward to being with you. I think we could be happy."

"Did you ask the lady in Europe to marry you?"

"Ah . . . As I think I told you, she was already married."

"People get divorced nowadays."

He shrugged uncomfortably.

"I read in the paper that Mrs. Athlone is going back to Greenland this year."

Jakob went cold, and hoped she didn't notice. He hated the way his whole being jerked at the name.

"Yes."

"I always wondered if it was her."

Jakob swallowed. He lifted his eyes to her with an effort.

"It was. I think it's unlikely that we'll meet. It's a huge country, and, even if we do cross paths . . . It was all over, two years ago."

"But you're . . . concerned about seeing her?"

Jakob shrugged. "A little. But it will go. And we may not meet at all."

"I still care for Lucille. I don't know if that will change. It would, if I could will it so."

He nodded.

Clara reached for his hand. "Jake, dear . . . I'm touched by your kind offer. By the time you come back, we may both feel the same—or we may feel differently. Let's wait until then."

Jakob looked around and summoned a waiter. He ordered dessert. They sat without talking, then Clara said, "I suppose I wonder what you are thinking. If we were to marry . . . where would love be? The kind of love . . . You know what I mean."

"The kind that is painful, and short-lived, and against our better judgment? I don't believe I will feel that again. I believe we can do better."

Clara looked at him in surprise, amusement pulling at her mouth.

"You're talking like an old man, which you are not! Do you really think I would save you from that?"

He was startled, and a little hurt. He said, "You make it sound selfish."

"I think it a reasonable question."

"Perhaps wanting to be with someone is always selfish. Your company is dearer to me than anyone else's. So, to answer your question: yes."

"And you think you could save me from that?"

He was shocked (though why should he be?) by her question. "I don't know. I know that I want to protect you from all unhappiness."

Clara smiled sadly. "I don't know that affection, however deep, is sufficient armor against that sort of love. I don't want to believe I'll never feel it again, however painful or ill-judged it may be."

Jakob couldn't think of anything further to say. Clara appeared to be thinking deeply, a slight frown on her forehead. After a few minutes, he said, "I'm sorry. It wasn't my intention to upset you before I left."

"Oh, I'm not upset . . . I'm not used to this sort of thing! I should thank you."

"Oh, God . . ." He waved his hand in dismissal. "Please don't think about it again—or do, if you want to. As you say, who knows what will have happened by the time I come back."

He smiled to cover his despondency. It wasn't that he'd expected a declaration of love, but the idea had seemed, in his mind, something entirely good—a solution, a talisman.

"I'm sorry I surprised you like this. Knowing I'm going away for so long, I wanted to . . ." He shook his head. "It was selfish. I'll miss you, Clara."

"I'll miss you too."

He did not regret asking her. Whether she said yes or no (it would almost certainly be no), there would be *something* to happen on his return, which made his return somehow more certain.

After lunch, their ways coincided for a block, and when they paused on a corner under a linden tree, he asked if he might kiss her goodbye.

"No, certainly . . . Oh, all right," she said, and so he did, gently pressing his lips to hers, and was sure he felt an answering tremor. He looked into her eyes, noted her quickened breathing. He grinned, suddenly heartened.

"There, was that awful?"

Clara laughed. "I must go. I will be late! Come back safely."

Why securing some sort of avowal had mattered so much, he couldn't afterward say; perhaps she was right and he was afraid, although what he was afraid of, he didn't know. Much later, he remembered how he had said to her, "I do love you." The small word did not seem significant at the time.

Chapter 45

The air smells of saltwater and root fires. The sand on the beach is a warm, pinkish white—a crescent curving out into the bay. The bare hills rise steeply, pockmarked and crimson. The water, a sheet of tarnished silver. Across the bay, dark cliffs, scored and wrinkled, their gullies highlighted by the sun; overhead, a pale sky—all mirrored in the stillness. To the east, at the head of the fjord, the white tongue of a glacier protrudes into the water. It looks inviting—such a gentle slope—a broad highway beckoning her into the interior. Above the cliffs—above even the circling, crying dovekies that speckle the pure sky—like a sleeping giant, always the line of white—winter in abeyance: the ice.

The air is as clear as gin, and plays tricks—it turns a white Arctic hare into a polar bear, a black turd into a seal. Flora can make out the contours on a rock, miles away; she has the sense she could reach over and pick it up. Beneath the skin of her kayak, the sea moves like the flank of an animal. Slicing the surface with her paddle, careful not to trouble the stillness, she spins her unstable craft around in a circle. Now she is facing the village of Siorapaluk—"pretty little sandy beach"—with its drunken sod-and-stone houses and their own wooden hut, awkward in its right-angled newness. A dog fight breaks out behind someone's house: a volley of sharp barks, a shrill yelp. Silence again. Juniper smoke stains the air, and, in the north, she notices a faint darkness above the horizon. This calm will not last.

Sighing with mingled delight and regret—that she is here, that she cannot stay here in the boat, all day, sliding through the water as easily as a fish or a seal—she steers herself lazily toward the shore. A figure on the beach ambles toward her, and she gets her smile ready. Although she is at the edge of the world, her kayak, out on the water, is the only place she can be alone.

She runs the kayak on to the sand and struggles gracelessly out of the boat. Gilbert Ashbee is a few yards away. When she is on her feet, he says, with the amusement in his voice she has come to detest, "Mrs. Athlone, allow me . . ."

"No need, Mr. Ashbee . . ."

Flora is quite capable of picking up the kayak, and begins to do so, but he strides toward her and plucks it out of her hands. The only way she could prevent him is by a physical tussle.

"Thank you," she says, as if she meant him to do so all along.

"Did you have fun?" he asks politely. He has an unerring sense for the thing that will most irritate at any given moment. She cannot believe it is accidental.

"I am becoming more proficient."

They walk up to the hut and, despite Ashbee's presence, Flora feels her heart toll with delight and the thrill of ownership. Every annoyance, every hardship, every sacrifice is worth this: to have come back.

They are all proud of their base—a prefabricated wooden building of a design chosen by Flora, who did not see why a hut built for the Arctic should be cold or cramped. Admittedly, it is not large: inside it measures thirty feet by eighteen. At one end is a tiny room, Flora's private domain, containing bunk, desk, and chair. The internal walls are of boxes that act as shelves. Her bunk is inspired by the maritime model: a structure with the bed at the top, a desk underneath, and lockers that fit snugly below that. There is enough room to bring in the bathtub. There is a tiny window and a door, which can be bolted from the inside—not that she has discovered any need to do so.

The main room has three more bunks ranged along the walls. Rails are rigged from the ceiling, and from these hang blankets so that each man can draw himself, when he has had his fill of his companions, into a nominally private space. The stove is ducted around the hut so that, by the time it reaches the outside, all warmth is spent. Next to the stove is the table, and, at the other end of the hut, another room serves as laboratory and darkroom. The whole structure is, in effect, a hut within a hut—the outer shell forms an enveloping lean-to corridor, where stores are stacked. The main entrance is to the southeast; they turn a corner to enter the inner hut by a door on the north side, by which time—the thinking goes—most of the cold will have been left behind. On three sides, the corridor is full height, but the fourth is lower, to allow daylight in through four high-set windows, facing southwest, over the fjord.

The most unusual part of the structure is the tiny hut perched at the northwest corner, by the second entrance door: a makeshift lavatory, positioned over a stream. In winter, when the stream freezes, they will build a snow hut, and let the dogs clean it out. To the villagers, the convenience is a source of hilarious fascination; they are used to squatting on the beach, protected only by their sense of discretion. Flora did the same when she was a child; it is one of the freedoms (not the most precious) that growing up has stolen from her.

Flora is delighted with the hut. She loves the golden brown of its raw planks. She loves the neatness of the joinery and the dull blue-black of the stove. She loves the patterns of frost that build up, inaccessibly, on the inside of the outer glass panes (and which, thereafter, will never entirely disappear). She delights in the painstaking ingenuity on display all around them. It is solid and functional and clever—perfectly without history.

Flora knows every family in Siorapaluk, and there are old friends among them—Simiak and Apilah, Meqro, Tateraq, Pualana. Not Aniguin. Since his return from America, Aniguin lives up the coast, at Neqi. A month ago, when Flora and the others disembarked, they learned that two Americans—white-haired de Beyn and another man—had set up a base there, and that they had already left on a trip over the inland ice. It was late in the season to attempt such a journey.

Flora is usually too busy or tired to think about this, but as the sun loses power and the days become shorter, she feels a deep-lying concern. Toward the end of September, Aniguin visits for the first time, and brings news that no one wanted to hear: the Americans have not returned, and autumn storms have begun.

Perhaps it is this that casts a pall over their reunion. Or it is that, when she first saw him, she expressed sympathy for Ivalu's death, and he looked away, as though bored. Flora knew it was not done to name the dead, or even refer to them, but to ignore her death completely was impossible.

Over supper, Flora tries to forget her worries and be happy that she is finally seeing her friend again, but every question she asks is overshadowed by the ghosts of the dead, or by the ghostly presence of Jakob. Aniguin tells them how de Beyn helped with the museum, with the hospital, with the farm where he lived over the winter . . .

Flora becomes depressed, and as the evening wears on, irritated. America seems to have changed him; he was always a subtle youth, but he was tactful, too. Either he has lost that perceptiveness, or he does not care that she is silent as he boasts of the many rich women who told him what a fine fellow he was, never mentioning his dead wife at all, as though she never existed.

As he talks, he barely looks at her—as though she doesn't exist either. She remembers her fear that she might not see him again. This awkwardness, her discomfort, his changed attitude, make that fear seem foolish.

The wind has kicked up—sudden gusts slam against the walls like blows—winds from the east: from the ice cap. The steel shutters rattle continually. During one vicious gust, when the shutters make a frenzied, high-pitched whirring, Flora snaps, "God, Ralph, we must stop that infernal din. I can't hear myself think."

Everyone looks surprised. Ralph jumps up immediately. "I'll go and have a look. The wind must be coming from just that angle . . ."

"Oh, you can wait until morning; I didn't mean . . ." But he has gone. She is embarrassed. She smiles at the others. "I didn't mean him to go outside in this . . ."

Ashbee pushes back his chair. "I'll go and help. He could probably use a hand."

He goes, leaving Flora feeling worse than ever. She has to be so careful not to diminish her status in their eyes. She helps Aniguin to more stew.

"Did the Americans go in the same direction as the trip they made before, with Armitage?"

"*Ieh.* They wanted to go north, to the big cliff. If they don't find game up there, they will die."

Flora smiles quickly. "They found game before. Who is with them?"

"Metek went again, and your brother, Sorqaq. He's young. He needs to prove himself. I expect, if he comes back, he will work for you too."

Flora freezes, and feels the puzzled stare of Henry Haddo turn toward her. He says, "Why does he call this man your brother? Is it a term of friendship?"

"Oh . . ." Under the table, Flora crushes her napkin in her hands. "It can mean many things. There are all sorts of adoptions here, and a child can be allied to another family, and is known as someone else's 'son' as well as his own father's. Aniguin was adopted by Apilah and Simiak after his parents died . . ."

Haddo nods, diligently filing away information.

"What Fellora says is true," says Aniguin, "but I say Sorqaq is her brother because her father, Mackie, *kujappok* many times with Asarpaka. Everybody knows this."

He laughs. Haddo looks down. Flora keeps her face utterly still. She has heard this rumor before, more than once, but always managed to hold the thing at arm's length, without deciding whether or not it is true (she has never, of course, asked her father about it). But no one has brought it up in such a coarse way, in front of a member of her expedition.

"Such things are normal here." Aniguin is addressing Haddo. "Many children are both *kallunat* and Inuit. Is it not so, Fellora?"

Flora attempts to smile in Haddo's direction, without meeting his eye.

"It has happened, but not everybody does it."

"Not you, Fellora."

She manages to laugh. "I'm a woman, and I have a husband."

"But a husband who is ill. Who cannot give you children. You should take another husband—one who is strong."

"Dr. Haddo"—Flora reaches for the seal stew—"can I help you to a little more?"

"Thank you. It's very tasty." Haddo drops his voice. "I think he is announcing his candidacy, Mrs. Athlone."

Haddo smiles at her in a way that unites them in the face of Aniguin's boorishness. Flora feels a wave of gratitude.

"Men all do it—Armitay, Te Peyn, Mackie—they all *kujappok* here." He smiles at Haddo. "We will find a nice fat girl for you!"

The door opens with a blast of frigid air, and Ashbee and Ralph come back in, their faces red with cold.

"How's that?"

Ashbee claps his hands together, pleased with himself. Flora stares, cannot think for a moment what he is talking about, then realizes that the whirring of the shutter has stopped.

The next morning, they wake to find the water in the fjord changed. The first signs are subtle; something indefinable is off, somewhere. The sea becomes matte and still, or it heaves like the flank of a great gray mammal. Then the sea's ally, the wind, gets up; a swell pushes in from the sound and the skin of ice is mashed into insignificance by the sea's greater power. The choppy water looks dark and powerful. But the cold comes back—a stealthy opponent, tireless—under cover of night. The sea is stilled once again. A milky belt of ice rings the coast, on which meadows of frost flowers spring up one morning, only to disappear, washed away, the next. But it comes back, and comes back; the ice thickens as October wears on, it turns white and begins to beckon: Come—while there is still daylight! . . . But it is heavy and waterlogged; it sags beneath the body's weight, is not to be trusted.

Halfway through the month, the cry of "*Qamiut!* Sledges!" goes up. It has been a raw, overcast day; mist lies heavy on the hilltops. There is one sled, rounding the ice foot from the north. It pulls up in a cacophony of barking as the dogs of Siorapaluk greet their kin. One fur-clad figure steps off the back of the sled. Under the fur hood, his eyebrows are white with frost. It is Tateraq, Flora's childhood friend. His feet and legs have been soaked and frozen; his bearskin trousers are as hard as wood. He went through the ice three times on the journey from Neqi. The dogs saved his life. This is nothing remarkable.

"Has something happened? Have the Americans returned?"

Enjoying his importance as the bearer of news, Tateraq takes his time as they ply him with food and tea. At last, he says that all have returned, alive, from their journey on the inland ice. But the *kallunat* need a doctor. They suffered for their foolishness—as everyone told them they would. Tateraq has a note.

"Do you have some of that nice, piss-colored paste? *Ieh*, that stuff . . ." He scoops a dollop of apricot jam onto a chunk of seal.

Flora opens the crumpled, greasy envelope, and turns away from the others to read it. It is addressed to Mrs. Athlone, and deeply regrets the necessity, but asks for the services of her doctor, as they need treatment for frostbite. It is signed Jakob de Beyn, but the handwriting is unrecognizable.

"Of course, we must go," she says to Haddo, with a glance up at the frost-gray windows. Outside, the sky has darkened.

"Tateraq, tell me how you left them?"

"They are hungry and exhausted, and the *kallunat* have frostbite." He indicates his face, hands, and feet.

"Were they walking?"

"They were walking. But the spirits got them up there; they look like dead men."

Neqi, 77°52' N, 71°37' W

They arrive in a soft, amorphous twilight. Without guides, they would have had no idea where they were—the horizon invisible, the cliffs swallowed by fog. Neqi crouches on a sliver of land under high cliffs, exposed to the winds off Smith Sound. Under dark cloud, it is cheerless and unwelcoming.

The Americans' home is the same hut she came to five years ago, much weathered and rebuilt. When Flora knocks on the door—with trepidation, but she *had* to come—it is opened by Ainineq, with a smile of welcome. Flora and Haddo are dazzled by the lamplight, then Flora sees two scarecrows sitting at the table with bandaged hands and feet and blackened faces. Her first, shocked thought is that Jakob is not here—and then she realizes that one of the scarecrows has gray hair. Like his companion, he is very thin, and his face is blistered, with red-rimmed, hollowed eyes. Their state renders them frightening: outcast lepers, mendicants returned from a place of dreadful privation. She stares (no, she should not have come), aware that no one has yet spoken. Jakob struggles to his feet.

"Please, don't get up," says Flora, finding both his appearance and his initial look of shocked hostility intensely painful.

"Mrs. Athlone, how nice to see you again. It's very good of you both to come. This is Mr. Welbourne; Mrs. Athlone, whom I met on my last trip here. Forgive us for not shaking hands . . ."

He raises bandaged hands, untidy and stained. Flora shakes her head.

"Very happy indeed to see you, ma'am. I've heard so much about you." Welbourne's voice is deep and melodious; his accent tickles her ear. "I'm sorry not to stand . . ."

"Oh, please, good heavens . . ." She is slightly hysterical at the general politeness. "This is Dr. Haddo."

"Mrs. Athlone," says Jakob. "I apologize for taking up your time and for bringing you both here in such weather. Mr. Welbourne and I appreciate your promptitude." He attempts a smile, but his face is too raw to respond. Even his voice seems cracked.

"There's no need to apologize, Mr. de Beyn. None at all. I'm glad we can be of help. When we knew you were out on the ice cap so late, we were concerned . . ."

Haddo unpacks his medical bag. Welbourne says, "You must see to Mr. de Beyn first—he is worse afflicted than I."

"All right. Stay there, under the light, Mr. de Beyn. Perhaps we could have some boiled water?" Haddo turns to Flora.

She nods with relief, asks Ainineq to set about some hot food, then occupies herself with heating water and scrubbing the surface of the table, glad to have an occupation. She has thought of this meeting many times, tried to armor herself against it, but it is worse, even, than she imagined.

Haddo sits in front of Jakob, unwrapping his hands, which are swollen with frost blisters, the fingertips blackened, skin peeling off.

Flora turns with a firm smile to Welbourne, whose overgrown hair and beard cannot entirely disguise the handsome features and bright blue eyes beneath. She begins to unwrap the bandages from his hands.

"Are you a nurse, then, Mrs. Athlone, along with your many other qualifications?"

"No, but I have experience with frostbite. You can't spend much time here without gaining that."

She turns his hands carefully. They are raw, but seem not badly affected. She kneels on the floor and begins uncovering his feet.

"My goodness . . ." He laughs. "I apologize for the state of them. They're not a pretty sight."

"Please don't worry. I'm sure I've seen worse."

She has seen worse, although the middle toes are blackened and nailless. She bends forward to sniff them. Welbourne manages to laugh; she admires his spirit.

"Your reputation for courage is well deserved, ma'am."

He has great confidence—the air of one who would be at ease in any situation. Jakob, on the other hand, keeps his eyes downcast, and is silent.

"There doesn't seem to be any necrosis." She gathers up the stained bandages. "Dr. Haddo will examine them. Then we'll need to debride the dead tissue."

"I look forward to it. Thank you, ma'am."

"How long were you on the ice cap, Mr. Welbourne?"

"Eighty-eight days."

"My goodness. That's a long time. Did you find game?"

Welbourne barks with laughter. "That's what the Eskimos ask! They don't care about . . ." He glances at Jakob. "Are we allowed to say where we have been?"

"I don't see why not. Mrs. Athlone is familiar with the territory."

"So I gather." Welbourne looks at her—despite the pain he must be in—with decidedly chivalrous appreciation. "Well, ma'am, to answer your question, we did find game, in the vicinity of Sherard Osborn Fjord and Victoria Inlet. We managed to shoot some musk oxen and two caribou. Good thing too. It was nip and tuck. We've been to the north coast of Greenland and we looked at the Arctic Ocean. We saw a bear on the sea-ice up there, but we couldn't bring him down, I'm sorry to say. I think that would have been the most northerly kill in the world! But we've proved there's no land farther north in that vicinity. Or, rather, Mr. de Beyn proved it. I was just along for the ride."

"Mr. Welbourne speaks less than the truth. I couldn't have done it without you—or Metek and Sorqaq."

"I congratulate you. That's an enormous achievement." Flora glances toward Jakob, who is looking at his right foot, now in Haddo's lap. He doesn't answer. He must be pleased to have proved Armitage a liar. He doesn't look pleased.

"Are Metek and Sorqaq still with you?"

"Metek has gone to his family in Etah. Sorqaq is here."

All through this exchange, Jakob keeps his head turned toward Haddo, as if he can't bear to have Flora in his sight.

"Do they need medical treatment?"

"They seem well. Tired, of course, but no frostbite at all. Remarkable."

"I don't think I've ever known a case of an Eskimo with frostbite. They seem to have an immunity to it, perhaps through being acclimatized from birth. Or maybe there's something in their blood. It would be an interesting field of study . . ." She addresses Welbourne.

"It was certainly extraordinary how they could perform quite intricate maneuvers without gloves, when it was so cold we couldn't do anything at all."

Haddo finishes his examination of Jakob's face and ears.

"Well, Mr. de Beyn, the damage is not deep. If I may, while I take a look at Mr. Welbourne, I will let Mrs. Athlone take over; you needn't worry . . . you're in good hands."

"I know what an accomplished nurse Mrs. Athlone is. She helped to take off this finger—when we met before."

Jakob holds up his left hand. His eyes meet hers, as if challenging her to deny that that was the last time.

Haddo moves on to Welbourne, and Flora sits in the chair next to Jakob with a bowl of water and a sterilized cloth. He holds out his right hand, and she begins to rub the dead skin off his fingers. Underneath, the flesh is red-raw.

"Tell me if it's too painful."

"It's fine."

"I'm sorry these are the circumstances of our meeting again."

He makes a noncommittal noise—hardly reassuring. Damn you, she thinks, and then chastises herself.

"Do you remember the geologist on our previous expedition—Mr. Dixon?"

"I do: a big, black-haired man. I liked him."

"He is here. He's eager to meet you again. He remembers you very kindly from before."

"Oh." A faint smile crosses his face. "I'd like that."

She smiles at him, catching his eye briefly. He looks away.

"I'll tell him. I'm sure there will be opportunities over the winter. There, that hand is done." She takes the other one. "Was the weather very bad on the ice cap?"

Jakob blinks, sucking in his breath, and says, "Not too bad, but one of our fuel cans leaked. We had to make do with what we had." After a pause, he adds, "I should have allowed a greater margin for error."

She finishes the left hand and kneels on the floor to work on his feet. It feels more intimate to be holding his foot in her lap like this, more than touching his hands. Because we are used to shaking hands, she tells herself. Possibly, also, because she remembers kneeling in front of him, in another time and place. She is vividly aware of the pulse in his ankle. Her throat knots with an emotion she does not care to identify. She looks up once—his eyes are closed, his expression remote. She concentrates on sloughing off the disgusting tissue, makes her movements brisk and ungentle. She stokes her memories of anger and despair and fear. Nothing else is of any use to her.

Jakob describes for Welbourne something of the circumstances of the Americans' last night in Siorapaluk, five years ago. He says the missing finger was his own fault.

"Mrs. Athlone must think me a poor excuse for an Arctic traveler."

"Of course not. Anyone can suffer frostbite, if conditions are bad enough. It is often a matter of luck."

There is a silence, and she realizes that her remark has not come off; she has come across as patronizing, or worse. She is grateful when Haddo turns to her and asks, in a low voice, if she can leave the hut so that he can ask the men "some more . . . ah . . . questions."

She steps into the pitiless night. There is no prospect of immediate escape—they have to stay at least until tomorrow morning. She is exhausted, but feels overwhelming relief to be out of the hut and his presence; at one point, she thought she would succumb to the threat of tears, but conquered them. She maintained a professional and friendly demeanor—she thinks—despite his behavior, which was so terse it verged on rudeness. On seeing her, he had looked . . . appalled.

What did she expect? She should not have come.

Chapter 46

Siorapaluk, 77°47' N, 70°38' W
October–December 1897

It occurs to Flora over the following weeks—when she and Haddo are back in their own house—that she is not the only one wearing a mask. Here in Greenland, clamped into this sliver of shore between ice cap and frozen sea, everyone hides their feelings behind a smile. Indulging in strong displays of opinion or emotion is too costly when life is so precarious. No one can survive alone. She has the impression that everyone walks on thin ice. Their presence—the British, the Americans, and the whalers, when they came—has made the smiling mask worse. No one disagrees with them, or denies them. The Eskimos can't afford to offend. We cannot form real friendships, she thinks, no matter what we say, because friends should be equal, and here—except for a few rare moments—we can never be equal.

The possible exception—she hopes—is her friendship with Meqro, who was delighted to see Flora again. Despite being an unmarried woman with a child, at the bottom of the pecking order, Meqro has grown in confidence since they last met. She lives with her widowed father, Ehré. She is lucky that he is still a good hunter, and that he has not remarried, which would make her position difficult. Aamma is four years old and shows traces of her father in her features. They live near the British hut, so Meqro can work for them, making winter clothes and helping with their housekeeping. A couple of other women are employed in this work—Flora tried to employ those who most needed help: women without husbands, like Meqro, and a young girl called Atitak, who has a terrible, disfiguring squint. Flora is generous (generosity is easy to show here); there is not enough work for everyone who wants it.

Often, there are three or four of them sitting on the floor of the hut, sewing and talking, but Flora is happiest when it is just Meqro. Then, if she has finished her work, she sits on the floor beside her and takes her *ulu*—her crescent-bladed knife—and joins her in scraping the inside of a raw pelt. No Eskimo woman ever sits idle, and Flora has picked up the habit of finding something to occupy her hands. She is clumsy at such work, but it is soothing to do something useful. Aamma plays nearby with seal vertebrae, or, encouraged by Flora, scribbles with a pencil on scraps of paper.

One day, Meqro says, "Te Peyn brought me a letter from Ferank's mother and father. They say they are happy to hear about Aamma, that it comforts them to know of her. They say they wish to help her. They say that, if I want her to come to America, they will look after her and give her a life there. I don't know what I should do."

"What do you want to do?"

"I don't want her to go, but I ask you, Fellora. If you think she would have a better life there, then I will make her go."

"Would you go too?"

Meqro looks down at her *ulu*. "I don't think I would like it. I think of what happened to my friends . . . It's dangerous for us there. But perhaps it is different for Aamma. Ferank was her father. If something happens to me, or my father . . ." She shrugs.

"I can't tell you what you should do, Meqro."

"But, Fellora, you know what it is to be here, and you know what it is to be there, for a woman. Here, life is hard."

"It's not easy anywhere. I don't know America, how much it is like Britain. I don't know the Urbinos, but . . . I would have thought

Aamma would be better off with her own people, and certainly better off with you."

Meqro smiles her delightful, sweet smile. "But her people are also Ferank's people. And they are rich. They sent many presents to her. Little figures . . . *Aja*—so beautiful!"

Flora has seen one of these figures: a china-headed doll with a cross expression, dressed in silk and lace. It has been stripped, dismembered, and disemboweled, the head broken in several pieces.

"What did Te Peyn say? He knows them well."

"He was like you. He said he couldn't say. But they are kind."

"I think it would be hard in America for a child who looks like her, who looks different from most people. Here, she looks like one of you—she is one of you."

Meqro nods vigorously.

"*Ieh.* It's strange how the children look more like us than like you. The *kallunat* are strong in many ways—but in this, Inuit are the stronger!" She laughs.

"Yes, it's true." Flora agrees, blushing, although she isn't sure why. "You could both go to America and see what you thought. If you didn't like it, you could both come back. It's always possible to change your mind. America is not so far away: three, four weeks' sail."

Meqro grows serious again. "I don't know. I cannot see what life is in America, without my people. I'm afraid."

"I know it was terrible, what happened to Ivalu and the others. There are diseases there. *Kallunat* diseases are bad for Inuit."

"*Ieh.* She is safer here."

They fall silent. Aamma tears her drawing into small pieces and throws them in the air. Despite Flora's efforts at teaching her to draw dogs and seals, destruction is her favorite game.

"*Qaniit!*" she says, and laughs. Snowflakes!

"Has Aniguin spoken about his time in America?"

Meqro shrugs. "He said people listened to what he said." She jerks her head, as though finding this hard to believe.

"He gave an interview to the newspapers," Flora says (she has to explain 'newspapers' to her friend), "and many people read it. So they did listen." She scrapes at a stubborn piece of membrane. "I know he suffered much there. Is he happier, now?"

"Aniguin is never happy. Not from when he was born. There's something wrong in his head." Meqro shrugs.

"But something in him has changed. Have the Americans helped him, since he came back?"

"Yes. Te Peyn is very kind. He has given him many things. Te Peyn is nice . . ." She smiles, and sees Flora's raised eyebrows and giggles. "No, no! Natseq tried to sleep with him again and he said no! He is married, now, to the sister of Ferank. No, not married . . . What do you call it in your country, before?"

"Engaged," says Flora.

"*Ieh.* He doesn't want a friend anymore." She shrugs. "Perhaps he's too old."

Flora peers at her pelt, at the traces of fat that cling to the inner surface. She puts it down. Her *ulu*, its curved blade bright as the quarter moon, weighs in her hand. She pictures it slicing through the skin of her wrist—up and down: she knows how—into the vein, bringing forth dark blood. She imagines slapping her friend's smooth, round cheek, and is so horrified that she stands up, muttering an excuse, and walks out of the hut. Not that she would ever do that—not that she would ever do either of those things—but she wants to commit an act of violence, on something.

At the beginning of November, they throw a feast for the village to celebrate—or commemorate—the setting of the sun. This is the occasion at which someone suggests they invite the Americans to Siorapaluk for Christmas. The others second the idea, eager for new faces. Flora is noncommittal. She has a horror of seeming forward. But she cannot tell the others why, so she assents. The odds are the weather will prevent it, anyway.

The four-month night begins. At first, it is not true dark; there is a month of perpetual twilight, but the twilight deepens as the sun sinks further below the horizon. It is the time of year when one has to be careful. At first, everyone pretends that it is no problem—the Eskimos have been looking forward to it! It's a relief after that endless light, which never lets them rest, and winter is the season for traveling by sled, for visiting. However, there is also something oppressive. Flora wonders if the oppression comes from the people as much as the darkness. In the past, in winter, she and her father could sit for hours with Apilah and Simiak while neighbors came to their *illu*, sat around the fire, ate, smoked, repeated the same anecdotes and scraps of news . . . A neighbor might visit five times in a day. There was nothing new to say. They were sick of each other. But still they came. Flora discovered extremes of boredom she had never imagined. As far as she could tell, everyone was bored. In the ship, after such a visit, she was drunk with solitude.

For the explorers, the cold and the darkness are just two of the challenges to be met. But the transition from endless day to endless dark is a hard one. They have their work: they set up a weather station on the frozen sea; Ashbee and Haddo bring samples of seawater to study in the laboratory—it teems with busy, microscopic life—and Flora has set herself the task of photographing the peculiar clouds prevalent here. After the sun sets, there is less she can do on that project, but, the day after the feast, she records a breathtaking display of noctilucent clouds over the strait. The sky is dark, but the cloud is so high it catches the sun's rays over the curvature of the earth and glows like white fire. Next to it, Deneb and Vega are crisp and bright. She makes exposures of different lengths, hoping one of them will capture it. She wonders whether, in Neqi, anyone else is doing the same.

Ralph is as steady as ever. Without him, Flora wonders if any of this would be possible. And she is pleased with Henry Haddo, a young man whose reticence (like her, he is Scottish) reminds her of herself. He is a skillful doctor, a scholar—he coauthored a paper on the incidence of scurvy in prisons—and he is unfailingly kind and patient with the Eskimos.

Ashbee is a different matter. On occasion, Flora hears him shouting at the girls for some real or imagined blunder. Once, he storms out of the hut, sees Flora, and walks in the opposite direction without a word. She goes into the hut to find Henry coming out of the lab, rather red in the face.

"Has something happened? Ashbee just glared at me and rushed off without speaking."

Haddo takes a deep breath. She thinks he is on the brink of tears.

"It's nothing." He tries to smile. "Nothing of importance."

Flora puts it out of her mind. Later, in the laboratory, she discovers that the floor is wet—as though a lot of water had been spilled, or something had been cleaned.

"I want to talk to you about Ashbee."

Ralph and Flora have come for a walk along the beach, for privacy. The cold is metallic and a wind blows snow crystals into their faces.

"You said, when we talked of inviting the Americans for Christmas, that we are not rivals, but we don't know that, because we don't know what their aims are. What is more ridiculous, we don't know what *our* aims are, because I don't know Ashbee's purpose. I had to accept that when we left, but here it is no longer acceptable. We cannot deal with them honestly, not knowing."

She sighs, her breath rushing into a white cloud.

Ralph shrugs. "Do we need to be honest with them?"

"I . . . You surprise me, Ralph. I can't make that decision without knowing. I want you to back me when I ask him to tell us the truth."

There is a pause. "Of course."

Over dinner, Flora brings up the subject, with the affectation of a levity she does not feel. If he refuses, she does not know what she will do.

"Mr. Ashbee . . . Gilbert . . . I think the time has come for you to tell us your purpose in being here. We all assure you of our complete discretion. But if I don't know what your purpose is, I cannot deal honestly with the Americans. There is a certain etiquette to be followed. In spring, we do not want to get in each others' way."

Ashbee looks around the table at the others.

"I gather you have discussed this."

"In the conditions that prevail here, our lives are in each other's hands. There must be trust. And, for that, there must be frankness."

There is a silence. Ashbee purses his lips.

"I suppose it can do no harm now. Although I must insist you do not repeat to the Americans what I'm about to tell you. I reiterate that I am an envoy, and my sponsors have told me only what I need to know. As you're aware, they are interested in new lands—islands—that are, potentially, habitable."

Flora can't prevent a slight, incredulous smile. "For what purpose? I fear you have come to the wrong place."

"New ideas are often mocked simply because they are new. From being thought absurd and unworkable, they are gradually accepted, until they come to seem commonplace."

No one speaks.

"As you know, transportation came to an end thirty years ago. But the problem of prison overcrowding has not come to an end—far from it. British prisons continue to grow; convict hulks are bursting at the seams. There are those in our government actively looking for alternatives, such as undiscovered islands in the Arctic."

He holds up his hand in Flora's direction.

"I realize that conditions here are harsh, but, in some ways, that is all to the good. Prisons should be punitive. People survive here—the natives prove that. And there are vast areas of the map that are uncharted. It seems likely that any new lands will be, like Ellesmere, uninhabited. The first step—the reason for my presence here—is to see if there are any such islands."

Flora breaks the silence: "The sea is no barrier when you can walk on it. It is more in the way of a road than a prison wall."

"But you need dogs and sleds to travel on the ice. If it is sufficiently far from the inhabited portion of the Greenland coast, then distance and difficulty themselves will be the barrier."

"You say that people survive here, Mr. Ash . . . Gilbert—they do, but they survive only by being nomadic. They go where the food is—they go to Neqi to hunt walrus, they come here for auks, to Pittufak for seals—and there are only . . . two hundred people, perhaps, in this huge stretch of land. That is all the land can sustain. Two hundred, spread up and down the coast. Even so, they sometimes starve."

"You're right in what you say, but with new ideas there are always obstacles to be overcome. I'm sure that, like me, you believe the British race supreme in overcoming obstacles that seem insurmountable to others. It is the harshest, coldest place on earth. The prospect of living in such a place fills you with fear. A perfect place, then, for prisoners and degenerates, the detritus of our mills and factories, the dangerous, and the damned."

He leans back and looks around at them. His eyes are shining. Flora takes a deep breath. In her wildest speculations, she never imagined this.

In the silence that follows, Atitak brings the jug of tea and refills their mugs. Ashbee's eyes pass over the girl's face as if she did not exist.

The weather in December is so bad that the possibility of inviting the Americans begins to seem out of the question. But, after a week of storms, the wind drops, the temperature rises, and Haddo sets out to check on their recovery. Flora tells herself they won't come. But Haddo reappears after four days with a written acceptance. Even without his report, Flora can tell from the handwriting that Jakob's hands have recovered. Haddo is touchingly pleased with himself, as if he has pulled off a major diplomatic coup. Flora smiles as if she too is pleased, thinking, It will be all right; there will be so many people here; and, anyway, it doesn't matter.

They plan an elaborate meal, and Flora wraps presents of cigars and sweets. On Christmas Eve, she, Haddo, and Meqro decorate the hut with sledging flags. Flora surveys the warm, colorful room and thinks that this hut feels more like home than her home has ever done.

It does not seem, despite her incoherent hopes to the contrary, that anything is going to prevent the guests' arrival. The weather on Christmas Day is cold and still. At around three o'clock, there is a shout of "*Qamiut!*" and the dogs go into a frenzy of barking.

The terrible scarecrows of a few weeks ago have gone; they have shaved off their beards and put on weight. Their faces and hands still show scarring, but they look human again. Jakob shakes Flora's hand with a smile and apologizes for his manners at their last meeting. Welbourne is effusively charming; he holds her hand in his and raises it to his lips, saying he will never forget her kindness to him, and if she would only deign to call him Scotty, it would make him extremely happy. In another man, such heavy-handed gallantry could be ridiculous or even offensive, but Welbourne carries it off with style.

"Mr. Welbourne is from North Carolina," says Jakob. "Southerners get away with the sort of behavior we northerners never could."

The men laugh. Flora hopes that, in the dim light of the hut, no one has noticed her blush.

After midnight, the wind rises. The hut is full of the shuffling and grunting of men and women asleep after a long, rich meal. The villagers have curled up on the floor rather than go back to their cold houses. Flora, awake, is aware that there is someone only a foot away from her, on the other side of the wooden wall. She hears a creak, the slither and hush of outdoor clothes being pulled on, the pad of footsteps: someone going out to the *illu*. She knows the hut so well that she can tell from the number of footsteps, the creak of particular boards, where he has come from. She sits up, takes her parka from its hook, pokes her feet into her *kamiks*. The wind has driven away the clouds, uncovering a moon two days off full and allowing a faint, silver light to bleed through the window.

Closing the inner door behind her, she is in the denser darkness of the corridor. To her left is the back door that leads to the convenience; he must have gone through there. The storm is getting worse. She steps outside into a freezing wind.

"Can I speak with you?"

The figure straightens up from the *illu* entrance, ghost-haired in the moonlight.

"You gave me a fright."

"I'm sorry. I wanted to talk to you, without everyone else around. It's so difficult."

"Now?" The wind rips his words away, but not the incredulity.

"We could go to Meqro's *illu*. They're all in there."

Hunched against the wind and stinging ice crystals, she fumbles her way to the stone house and dives into the low entrance tunnel. She hears Jakob behind her. When she can lift her head, she is horrified to see the flame of a lamp, and the creased, polished face of Pualana peering at her from the sleeping platform. If he is put out to be disturbed, he does not show it. In the storm, she has taken a wrong turn. Jakob, crawling blindly, bumps into her.

"Fellora. Te Peyn. You are welcome in my poor house. Sit. Eat."

"Thank you, Pualana. Thank you."

They sit on the sleeping platform and Pualana, who has no wife to cook for him, pokes at the flame and throws seal meat into the pot over the lamp. After a few general remarks, she asks Pualana if he minds if they speak in English. He nods acquiescence.

"I'm sorry; I mistook the house, but he can't understand English. I want to discuss plans for the spring tomorrow, but there are also things I want to say to you alone."

Until yesterday, she thought she would not speak of their past. But at dinner she happened to look up—Jakob was on the other side of the table—and their glances met. To her right, Welbourne was playing the gallant and flirting with her; he was the type to flirt with any woman, but he was charming and she enjoyed his attentions. Jakob's look had frozen the smile on her mouth.

"I hope we can be friends, as before."

"Of course." His face is stiff. He seems irritated that she has dragged him out here, and embarrassed by her mistake over the *illu*. Neither can be helped now.

"Good. I hope our expeditions can work in a complementary way."

Jakob nods. "I'm sure they can."

"I don't want there to be a misunderstanding between us because of . . . before."

She watches his face. He looks slightly abashed.

"I'm sorry. When you came to Neqi, I wasn't pleasant. It's not that I want to . . . deny the past—but not in front of the others. I assume they don't know?"

"No, of course not. I want to apologize to you. I know it's all past, but I should have answered your last letter. It was unforgivable of me not to have done so, and I'm sorry."

Jakob smiles briefly. "There's no need to apologize. I understood perfectly."

Flora glances at Pualana. He is staring into space, sucking on his pipe, as though he were alone with some pleasant thoughts. She speaks in a low voice, looking at the wall of the hut.

"I think there is. Your last letter was so kind. I had misunderstood . . . some things. I should at least have explained properly. I don't think I gave you the right impression."

He shakes his head. "I quite understand how difficult your situation must have been. The quickest way to break it off was not to respond. I should not have pestered you."

She is stung by a hard note in his voice.

"I didn't want to break it off," she says in a miserable little voice that she despises. "I wanted to come to Switzerland more than anything; I kept thinking, if I went, and he died . . ."

Jakob sighs, a little impatiently, it seems to her.

"Well, it's water under the bridge. I accept your apology, which was unnecessary. As you said, it's all past."

"You seem angry."

"I'm not angry." His smile is no more convincing than before. "I don't know what else I can say."

"No, I . . . I wanted to . . ." She stops, because, although what she wanted to say had been clear to her when she lay awake in her bunk, it no longer is.

"I'm not angry in the least, but I'm embarrassed to be keeping Pualana from his bed."

They walk back in silence, but, in the lee of the hut, Flora turns to Jakob. She has to raise her voice to be heard over the wind.

"It wasn't just Freddie's illness that made it impossible. There was something else."

"What?"

The fact that he so clearly wants to end this conversation makes it easier to say: "I thought I was safe, but I wasn't."

"What?" He is almost shouting over the wind.

"When we were together—I thought I was safe . . ."

As the realization comes to him, he seems to shrink away from her. Flora thinks, Yes, they say they want us to be weak, and womanly, but when we are, they despise us.

"It was my fault. I believed it was safe. I was wrong."

Jakob seizes her by the arm and pulls her toward the convenience—the summer lavatory, unused now. The door is stiff with disuse. He forces it open and pulls her in out of the wind. Moonlight fills the shack with silvery luminescence, turning his hair into a halo.

"Do you mean . . . You mean that you were pregnant?"

She nods once, without looking at him. There is a silence. When she looks at him again, he is staring at the ground.

"Why didn't you tell me?"

"Why? What would you have said?"

He doesn't seem to have an answer, but looks at her fearfully, the question in his eyes.

"There was no child."

He lets go of her arm—she hadn't noticed he was still holding her.

"I was desperate. Alone. I didn't want to seem to be importuning you, or asking for anything. What could you have done? It was my fault."

She looks out to where the moon casts sharp shadows on the spoiled snow.

"No, it . . . I should have known, better than you. I only meant, if you had told me, perhaps you wouldn't have felt alone."

When she looks at him again, he looks anguished, his face pinched. His voice is quiet. She had expected anger, condemnation, shouting.

"Flora, I'm . . . sorry."

With an effort, she pushes down the lump in her throat.

"It was all right, in the end. It was . . . difficult for a while, that was why I couldn't . . . Do you see now?"

"I don't know what to say."

"There's no need. I learned a lesson. Not to be so . . . rash."

Jakob looks at her with a wrinkled forehead. "Rash . . . ?" he repeats. He looks winded, aged, his skin the same gray-white as the snow.

"Things have to be paid for."

It was something her father might have said. She had not set out to tell him; God knows, she'd thought that would never happen—but his anger kindled her own. She wanted to shock him. To punish. Now he frowns, having recoiled from her as far as the confines of the shack allow. He is shivering.

"You must go inside—your hands will get nipped."

He is holding them curled protectively in front of his chest.

"Go in!" She nods, emphatically. "I'll wait awhile."

"Flora . . . we'll talk tomorrow . . . ? Flora, for goodness' sake!"

She nods at last, so that he will leave her alone.

Chapter 47

Conflicting emotions keep him awake. Initial shock and horror—which he could see she had read on his face—then pity, and chagrin as he has to revise everything he had thought. Then he is overtaken by anger that she had not seen fit to tell him such a thing—braided with the old anger: the hurt he had felt at her silence, her rejection. Do her reasons explain it, really? A terrible, craven relief when she said there was no child. (Is that wrong? Human, surely . . . Anyway, that is what he feels.) But also, beneath shock and sorrow and anger and relief, under all that, deep and glittering, a dark nugget of pride.

He does not know what she must have felt. Surely, it had been a dreadful dilemma. She was right, though—what would he have said? And now? Out there, she was brittle, defensive, matter-of-fact. Dry-eyed throughout. He finds himself both admiring and resenting her unwillingness to share the blame, as though he were not really involved, as though he were not . . . important enough. Yes, perhaps that is what she thought.

Throughout the night, he comes back to his first question: Why hadn't she told him, when they had made those promises to each other? When they had shared something extraordinary? When he, for one, had been in love?

There is no dawn, no breaking of day, but the morning after Christmas begins with a strengthening of the storm. The wind has got up overnight, the noise outside the hut has risen to a tremendous howl; Jakob estimates it is blowing fifty knots. No chance of an early departure.

The first person he sees on pulling aside his curtain is Dixon, stirring something in a steaming jug. Already dressed, Jakob swings his legs to the floor and joins him at the table.

"Good morning, sir. Coffee?" Ralph hands him a mug.

"Thank you."

He looks around at the landscape of frowsy humanity, most still asleep, muttering and exhaling. One of the curtains twitches, and Jakob looks away as Meqro slithers, half-naked, from the bunk behind it—Ashbee's bunk. He feels a stab of irritation, but knows it to be irrational. It is hardly as though she is being unfaithful to Frank.

"I guess it's not usually this busy in the mornings."

"No. High days and holidays only."

Ralph, too, pointedly ignores Meqro's appearance. He smiles at Jakob. Over last night's dinner, Jakob's liking for the man was confirmed. Dixon's shyness dissipates when talking about his work. He is modest and painstaking, eager to hear about Jakob's experience. Jakob has brought a copy of his book of the Gorner Glacier photographs, and thinks he might make a present of it to Ralph on parting. (Hard to believe that, on leaving Neqi, he had toyed with the idea of giving it to Flora—to show her what she had missed.) Ralph promises to show him his notes and specimens from Melville Bay—a prospect that fills Jakob with uncomplicated pleasure.

Meqro is at the stove, melting snow in a pan. She keeps her eyes down, as if she is embarrassed to have been seen with Ashbee. Although, Jakob reflects, she is probably not in the least embarrassed.

Aamma shouts for her mother. Jakob finds it almost incredible that she is also Frank's daughter; he can see no trace of his friend in the little girl. If Frank's parents could see her now, yelling, with snot dribbling over her lip, he can't help feeling they would blanch at offering her a home.

Does any part of Frank live on in this child? She will never know her father, or understand what he was like. He was never aware of her existence. If Frank lives on in her, then the lunatic Arent de Beyn lives on in Jakob, and that is something he cannot countenance. That is why, perhaps, he has never imagined himself having children. But Aamma is not Frank, just as he is not his father . . . He glances up to see Flora emerge from her room, and drops his gaze to stare into his coffee, terrified that she might look into his eyes and be able to read his thoughts.

Like Greenland, Ellesmere is known by its edge. The eastern coast—facing Greenland across Smith Sound—is well explored, and the north coast was mapped in its rudiments by the British naval expedition under Nares, and by Greely, before his expedition ended in disaster. A further portion of the northwest coast was completed by Jakob's own journey, five years ago. The rest—the massive interior, the south, the west—is a blank. The map that Flora now spreads on the workbench in their small laboratory covers the known coasts, Smith Sound, and Greenland, feathering out into obscurity from Whale Sound, where they stand.

"You've already added to this," she says. "Thirty-nine degrees west."

She taps her fingernail on a point in the whiteness at the northern edge of the map.

"How much coast did you survey?"

"Can they hear us in here?" Jakob asks in a low voice. He is sure they cannot be overheard, what with the wind crashing and banging against the walls, making it resound like a drum, but he has to say something.

"Not unless the wind falls." She speaks—also in a low voice—while peering at the map, as though she thinks she is being watched. "It was a remarkable journey. Bold of you to leave so late in the season—"

"Flora, please . . ."

She stops, becomes very still.

"I've been thinking over what you told me last night . . ."

"I'm sorry about mistaking the house. I didn't mean to embarrass you like that. I was sure it was Meqro's."

"Heavens, that doesn't matter." He looks at her in puzzled frustration. "I've been trying to understand . . . I realize that nothing I can say will help, now. But I am . . . enormously sorry for the suffering you must have undergone. I was as much to blame as you; more so."

She places her fingertips on the map and speaks quickly, her eyes on a row of glass jars on the shelf in front of her.

"It's all right; it doesn't matter now. It was what no one would have wanted, but . . . I didn't intend to tell you." She glances briefly at him, then her gaze goes back to the map. "But you seemed so angry with me. It wasn't . . . fair. I wanted you to understand how . . . impossible everything was. I realize that was perhaps selfish of me," she adds, in a slightly waspish tone.

"I wish you had told me at the time."

"I'm sorry," she says stiffly. "If I must apologize for that as well."

"No, I . . . That's not what I meant." Although, perhaps it was.

"Can you at least see why I did not?"

He sighs. This conversation is like walking through nettles, without clothes. The slightest touch stings. A part of him fills with a frightful tenderness; if only she would shed tears, if she would soften, he could put his arms around her and she could rest against him. If she would weaken, then he would be strong. Another part of him wants to walk out of the laboratory and slam the door in her face.

"I don't know. It makes me wonder what sort of person you thought I was. Someone who would have been angry? Who would have run away? Did you think that of me? Or did you not think my opinion mattered at all?"

She frowns at him; exasperated, or hurt—he can't tell.

"No . . . I wasn't only thinking about you, if you can believe that—I was in the most desperate trouble! Freddie was dreadfully ill—possibly dying! I was near despair."

Jakob winces. "I'm sorry. I meant, I thought we knew each other, and you would turn to me for help. I thought we shared something. From the beginning. From Neqi."

"Did we, really?" She is suddenly sad. "It was like a dream, and Freddie's illness . . . that was real. It was all so fast—there wasn't enough time."

It seemed to him that there had been plenty of time. More than enough time for him to know he had arrived at a place he didn't want to leave.

"And your letters . . . I was trying to read your thoughts, but they were so . . . stiff. So formal. I thought perhaps you had changed your mind—had second thoughts."

He curses those letters. "I hadn't changed my mind. I don't write a good letter. I was waiting until I saw you, to tell you . . . to show you—"

"I couldn't be sure of you, you see! I didn't know what to think. Sometimes I couldn't believe it had really happened. You were like nothing I had . . ."

And there it is—the hint of feeling threatening to break through. She looks down and lets out a deep sigh. Jakob looks at the curve of her cheek, an escaped strand of hair snaking down past her collar.

"I understand, Flora . . . but now . . ." He takes a breath.

"Yes. It's past."

An immense crash—almost an explosion—as something huge and solid is hurled against the hut wall. They later discover it was a sled, picked clean off the ground by a tremendous gust of wind.

The whole building shudders, the noise so sudden and violent it makes Jakob flinch. He had been on the brink, he knows, of reaching his hand across the space between them to touch her gently on the sleeve. Or, no . . . not gently: to seize her wrist and say, "Stop this! Stop talking like this! We are still the same, you and I. Can't you feel it?"

The crash pulls him up short. The moment is gone. They turn their attention to the map.

On reflection, it would have been a mistake.

Chapter 48

Diary entry, February 20:

Personnel. Ashbee worries me. He is unhappy about the sledging plans, at times unpleasant. He continually reminds me of the funding he brought with him, and argues that this entitles him to a final say in our plans. In order to cover more ground, we shall have to split into two parties, and, due to the nature of relations between Ashbee and the rest of us, I think I have to go with him. To partner him with Henry is out of the question. Ralph came to me privately and offered to partner him (a generous gesture—he likes him no better than I do), but this seems to me a matter in which a leader must accept the most onerous tasks. In all other ways, he is an excellent member of the expedition. No word from Aniguin. I am more than ever inclined to take Tateraq as our hunter. He has been steady and reliable and has the best dogs in the village.

N.B. I must speak to Meqro about Ashbee—but how to go about it?

Flora sits back in her chair. Since Meqro and Ashbee began their liaison over the winter, he has treated her as his personal slave, getting her to fetch him things, or make him tea. It is awkward, as Meqro does these things and more for all of them, but the way Ashbee talks to her is curt and peremptory. Again, yesterday, Flora heard him shouting when they were alone in the hut. There was a bullying note in his voice that she hated. Meqro does not react; she bows her head and meekly goes about her tasks. Perhaps she is simply thankful that he does not strike her, as her father used to strike her mother—a not unusual occurrence here. Ludicrously, they both act as if their liaison is a secret that Flora does not know.

Today should be cause for celebration—shortly after four, the sun showed itself for the first time since November: a pink, hazy glow above the cliffs. But Flora is not inclined to celebrate; so many preparations are still to be completed, and time vanishes with astonishing speed.

The problem of Meqro and Ashbee is an additional awkwardness to the worsened relations between Ashbee and Haddo. A few weeks ago, Flora had cause to confront Ashbee about his temper. It was dark, very cold, and they were all feeling the effects of being confined to the hut. Flora was in her room, while Ashbee and Haddo were in the laboratory. She heard breaking glass, then Ashbee yell, with shocking venom, that Haddo was a "fucking clumsy cretin."

Unfortunately—they have all noticed it—Haddo does have a tendency to be clumsy. Never when he is treating someone, as a physician, but often, afterward, he will cough, blink rapidly, and shrug his shoulders in an odd manner. Sometimes he moves jerkily and knocks things over—this habit has seemed to worsen over the winter months. It is irritating, but Flora is well schooled in hiding irritation.

When she spoke to Ashbee about his outburst, he said, "The man's a menace when doing fine work. I spent hours classifying marine animalculae, and he destroyed fully half of them."

"I'm sorry about your specimens—that must have been trying, but when we are so closely confined, it behooves us all to exercise even more than the usual restraint."

Ashbee bares his teeth. "I will endeavor to restrain myself, Mrs. Athlone, although the provocation is extreme. I'll try and make even more allowances for the poor man. I suppose it is hardly surprising."

Reluctantly, she said, "Why is it hardly surprising?"

Ashbee gave a slight smile. "Well, if you choose to employ some-one like that . . ."

Flora was angry. "Do not make mysteries, Mr. Ashbee."

Ashbee actually looked surprised. "Can it be that you don't know?"

"Don't know what?" she said.

"Why, that our young friend is a laudanum drinker."

Ashbee had a look of sly delight on his face. Flora was about to remonstrate, then realized that he was serious.

"Dixon knows. I assumed you did. He says he takes it to control the nervous tics. It doesn't seem to be working quite so well these days."

If Ashbee hadn't told her, Flora would not have known anything was amiss. Henry is a scrupulous and painstaking doctor. He insisted on visiting the Americans at the end of January, to check on the progress of their injuries. She considered giving him a letter for Jakob, but in the end had not. The salient fact was that Jakob was engaged to be married. He had not mentioned it, perhaps out of a residual delicacy for her feelings, but that was neither here nor there. Their affair was in the past, and raking up that past was futile; when she had tried to clear the air, she ended by regretting what she had said.

The news about Henry had to be dealt with. When she brought up the subject, as kindly as she could, he went white with horror. He apologized profusely, but assured her that his use was entirely within safe limits, purely to alleviate the nervous tics from which he had suffered since childhood.

"I know it's gotten worse since the sun set," he said in a stricken voice. "But it will get better when I can go out more and there is less of this being cooped up in here. Such pressures tend to make it worse."

"Henry, I have to rely on you, as our doctor, to be honest: Will it impinge on your ability to perform sledging duties? Ralph and Kudloq will be relying on you. Any failure on your part could endanger their lives."

Henry swallowed. "I know that. And I'm quite sure. Being outside and being physically active has always made the tics disappear completely. But I realize I haven't been frank with you, and I want to offer my resignation, in case you feel you can no longer trust me."

Flora looked at him dryly. "I'm hardly in a position to dismiss my medical officer, Henry. But I will ask Mr. Dixon if he is happy to have you as his partner. It will be up to him."

Henry blushed miserably, and his cheek twitched. "I've put you in a difficult position, Mrs. Athlone, and I will of course continue my duties as a doctor. But, under the circumstances, I can no longer take payment for those duties."

"Henry, please. The matter is closed."

She finally speaks to Meqro about Ashbee a few days before they are due to leave, when the subject of their relationship is little more than academic.

"Is Ashbee nice to you, Meqro?"

"Yes." She smiles shyly. "You know about us? He didn't want you to; he said you would be angry."

"Of course I know, Meqro; everyone knows. I'm not angry—not at all."

"But you do not like him, Fellora. He is a good man!"

"I know he's a good man." Flora is embarrassed she has let her feelings be apparent. "I just don't like the way he shouts at you. The way he tells you to do things for him," she adds, when Meqro looks perplexed.

"But I do those things for you all, so . . ."

"I know, but he talks to you as though you were his *kiffak*." She uses the derogatory word for a menial servant.

"But I am your *kiffak*, Fellora." Meqro laughs.

"What if you had another baby? Wouldn't that be difficult?"

"Oh, no, it's not like before! I loved Ferank. With Gilbert, it is . . . like, not love." She shrugs again. "So there will be no baby."

"It can happen anyway, without love—without even like. You know that, no?"

Meqro laughs, highly amused. "For the *kallunat*, I don't know how it is, but for the Inuit, there is no baby without love."

"Oh," says Flora, and changes the subject.

On their last evening in Siorapaluk, Flora allows herself a hot bath. She sits in the tub in her room and contemplates her body with a mixture of vanity and regret. Late March sun fills her room with light. Her skin is white, matte and soft, with nothing of Meqro's oily, golden sheen. She feels flabby after a winter of little physical activity, but that will soon change; what makes her sad is that no one else will caress these smooth, fleshy curves, her round, pretty breasts—or, what he had claimed, after some deliberation, was his favorite part of her body: her "cross." She hadn't known what he meant until he rolled her on to her stomach and traced the ticklish crease under her buttocks and the more than ticklish cleft between her thighs. Then he had traced it with his tongue . . . She slides her fingers between her legs and starts to stir herself, knowing that this, also, may be the last for a long time. She tries to think about something other than him, but her thoughts go where they will. And then she is in the bath, as she was that time in the Victoria, when she leaned on the sweating, sea-green tiles, possessed by such hunger . . .

She makes it very slow, because that way it will be better, and she wants to remember every single thing—every caress, how it felt. Most of all, she wants to remember his desire for her, his abandon, and her answering want—not just want, but an onrushing force—an energy so powerful she had no words for it, has none now, but knows it, can almost relive it, and does not want it to end.

Afterward, she wallows in the tub in a drifting trance until the water grows cool and she is driven to clamber out, stiff, with shriveled hands.

She rubs herself dry, feeling both calm and jumpy—an alert excitement that is first cousin to fear. She has always felt like this on the eve of a departure. This adventure, she reminds herself—not worries about Ashbee, or Aniguin, not anything and certainly not any*one* else—this is why she is here.

Ellesmere Land, 78°22' N, 83°54' W
April 1898

That is why she is here, but there is an odd atmosphere in her camp, and she does not know what she can do about it. It has been ten days since they split from Henry, Ralph, and Kudloq: ten days in which the atmosphere in her party has slowly worsened. Ashbee is by the tents, writing his diary: a diary he is not, under the terms of his contract, obliged to show her. Tateraq is miserable and withdrawn. She goes up to him as he examines the dogs' paws, his face grim. She squats beside him.

"How are they?"

"Alineq has cuts on her feet. She won't last much longer."

Flora nods. Once the snow melts, they will have less use for the dogs.

"Is everything all right, Tateraq?"

"*Ieh.*"

She can't remember when he last looked her in the eye. "You seem worried. Is something bothering you?"

"No. I'm happy."

Flora hesitates, knowing there is little point in pursuing it.

"If there is, I hope you'll tell me."

He murmurs, but to the doomed dog. He will kill it tonight, to feed the others. She trudges over to the tent Ashbee shares with Tateraq; Flora has her own, pitched five yards away. He looks up.

"Tomorrow we should get to the head of the fjord we saw from up there." He is excited. He has already begun to sketch the fjord on his map—their first glimpse of new coast, beyond which they may find—who knows?—islands suitable for the "dangerous detritus." "Perhaps it will be called Athlone Fjord!"

"We'll see. Has Tateraq said anything to you? He seems unhappy. It's not like him."

"He's more likely to tell you than me. His English isn't that good."

"Mm. Will you have a look at the ignition on the stove tonight?"

"Of course."

Half past ten and the sun has just set. Every day there is another half hour of daylight. They've made good progress. She tries not to think about how much she wishes her companion was Ralph. Or Henry. She tells herself that Tateraq will get over whatever is bothering him—sled travel has that effect, scrubbing the mind bare of all that is not immediately present. Probably, it is the dogs . . .

When she finishes her diary entry, Flora crawls into her tent, eats a square of Fry's chocolate, then, turning several variables over in her mind, falls asleep, the taste of sugar in her mouth.

Chapter 49

New land, 79°27' N, 86°19' W
May 1898

"There . . . to the left of the dark cliff."

It is Sorqaq who sees it. Jakob and he are making camp on a stretch of gravel beach. Their fourth day on new land—the land he saw six years ago, a lifetime ago, from a hilltop.

For days they have walked through thick weather, but today, for the first time since crossing the strait from Ellesmere, the clouds have blown out and granted them their first real glimpse of what they have found. Inland, the ground rises to an ice cap that glistens in the sun; on south-facing slopes, snow is melting. Jakob can hear the gurgle of hidden water, feels the tenuous warmth on his face.

"I don't see it."

Sorqaq points east, back across the frozen strait to Ellesmere.

"Smoke. Black smoke. A fire."

Jakob takes off the blue-tinted glasses that protect his eyes and shields them with his hand; the glare off the sea-ice is intense.

"Damn, you have good eyes, Sorqaq. Oh, wait . . ."

There, faintly visible against the snowy hills, a dark stain rises straight into the air.

"I suppose it could be the British."

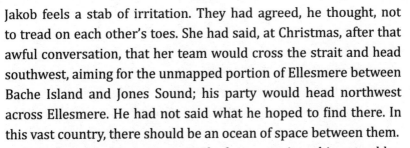

Jakob feels a stab of irritation. They had agreed, he thought, not to tread on each other's toes. She had said, at Christmas, after that awful conversation, that her team would cross the strait and head southwest, aiming for the unmapped portion of Ellesmere between Bache Island and Jones Sound; his party would head northwest across Ellesmere. He had not said what he hoped to find there. In this vast country, there should be an ocean of space between them.

Four days ago, his party crossed a frozen strait to this untrodden land, then he and Sorqaq turned south to follow the coast, while Welbourne and Aniguin headed north. If it is indeed an island, they will meet on its western shore, some time in the future. They had held a brief celebration, trying not to get ahead of themselves (it could be only a peninsula), but, standing on the desolate shore, Jakob experienced an excitement, an innocent glee he had thought gone for good.

He takes out his sextant and begins to plot their position. What he wants to do more than anything is crawl into his sleeping bag and pull a blanket over his eyes, but you don't give in to tiredness while there is work to be done. He has learned the Eskimo trick: you tell yourself that to behave in any other way is impossible, and then it is.

Next morning, the smoke is still there. It's very odd; odd that there should be a fire at all, doubly odd to be a fire they can see from so far. It is not a regular campfire, and there is no wood here, nothing that burns. He asks Sorqaq what he thinks. He has heard of burning cliffs in Greenland—seams of coal that smolder of their own accord.

Could that be what this is? Even studying the smoke through binoculars until his eyes water, it is too far off to learn more. Jakob feels a stirring of unease.

"How far is it, do you think?"

Sorqaq stares. "If the ice is good, a day, maybe."

"I think we must go and see what it is. Maybe someone is in trouble." He looks at Sorqaq with the hint of a plea. "Just in case."

By the time they have crossed the ice again, the smoke has vanished, but having fixed its position, they strike south. They finally round a headland to see a narrow valley running up to the mountains. Their best guess is that the smoke came from here. The snow on the northern slope is melting; patches cling on in hollows, dappling the gray gravel. There is no sign of anything else, no hint that anyone is here or has been here. Beyond the valley, the coast steepens to forbidding cliffs. Jakob decides to trek up the valley for a few hours, and then, if he finds nothing, they will give up, go back. He tells Sorqaq to stay with the dogs, who deserve a rest.

Convinced, after a couple of hours of stiff climbing, that he is wasting his time, Jakob stops for breath. It is a still day; there is no sound other than his breathing, and the trickle of snowmelt under the gravel. No sign of smoke. Perhaps they imagined it, or—whatever it was, some oddity of the north—it has vanished as mysteriously as it came. He takes out his binoculars, scans the valley, and there it is again: a dark feather, barely distinguishable from the gray gravel. He finally identifies a tiny smudge nearby as a tent. Surely the British? But nothing else. No movement. If the occupants are gone, why the fire? He starts to climb again, regretting the rifle he left with Sorqaq. The unease he felt earlier returns, sharpens to a point. He stops, fills his lungs, and shouts to the drab, silent valley. After several seconds, someone crawls out of the tent, stands up. Even when they are on hands and knees, in trousers and parka, and are far away, he knows it is her.

As he approaches the tent, she comes toward him. He hasn't seen her since Christmas, when they parted on terms of something like armed neutrality—a hopeless impasse. There has been no reason for them to meet again. He notices her hair is in an untidy braid down her back, that her face looks odd, her eyes reddened. He realizes with a shock—a cold premonition—that she has been crying. She says, in a voice that trembles and almost breaks, "You came."

He goes up to her and then, somehow, without any thought at all, she is in his arms. Her hair flutters against his mouth. He is breathing hard, his heart pumping with the effort of climbing uphill.

"What's happened? Are you all right?"

She pulls away, and he can see the gleam of tears on her face. She turns to look over her shoulder.

"Yes, but . . . he's dead."

"What? Who's dead?"

"Come and see."

She leads him toward a second tent, which he hadn't noticed until now—it has been collapsed into a heap of canvas. Jakob smells a sweetish odor before she lifts the open end of the tent. He sees a single, stockinged foot, crouches down, and pulls up the canvas. A cloud of flies bursts out and hits him in the face. Holding his breath, he pushes up the canvas again until he can see the rest of the body—and a man's head, spoiled and blood-matted and crawling with flies. Glints of blond hair are visible in the brown mess. He drops the canvas back over the awful thing, crawling out backward, brushing flies off his face, spitting them out of his mouth. He has to walk away to gulp clean air before he can turn back to her.

"Three, four days ago, we camped here. I was in my tent . . . I was woken by a shot. I came out. Tateraq was standing here, holding his rifle."

She hesitates.

"He said Ashbee shot himself."

"Where is Tateraq?"

Flora looks up the valley, to the ice cap. "He left. He took the dogs and left."

"He left? When is he coming back?"

"I don't think he's coming back."

Jakob is silent. To abandon someone alone, here, without dogs, is unthinkable. Without dogs, you cannot travel. Without dogs, you die.

"You're sure he didn't go for help?"

She nods.

"What do you think happened?"

She exhales sharply.

"I suppose it's possible that Ashbee shot himself, but I can't think why he would. He gave no sign. And to do so in a tent, lying down like that, with a rifle . . ."

"Is his rifle here?"

"Yes. I tried . . . you know, to see if you could pull the trigger . . . Perhaps someone taller could do it, or if you used something . . ." She shakes her head; she doesn't believe it.

"Can I see it?"

She walks back to her tent and picks up a long-barreled Martini-Henry. The gun is more than four feet long; Jakob knows perfectly well that a man could not reach the trigger while holding the barrel to his head.

"This was in the tent with him?"

Flora nods. "Beside him." She pauses. "It hadn't been fired."

"So Tateraq shot him."

She half laughs. "I don't . . . know!"

"Do you think he shot himself with Tateraq's rifle?"

She shakes her head. Jakob looks around, up the valley, where the snow is still thick. Tracks are visible, leading into the mountains. That was the way they came, and the way the sled went back.

"Was there any reason why they might have quarreled?"

There is a long pause, then she says, "I think they might have quarreled because of me."

"Can you explain?"

She keeps her eyes on the hillside. Her voice is flat and quiet.

"Ashbee came to me a few days ago and said that, of all the things he had to do, he didn't expect to have to defend my honor. I told him that people make silly comments, but it doesn't mean anything. I'd heard harsh words between them. Tateraq was sullen. I didn't know why. I thought, anyway, with Ashbee there, there was no reason to worry . . ."

"Nothing else had happened—before this?"

"Not that I know of."

"Then, after Ashbee died?"

"The thing was . . ." She closes her eyes for a moment, her voice no more than a whisper: "He didn't die. Not right away. I went into the tent and he was making a terrible noise, a kind of snoring, but his eyes were open . . . He looked at me and, it wasn't clear, I think he said, 'I tried . . .' then he started swearing. I told him he would be all right . . ." She looks at Jakob at last, her face collapsing. "But I knew he wouldn't be."

He lays his hand on her arm. She takes a great, shuddering breath.

"I went outside again, and Tateraq said, 'We have to go; there's nothing we can do.' I said we couldn't leave while he was still alive. Tateraq was harnessing the dogs to his sled—all the dogs. The way he looked at me, it was . . . I thought he might kill me too. I got my rifle and . . ." She grows suddenly calm. "I told him to go, and, if he didn't hurry, I would shoot him. Then he left."

"He didn't try to hurt you?"

She shakes her head.

"When was that?"

"I don't know. Three days ago?"

"And how long was Ashbee . . ."

"He died the next day. I think. I gave him laudanum. I started burning the other sled. I thought Ralph might see the smoke, and come." Her voice breaks up into a moan of anguish. "I stayed with him, as much as I could, but I couldn't do anything for him!"

Jakob glances toward the heap of canvas. He cannot imagine what that would be like.

"That injury was bound to be fatal. He probably wasn't even aware."

"Then the noise stopped. I thought I must bury him, before I . . ."

Jakob looks toward the ice cap. Without dogs, she could never have gotten back—she would know that as well as anyone. He feels a surge of fury against Tateraq. To abandon someone here is as sure a way of killing them as a bullet.

"I started digging a grave, but it's so hard."

She shows him a shallow trench in the frozen gravel.

"I'll do it. Do you have food?"

She nods.

"Can you get something to eat? And water."

He takes off his parka and, picking an unburnt slat from the fire, starts to dig. The ground is like iron; an inch below the surface, the gravel is frozen solid. He kicks away the smoldering timbers and attacks the earth where the fire has softened it. When he has hacked and scraped a big enough hole, he drags Ashbee's body into the trench in its canvas shroud and piles gravel over it. Then he hunts for rocks to cover the grave, to keep foxes away from his remains. Despite the low temperature, he has to take off his shirt, and, by the time he is finished, his skin is gray with sweat and dust. Flora hands him a towel and he scrubs off the worst before putting on his shirt and parka. She has made stew and tea, and brings out a bottle of brandy. They sit at some distance from the grave.

"Where are the others? How did you come to be so close by?"

"Sorqaq is down at the shore, with the dogs. We were across the strait. He saw the smoke. I had a feeling something was wrong."

He looks at her and sees a tear slide down her face.

"It must have been terrible, but it's all right now. We'll see you safe."

"You can't change your plans for me."

"We'll find a way. Don't worry."

Jakob rolls a cigarette and works his shoulders, muscles complaining from the digging. Tomorrow it will be worse. He looks at his watch: already three o'clock in the morning.

"I keep thinking I should never have come."

It is the first time he has heard her express doubt. He looks at her, but her face is half hidden by hair.

"It wasn't your fault."

"If I weren't here, or if I weren't a woman, there wouldn't have been this quarrel. Ashbee would still be alive. All I wanted was to be treated as anyone else would be treated. I love this place. But no one can forget what I am. My father stopped bringing me north, because of the men . . . They changed. I tried to be just like them. I dressed like them, but it made no difference. A child is just a child, but a woman is a . . . danger. I poisoned the ship by being there. I've fought it, and Freddie fought it for me, and Ralph fights for me. But even Tateraq, even he, whom I played with, who was my *friend* . . ."

She puts her face in her hands and digs her nails into her scalp until the knuckles go white.

"I didn't like him," she says, and bursts into tears.

Jakob moves to sit closer to her—rather gingerly—and puts his arm around her shoulders. She doesn't resist. Her whole body shakes.

"It isn't your fault," he repeats, his mouth close to her hair.

It isn't her fault, but there is an extent to which what she says is true.

With what they can carry, they walk down to the shore. They agree to say little about what happened—Jakob tells Sorqaq that Ashbee died in an accident, leaving Flora on her own. Sorqaq gazes shyly at her and says he is most happy—*qooviannikumut*—to see her safe. Then he takes an empty sled to fetch from the British camp whatever they can use.

Flora sits on a rock on the shore, gazing out over the strait. The sun shines relentlessly. Jakob wonders how much she could have slept over the last few days. When he asks her, she doesn't reply right away. He himself is so tired his head keeps dropping forward onto his chest. Sorqaq pitched their two-man tent, but he doesn't want to leave her out here alone, and she refuses to take it. He is half asleep when she finally speaks.

"I lost hope, more than once. After I'd had the fire going for two days, it seemed impossible that anyone would see it. I was going to leave, try to get back, but, you know ... I thought, Is this where it ends? I thought, What have I done in my life that I want to remember?"

Jakob waits for her to go on.

"All I kept thinking was, at least I spent a small part of it with you. That was what I wanted to remember."

Her voice is so quiet, he isn't sure he's heard correctly. All he can see of her face is the curve of her cheek.

"With me? Did you say—?"

"That's why I never congratulated you on your engagement."

"What?"

"I couldn't."

"I'm not engaged, Flora."

She turns her head slowly. "Meqro said you were engaged to Dr. Urbino's sister."

"No! We are friends, but . . ." God, I said that to discourage . . ." He groans. "God almighty!"

"You're not engaged?" She turns her head toward him, just a little.

"No! Did you mean that?"

She looks at him with a fierceness that is almost menacing. "I couldn't bear to think of you with someone else."

Jakob pushes himself to his feet, wondering if he has fallen asleep and is dreaming. He goes to her.

She looks up at him and says, "I'm sorry I wasn't braver."

He kneels beside her and puts his arms around her, filled with new strength, an unstoppable power, and she leans into him with a sigh. Her hand closes tightly around his forearm, and he hears her say, "Oh."

"My dearest, darling Flora."

Her forehead is a cold stone against his cheek; his hand is on her hair, pressing her to him.

"I never stopped thinking about you."

Chapter 50

Thule, 79°12' N, 93°50' W
June 1898

An ice cap covers the high parts of the island, but it is a gentler land-scape than that of Ellesmere or Greenland. Glaciers ooze off the mountains and, by early summer, rivers pour down the valleys; hill-sides are bare of snow. Under the sun, it seems a land of plenty: they find the first grasses poking through gravel, the first moss. Birds and animals appear with the new growth—ptarmigan and snow bun-tings, foxes and hares; gracious, ceremonial musk oxen. Where they have come from, how they survive the winter, is a mystery.

They cross a plain where every piece of rock shows traces of life—fossils that tell of a temperate ocean, swamps, forests, a multi-tude of creeping things—but there is no sign that humans ever lived in this place. It is possible that they are the first people to set foot here. Jakob is torn between frustration and joy; each place they stop offers untold riches, but, if they are to keep to his plan, there is no time to do more than wonder at them.

After weeks of traveling, they know that what they have found is indeed an island. The tortuous coast took them south, west, north again—until they reached the shore of this wide fjord, facing west over the Arctic Ocean. The island is huge: their part of the journey alone has covered three hundred miles. On the far side of the fjord, they can just make out some black dots, and those dots are Welbourne and Aniguin. When they join them, they will, between them, have completed a circumnavigation of this new land. Staring through binoculars to the west shows an unbroken plain of sea-ice. There is no land visible beyond this. He calls the island "Thule."

They take turns to study the moving figures on the opposite shore—too far to know if they have been seen, in turn.

"We'll camp," says Jakob. "Tomorrow will be soon enough."

Sorqaq offers to cross the fjord right away; although there is no darkness, at night the ice will be safer.

"I'll bring them back tomorrow," he promises, grinning. "Not too early."

The ice in the fjord is covered with a film of meltwater that reflects the sky like a sheet of metal. Sorqaq says it is safe, but watching his sled set out across the sheet of water brings Jakob's heart to his mouth. They have both become very fond of him. The sled skims through blue and white space, sky above and sky below, shimmering into insubstantiality. They watch him dwindle, until he too is a dot.

Jakob and Flora are alone for the first time in three years. He turns to her, takes her by the hand, and says, "Come."

Sorqaq offered to leave them alone almost at once. On that first day, he arrived back at the beach in the morning to find Jakob asleep, slumped against a rock, with Flora curled on her side, her head in his lap and his hand on her hair. Jakob started awake to see Sorqaq's delighted grin, his pantomime of being quiet.

"I knew!" he claimed, later. "I'm happy—my friend and my sister! *Aja*, it is good."

Once they had crossed the sea-ice again, Sorqaq assumed that he would be sleeping in Flora's one-man tent—in the natural course of things, when a man and a woman married, they went off on their own, so that they could get to know each other. Jakob said he would ask Flora what she wanted; the *kallunat* did marriage, as they did many things, differently. Their ways were inexplicable. And when he related Sorqaq's suggestion, Flora looked at the ground and shook her head.

"I'm already inconveniencing you by being here. I don't want to disrupt your plans any further. I don't want to . . ." She didn't finish the sentence, but Jakob thought he understood. Despite his reassurances that she wasn't inconveniencing either of them, that her belongings weighed relatively little and that nothing could make him happier than her presence, she was as tense and serious as when they had first met. For his part, Jakob found the horror he had seen in the tent almost embarrassingly easy to forget: Ashbee was a man he had barely known and hadn't much liked. And there was so much to see, so much to be done. Every few hours, they stopped so that he could take readings and sketch the outlines of the coast, to photograph the mountains and glaciers, to collect specimens, but then they pressed on, hurrying to make their miles. There was more work than he could accomplish in a dozen seasons, and he found that he had forgotten the dead man for large chunks of every day. But Flora was accountable for him. She had sat beside him as he died, listened to his last, appalling breaths.

For three days after crossing the strait, they walked side by side, but she slept in her own tent and made herself as unobtrusive as possible. She got up earlier than the men, was packed and ready before they finished breakfast; she checked navigational readings, made sketches, and did her share of camp tasks. She was unnervingly helpful and rarely spoke unless one of them asked her a question. Then, one evening, they were crossing a stretch of sea-ice that was covered in inches of slush—they should have waited until morning, but the day had gone slowly—and, out in the middle of the fjord, a floe opened under Sorqaq's sled like a mouth. Flora, just behind him, ran to catch hold of the upstand and they both threw themselves flat on the ice to spread the weight. Then the piece of ice Flora was lying on cracked, tilted, and she slid into the water. A slopping wave hit her full in the face, choking off her cry. Sorqaq grabbed her by the hair and held her head above the surface until Jakob joined them and they pulled her back. The dogs struggled out of the water and the twelve-foot sled teetered for long moments, the ice quaking underneath, as they yelled and strained on the traces, at last hauling it to safety.

Afterward, Sorqaq laughed. They were lucky—*aja!*—were they not? And Flora had looked very surprised when the wave hit her face—funny! He mimicked her expression. Flora laughed too. They were soaked, shivering, and exhausted when they arrived on the far shore, but a layer of reserve had been washed away. As Flora and Jakob crouched over the stove, warming their hands by the boiling kettle, she said, almost in passing, "I've been thinking: we could die tomorrow. If you still wanted, perhaps . . . if Sorqaq doesn't mind, that is . . ."

Jakob looked around to where Sorqaq was throwing chunks of meat to the dogs amid frenzied barking, and tried to suppress his smile.

"I'll ask him."

Sorqaq nodded. "Of course. She will make a good wife, that one—did you see the way she ran to grab my sled? No holding back!"

Flora was under the blankets when Jakob crawled into the tent. It had become colder, with a keen, gusting wind, and the night sun was obscured by cloud, but gray light bled through the canvas, and he could see her expression, which was solemn.

"Are you all right?"

"Yes. I don't know. I'm . . ."

"We don't have to do anything. I'm happy just to lie next to you."

"If I die tomorrow . . ." She laughed at herself and looked away from him, as she always did when she was embarrassed. "That wasn't what I meant. But, what happened before—it can't happen again."

"No. Of course. And it won't."

He had thought to bring the Paragon into the tent with him, explaining rather pompously that he found the rubber sheaths an efficient way to keep rolls of film dry. Not to mention their other uses: ammunition, salt . . . "I'm just telling you because you might think it odd that I brought such a thing on a sledging trip," he finished lamely.

"Oh." She had an infinite number of inflections for the word. There was a ghost of a smile. "I wish I could have a bath. I'm horribly unwashed."

He laughed. "You're perfect. You couldn't be anything else. And I'm horribly unwashed too."

He peeled off his underwear and slid, shivering, into the nest of blankets beside her. The touch of her bare skin was electrifying; he pressed himself against her with a moan of frantic, greedy joy. She wrapped her arms around him, but her body felt rigid, and she hid her face, seemingly avoiding his kisses.

"Flora, what is it?"

She sighed. "It's just . . . I know I shouldn't be, but I'm ashamed."

"Why?"

There was a long pause, in which she loosened her embrace, kept her eyes on the blankets.

"I can't help thinking—I know it's absurd—that I wasn't faithful."

He was pierced with a hideous thrust of shock and hurt. He kept silent, not knowing what to say. She went on in a small voice, "I missed you so much. I took a lover. I thought it might . . . But it was no good."

"When?" He found himself demanding, thinking, with a spurt of anger, Ashbee! No, Ralph, of course it was Ralph . . .

"The autumn before I left. It wasn't for very long. It—"

"It doesn't matter," he said, his voice stiff and unconvincing.

He tried to steer his anger toward this unknown man. His erection cared not a whit for his thoughts, but throbbed imperiously against her thigh; he shifted his body, as if casually, to move it away from her. Under the circumstances, it seemed inappropriate. She felt his withdrawal and he knew she was wounded by it.

"Please, listen. You see, I tried to tell myself that it was . . . the intimacy I missed, and I would get over it if . . . but it wasn't true. I discovered that." She looked at him, until he was forced to meet her gaze. "You were always my beloved. I knew then, but it was too late."

Jakob shook his head.

"It doesn't matter. It wasn't a question of being faithful . . . We both thought it was finished. I went with women, a few times."

"Oh!" It was as though he had struck her. She swallowed. "Who were they?"

Jakob thought this unfair. Moments ago, he had thought nothing on earth could stem his desire, but here he was, ebbing. It was not how he had imagined this reunion.

"Does it matter? All that is over now, isn't it? It's past. We are here."

They stared at each other, frightened. He realized his voice sounded severe, and lowered it.

"I don't understand why we are talking about what is past, now."

Flora shook her head, which made the tears run over her cheeks and into her hair.

"I wanted you to know, so that it wouldn't be in my mind, and I wouldn't think: I will have to tell him, one day. I want to start with a clean slate. There have been so many misunderstandings. I don't want there to be any more."

They were subdued. Jakob thought it would be so simple; now he was burdened by the need to confess.

"I should perhaps tell you, then, for the same reason, that, when I left New York, I had asked Clara Urbino to marry me."

"Clara?" She looked at him with a terrible anguish. "It was true! You are engaged."

"No, of course not! I wouldn't lie about that. She said no—for which I will always be grateful. I wasn't in love with her, nor she with me. It was a strange thing to do, it seems to me now—and seemed to her then. It was an impulse of fear, I think—I was trying to . . . inoculate myself."

Flora was silent for a minute. "So there's . . . nothing? You don't wish that you were with her?"

"Darling, no. She is a good friend, but that's all. Please don't look like that. You have no cause to be uneasy."

But Flora looked stricken. He picked up her hand and kissed her fingers, one by one.

"I think she would forgive my saying this if it set your mind at rest, so I will tell you . . . She is not the marrying kind—do you know what I mean by that?"

Flora nodded. "I think so, yes."

"And she's one of the few people I want to invite to our wedding."

"What?"

Flora frowned, and for a terrible moment Jakob thought he had misjudged it. Then, as a gust of wind slammed into the canvas and made the tent writhe, she smiled, with that slow, reluctant smile he loves, that seems to rise up from her very core.

"I want you beside me for the rest of my life. I'm sorry, I should have asked. Will you marry me, Flora?"

There is a pause.

"I will have to get a divorce."

"That is advisable, I believe."

"Isn't it too soon to know if that's what you really want?"

"No. It's late. I should have said it in London. I wish I had."

She let out a sigh—almost a sob.

"Yes. As soon as I can." She kissed him and wiped away her tears. "Yes, my love."

"There's one condition, darling."

"What?"

"Promise not to leave me again."

"I promise. Never."

"Clean slate, then? Fresh start?"

She nodded and sniffed away her tears. He took her in his arms again, as the wind howled about them, and they lay quietly, hardly daring to move. Jakob felt as though his chest contained a heavy bowl, full to the brim; one move and it would spill over, and then he didn't know what would happen—whether it was finite and would leak away; whether he would laugh or cry. Then this seriousness struck him as absurd.

"Although"—he rubbed his mouth against her still-damp hair—"I'm neither clean nor fresh, I'm afraid. Also, you may have missed your chance . . ."

He glanced toward his groin, and she laughed, and he felt some of the tension go out of her, and he thought, No, it is infinite, this feeling; nothing can exhaust it. Then he felt her hand slide down his body, softly stroking him. Her touch was light yet deliberate, soothing and thrilling. She whispered, "In my tent, I couldn't stop thinking about you. You were a few feet away, but I couldn't touch you. I thought, We've wasted so much time . . ."

Her hand brushed shyly over his cock, stiffening back to urgent life.

"Not anymore."

She moved to lie, full length, on him, resting on her elbows, her hands lightly grazing the sides of his face. He could feel the weight of her breasts on his chest. The heat and heft of her body was divine—a blessing. It gave him back his strength.

"One last thing . . ."

"What?" She was alarmed.

"You're not going to die tomorrow. We have the rest of our lives."

They kissed, clumsily, hipbones and kneecaps colliding in the cramped confines of their bedding. They were apologetic, awkward; blasts of cold air struck at their skin and made them gasp. He wanted to throw off the blankets and move freely, kiss her and taste her as thoroughly as he wanted, but the wind was howling and punching the canvas like a jealous husband, knifing through the tent flaps, icy and venomous.

"Lie still. Let me warm you." He pushed her onto her back and pressed himself into her side, tucking the blankets around their necks, the head of his penis rubbing deliciously against her hip. He caressed her body stealthily, mindful to cheat the wind of her warm flesh—her throat, her beautiful, opulent breasts (his memory hadn't lied), the soft flesh of her belly, her velvety thighs—and then his fingers slid between her labia and were bathed in slippery warmth. He stroked her clitoris with tiny, tender movements, his forehead pressed against her cheek, until he could feel as well as hear her breathing become shallower and more rapid, her heartbeat accelerating, her muscles tensing. After several minutes, his left arm, awkwardly bent beneath him, had gone to sleep, his fingers ached and he was dying, *dying*, to thrust himself inside her hot, lubricious cunt. Then he felt her muscles gather into shuddering spasms and heard with delight the wrenched cries she tried not to utter. When she was calm, he pressed his fingers hard and unmoving against her swollen flesh—he remembered how she liked this—and kissed her face over and over. At last, she turned to him and kissed his mouth, her tongue reaching for his. He held her gaze as he sucked his wet fingers, inhaling her warm smell until his lungs were full with it.

"You taste like a liqueur."

Her face was flushed, eyes wide, the pupils big and black. She smiled—a smile that came from a different part of her being; the smile he thought that only he saw.

"Warm?"

"Nearly," she said, and reached for him.

He fumbled to tie the Paragon firmly onto his rigid cock, and then she pulled him almost roughly onto her and guided him between her thighs. The wind rose to a scream. Neither wind nor cold nor covering was going to stop this. No sooner was he sliding into her, into a heat that exploded out beyond the boundaries of his skin, no sooner had he felt rather than thought, "Home," than he was gliding beautifully and inexorably toward the precipice.

He heard moans and exultations; he saw himself in her eyes, inscrutable mirrors, dark as the northern sea—as deep and unpredictable. He remembered water shining at her temples, and then he felt himself fall.

Chapter 51

Onmogelijk Dal, 78°14' N, 88°32' W
July 1898

Midsummer. Meltwater from the glacier forms a shining braid over the valley floor. The hills surrounding them are mottled with a kaleidoscope of introverted colors: fawn and ocher; gray and dun; slate, bronze, and taupe. The hills open to cup this south-facing valley: a bowl tilted to the sun's mouth. It captures its heat and holds it, and the air is warmer than she has ever known it in Greenland. In between the streams and on the hillsides, the gravel is flushed green with grass and mosses, spangled with tiny white heathers, tufts of bog cotton, lemon-colored, tussore-petaled poppies. In the endless light of midsummer, flowers are everywhere: tiny matted willows, miniature tussocks of astonishing brilliance. Nothing is more than ankle-high. They are giants who have blundered into a tiny Eden.

Like Eden, there is an innocence here. Because they are alone and the sun shines without ceasing, and it is as warm as a spring day in London, Jakob peels off his clothes when he is in camp and lets the sun darken his skin. Flora is secretly thrilled by this, but when he suggests she do the same, she demurs, glancing anxiously around the empty valley, as if expecting tea-time callers.

"Who do you think is going to appear?" Jakob is amused.

"I don't know. Sorqaq, perhaps . . . Any of them."

Sorqaq, Aniguin, and Welbourne have gone back to the north coast of the island to look for seals and musk oxen. They wanted to hunt. Welbourne was determined to shoot wolves and polar bears, so they went looking for permanent sea-ice. They were tactful, but could not hide their smiles as they said good-bye.

"They're probably a hundred miles away. Besides, I told them not to disturb us—at least, not until mid-August."

"You did?"

"Yes. Are you horrified? So you see, we are safe from intruders. And if by some odd chance they did come, well . . ." He looks at the denuded hillside: there is barely a rock big enough to hide a fox. "I think we'd see them coming."

He is right. In their valley, they inhabit a fortress of space, of silence and distance. First, she allows herself to take off her chemise when she is outside. It is actually hot—nearly seventy degrees, according to her weather station. Then—having made Jakob walk some way off, and turn his back—she takes off her heavy trousers and sits neatly on a blanket outside the tent. She can't quite bring herself to stand up, but she has to admit that baring her skin to the sun is pleasant. She is aware of the slightest movement of air; every nerve ending tingles with renewed life. Jakob walks back and sits beside her. He wears nothing but his boots.

"I'll have to make a picture of you here, sitting in our garden," he says, his hand warm on her bare back. "Looking over our domain."

They made their camp on a terrace on the hillside, from where they can see the fjord and the sea-ice. It has melted away from the shore, now lies in broken floes on the open sea. The fjord is dark and still; the water barely salt. Where the river flows out into it, the water has a milky, greenish hue, because the river comes from the glacier, higher up the valley. The glacier itself holds a meltwater lake, a miniature Gornersee, growing and deepening in color as the summer progresses. It is this glacier and this lake that brought them back to the valley.

Hypnotized by the light reflecting off water and ice, Flora leans against Jakob, knees drawn up to her chest, but he stands up and takes her hands.

"Come on, stand up . . . See, it's not so bad. Now: walking . . ."

She smiles and blushes as he leads her around the little plateau; he is laughing at her.

"No one can see, except me. And that can't count; I've seen you before."

"Yes, but this is *outside* . . ." she mutters. "And walking—it can't look *nice*."

Jakob stops and faces her, a smile hovering around his mouth, his eyes serious. "You have no idea how nice it looks."

She is aware of his gradually filling erection, and is glad that he doesn't find the sight of her unpleasant. She puts her hands on his waist and draws him closer, until the tip of his hardening penis nuzzles against her belly and her nipples graze his chest. A mild breeze wafts against them, a cool breath that makes the points of warmth even more delicious, urges them closer. Her skin is charged, no longer just her body's boundary; it is molten, intelligent, with its own appetite, its own will.

"You have to admit that it feels nice."

"Mm . . ."

"But I'm afraid you're cheating."

"Cheating? How?"

"Because you're using me as a modesty . . . apron."

She looks down and laughs. "You and modesty hardly belong in the same breath!"

"I didn't touch you."

"I know, but . . ."

She loves the way his cock rises springily to greet her. Worries, when his body remains indifferent, what she has done wrong.

He is smirking, with the bashful pride in his body that delights her. "It's not my fault. I'm not responsible."

"Oh . . . Well. What now?"

"I'm tired of telling you what to do. It's your turn."

She puts one hand on his breast, presses the flake of muscle over his ribs. With the other, she cups the delicate nape of his neck, feeling the bones in his skull. She puts her lips to the hinge of his jaw, brushes them over his cheek until she finds the ticklish corner of his mouth and opens it with her tongue, probing the smooth, satisfying gap where a molar is missing. Penetrating him like this, she unfurls urgently, an intemperate rose.

She invites him to lie on the blanket and kneels astride him, positions herself until his tip just nudges against the most sensitive part of her, and leans forward so that he can warm her cold breasts in his mouth. She moves back and forth, sliding faster, striving until she cries out and collapses, her thighs shaking too much for her to stand.

The only spying eyes on them are those of the fox who comes to sit on a knoll near the tent, a pretty creature with black eyes and white fur. Flora has named it Imaqa, which means "maybe." Before now, Flora has turned her head, on all fours, her fingers anchored in tufts of willow, knees bruised from roots and stones, moaning at every thrust, to find the animal regarding them with a bright, incurious gaze. She gazed back, feeling no shame.

The weeks slide away, even as time seems to stand still. They work: they explore and name the salient features of the valley they have colonized—the glacier, he has named after her, together with its evanescent lake, the "Florazee." The highest peak, she calls after Ashbee. The valley itself, he christens "Onmogelijk Dal." He teases her, for days not telling her what it means, but at last she finds out.

It means, in the Dutch of his childhood, "Impossible Valley." When she asks why, he says, with a fond smile, "Because it's the valley where impossible things happen," and she is sobered, reminded of her letter.

Happiness astonishes Flora. It also makes her suspicious; she worries about time, about what she should do, how she will account for Ashbee's death—about the future.

"I see no problem in maintaining that his death was a tragic accident. Such things—God knows—happen here."

"Not for those reasons," she mutters. She blames her femaleness, which leads her onto her other recurrent worry—that she is not behaving like a leader, or a scientist, that she has abandoned their plan of work for the summer, weakly given it up, to be with him.

"Don't you see? They will say, 'This is what happens when a woman goes to such a place. She fails. She cannot overcome adversity.'"

"What happened with Tateraq could have happened to anyone. It could have happened to me, Flora, and I couldn't have continued on my own. It was bad luck."

"Perhaps I could have gone on with something else . . . but instead, I'm here. Not doing anything useful."

"I'm not doing anything particularly useful."

"You're studying the glacier."

They have been measuring and monitoring its rate of movement and decay, watching the Florazee and its apparent, imminent demise.

"You're helping me. I couldn't do this alone."

"You would have managed. No one will know what I've done."

For the sake of Jakob's notes, with an eye to the future, they have invented a native companion, whom he has named Naasut. It is Naasut who positions the stakes on the glacier surface, who measures the temperature and wind speed, who takes the photographs of him posing by the theodolite. *Naasut* is the Eskimo word for "flowers."

"It's the north, Flora. We're at the mercy of the place. If you think you won't have done enough, why don't you stay?"

Sometimes he is infuriating. He and Welbourne are staying for another season—but they have no one but themselves to answer to. Flora thinks of Ralph and Henry and . . . everything. Freddie.

"I can't. You know that. It's just . . . I have to account for the time. I have to have something to *show*."

"Do you regret coming here, with me?"

"No, of course not! I'm not saying that. I am not . . ."

Jakob gets up and stalks away without speaking. In the ensuing silence, she goes to check on her weather station, to reaffirm her independent purpose in the world—to remind him that she has one.

She likes to watch him as he sleeps in the sun, lying on his back on the blanket, one arm flung over his head in a gesture of absolute trust.

Sometimes, looking at him feels bolder than the most intimate caress. Embraces bring their own oblivion—they forget themselves, they are no longer she and he—but when she looks at him, it underlines the distance, the difference between them. She contemplates his lovely, urgent body, taut in its brown skin, the shapes his bones make. She knows it so well: each scar, each mole, each plane and curve and slope, the bruises on his knees—worse than hers. She is never going to stop looking at him.

When she looks at his face, he has opened his eyes a crack and is looking at her.

"What?"

"Nothing. You're asleep."

"You look as if you're up to something."

She shakes her head.

This is an untruth. She likes looking at his sleeping penis, nestled in its ruff of hair. She lies with her head on his thighs, inhaling its sharp, salty odor. At first, the smell repelled her. He sighs, eyes closed, as her fingertip lightly strokes his flaccid stem—the skin that feels as delicate as silk, as soft and tender as a newborn animal.

"I like it when it's soft," she murmurs, and feels a quickening under her fingers.

"Not my fault," he mutters, from somewhere up above. "I'm sure that when we're ... married ..."

She loves that his body is like a musical instrument; his breathing varies according to her touch. His cock grows under her fingers. Swells. Like magic. A creature with its own will. She lifts her head, and the glossy, bulbous tip strains toward her.

His eyes are shut. His chest rises and falls, slightly too fast. She doesn't feel closer to him, despite this intimacy; if anything, he seems distanced, preoccupied by some complicated, internal conundrum. And yet she derives a thrill from this slipping away. He is in her power. She brushes her lips over the shaft, now hard and full. She inhales again with eyes closed: under the brine, there are deeper notes—vegetal, musky—dark, sun-warmed earth. With the tip of her tongue, she follows the vein that travels up the length of his shaft. His hips lift slightly, his mouth opens, and her hand closes around his root. Her tongue teases the rim of the bulb; firm but spongy, it bucks optimistically at her lips, and she responds by taking it inside her mouth, where he fits as snugly as an acorn in a cup.

A wet, cold, cloud-confined day. They talk about the terrible meeting last autumn, when she and Haddo came to treat the Americans for frostbite. She says, fishing for sweet words, "I nearly cried. I thought you hated me."

"Did you? Darling. Of course I didn't hate you. I hated you seeing me like that. That's why I was horrible."

He has a cough. He says he is fine. They entwine in the tent for warmth, listening to the tapping grace notes of rain against the canvas.

"I couldn't bear to see you like that. I'll never let that happen again. I will keep you from harm."

He grins. "You keep *me* from harm? I'm supposed to say that to you."

"I'm as tough as old boots."

He looks at her, coughs, picks a strand of her hair and wraps it around his finger, where it gleams like a ring.

"True."

Each of these moments a bright bead, to be collected and cherished. They have a shared past to turn over and polish with telling, but now it is all the sweeter because they have a future, also—shyly, tentatively referred to. They talk of living in the mountains. Somewhere they can see the snow. They will come back here.

There will be days when they will say to each other, "Do you remember the valley . . . ? The fox who used to come and watch us? Do you remember the lake?"

As if these things could ever be forgotten.

PART EIGHT

DESTRUCTIVE INTERFERENCE

Two systems of sonorous waves can be caused to interfere
and mutually to destroy each other; thus, by adding sound to
sound, silence may be produced. Two beams of light also may
be caused to interfere and effect their mutual extinction;
thus, by adding light to light, we can produce darkness.
—John Tyndall, *The Glaciers of the Alps: An account
of the origin and phenomena of glaciers, and an exposition
of the physical principles to which they are related* (1860)

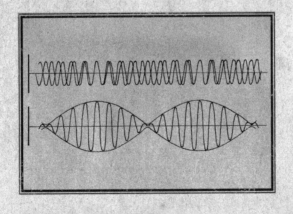

Chapter 52

The two of them have walked up to the low wooded rise, covered with spruce and bilberry, that divides the air base from Gander Lake. There are glimpses of water through the trees. The lake is still cara-paced with winter's ice, blotched like a moldy cheese, but the ice is old and weak, a cloudy and tarnished gray. There are traces of tracks, but no one would think to trust it now. Randall rubs his hands; fool-ishly, he didn't bring his gloves. Yesterday, in Trenton, he was warm. She doesn't seem to feel the chill, even though they have stopped to rest on some humped rocks overlooking the lake, and their breath condenses in soft clouds. She looks at the white sky.

"It's going to snow."

"Certainly cold enough." He blows into his cupped hands.

"Not as cold as it'll be up there."

"I guess not. Are you looking forward to it, Mrs. Cochrane?"

"To the Pole? Yes. Although I'm not expecting very much."

"What do you mean?"

"Well, it has no intrinsic importance, other than symbolic. It's not new land. It can profit nobody. And we're not reaching it in a way that reflects any credit on us."

He grins. "I'll try and remember that when I write the article. But its symbolic importance is not negligible."

"It's a point in the sea, on a map devised by men."

"I don't think you're as down on it as you seem."

"We'll see—if we actually get there."

They walk back through the woods in silence. Randall is trying to absorb all that she has told him: that she and Jakob met again, in the north, that they had planned to marry. That, after a period of time together (he thought of the photograph; said nothing), she went back to England to obtain a divorce.

When they reach the road, something prompts him to say, "Did you ever hear what happened to Jakob's brother, Mrs. Cochrane?"

"To Hendrik? No."

"It was strangely . . . Well. Grandpa had a business selling meat wholesale. They kept the stock in these big walk-in freezers at the docks. One Saturday, he was at the warehouse by himself and—no one knows exactly what happened—he managed to get himself locked inside one of them." He shrugs. "No one knew he was there. They found him on the Monday morning. He'd frozen to death."

"Oh my goodness. I'm sorry."

"Thanks. Kind of ironic, though, isn't it? Him dying of cold. His whole life, he never went north of Boston."

"Did you get to know him?"

"Sort of. I was eleven when he died. He was so proud of his brother, the explorer."

She nods. "Jakob loved Hendrik. He talked of him as one talks of a father."

"He was protective of Jakob's memory too. For himself, Grandpa couldn't have been less interested in the Arctic and that sort of thing. He never traveled. I don't think he understood why Jakob wanted to do it. Can you tell me?"

"He wasn't particularly ambitious. With him, I always thought it was primarily escape. I think he was only truly happy when he was away from civilization. The wilder and more uncomfortable it was, the more he liked it."

"What did he want to escape from?"

She walks in silence for so long he thinks she isn't going to answer.

"He loved his brother, but he didn't want to be like him. Settling down. Working six days a week in an office. The same thing, day after day."

"But then he met you. You were . . . equally unconventional, would you say?"

"Oh, I don't know."

She sounds cross, and won't meet his eye.

"Sorry. I'm just trying to get a sense of what impelled him to leave."

"What do people usually want to escape from?"

"Well, speaking generally, I would guess, their past, sometimes . . . An unhappy family?"

"I think it's more often the sense that you don't fit with what is expected of you. You don't want to be *that*—whatever *that* is."

She looks up ahead, to where lights are winking through the tree trunks. The sky has become murky.

"Of course, there was their father . . . That was very difficult. He could hardly bear to talk about it."

Randall stops walking. She too stops, turns to look at him.

"You know what I'm referring to, don't you?"

"You're talking about Hendrik and Jakob's father—my great-grandfather? What do you mean?"

"You should ask your parents about this."

"No, you can't just . . . You have to tell me now. I know both their parents died when they were very young. They were brought up by relatives."

"Their mother died—this is what he told me. Their father spent the greater part of his life in a lunatic asylum. But the boys were told he had died in an accident. Years later, they found out the truth—I think Jakob was in college. I know he visited him, but he found it very painful. Apparently, he was a hopeless case. So, yes, I think he was escaping that, too."

Randall feels hot, despite the louring snow clouds.

"What do you mean, 'a hopeless case'?"

"It's a long time since I thought of this, you understand. You'll have to ask your family. I understood him to mean that there was no hope of recovery. You can imagine how distressing that discovery must have been, for both of them. I'm sorry. I assumed you would have known."

Randall stares at the ground.

"What was wrong with him?"

"I'm sorry, Mr. Crane, I don't know. There's not the slightest reason to think it was hereditary. I think Jakob was afraid of that, but he was the sanest person I ever met."

Randall goes back to his room to change. He is freezing; his hands and feet feel like ice. He washes in his little private bathroom but feels soiled, his earlier excitement quite gone.

Some months ago, when he knew he was coming on this trip, he reread the Snow Queen's book, the one she published at the end of 1899. It is a strangely lackluster read, quite unlike the lively account of her first expedition. Perhaps this is because, according to what she has just told him, she left out everything of importance. There is no mention of the island she said Jakob and Welbourne discovered and circumnavigated (according to her, the one later mapped by a Norwegian expedition). The only mention of Jakob is in the brief account of a visit made by Flora and the British doctor to treat Mr. de Beyn and Mr. Welbourne for frostbite. It is bland, unrevealing. You would never guess.

A sustained, even impressive feat of misdirection. It is hard to work out who went where, and when. The book gives the impression that she, Dixon, and Haddo were all present when Gilbert Ashbee died—and that his death was due to a tragic accident with a gun. No mention of murder, or the Eskimo driver; no mention of her lonely vigil, of Jakob's arrival and their subsequent reunion. (How romantic that must have been, although, in telling him, she was matter-of-fact.) She wrote that the British spent the summer mapping the coast of Ellesmere. It is a remarkably anodyne piece of fiction.

He leafs through his collection of newspaper clippings, looking for any hint of corroboration for what she has just told him. Astonishing how many inaccuracies were peddled in the papers of the time. Some of them subsequently came to light. This, for instance, from the *Toronto Star* of September 1899:

> . . . Reports have reached the *Star* that American explorer Lester Armitage has reached an unprecedented Furthest North—having traveled for hundreds of miles over the frozen Polar Sea with his sturdy native companions, he has stood within three degrees of the Pole itself, marking another record for the Stars and Stripes . . .

But Armitage almost certainly got nowhere near eighty-seven degrees north. The surviving members of his team returned, in bedraggled confusion, in the fall of 1900, by which time the disappearance of three men was more newsworthy than where they had actually been. Armitage's men seemed embarrassed to have lost their leader in such circumstances (they returned from a musk ox hunt to find him gone), but their reports suggested that the expedition had not traveled far from land, perhaps not even as far as Armitage's previous attempt.

There was the odd thing in Armitage's first book, the climax of which was his announcement of having discovered a new island off the north coast of Greenland in 1892. Years later, Dupree Land was proved not to exist.

What other mistruths lurk in these old clips? Omissions? Downright falsehoods? You can't believe something because it is in print. How did Armitage get away with his claim for so long? It's hard to avoid the inference that explorers were prone to telling lies because—well—because they could.

The first hints of trouble appeared a year after the Snow Queen's return:

ACCUSATION OF FRAUD IN THE NORTH

Mr. Lester Armitage, the man who reached humanity's Furthest North
this year by achieving 87 degrees north, less than 200 miles from the
North Pole, has claimed that reports of the new island discovered by
explorer Mr. de Beyn are false. The records at the center of the claim
cannot be traced, and Mr. Armitage has stated that they never existed,
and that Mr. de Beyn's Esquimaux companions have denied seeing the
putative island.

New York Leader, September 1899

Here is a mention of the new land she talked of. But Armitage
disputes it. (Why? How would he know?) It seems premature—to
say the least—to question a claim that has not yet been made. But
the *Leader* was one of the worst examples of yellow journalism
(it eventually folded after a number of lawsuits). At this point,
Armitage seems to have been alive and well—and communicat-
ing in some way with home. De Beyn and Welbourne were also
still in the north. So far, the only reason to believe that something
untoward had happened was that no one knew precisely where
they were.

A few weeks later, bad news was growing:

HOPES WANE FOR LATEST ARCTIC EXPEDITION
MR. ARMITAGE'S SILENCE LEADS
TO QUESTIONS IN SENATE
NORTHERN EXPLORATION—WASTE OF MONEY AND LIVES?

Patriotic Americans are on tenterhooks as to the fate of the latest
attempt to plant the Stars and Stripes at the top of the world. Eighteen months ago, Mr. Lester Armitage set sail on his brave quest to
fill in one of the last remaining blanks on the map, to claim the North
Pole for the United States of America. The relief ship that attempted
to make contact with him this summer was stopped by heavy ice and
had to leave supplies at Pym Island, far to the south.

On a further somber note, fears are growing as to the fate of the explorers Mr. Scott C. Welbourne II and Mr. Jakob de Beyn, who failed to make a rendezvous with the ship hired to bring them home. There is no news as to their whereabouts.

New York Mail, December 1899

SPIRITUALIST CLAIMS KNOWLEDGE OF HEROES' FATE!

Mrs. Eliza Jupp, the well-known New York spirit-medium, has told our correspondent that she has vitally important messages for the families of Mr. Armitage, Mr. de Beyn, and Charleston banking heir Mr. Scotty Welbourne II, the Arctic explorers who have not been heard from since the summer of 1899, when all three disappeared in Arctic mists. She claims that she has information as to their whereabouts, which she will communicate to them privately.

New York Leader, April 1900

Only a few months after claims of success and extraordinary feats, Armitage, Welbourne, and Jakob joined the ranks of the lost.

He has found only one photograph that shows his great-uncle and Lester Armitage together, and that is from the first expedition, in 1892. The five men pose in front of a dark stretch of water, two dogs at their feet. It is summer and little snow streaks the dark hillsides. Randall has stared at their faces for a long time, has judged them according to his lights. He thinks Armitage looks severe and arrogant—a frown is apparent, even on a face half-obscured by a handlebar mustache that makes him look old-fashioned, self-consciously heroic. Perhaps his judgment is colored by his reading of Armitage's book—all those things are evident in his writing. As for Jakob, it is hard to say. He looks rather weedy in this company. He is clean-shaven, a young man, smiling. He looks, unlike the others, as though he is having fun.

Other than that, the picture tells him nothing. And the Snow Queen has told him nothing that throws light on the men's relationship with one another.

He is angry with her. He doesn't want to be angry with his parents, or his grandparents, and he needs to be angry with someone.
The truth is, he has not warmed to her; he finds her cold and unsym-
pathetic, rather elusive. And—sometimes—he wonders if she is
playing with him. Perhaps—this occurs to him, suddenly—she lied
about his great-grandfather. Or is mistaken—an old woman, confused, telling stories . . .

What if nothing she has told him is true—she and Jakob were
never reunited in Greenland, never going to be married? What if
the account she gave in her book was the true one? What proof is
there that any of it really happened?

Chapter 53

Kennedy Channel, 81°11' N, 67°53' W
July–November 1898

People said Lester Armitage was looking older. He'd heard mutterings to this effect and pretended not to care. It didn't help that when his wife, Emma, welcomed him home after his last trip to Washington, she had kissed him with a tender frown on her brow. "Darling, your poor little gray face!" she had cried. "What have they done to you?"

In fact, the senators had given him good news. Obstacles began to melt away, and a replacement for the *Polar Star*—another expensive, heavily reinforced, and over-engined ship, the *President McKinley*—was nearing readiness. He had gathered a new team of helpers; money came in to provision them for a three-year sojourn. Three throws of the dice. This time, even allowing for mishaps and false starts, he would—*must*—be the first man to reach the Pole. As he was only too aware, he was forty-five years old, and he was running out of time.

He knew that de Beyn had gone back to the Arctic the previous year. There had been little fanfare; in fact, the whole thing had a slinking, hole-in-the-corner air about it, as if he and his playboy friend were doing something underhanded. When he learned that their ship had dropped them off in Neqi, the very village he had chosen for his base seven years ago, Emma could hardly contain her indignation.

"But Neqi is *your* village! How dare he . . . horrible little man!"

"I agree he could have at least, ah, consulted me about it." Lester tried to control his anger. "But, of course, he was taking the Eskimo back home."

Emma pursed her lips. The whole affair of the Eskimos had been most distasteful. He knew she didn't like him to talk about it. The hurtful thing was, people probably thought he was unfeeling. They didn't know what torments he had suffered when he heard of their fate, particularly that of his little Arctic dove; there was no one on earth with whom he could share that grief. It had been essential to cut himself off from the whole thing in order to pursue his plans for the next trip. He could not be tainted with mess and failure when raising funds.

He had felt old and tired when they set sail, surrounded by bright-eyed young men, with their taut muscles and smooth skins, but once he smelled the ice and saw the red cliffs of Melville Bay and the great, phallic spur of the Devil's Thumb—he felt it a signpost that they were arriving in the proper country of men—he felt his spirits lift and the years seemed to fall away.

That feeling of exulted and rejuvenating purpose lasted until they had moored off Siorapaluk to take on board as many dogs and men as they could muster. All the hunters in the area heard that he was there and came to see what he was offering. Dogs, hunters, and their families came on board, and the decks of the ship turned into a filthy, floating village.

Among the familiar faces was Metek, that fine dog driver, resourceful companion, and veteran of the first northern journey, but this time he did not want to come—no, not even for two rifles! He has done with such things. He is a grandfather now and too old (he is younger than Lester, but, of course, these things are not comparable). He did not want to go away from the hunting grounds for so long. Only last year, he went with de Beyn on a repeat of that first northern journey—they reached the big cliff again, only this time there was no fog, and they could see across the sea-ice for miles and miles. A desolate place. No game. It had been a hard journey, very hard . . . He did not know why de Beyn wanted to go somewhere that Metek had already been with Armitage and Urbino, when they had found nothing there, but that was what they did. That was the last time for him. So *naamik, kooyounah*—thank you, but no.

Lester's jaw ached from smiling. When he heard what de Beyn had done, he was almost overwhelmed with nausea, and gritted his teeth. He knew why de Beyn had gone there: there could only be one reason.

As they battle their way up the ice-choked strait until the ship can go no further, as they build a winter camp and Lester makes his endless calculations, as he sets his team to hunting and making clothing and adapting equipment, as he does all these things with the energy of his relentless purpose, the boring beetle that Metek unknowingly—smilingly!—passed him worms deeper, gnawing at him, stealing his sleep. The days grow shorter and so does his temper. When he falls into his bunk, long after midnight every night, he closes his eyes and sees de Beyn's face (or rather, the hazy approximation of it that he remembers) and wonders why the geologist should have it in for him. He gave the man his big chance—why isn't he grateful, instead of trying to steal a march on him? Trying to snatch the prize of the Pole from under his nose? Now de Beyn knows what, for the last six years, even Lester has not allowed himself to know—that Dupree Land was a figment of his desire. He conjured it into being with his will and told himself that perhaps it *was*, after all, there—since they could not see through the fog, they could not assert that it did not (like God) exist. De Beyn must have hoped to find in it a viable road to the Pole, and when it failed to provide one, turned his attention elsewhere. That must be what he was doing on Ellesmere: looking for an alternative route . . .

Ticking away, gnawing at him . . . Even if de Beyn does not get to the Pole (and without a ship, without a far northern base and without a large infrastructure behind him, Lester does not see how he can—surely?), even so, he now has the means to ruin Lester's reputation. He will go back to New York and brand Lester a liar—or, at best, a fool. If Lester comes back with the prize, afterward, will anyone believe him?

Time flows like a torrent. His busily ticking watch strikes off the seconds as they rush past, each one a reminder that he is a fraction closer to death. If timekeeping were not essential here, he would have silenced it under his heel.

Lester, long ago, persuaded himself that he *had* seen something in the dreadful murk: a high outline . . . a faint solidity, tantalizingly indistinct. He *had to* have seen it. He convinced himself that it was true.

It is November, but traces of pallid dusk still stain the southern horizon. For the last two days of the trek south, made with two of his hunters, they have seen moon dogs—arcs of light and false moons refracted in the taut sky—hanging like cold lamps over the velvet rubble of the frozen sea. One of the men, Kussuk, says it is a bad omen.

His old hut at Neqi, much pillaged and rebuilt, is banked high with snowdrift. He raps on the hut door, surprised that no one has come out to see the visitors and their howling dogs. The door opens, and there, in a shapeless sweater and bear-fur trousers, is the geologist, staring at him as though he, Lester, were a ghost.

"De Beyn. It's Armitage."

"Of course . . . Good heavens."

"Surely you knew I was here."

"We heard you were up north. I suppose we didn't think to see you here . . . Come in!"

De Beyn steps aside to let Lester enter his old domain, and bangs the door closed. Lester pulls off his snow-caked boots.

"I'm surprised to see anything left of the place."

"We had to patch it up. It was a wreck."

"I'm sorry to be so unexpected. I hope it doesn't inconvenience you?"

De Beyn laughs then, and Lester is reminded of how his high-pitched laugh grated on him during the winter they spent together.

"Inconvenience me? No, not much at all. It's always a pleasure to have visitors, but I'm afraid Mr. Welbourne isn't here—he's gone hunting for walrus, again. I would have thought he'd have tired of the sport by now, but apparently not. He thinks it quite the most exciting hunt in the world—better than lions, even."

As he chatters on about nothing in particular—another habit that irked Lester in the old days—de Beyn puts on a kettle of water to boil, finds mugs and biscuit, and carries it all to the table. Lester watches his former colleague. To look at, he is very much as he remembers him from their last meeting—when was that? The memorial for poor Urbino, it must have been—six years ago. He is just as slender, with that easy movement that belies his delicate appearance. His uncanny white hair is rather long, his face a little harder than it was; much like himself, he supposes, although de Beyn must be the younger by a decade.

"You have no women to do for you?"

"Oh, yes . . . try stopping them. But they come and go." De Beyn gives him an insouciant smile. "I'm working on my photographs at the moment, and it's easier to do that on my own."

"Ah . . ." Lester's eye wanders over the walls of the hut. A couple of prints are pinned up, on display. One seems to show the inside of a cave, a vertical shaft of light falling on a fur-bundled figure. There is something odd and theatrical about it that draws his eye.

"I hear the British woman has been here again."

"Yes. The British were at Siorapaluk earlier this year."

"Extraordinary thing. And the, er . . . husband? Was he recovered from whatever had befallen him?"

"As to that, I don't know. He wasn't with them." De Beyn looks at the table.

Lester shakes his head. "Blind folly. I shudder to think what could befall a woman here, don't you?"

De Beyn gives a noncommittal smile. "I suppose anything could befall any of us."

"Well, with certain exceptions . . . You saw them, then?"

"A couple of times. They spent most of their time to the south-west, I believe."

"The boys told me that one of the Britishers died."

De Beyn hesitates, before drawing a cigarette out of a pouch.

"Yes, apparently some sort of accident with a gun."

"Dear me. I suppose we should be glad it wasn't worse. When we met them, before, the whole thing struck me as a very queer affair. I must say, I cannot readily conceive of the sort of men who would agree to be part of such a . . . cheap stunt."

"I found the men to be good sorts. Certainly their geologist—that's the only field where I'm qualified to judge, of course—seemed to be doing excellent work."

Lester shrugs. "I would have thought a woman would limit them too much. One would always be worrying, having to look out for her. One would be dreadfully slowed down. And the idea of a woman leading a group of men—it's as ludicrous as a . . . an Eskimo leading a group of white men! It must be in name only—for the publicity, I imagine."

"It didn't appear so."

"Yet they lost a man."

De Beyn looks at him steadily. "Accidents occur in the best-run expeditions, as I'm unlikely to forget."

"All the more reason why women should not be allowed to expose themselves to such risks. I wonder at her husband allowing it."

There is a pause, then de Beyn says, "Well, it's not our affair."

His eyes flicker toward the partition that divides the end of the hut into a separate room—the room that used to be Lester's private quarters.

"So, you're going north again, Armitage?" de Beyn says at last.

"Yes. We'll make an attempt on the Pole in the spring. And you? I heard you had a successful season on Ellesmere."

"It was everything I could have wished."

"And what are your plans for next season?"

"More scientific work. Perhaps on the glacier, here. When Welbourne returns, we'll discuss it."

"I merely ask because I hope to avoid a conflict of interest."

"You don't need to worry about that, Armitage. I wish you luck with the Pole. It'll be quite an undertaking."

"We will do our best."

De Beyn smiles at him. What does that mean? It is conceivable, to Lester's mind, that de Beyn intends to launch his own polar attempt in the spring and is keeping quiet about it—that would be in keeping with his hole-in-the-corner style.

"Have you seen Aniguin, since you arrived?"

"No. How is he?"

"Well enough. He's settled in a village to the south. I think he's had enough of the *kallunat* for a while."

Lester nods. "I never thanked you properly for what you did in New York. For him and the other Eskimos. A dreadful business."

"Yes."

"I was only sorry I could not be of more help to them, but I was so busy . . . my commitments, you know, were so onerous . . . my hands were tied."

"So I understood."

Lester frowns. "It was a source of great personal distress to me, as you can perhaps imagine. If I'd had any conception of how dangerous New York would be to them . . ." He shakes his head. "But they were so keen to come. They earnestly petitioned for it."

"You couldn't have known," de Beyn says.

"No. Yet I feel responsible. And, ah—do you have news of the, er, of Dr. Urbino's child? I'd like to do something for it, if I can."

"Meqro does some work for us. You can ask her yourself."

"Ah . . . ?"

"The girl's mother. She is well, and the child too. Aamma is five now."

"Ah . . . Good."

"She's an independent soul. Dr. Urbino's parents offered to take the girl, but Meqro wouldn't give her up. I'm sure, however, any assistance you offered would be graciously received."

Lester nods. "I'm happy to hear it."

He stares into the bowl of his pipe.

"De Beyn, there's something I wanted to discuss with you. I was concerned by something I heard when I arrived." He tries a smile. "It may have been a garbled account, but I was told that, last summer, you went to the north coast; in effect, retraced my footsteps—is that right?"

"Yes, that's true."

"And did you cross the ice to Dupree Land?"

De Beyn looks at him steadily. "We saw no land."

"Then you can't have gone as far east as we did."

De Beyn glances down and seems to smile slightly.

"We went further along the coast from the coordinates you cited, about fifty nautical miles, and there was no land visible. I know the conditions you experienced were difficult. We were lucky in that respect; the weather was perfectly clear. We took several sightings to be sure."

Lester schools his face not to react.

"How very strange. I know what I saw."

"Perhaps it was a Fata Morgana. I've seen extraordinary effects: a range of mountains that weren't there, a city, even . . . I understand how one could be misled."

Lester shakes his head. "It is a great pity that Dr. Urbino is not alive to attest to what we saw."

De Beyn gives an abrupt laugh.

"It is indeed a pity that he's not alive! You must know that he told me what he saw—and that was nothing at all. The fog never lifted. He said you could not even swear that it was the north coast, and not the shore of a fjord."

Lester feels his heart pump strongly and steadily. He weighs his words. "No. Urbino did not see what I saw. But after he died, I wanted to share the credit with him. I wanted to do something for his family—for his name."

"A generous thought, but misguided. As it turns out, you have only shared the credit for a mistake."

De Beyn's eyes look very black in the lamplight, thrown into relief by his pale hair.

Lester shakes his head slightly. "It seems extraordinary . . . Do you have photographs taken from the coast?"

"Yes. Would you like to see them?"

Lester waves a hand ambiguously. He tries to collect his thoughts as de Beyn goes into the partitioned room and returns with a folder. The photographs are small but more than sharp enough. Each one is mounted and annotated with coordinates, date, time, direction. There is a precision, a thoroughness to the work that casts an unflattering light on his own efforts.

"These cover the area you describe in your book. We couldn't have missed an island such as you described. I'm sorry." He spreads his hands.

Lester is infuriated by the apology. As if de Beyn weren't delighted. As if he weren't *crowing*.

"You were certainly fortunate with the weather. I must congratulate you, then, for improving on my work."

De Beyn shrugs, and inclines his head. "One stands on the shoulders of those who went before. Metek was a great help, since he knew the country."

"Welbourne went with you?"

"Yes. He can navigate as well, which meant we could corroborate readings."

Lester tries to make his voice light and casual. "So, you plan to go home . . . when?"

"August." De Beyn smiles. "If you reach the Pole, Armitage, no one will care about my findings. You'll go down in history. I will be, at best, a footnote."

Lester lies awake as night turns toward morning. His brain whirrs, turning over the facts, looking for an answer. De Beyn will return to America long before he will. He will denounce Lester as a liar. In some way, the man seems to hold him to blame for Urbino's death. Behind the smiles and reasonable words, his dislike is clear. Lester wishes de Beyn would accuse him straight out, so that he could expostulate, show his real pain. Did people think he didn't feel? He is as sensitive as anyone. But, as leader, you cannot allow yourself to go to pieces. You have to do what needs to be done, and he had.

What, now, is the thing that needs to be done? Should he plead with de Beyn? Should he ignore the bad news, hope his relative insignificance will lessen the impact, perhaps bury it altogether? Should he bargain?

He listens until he is sure that de Beyn is asleep. He gets out of bed and pauses, waiting for any change in the breathing from the other bunk. When he is sure there is none, he goes and tries the door of the partitioned-off room.

He'd noticed de Beyn glance toward the room, earlier—wondered for a crazy moment if someone were inside . . . but the flame from his candle only reveals the paraphernalia of photography: chemicals, folders, prints strung up on the wall. He scans the photographs—permutations of ice, rock, water—then turns to the folders, labeled with locations and dates. De Beyn was always meticulous. He reads the titles and pulls out one marked *Thule. F. Glacier*. It contains photographs of a glacier in an unfamiliar landscape. There is a glacier lake, sunlight dazzling off it. He replaces it, pulls out the others. More landscapes, some with people: a bearded white man, who must be Welbourne; Eskimos—he recognizes Aniguin, and a younger, taller man he does not know; de Beyn himself. These four, in various combinations, in various places. Nothing out of the ordinary. Lester can be meticulous too. He searches further, on shelves, behind bottles, under the table. Maybe there is nothing—but that glance . . . Lester is not obtuse.

He opens a box that contains blank sheets of photographic paper. He is about to replace the lid when he notices that the stack inside looks uneven. He empties it out. Underneath the blank sheets is a packet wrapped in brown paper. A single word is written on it in pencil: *Naasut.*

The word has no meaning for him. His heart begins to race as he unfolds the paper. He is puzzled by the first photograph he sees. He is astonished by the second.

It comes to him that *"naasut"* is the Eskimo word for "flowers." But they are not pictures of flowers.

Chapter 54

Neqi, 77°52' N, 71°37' W
November 1898

He struggles awake through meshes of dream. Fresh in his mind is a morning three years ago: his first, waking in England. He had no idea where he was, knew only that he could not hear the grinding of the engines, nor feel the sickening heave of the *Etruria*. Perhaps he had drowned, and this was the afterlife; why had he been afraid of this? He luxuriated in the silence, the solidity, the strip of sunlight bleaching the wallpaper in front of him. And he thought, how glorious to have arrived . . .

Blissfully, he stretched out his limbs in the bed—a soft, generous bed, wonderfully unlike the mean bunk in second class—until his foot touched something firm and warm, which moved. And he remembered, in a brilliant rush, everything. He rolled over—Flora lay with her back to him, but he knew that she was awake, that she was waiting, that she did not know what to do. He stroked a hand down her bare shoulder, murmured her name (amazing, saying it out loud), and she turned over and looked at him. Her eyes were wary, but when he smiled, as he could not help doing, an answering warmth kindled in them. In the past, whenever he had made an amorous conquest, the morning after was clouded by doubts, misgivings, second thoughts, but that morning, he felt none of those.

He said, "I was afraid I was dreaming. Are you flesh or are you spirit?"

She dropped her eyes, smiled as she said, "I am flesh."

The three surviving members of the British expedition—Flora, Dixon, and Haddo—left for home in August. Although painful, it was also, in his heart of hearts, something of a relief when the *Clansman* finally bore them away. Flora had been intent on keeping their relationship hidden from Ralph and Henry, worried that she would lose all authority. Jakob thought he understood, but was still hurt by the way she withdrew—layers of reserve sweeping in and hiding the happy, uninhibited girl of the valley, until she would barely look at him in company. Frustrated and uncertain, he was driven to ask if she regretted their promises. He accused her of being ashamed of him, even (he knew this would wound) of being a coward. She reacted with such passionate, furious denial that he was chastened, and then she cried. As he held her in his arms, he was gladdened, relieved, and ashamed.

There were few private moments once they were back on the mainland, and those they had were charged with something akin to desperation. She reminded him of how he had sometimes been when he was younger, the way she threw herself into loving as if passion could obliterate doubt. He was concerned, although not to the point of saying anything. But, the night before she was to return to Siorapaluk, when Welbourne had tactfully slipped away, she went limp and turned away from him in his bunk, mid-embrace.

"I can't. It won't work. I can't."

She was on the verge of tears.

"Shh. It doesn't matter. I won't either."

"I don't want the last time to be like this."

"It isn't the last time, darling."

He pulled her back into his arms, but she would not be consoled.

"You were right. I'm a coward. I'm afraid."

"No. What are you afraid of?"

"Of people, censure, everything. Of being alone and having to . . . protect us."

"Well, I don't need protecting. And it won't be as bad as you think. You won't need to talk about us. You don't have to say anything about it."

"I'm not ashamed."

"I know."

"I'm not afraid that I'll change my mind."

"Good. I'm not afraid of that either."

She caressed his hip. In the light of the hurricane lamp, her eyes were sad. She pulled him toward her.

"I want you to, even if I don't."

"I'm fine."

"You don't want to?"

"It's okay, really."

She began to cry in earnest.

"I wanted you to have this . . . to remember—and now I've spoiled it."

Her eyes spilled over, cheeks gleamed in the lamplight.

"You haven't spoiled anything. It's going to be all right. You are my wife, Flora."

"Yes."

"And when you're in London, you should know I will think of you every night, like this."

"Sniveling?"

He laughed. "In my arms. Naked. Remember the Pope?"

To his relief, she smiled. "The good old Pope."

"I thought I'd ruined everything, that day."

"No . . ." She kissed his shoulder and said, more fiercely, "No."

"Remember the bathroom, in Liverpool, with the green tiles?"

Her eyes changed; a different kindling.

"When you washed me . . ."

"I think about that."

She looked down, and spoke into his skin: "So do I."

"What do you think about it?"

She smiled and pressed her lips to his chest.

He stroked her hair. "I will think about it when you're not here. Every wonderful thing."

She lifted her face a little.

"No time since then?"

"Oh, yes, lots of times . . . Like when you were so cold after swimming in the lake . . ." He felt suddenly, uncharacteristically, shy.

"Are you blushing?"

He laughed, feeling caught out. "I'm just saying, I don't need . . . and I will think about the next time, when I see you again; that will be best of all."

She had wriggled to face him again, was stroking him lightly, her thigh pressed against his.

"I will think of that too."

When they said their good-byes, with dry-mouthed kisses, she held him so tightly it hurt, and her eyes were wet as she said, "Don't doubt me, my darling. I will not fail you." Such a fierce look, as she held his face in her hands, that even after the awkwardness and uncertainty and unease, he didn't.

And they exchanged letters, to be parsed out; thin fare, over the next year. The two he has read so far are soft with handling; in them, she begs his forgiveness; he knows the real her, the Flora of the valley, and when she is free . . . He loves her letters; they keep him warm on the coldest night. He carries them buttoned in the breast pocket of his shirt. He wrote his own swiftly, in the hope that, by doing so, they would reveal him more truthfully. He found himself writing phrases that seemed old and threadbare. He did not discard them; after all this time, clichés no longer frightened him.

Quiet in the hut. Still early. He sends out his thoughts toward her, imagines them winging over a map toward the dot where she is, succoring her ... Swooping into her house in London, whatever that is like (down the chimney? Through the window?), into her bed, which he has never seen . . . and, then what? Words trickling into her ear? Ghostly hands sliding under her nightdress? In London, it must be lunchtime.

He hopes she is all right, that things are not too difficult, that she is not doubting, or suffering. He has the easy part. He shifts in the warm blankets, feels longing—a tender, beneficent desire . . .

He remembers lying with his head in her lap, sun in his eyes, undoing the buttons of her blouse. (She said, smiling, he looked as though he didn't know what he might find.) With a fingertip, he traces a contour around her breast, marveling that it can be both weighty and delicate. Areolas flushed the colors of Alpine dawns; tender cushions. He cups her breasts as gently as he can to—just—heft the warm weight, prolonging the moment until he brushes his lips across that fleeting, rosy softness. He craves the instant of stiffening, but wishes he could delay it, a little, because then the hard, round bead causes his lips to purse and his cheeks to hollow and his tongue to pay tribute. (She looked down, laughed, without explanation; he didn't care.) She stopped laughing, pressed his head to her breast; he sucks her hard enough to make her moan.

The Eskimo name for this time of year, *tutsarfik*, means something like "it is listening," and this morning, it is apt; the single bark of a dog is the only thing that interrupts the stillness. Jakob stamps down to the frozen shore, his breath smoking in front of him, a bucket dangling from one hand, a lantern in the other.

It was to be expected, perhaps, that Armitage would seek him out, once he had heard news of the northern journey; and yet, he had thought the man would be too proud, or too embarrassed, to show himself. When they first heard that Armitage was back in the north,

Flora worried for him: Did he pose a danger? What might he do? Jakob had laughed—Armitage wasn't that much of a villain. As for himself, after he and Welbourne had discovered the non-existence of Dupree Land, he felt his animosity toward Armitage diminish. It was strange; for so long, he had burned to prove the man a liar and had dwelled on Frank's death, blaming him; had hated him, really, as he hated no one else—his very existence a painful burr . . . Now that proof is in his hands, the burr has gone. So what if Armitage claimed he had seen a chimerical island, simply to raise money? And if he exploited Frank's death to do so (perhaps the reason he gave last night was genuine—it is possible), somehow, it no longer seems of overwhelming importance.

Jakob sweeps the lantern from side to side, searching for a bank of clean snow—no easy matter in the village. When he finds a patch that is still unblemished by dog or man, he squats, and, with mittened hands, scoops it into the bucket. Fresh snow vanishes when it melts; to make one pot of coffee requires a bucketful. Collecting it is one of the tasks that give him satisfaction, that he refuses to delegate.

Armitage is as arrogant as ever—dismissive and overbearing—but Jakob can see him now as a man bent under an unendurable lash, harried by an ambition so voracious it burns up everything in its path. His eyes have always been haunted; last night, they seemed to beseech him.

Before he leaves, Armitage asks Jakob if they can have a private word.

"Do you give me your word of honor that you're not going to try for the Pole?"

"We have no interest in the Pole, Armitage. You can rest assured."

Armitage nods. "I intend to. I would like to put something to you, de Beyn. I suggest that, when you get home, neither of you mention anything about your northern journey, or about Dupree Land."

"Do you? Nothing we could say can make any difference to what you do here."

Lester blinks. His eyelids are red, as if he has not slept. "I rather think you will not mention it. After all, Dr. Urbino's reputation rests on it."

"Only by your say-so. And I find your suggestion inappropriate in the extreme."

Armitage lets out a huff of air and smiles.

"An interesting choice of words. In any case, I think you will not."

"Why?"

"I suppose that, ah, I think . . ." His tongue appears and moistens his lips. "Because Mrs. Athlone is a woman with a very public profile."

Jakob feels something cold at the base of his spine.

"What do you mean by that?"

"Simply that, if you do not mention anything about your northern journey or Dupree Land, then I will not mention your . . . liaison with her. If you talk or write about it, in any way that damages my reputation, then I will be compelled to do the same."

Jakob discovers that his throat has turned dry, and it is an effort to get words out.

"This is nothing but foolish gossip. I don't know what you may have heard, but it is iniquitous to suggest—"

"It probably would be nothing but gossip, but for your penchant for making evidence."

Armitage's eyes betray him—they slide toward the darkroom. Jakob's follow. When did he go in there? Last night? This morning? He must have turned the place upside down . . . He feels his gorge rise.

"You wouldn't be that low."

"I'm not the one who has made a whore of Mr. Athlone's wife. That, I would say, is inappropriate in the extreme."

Jakob is silent for several moments, then makes a gesture of defeat.

"Very well. I give you my word I won't mention Dupree Land. I will say nothing about the north coast. Neither of us will. Now give me back . . . what you have taken."

Armitage stares at him. "After it's all over, of course I will."

A plank creaks. Jakob takes a step forward, and Armitage takes a step back. It is that that makes him sure that he still has the photograph on him—he wouldn't have trusted such a thing to his men . . . Armitage watches, eyes almost starting out of his head, and then a thought that had not taken concrete form launches Jakob across the space between them. He seizes the man by the arms, the impetus propelling them both against the wall; Armitage's head knocks against the wood with a crack, breath explodes from his lungs in a loud "*hunh.*"

After a moment's stunned passivity, Armitage twists like an eel and grabs Jakob's jaw in his fingers. His teeth are bared in a rictus that looks like a smile. They wrestle in silence—God, Armitage is strong, his arms sinewy and hard, his grip agonizing—Jakob grabs for his clothing, yanks at his sweater, his belt . . . Where is it . . . ? Where? A chair spins across the floor. Something breaks. Jakob has the clear thought that he has never hit a man in anger in his life—why ever not? He makes a fist and aims it at the grimacing face, makes contact with flesh and yielding gristle, and then feels a ringing blow on his left ear and jaw. His teeth rattle, his head sings, he stumbles, momentarily unable to hear, or see, but launches his weight onto Armitage and they both fall. They land against something low and dark and hard. The stove. Armitage lets out a shrill scream as his back makes contact with heated iron.

Armitage rolls away, holding his back; Jakob drags at his trousers, falls to his knees astride Armitage, tearing at his pockets, feels a square of stiffened paper in his breast pocket, fumbles it out, crushed. There is blood on his hand. A swirl of cold air; another yell—a woman. When he sees what he took, he attempts to land another punch on the man's face. No more than he deserves. The fist connects, but hurts abominably. There is numbness in his head. Armitage's face is twisted. Red teeth . . . An arm goes around Jakob's chest and he finds himself dragged backward. Men are shouting.

Kussuk is leaning over Armitage, who slowly sits up, shaking his head. He is speaking, but Jakob can't hear for the ringing in his head.

"Is that it?" he is shouting, holding the photograph in front of him. "Is that it? You unspeakable . . ."

The arms around his waist are Sorqaq's. Jakob goes limp and turns away, freeing himself. Amazed faces stare at them both. Jakob looks down at Armitage. Blood flows from his nose, staining his mustache and beard a deeper red. He looks up at Jakob, eyes burning like lamps in a house where someone has died.

"Get out," says Jakob. It comes out as a weird mumble.

In silence, Kussuk helps Armitage to his feet, whereupon he shakes off his arm and tugs at his disordered clothing. One of his sleeves hangs by threads. His shirt is dragged out of his trousers, the breast pocket almost ripped off. He walks stiffly to the door and goes out. He doesn't look around.

Sorqaq looks at Jakob. "What happened? Are you all right? Did he attack you?"

Sorqaq is not accustomed to thinking of Jakob as a man of violence. It is not how Jakob thinks of himself. He sits heavily at the table and shakes his head. It can't be real. The fight between him and Armitage can't have happened. And yet, apparently, it has. The crushed photograph that Armitage stole is still in his fist—the fist he hit Armitage with, breaking his nose, from the look of him. It throbs hotly, the fingers already swelling.

"Ah . . . I . . . He tried to steal something of mine."

Sorqaq nods and exchanges a knowing glance with Meqro.

"Will you go and make sure they leave?"

His gaze falls on the rifle hanging on the wall. Good thing he didn't think of it before now. God knows, he was angry enough . . . Is angry enough. He can't seem to loosen his fist.

Unable to sit there, not knowing what is happening, Jakob pulls himself to his feet and follows Sorqaq. The whole village is outside, talking, gesticulating, and watching as the visitors load up their sleds in the darkness. The dogs make their own cacophony, eager to be off. The atmosphere is excited, almost festive, with an undertow of alarm. Jakob stands back from the others, feeling their eyes turn toward him, hears them muttering. But nothing, not even something as extraordinary as a fight between two *kallunat* can make an Eskimo hurry when he isn't ready. The tall figure that is Armitage bends over his sled, tugs on cords. He doesn't look at anyone. His two hunters argue about something to do with the dogs. Jakob watches, until embarrassment and cold overcome him, and he goes back inside.

By the time Armitage has left, Jakob's whole body aches. Every muscle feels as though it has been put through a mangle. His jaw is swollen and tender; two of his teeth are loose and he has the taste of blood in his mouth. His right hand hangs like a heavy club. But, at first, reaction makes him euphoric. I won! he thinks. I had to fight and I won . . . He replays the fight over and over in his head, each grab and blow . . . although large parts seem to be missing. Admittedly, he was lucky. Then the euphoria fades.

Alone in the darkroom, he smooths out the crumpled photograph. It shows Flora sitting on a blanket in the sun, their tent in the background, her knees folded to one side, smiling up at the camera with a look that pierces him—she never looked more carefree, or more trusting. It captures the essence of Onmogelijk Dal. Their place. It is that, even more than her nakedness, that makes him tremble with anger and shame. You can see in her face what they found.

When Welbourne returns from his walrus hunt, bearing tusks, the pelt of a fine bear, and stories of his near drowning, Jakob tells him about the bizarre incident, and Welbourne laughs. He makes him recount the fight in detail, terms it the sporting event of the season, and is sorry he missed it. He treats the whole thing so lightly that Jakob ends up laughing too. The fight with Lester—but especially the fact that he appears to have won—takes on the quality of a vivid, unbelievable dream.

"He won't come back," says Welbourne. "He'll be too humiliated."

Jakob agrees. He thinks Armitage is afraid of him, having been seen in such a light. Anyway, from now on, they will be on their guard. He thinks of him less and less, and soon, barely at all.

There is another visitor, before the turn of the year. Jakob has not seen Aniguin since the summer. He brings his new wife—very young and silent—to show off. They sit around the table, eating and smoking, then Aniguin says, "I have to ask you something, Te Peyn. About the bad men."

"What bad men?"

"The bad men that Fellora wants to bring here. When will this happen?"

"I don't know what you mean, Aniguin . . ."

Then he remembers what Flora told him in Onmogelijk Dal: that Ashbee was the agent of those who wanted to build a penal colony in the Arctic. She hadn't known, when he signed up, and thought it both unworkable and abhorrent. ("But without the money he brought, I wouldn't have been able to come.") Later, as they watched a snow bunting on her nest, a few feet away, she said, "I'm glad he never got to see this. I'll never tell anyone. They won't spoil it."

"It's not what you think, Aniguin . . . Who told you that?"

"Tateraq. Ashbee told him—when he and Fellora and Tateraq were on *Umingmak Nuna*. He told my brother bad men would come and live here—*kallunat* thieves and murderers—and we would be their servants. Tateraq was afraid, so he killed him, to stop them, but he did not want to shoot Fellora."

Jakob is stunned. Welbourne stares; Jakob had not shared this confidence.

"Aniguin, no, that will not happen. Ashbee was wrong; he didn't know this place, and Flora would never have allowed it. That's why he killed Ashbee? Is that what he said?"

"He was trying to protect us. But perhaps . . ." Aniguin shrugs. "We cannot stop you coming here; we have to change . . ."

Jakob shakes his head. "Not like that, Aniguin, I swear. It was a mistake. It was only Ashbee who thought that. Not Fellora. Or Dixon or Haddo. None of them knew before he came. That will not happen."

Aniguin looks at him with his shrewd gaze.

"The *kallunat* will do what they want. I don't mean you, Te Peyn, but others—men like Armitay. You have guns and everything. You are implacable. We are only silly Inuit."

Jakob shakes his head, and smiles, wanting to disagree, but his main thought is, His death wasn't her fault, after all . . . If only I could tell her now . . .

Aniguin shrugs. "*Ayornamut.*"

It cannot be otherwise.

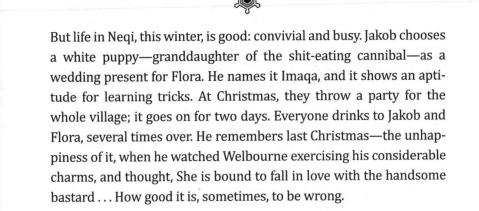

But life in Neqi, this winter, is good: convivial and busy. Jakob chooses a white puppy—granddaughter of the shit-eating cannibal—as a wedding present for Flora. He names it Imaqa, and it shows an aptitude for learning tricks. At Christmas, they throw a party for the whole village; it goes on for two days. Everyone drinks to Jakob and Flora, several times over. He remembers last Christmas—the unhappiness of it, when he watched Welbourne exercising his considerable charms, and thought, She is bound to fall in love with the handsome bastard . . . How good it is, sometimes, to be wrong.

He misses Flora, but since he has faith, it is, on the whole, a pleasurable ache. He and Welbourne have become close: he enjoys his company, and that of Sorqaq and his other friends. His fluency in their language improves. He has his work: he writes up his field notes from the summer, starts to write an account of the circumnavigation; and he indulges in a certain amount of self-congratulation. He experiments with the camera—tries to capture the Siren-like aurora, the effects of winter half-light. The results are frustratingly uneven, but in the summer he took photographs of the valley, of the lake, and of caves and tunnels in the glacier, which he is proud to show the others. He made a record of something that cannot last, that even now no longer exists, but he has done it: caught the essence of something fleeting and sublime.

And then there are the photographs that he shows to no one: of her, in the valley. There are photographs of himself, as well, that she took. Unnerving to see himself like this—as she sees him. Astonishing but . . . not unpleasant. Each time he pulls a print from the water bath, he shuts his eyes to remember the moment with greater clarity—opens them, to look at what *she* is remembering—shuttling between past and present, between he and she. He understands that this is how he has always felt: as though the distance between them is meaningless.

Between past, present . . . and future. He believes the question she asked him, years before—"Is it really possible?"—has been answered.

PART NINE

THUBAN IN DRACO

The constellation Draco represents the dragon, Ladon,
which guarded the golden apples of the Hesperides and was slain
by Heracles. It wanders eternally around the celestial North Pole.
Five thousand years ago, its star, Thuban, was the pole star.
The great pyramid of Gizah was configured, it is believed,
so that light from Thuban shone into its heart. Of all the
pole stars, it is the faintest, but the most perfectly placed.

Chapter 55

Gander, Newfoundland, 48°57' N, 54°36' W
1948

When the next report comes over the wire, from Station Eureka on Ellesmere Island, the weather forecast has worsened—poor visibility, snow, and winds. They are informed that the flight has been delayed until the following day—if conditions permit. Inside the base, the atmosphere has likewise deteriorated: the scientists start to grumble about the valuable time they are wasting.

Flora walks slowly back to her room. Last night, she barely slept. She had forgotten how hard it is to sleep when it is not truly dark. She could have closed the blinds, but she wanted to look at the stars. She watched the sky slowly lighten.

At one point, Gemini—the Eskimo doorway—was perfectly framed in the window. Aniguin had likened him and her to the twin stars; she was enchanted, and never forgot. Could he still be alive? The latest she knew of him was on her most recent visit—eight years ago—when she heard he had moved to Thule, the trading post, and converted to Christianity. This last, she took with a pinch of salt.

Talking to the young man has exhausted her. She said things today that she has never said to anyone. She tried to be truthful, while protecting *them*—her most precious jewel. She always believed that, by keeping it hidden, she was sheltering it, keeping it intact; but now, talking about him has brought a deluge of memory, more vivid and overwhelming than she has experienced for years. After all this time, things have become . . . slippery. Sometimes, she doesn't know where she is, or when.

The window is suddenly full of tiny white flecks that spiral and float downward, each lonely spicule reaching for another with outstretched arms . . . and clotting, and clumping, and falling.

In Gander, it has started to snow.

Do you remember the lake?

(Strange, it sounds exactly like him.)

When you nearly killed yourself?

Of course. How could I forget?

The colors of the glacier lake, caught between the ice and the dark hillside: sometimes a milky turquoise, sometimes the green of polished agate, sometimes—rarely—the hot blue of cornflowers. He named it after her, and it held her in its spell. Its opacity frustrated her gaze, increased its allure. After days of contemplating her foolishness, and her desire, she tried swimming in it—with painful, paralyzing consequences. The floor of the lake was ice—where it had a floor. Then it shelved away into invisible depths. Its cold was not like the bright, snapping cold of the river where they—quickly—washed, but crushing and brutal, like iron swords. He rescued her. It was the one instance where his anger delighted her. He had carried her all the way back to the tent, despite her shivered protests that she was too heavy, that he would strain his back (he had). She remembers the hardness of his arms, the pounding of his heart through her ribs, the crease pinched in his forehead. It was the anger of fear, of love. The medium she had stepped into, feeling its silken, deadly embrace that numbed her limbs and choked her breath—it wasn't water, after all; it was liquid ice.

In the tent he said, "Don't ever do that again."

He was chafing her cold flesh; for once, she could barely feel him.

She said, dreamily, "But you would save me again. And pick me up and carry me again."

"I wasn't going to let you fall."

But that is what she had done to him.

After the lake drained away, they walked into the glacier. The shoulder of hillside plunged into an empty socket of ice: pale green walls; dank, gravel floor. At one end, a dark slit beckoned: the mouth that had swallowed the lake. Stepping inside the tunnel mouth was to go from one world to another—one where the air was hard, with a harsh smell and metallic chill. Inside the ice was silence. If you put out your hand to touch the walls, they felt dry. Sometimes the ice was rough, opaque, granular; sometimes, so smooth it was barely there at all. Glossy crevices, cracks filled with frozen water, tinged with indescribable colors, revealed fault lines and bubbles, held suspended within them tiny fragments of gravel, or vegetable matter, or dust. Or, once, a drowned mosquito, enshrined in lifeless perfection.

They walked farther in. The space swelled and shrank. Bullied and caressed by water, the ice had made shapes like nothing she had seen, no human architecture: bubbling and rounded, rippled like the roof of a mouth; bowl-like concavities, bulbous swellings, sharp ridges; gleaming, glassy. And the light . . . bleeding softly through the ceiling, revealing weakness, drawing their eyes upward. And in the unexpected high chamber halfway down, there was a fissure in the glacier surface—a chimney worn by surface melt. At certain times of day, the sun sent its sword into the glacier's heart; its rays found them out like the gaze of God.

Flora had the unsettling sense of being inside a living body, something that had, on an infinitely greater scale, its own perception of time, on which they—tiny, darting specks trapped in its gullet—barely registered. Some creature of unimaginable vastness and slowness, terrifyingly patient. Sometimes the ice would creak or crack, groan or hiss. Inexplicable currents of air wafted past them, as though, once in a while, it breathed.

Despite the unearthly beauty, she was twitchy, could not shake off a nervousness as the ceiling pressed down on them the farther they went. Jakob crawled on alone under the lowering roof until he was lost to sight and hearing. He refused to take the rope—it would only snag on the rough floor. After what seemed an age, she shouted to him, and there was no reply. She was cold, waiting. She crawled into the narrowing crack as far as she could bear, shouted herself hoarse. Tears froze before they could fall. At last, she heard something and called out to him. When he crawled out, he was shaking with cold. He had gotten stuck in a particularly tight spot and became disoriented in the darkness. He laughed, but she knew he had been afraid. As they walked out, they came to a smooth stretch of wall just as the sun illuminated it with gorgeous striations of color, as though cobalt pigment had seeped from above, saturating the lowest levels. He asked her to take a photograph (his hands were too cold). Then he wrapped his arms around her from behind, put on a terrible English accent and quoted a passage they both knew from Tyndall:

"Could our vision penetrate the body of the glacier, we should find that the change from white to blue consists in the gradual expulsion of air. Whiteness results from the intimate and irregular mixture of air and a transparent solid, a crushed diamond would resemble snow . . ."

When he said "intimate and irregular," he buried his face in her neck. His skin felt like ice.

Instead of laughing, she wrested herself away.

"We have to hurry. You need something hot."

"Flora, it's all right. No damage done."

Buoyant with relief, he smiled. She could not smile. He had never been happier.

* * *

When they got back to camp, his hands were aching. He still felt cold as they got into bed and he wrapped himself around her, pressed every inch of his body against her bare flesh. She willed her warmth into him and felt the shudders of cold lessen. Separateness seemed a thing of the past, as though they shared the same blood.

She said to the tent wall, "I kept thinking, What if he doesn't come back? I couldn't bear it."

"Shh. I'll always come back." His arms tightened around her, and he nuzzled the nape of her neck. "I like that you worry about me. I worry about you, too."

"If the roof had fallen in, or something, I couldn't have saved you."

"Glaciers don't do that."

"I wish you were coming with me."

They had talked about her imminent return to England. Both agreed that his presence there could serve no purpose. Besides, he couldn't afford it.

"I wish you were staying. Can I put them here?"

She shifted so that he could tuck his cold hands between her thighs.

He said, into her hair, "I won't do anything stupid, I promise."

Flora pushes herself into a sitting position and fumbles for the glass of water by her bed. She is thirsty, her throat painfully dry. Was she asleep? She has to dab at her eyes, which have a tendency to leak when she lies down. Something wrong with the tear ducts, she has been told. Not crying. She doesn't do that anymore. Never did, really.

Jakob planned to return to New York in September of '99, a year after Flora had left Greenland, but by the end of that month, there was no word—no letter or telegraph. She ordered herself not to worry. To wait, believing that all would be well.

After a few more weeks, she wrote to his brother in New York. Just in case—she told herself—he had changed his mind about her.

It was unthinkable, but it was also possible. It would not be the end of the world, but she had to know. Hendrik de Beyn's reply confirmed that Jakob had not returned. He too was worried, but he knew that the north was an unpredictable place. His letter both relieved and depressed her. So Flora waited, starving her imagination. Freddie, who had agreed to a divorce, said nothing about it, until after the rumors and reports began to appear in the papers, late that winter. Flora ignored them; what were rumors, after all? But she wrote to her father: she was going to Greenland in the spring; please, please, Daddy, this time you must help me . . .

One day in February, while they discussed a clause in the contract for her book, Freddie said, without looking at her, "Am I to take it that you no longer wish for a divorce? It's quite all right. Up to you."

Flora walked out of the room without another word.

Chapter 56

Siorapaluk, 77°47' N, 70°38' W
July 1900

The air smells of salt water and juniper. The *Vega* noses her way between floes and drops anchor in the fjord, where she hangs, doubled by her reflection, like the icebergs, like the red hills. Ice clings to the shore in places. It is strangely quiet—no dogs bark, there are no shouts of welcome. Only the distant cries of wheeling dovekies disturb the stillness. The village, on its quiet sandy beach, looks deserted. She wonders whether some wholesale calamity has befallen it.

Flora rows herself ashore. She would not let anyone come with her. Her father has brought her here—reluctant, critical, generally disapproving, but unable to deny her. He called in favors, made claims on men he hates to be indebted to, so that the *Vega* would be leased to him for the season. He doesn't know what this will end up costing him. The crew, most of whom know, or know of, the renowned Captain Mackie and his oddly celebrated daughter, must have formed some idea of why they are here, on what strange mission that has nothing to do with whales, but they say nothing.

When she came to Dundee to beg for help, she knew he would not—in the end—say no. Her father did not rage and shout—that would have been out of character—but he was tight-lipped, judgmental, his face pinched with Presbyterian disgust, as though this were merely the last of very many straws: that was her payment.

"What about your marriage vows? You made a vow before God to support your husband in sickness and in health. Till death do you part."

Flora refused to admit that hope was lost; she was divorcing Freddie to marry another man, who was . . . temporarily mislaid.

"You assume the fault is all mine."

"No, I don't. But no marriage is perfect, Flora. Life is not meant to be a picnic party."

"I know that!"

Her father made her feel and behave like a child.

"Life isn't meant to be purgatory, either. I shouldn't have married Freddie. I was twenty years old and unhappy, and I made a mistake. It never worked, not even before his accident. I deserve a chance to be happy, Father. Marrying Mr. de Beyn will not be a mistake."

If she hadn't married Freddie, she would not have gone north—would never have met Jakob. And if Ashbee hadn't died . . . There is no unpicking the weave of causality in her life.

"And you say you intend to move to America"—he seemed to find this more outrageous than the divorce itself—"where you know no one! Where you have no family or friends. You would cut all natural ties and be absolutely dependent on this man?"

Flora sighed. "I'm not cutting all ties. The boat to New York only takes a week. And I don't mean to be his dependent—I will work."

"How do you know you will be able to?"

"I've as much chance of doing so there as here."

"There are storms in every marriage . . . temptations. It is almost always better to weather those storms. You've been a fortunate young woman, Flora. Perhaps that was my fault; I indulged you too much. You've not had to learn about sticking it out. That's what most people do—they make a promise and they make the best of it."

Flora was goaded into attack, at last.

"I 'stuck it out,' as you put it, for eight years! And do you claim you made the best of your vows—your promises? Do you think I don't know about Sorqaq and Asarpaka? What you did up there?"

Her father's face went very still, his eyes fixed on the wallpaper. Only his nostrils moved. For a moment, she was afraid of what he might do.

"I never set up to be a saint. Your father is weak, Flora. But your mother, God rest her soul, never knew or suffered for it. I stood by her. I didn't walk away."

"You did not stand by her! You were gone for two years at a time! Did you know that I blamed her for driving you away? I hated her for it! I didn't know, then, that you were ... For all I know, you spent as much time with them as you did with us!"

Captain Mackie looked at her again, and she quailed.

"No. I was away so much because my job entailed it—that was all. I regretted my weakness, every day. I am sorry if you ... I didn't know ..."

Flora glared back at her father, but her indignation was waning. It occurred to her that he would miss her—not that he would say so. She felt stirrings of pity for him, and did not want to.

She rows the dinghy as slowly as she can across the quiet surface, attuned to the dip of the oars, the hollow sound of the rowlocks, the soft glitter of water falling from the blades. She notices everything about the boat, and the fjord, and the ship drawing away from her. She is backing blindly into a future she does not want. She stops rowing. As long as she does not land, perhaps it will not happen.

The boat grounds itself on the sand with a rasp. She climbs out. She has thought of all the bad news that she might hear, and how she will survive it. Except that, after a certain point, she cannot imagine herself surviving. She has forced herself to imagine terrible things—he is living with a woman here, with a half-Eskimo baby, having changed his mind. She has imagined him stranded on the other side of Smith Sound, like Greely and his men, weak, ill, starving . . . And she imagines—she can't help it—Jakob walking out of an *illu* toward her. Seeing his dear smile. ("Darling, I couldn't write . . . I hoped you didn't worry too much . . ." How long his hair? Bearded or clean-shaven? How tanned?) She can feel, physically feel, his arms around her, his body against hers. For how much longer can she believe any of these things?

Things have to be paid for. She has told herself that, as long as he is all right, she can bear to give him up—if that is what it costs. As if the outcome could be anything to do with what she wants.

Now there is a barking from behind one of the *illu*. A small, half-naked figure runs out, stops and stares at the stranger. It is Aamma. Seven years old, tall for her age, fine-featured, imperious. Flora calls out to her, "Aamma! It is I, Fellora, remember? Fellora."

The child stares back without recognition. Then she calls out the question you ask of people you don't know, of whom of you have reason to be suspicious: "Are you flesh or are you spirit?"

Flora says, "I am flesh."

Aamma calls over her shoulder. And Flora is thinking, not of the last time she saw him, but of the time they said good-bye in the London hotel, when she did not know when or if she would see him again. The force of it: not now . . . not now . . . please God, *not now*.

Now Meqro is coming out of an *illu*, her face changing from worry and surprise to pleasure as she recognizes her old friend.

"Fellora!"

Now Flora is walking up to her, smiling at Meqro, but her face feels like a mask.

"Meqro, dear friend . . . Oh, tell me—is he . . . ?"

But then it is now.

Chapter 57

The hut, with its honey-colored walls, is still standing, although parts have been dismantled and carried away. The foodstuffs they abandoned have gone and there is little of anything left. Furniture has been broken down for timber, planks pried away, nails pulled out, and the orphaned things—stove, mismatched bottles and tins—are broken, rusted, and dirty, scattered in squalid confusion. Flora looks at it and feels rage and sadness, although what does it matter? She cannot cry. She is too angry—with Jakob, with herself. How could he have left her, after all those full-hearted promises? How could she have failed to keep him safe?

Meqro can tell her little enough. She tells Flora about the strange incident when Armitage came to Neqi from the north, the winter before last, and fought with Jakob and then went away, angry. She thought they had fought because of Flora—perhaps Armitage was jealous. Sorqaq would know more. He and Jakob were like brothers. They had been working on the glacier at the head of the fjord. They had gone up there many times after the sun came back. Sorqaq said they had climbed down inside it, into its blue heart. Then, after

Sorqaq married, Jakob continued to go up on the glacier alone. One day, he didn't come back. The men went to look, but there was no sign of him. The glacier was of the inland ice: haunted by spirits, unpredictable and dangerous. Its crevasses could swallow a man.

Ayornamut.

The American *kallunat* must have angered the spirits. Some time after that, Welbourne went to hunt walrus with some of the men and was drowned. His companions, who included Aniguin and Metek, found his body too late. Another death, but unconnected. Bad luck.

"Sad. Both of them. I'm sorry, Fellora."

Meqro cries softly. Flora nods. Her throat has become too tight to speak. She keeps her lips pressed together. If she opens her mouth, she might scream.

Meqro goes on, almost as if she is talking to herself.

"He was a good man. And he was happy, with you. *Qooviannikumut.*"

Meqro's eyes are focused on her needlework. She does not look at Flora. She does not reach out and touch her. Flora did not expect that she would.

Her father is oddly tender with her—tentative, even—as if, robbed of disapproval, he does not know how to behave. He seems less sure of himself. Flora looks at him and thinks, in astonishment, But he looks like an old man! When did he become old?

When she wasn't there. All sorts of things happened when she was not there to prevent them: her father aging, Jakob dying. She should have been there to keep him from harm. She had told him that she would, and did not.

A few days before she left London, she went to see Iris. Her friend was in a terrible state. Helen Tomlinson had left her, which was no great surprise to anyone, but, in a stroke that seemed especially cruel, she had run off with Jessie Biddenden. They had gone to

Egypt, or somewhere like that—somewhere hot and full of history. Iris went to pieces. She frightened Flora; it was as though her brain was unspooling in front of her, her thoughts landing on the floor in a chaotic jumble. Her hair was unkempt, her clothing disheveled. Flora tried to buck her up, knowing it was probably futile. She couldn't believe Jessie's treachery; Helen's she could believe only too well.

"I know you used to warn me about Helen, Flora—everyone did. But you didn't know how she could be . . . I wouldn't have changed a thing about her. Not one thing."

Flora held Iris's bony, fragile hand. Her wrists were white and unblemished.

"Do you know, she had the temerity to write to me from Rome to say that she was missing me! *Missing* me!"

Iris looked demented, her eyes unable to focus on anything in the room.

"Can you believe it? No acknowledgment of the agonies she put me through, as though this pain I live in were nothing! The feeling that she might, after all, change her mind, come back . . . Oh! It's this constant *dangling* I can't stand."

"You can refuse to be dangled. You have a choice."

"I can't! I wish I didn't. I don't."

"You do."

"I couldn't not choose her. And it's torture."

Flora murmured in agreement. Iris lifted burning, tear-lensed eyes to her and gave her a ghastly smile.

"Do you know what I find myself wishing? I actually wish she were dead. I wish she had died. Then I could just be sad."

Her voice broke on the last word and the brimming tears flowed down her cheeks. It made her look more human.

"I would know that I would never see her again; she could never write and twist the knife once more . . . It would be easier than this."

She sobbed for a minute and then dabbed her eyes with a handkerchief. The outburst seemed to have restored a little sanity. Her voice was calmer.

"Oh, I'm sorry, Flora, I don't mean . . . I don't know what I'm saying."

Flora shook her head, meaning, It's all right. But she did know what she was saying. She knew.

There is a youth walking around the village in one of Jakob's shirts—an old flannel shirt, with thin stripes of red and green—walking around with it unbuttoned and flapping, as though it were nothing. Flora does not know this boy, but she goes up to him.

"You got this from the *kallunat* house at Neqi?"

"*Ieh.*" He smiles.

"That was Te Peyn's shirt."

He shrugs.

"He was my husband. It was his shirt. Could I buy it from you?"

The youth stares at her with shy curiosity.

"It is a good shirt," he says. "Will you give me a gun?"

This is so preposterous that Flora nearly laughs.

"I can't give you a gun for a shirt. I don't have a gun. I will give you . . . some nails, some cloth . . . I can give you another shirt. A better shirt. Thicker than this. This one is old and worn out."

She can see him calculating how much he can ask for. She could kill him without compunction. She reaches out her hand to touch the hem and he draws back.

"Please . . ."

Suddenly the tears are flooding down her face. The boy looks confused. Flora tries to explain but finds she can no longer speak. Not only that, she can't breathe. She is gasping for air, her throat working uselessly, making strange, inhuman sounds. She grows dizzy, but her throat has locked shut. She thinks, This is it; this is how I die. Grief will choke me.

The next thing, she is lying on the ground on her side, her cheek pressed into the cold gravel. Her hands are covered in grit, and they hurt. Above her, against the sky, the boy has taken off the shirt and is holding it out toward her. He looks frightened. He lays it down in front of her and backs away.

Flora puts her hand on the cloth. She washed this shirt in the river at Onmogilijk Dal. Molecules of their glacier are in this shirt, atoms from their lake. She brings it to her face and breathes it in. It does not smell of him, she thinks. Then she thinks, I can't remember what that was like.

Neqi, 77°52' N, 71°37' W

They camp beside the remnants of the abandoned American hut, as ransacked and dilapidated as her own. Flora stands in the cramped space that was his darkroom, its partition wall nibbled away, the glass bottles broken. There are the few pieces of photographic equipment that no one could find a use for: some chemicals, which she pours away; a box of blank paper, stained and swollen with damp; a piece of amber glass that he used to filter snow glare, broken in two. On the wooden walls, at head height, lists of numbers are scribbled in pencil: developing times, perhaps. His writing. His thoughts. She thinks about asking Sorqaq to cut out the piece of plank for her, then thinks, This is so, so stupid.

There is no sign of his cameras, his photographs, his films, notebooks, records. She can see where folders were once stacked on a shelf. There should be the photographs of his discoveries, his new land, the account of the circumnavigation of Thule, with his notes, drawings, painstaking measurements, samples . . . All that proof. These things are important. Less important, perhaps (but dearer to her), there are the photographs of the valley, the glacier and its lake. The caves of ice. The pictures she took of him (in his notes, credited to Naasut). And, somewhere, there must be photographs of herself among the flowers, and of him—the ones he promised no one else would see.

There should be the account of his northern journey and the evidence he has that proves Armitage a liar.

The bunks are partially dismantled, but the blankets have been left, unwanted. Wool does not do well here; the blankets are damp; mildew and other forms of decay have stolen into the hut and begun their work. Flora lies down on the bunk they briefly shared, listening to its creaks, breathing in the miasma of wet wool.

Sorqaq could add little to Meqro's account. Last spring, he married a girl called Megipsu and went with her to her village. Jakob worked on the glacier nearby. He continued to go up there after Sorqaq left. He knew it well, knew what to avoid . . . Glaciers are always dangerous, no matter how much care is taken.

But Sorqaq told her something else. Just after Jakob's disappearance, Armitage came back. He came to the hut and told Welbourne that he wanted to apologize to Jakob. He had failed once more to reach the North Pole. Welbourne said Armitage seemed shocked to hear of Jakob's death. But, Sorqaq added, it was possible he had come back earlier than he said.

"What do you mean?"

"Perhaps he came back here before Jakob died."

"Why do you say that?"

"I was there when they fought. I saw him. Armitay looked at Jakob like he wanted to kill him."

And, some months later, after Welbourne's death, Armitage and some men came back, saying they must take the dead men's belongings away, because their things should go to their families in America. If Sorqaq had been there, he said, not meeting Flora's eye, he would have stopped him taking Jakob's things.

"I put them in a box—his papers and pictures, his clothes, his camera. I knew you would come back. I'm sorry, Fellora. Of course, some things were with him. Tools, another camera . . . He kept your letters, here." He touched his breast.

Chapter 58

The last time Flora crossed the strait between Ellesmere and Greenland was two years ago, in August, after she and Jakob left the valley. They met up with Sorqaq, Aniguin, and Welbourne, and stared at the daunting sight of a strait made up of gray, sullen water. Winds from the north had blown out the ice. They had to use the collapsible boat, dug up from the cache and mended, although the warped timbers meant it leaked terribly. Dense fog rolled in, so they had little idea where they were. Heavy swells pushed them north and east. Without Welbourne's skill with the makeshift sails, and the untiring vigilance of Aniguin and Sorqaq, God knows whether they would have made it back to Greenland at all.

Flora, who had never been truly afraid in the *Vega*, even in the worst storms, struggled to stay calm. At one point in the sixty-hour crossing, they found themselves menaced by old, battered floes and near-invisible slabs of black ice—every piece larger than their fragile boat. They bailed continuously, or used oars to punt off the encroaching bergs.

Once, the wind tore a rent in the fog and, away in the northeast, there was a black scribble against the grayness: a bare-masted, thick-funneled ship. Flora squinted; the others looked at her in expectation. After peering hard through binoculars, she shook her head.

"It's not the *Clansman*. I don't think it's British. It looks wrong."

Whalers wouldn't venture this far north. And her ship, coming to pick her up and take her home, would have stopped at Siorapaluk. Scotty Welbourne took the glasses from her and studied the stranger, plowing northward.

"I think it's an American," he said.

He and Jakob exchanged glances. The swirling fog wrapped itself around them, blotting out the stranger, reducing their visible world to a few yards of gray, heaving water. No one said what they were thinking.

When at last they made it back to Neqi, the villagers came out to greet them. They were all smiles, laughing with relief, joking—until they saw Flora. They stared at her in consternation, even fear.

"Are you flesh or are you spirit?" they asked.

"I am flesh, Pualana!"

She smiled. No one smiled back at her. Aniguin and Sorqaq remonstrated with them, and it transpired that they had heard from Tateraq, who had told them that Ashbee had killed Flora and then turned the gun on himself.

"No, there's been a misunderstanding."

Jakob laughed, his hand on her arm. She had stepped carefully aside (this memory lacerated her), worried that they would *know*.

"You can see that Fellora isn't dead! She is flesh, like us."

They explained that Ashbee had died in an accident, that Tateraq had gone in search of Haddo and Dixon . . . A misunderstanding . . . The questions raised by this version of events floated away in the mist.

Now, as they steam north, the weather is glorious. The water is a deep blue, with small, skittish waves that slap playfully at the *Vega*'s hull. The sun sparkles off the glittering surface. A *qaqulluk* hovers in the air above the deck, a white ghost, delicate spider legs dangling. When it abruptly veers away, having given up on whatever purpose it was engaged in, the sun turns its flashing wings to silver. Flora stands in the bows, watching the line of white come nearer.

Flora broods on that exchange. She was presumed dead, but had returned. She cannot help wondering, even as she knows it to be impossible, What if . . . ? *What if . . . ?*

False hope, retreating in front of her like the ghostly mountains that have deceived explorers for centuries. Atmospheric delusions; desires made manifest. She must not let herself be dangled, like poor Iris. But what else is there?

When the ship can sail no farther, they leave the *Vega* moored in the lee of a grounded berg and continue over the sea-ice by dogsled. Captain Mackie lets it be known that he thinks her deranged. But his knees are too bad to accompany them (and she would not let him go), so he sighs and paces the deck, grumbling about the unpredictability of the season up here, the dangers of the ice to the *Vega*'s old timbers—the old girl is insufficiently reinforced for the situation in which she finds herself . . .

After two days, Kudloq sees something in the distance: on the gray western shore, a huddle of bleached timber—two or three huts. A skein of smoke leans to southward, but there is no other movement, no sound. The American camp.

When they are still some hundred yards off, Flora asks Sorqaq and Kudloq to wait. Sorqaq frowns, asks if she doesn't want him to come.

"I will see if he's there," she says, beyond which, she has not thought. She thinks that, when she looks into his eyes, she will know if he is guilty of murder. This belief is based on nothing at all.

* * *

Knock at the door, then push it open. A large room bisected by a table. A tall stove like an altar. It is quietly dark and she is aware of the smells of tobacco, green wood, unwashed men. Little light makes it in through the small, dirty windows.

"Mr. Armitage?" Her voice comes out strongly.

At first, she thinks there is no one here. Then there is a noise behind a partition, and movement through the open door. A figure stands up from a desk in the dimness and faces her.

"Who's that?"

She hasn't seen him for eight years, not since the day when Jakob and she wished each other well on the beach at Neqi—the day when they both *knew*. Armitage's reddish hair is faded, but unstreaked with gray. An overgrown beard obscures mouth and chin, but she can see that the cheeks are haggard, the pale eyes oddly prominent. Where he was spare, he is now gaunt; whittled down to the bone.

"Well, well ... Mrs. Athlone ... I didn't know you were in the north."

"Yes." She takes some steps toward him and sits down, uninvited, at the table. The wood is cold and greasy to the touch.

"What a pleasant surprise."

"Where are your men? Are you alone?"

He makes a dismissive gesture. "They've gone on a trip to the mountains. We must lay in meat for next winter."

"You're not with them?"

"I have too much work to do here, alas. Plans for next year. I must stay here until the work is done. So much to do, as ever. To what do I owe this pleasure?"

"You know why I'm here."

He shrugs. "No, I'm afraid I do not."

She pauses, wondering if Sorqaq is outside now. She thought she might be afraid, but she does not fear him. She wonders if he fears her.

"Why did you go to Neqi last June?"

"In June?" He blinks. "Let me think ... June ... It is usual to visit colleagues if they are in the same area. I knew Mr. de Beyn of old, as you know."

"You had had a disagreement with him. A severe disagreement."

"Ah . . . I see. That was when I was unwell in the winter. It's true, and I wanted to make amends for it. That was the reason for my visit then."

"What did you find when you got there?"

"I found, very sadly, that Mr. de Beyn had passed away before I arrived. Had I been only one or two days earlier, I would have seen him. Sad. He was a fine scientist, a fine man."

She tries to stare into his depthless eyes, to read his face. To *know*. He nods slowly, sorrowfully.

"What was the argument about?"

"I hardly remember. Nothing serious. As I said, I wasn't well. It was unfortunate. I'm sure he would have understood."

"Wasn't it about the fact that he had proved Dupree Land does not exist, which would damage your character when it became known?"

Armitage looks at her with a hint of impatience. Shakes his head.

"He could prove that you lied."

"Mrs. Athlone, I understand that you and he were—ah—close. His passing must have been a great shock."

"The proof is in his notes. You took those notes. And Mr. Welbourne's. Why did you do that?"

"I took all their belongings to return them to their families. As is right."

"So then you still have the proofs about Dupree Land?"

He spreads his hands, palms upward.

"I suppose so—if they in fact exist."

"Where are his things? I want to see them."

"I am not sure if I can allow that. They are in my care . . ."

"He was my husband!"

He gapes, wrong-footed. For all he knows . . . She stands and goes to the open door. Sorqaq comes toward her, his rifle slung over his shoulder. She looks at him, shakes her head minutely.

"Mrs. . . . . ah, I acted appropriately. The belongings were not safe left at Neqi."

"You're not going back this year. Give them to me. I'll take them to New York myself."

His pale eyes stare at her, register Sorqaq in the doorway. The eyelids are red and watery, and he blinks frequently.

"Well . . . a handsome offer. However, you would have to give me time to find them. They're in the stores, somewhere. Things have become rather confused—"

"They should be conveyed to the families as soon as possible. And something may happen to you before you go back. As happened to both Mr. de Beyn and Mr. Welbourne."

Armitage looks at her curiously, and smiles.

In uneasy silence, they watch as Armitage searches the store hut and unearths two tin trunks, painted with the initials of the dead men. He looks at them patiently, warily, as if he is at the mercy of lunatics who must be humored.

"There you are. You're welcome to look through them. I trust you will put everything back in order. If you'll excuse me, I have work I must get on with."

Kudloq goes to hover by the hut, to keep an eye on Armitage. Crouched on the floor of the stores, Flora and Sorqaq open Jakob's trunk. Inside are clothes and books, piles of folders, his field notes, his written-up notebooks, rolls of film, a camera wrapped in a sweater. There is the chemise she left behind, carefully folded. Avoiding the stacks of photographs, she skims through the notebooks. Because they are so clearly labeled, it does not take long to sort through them, putting them in order. Her heart is pounding, making her dizzy. At last she looks up at Sorqaq.

"The notebooks from the northern trip aren't here."

"You mean when we went to the north coast? What about these? I know he kept notes in these. Every night he wrote in them."

Sorqaq indicates Jakob's field notes—small, thin notebooks tied in bundles. Each is labeled, each in order, but still, she looks through every one, to be sure. Nothing.

They open Welbourne's trunk; fewer notebooks are among his things—he seems to have kept a diary, nothing more. The evidence against Armitage is nowhere to be found. There is no written trace of the northern journey. There are no traces at all.

Flora sits back on her heels, frightened.

Sorqaq says, "Well, Fellora?"

"It's all gone. He has destroyed everything."

Chapter 59

Gander, Newfoundland, 48°57' N, 54°36' W
1948

Snow continues to fall throughout the day, turning the windows white. It is soft and silent; it renders the air base picturesque and useless. Randall thinks of the dark lake he saw earlier and wonders about the snowflakes, millions of them, falling and disappearing in the gray water, or settling on the old ice, making it white and perfect, masking its imperfections, making it look safe.

Restless, he thinks of tramping out once more to watch, but the dirge-like grayness of the air and poor visibility—and the cold—dissuade him. He should use the time productively, he tells himself, but can't settle to anything. He catches himself staring at the window. Instead of poring over his notes or the clippings or the photographs, his eyes fasten on the pattern of flakes that drift into the corners of the frame. He feels their coldness from inside. If he looks very hard, squinting through his eyelashes, he thinks he can see individual crystals: tiny, exquisite hexagons, each conforming to order, yet each, supposedly, as unique as a face. They are, according to his girlfriend, Barbara, proof of God's existence. She is as pretty and untouched as a snowflake, and he finds it hard to argue with her.

He can't help thinking about "hopeless lunatic" Arent de Beyn. What does *that* prove? That his mother is a liar? His grandparents? Or Flora Athlone-Cochrane, or whatever the hell her name is?

Doesn't the truth matter?

He should concentrate on Jakob and Armitage, while he has the chance to ask her. But, somehow, his questing after truth, which felt so fine and noble, a pure torch he carried for his family, seems to have turned grubby. The more he reads and hears about them all, the more he suspects that those golden-age explorers were an unpleasant lot—selfish, elusive, ruthless. They left people in their wake while they ran to the ends of the earth, to beat their chests and show everyone what great men they were. Or women. He doesn't believe her claims of escape; she was as much after glory as Armitage, he can tell. No, not much fun to be around. Or if they were fun, perhaps, then (like his great-uncle) they weren't around. But imagine having a dead father who is suddenly resurrected as an incurable—a *hopeless*—lunatic. A taunt and a portent. A threat and a shadow.

He didn't tell her that his grandfather, Hendrik, was assumed to have taken his own life.

Randall presses his hand against the cold glass, making the snow melt, dissolving the fragile bonds between individual crystals. Clots turn back into stars, before they disappear.

Snowflakes: more beautiful when they are alone. People do not harp on *that* analogy, for some reason.

In the bar, some scientists and air officers are playing pool. Randall watches for a while, takes a couple of games and is roundly beaten by the Cambridge physicist. He plays badly, but still blames his final defeat on the fact that Flora Cochrane has come into the bar and sits by the window. She does not seem to be watching, but even her not watching bothers him.

In that frame of mind, he relinquishes the cue to one of the navigators and goes up to her.

"I was hoping to find you here," she says, before he can say anything. "I'm sorry about earlier. I didn't mean to upset you."

He shrugs. "I asked to be told."

"Have you spoken to your family?"

He shakes his head. "I can't discuss something like that over the telephone. If I could even get through." He glances toward the whitened window.

"Mr. Crane, there's something else I want to say to you."

"Oh?"

"Could we go somewhere more private? To my room—if you don't find the prospect too alarming."

She closes her door behind them and starts talking immediately.

"Mr. Crane, for a very long time, I could not speak about Jakob, or acknowledge what had happened. I was bereaved, but that cannot excuse my behavior. There were things I should have done that I did not, and one of them was, certainly, to send his things to your family. For that, I apologize."

"His things? You had his things—from Greenland?"

"Yes. I'm sorry. And I'll be sure to send them to your mother, when I get home."

"You still have them *now*?"

She nods. Randall is astonished.

"My goodness . . . That's incredible. It would be wonderful to have them."

"I'll write to your mother and apologize to her. I'm sorry it's taken me so long."

Randall shakes his head wonderingly.

"What sort of things are they? Records, do you mean? Or personal items?"

"Some of his records. Some personal things. His camera. Clothes. Photographs."

Randall finds that he is grinning. He shakes his head. "This is amazing. But I don't understand how you could have them? Did he give them to you?"

"No. In the summer of 1900, I went back, to look for him. You didn't know that . . . Well, why would you? I had to find out what happened. Eskimo friends told me that he'd gone missing on the glacier where he was working. A crevasse—that was the most likely explanation."

"Oh."

"But, at around the same time, Armitage was back in Neqi. He came to see Jakob, he said. But he was dead."

"You mean, Armitage didn't see him? He was too late?"

"That was what he said."

Randall frowns at her. He thinks, she could say *anything*.

"Are you alleging that Armitage killed Jakob?"

She is looking directly into his eyes, as if trying to impress him with her sincerity.

"I'm saying it's possible. I don't know."

"Welbourne, too?"

"No; Welbourne drowned, weeks later, and in front of witnesses. But when they were both gone, Armitage came to take their belongings away."

"Why would he do that?"

"According to him, to carry them back to America for the families. But I was afraid—and Sorqaq agreed—that what he really wanted was to remove certain things from their records that would prove him a liar."

"Um . . . Who was Sorqaq?"

"Sorqaq was a hunter. A good man, who spent more than a year in the field with Jakob. They were great friends. He'd already witnessed Armitage try to blackmail Jakob into keeping quiet."

"Good heavens! What do you mean, blackmail?"

She looks impatient. "What does it usually mean? If they hated each other before that, and they did, it must have been ten times worse afterward. What matters is that the attempt failed, so Armitage was furious, and desperate to make sure Jakob couldn't ruin his good name."

She looks meaningfully at him. "He was desperate to keep him quiet."

Randall stares at her, thinking of his earlier misgivings about her.

"What were these things he wanted to remove?"

"You know Armitage claimed, in his book, to have discovered a new land in '92?"

"Dupree Land—the island that was later proved not to exist."

"Yes. But at the time everyone believed it. Jakob and Welbourne discovered that it didn't exist. Armitage had lied. A deliberate lie. Jakob would have made that public—at a time when Armitage needed people to believe his word, if he got to the Pole."

"So you're saying he killed him to protect his reputation?"

"He had reason to, and he was there."

Randall sits on the bed and rubs his hands over his face. He asks her to repeat certain things. He takes paper and a pen and writes them down, to try to make them less unlikely. Blackmail, lies, murder—it wasn't what he was expecting . . .

"Wait; I'm confused. Did Armitage take the records or didn't he?"

"Yes, he took everything that belonged to Jakob and Welbourne. We went to look for him, Sorqaq and I. Sorqaq was devastated by what happened to Jakob. He felt responsible, I think."

"Why?"

"When I left Greenland, I asked him to look after Jakob for me."

Randall must have looked confused, for she adds, "Sorqaq is my half brother."

Randall gapes at her, stunned.

"I see."

Although he doesn't see, at all.

"So Armitage took the records . . . and then?"

"We found him, farther north. He'd just failed to get to the Pole for a third time. He looked ill. His men were away—he was alone. He had Jakob and Welbourne's trunks in his storehouse—photographs, field notes, and so on. But much of it was missing. Armitage had destroyed everything that could be damaging to him."

"How do you know?"

"I know what had been there. Jakob's journey to the north coast proved that Armitage had invented Dupree Land. But every record of that journey was gone. Every trace. Jakob was meticulous about such things. It couldn't have been a coincidence—not such a complete erasure. And much was missing about the new island he discovered—that brilliant circumnavigation—so that his notes were no longer coherent. It wouldn't stand up to scrutiny."

Randall feels horror.

"God damn!"

He lets out an explosion of air. He finds he has clenched his fists.

"Why have you never spoken of this in public?"

"There was no proof. There were only things missing. And I was the only one who knew they were missing. Armitage said that, even if Metek and Sorqaq swore to it, no one would believe them, or care."

Randall paces to the window and back. The room seems too small, and airless.

"What happened to Armitage?"

She gazes out of the window; already, it looks like dusk.

"I think he couldn't bear to come back. Not only a failure, but a cheat; probably a murderer. I told him I would expose him; I would recount in great detail what he had done. I had nothing more to lose."

"Are you saying he took his own life?"

She says, "It's easy to do. You walk out on the ice, where it's weak, in summer. You keep going."

Randall writes down: *Armitage—suicide—shame? Thin ice?*

She says, "He was a tormented man."

"So . . . you took Jakob's things with you then. Armitage didn't stop you?"

"All that was left was personal. It couldn't hurt him."

"You left Armitage there, and then went home?"

"Yes."

"You meant to expose Armitage; to ruin him?"

She nods, a little impatient. "Yes."

"But . . . when you got home, you didn't."

"After he was dead, what was the point? It would only have hurt his family. It wasn't their fault."

Randall looks at his notes; perhaps he has gotten it wrong. He shakes his head, to clear it.

"But, if you'd left him there, how did you know he was dead?"

There is silence. He looks at those gray eyes, but she is staring past him, over his shoulder. Her eyes are the exact color of the frozen lake, the last of the old ice: gray, clouded, dangerous.

"I don't remember. I suppose I must have heard."

Chapter 60

In the summer of 1927, Flora Haddo (as her name was then, although it would not be for much longer) arrived in Siorapaluk on the Danish packet steamer *Mjølner*. She had not been to Greenland for eight years. She disembarked, not knowing, as ever, who would still be alive. She was delighted to find her old friend Meqro, as well and as stubborn as ever, and to see Aamma, a schoolteacher, married to her second husband. After a few days there, she traveled north to Neqi and eventually found Sorqaq and the daughter he had named after her. She met his grandchildren. They joked about which of the sleek, black-haired infants were more like William Mackie, still living indomitably on in his nineties (she was delivering a case of Dundee cakes and Keiller's marmalade from that quarter).

The north was changing. Sorqaq still hunted for seal and walrus, and his wife, Megipsu, still prepared skins and sewed fur clothes as she always had, but the Danish village at Thule, a day's steaming down the coast, had an amazing new thing he called a "land-hat," which confused Flora, until she worked out that there was now a general store. There was also a church and a school (whose Danish names were easier to recognize). People were moving their families to be near them. Some of the children were learning to read and speak Danish, and to count money, so that they could work there one day. The packet brought goods from the south a few times a year, so they would never run out of flour and sugar, kettles, tobacco, and the like. There was a doctor all year round. People still died, but now when you died—if you went to the Danish church, that is—you went to a nice place called *Heemlin*, where there were flowers and sunshine and trees (Sorqaq had never seen a tree), and endless game animals that lay down to be killed, and nice things to eat, and you saw all your relatives who had died before you. But if you didn't do as the pastor told you, Sorqaq said, with a tolerant laugh, then his god would push you into a hot sea called *Hilva*.

Sorqaq had something else to tell her.

"A strange thing happened, Fellora, two . . . three years ago. Some of our young men were fishing near the end of Jakob's glacier, in summer, and they saw something on the beach. Something white. They went to look, and it was a bone."

Flora looked toward the end of the fjord, where the crumbling snout of the glacier shone in the sunlight. She had once watched as pieces of that cliff sheered away and fell into the sea, but had not thought, at the time, that with them would fall all the things that had traveled slowly, held inside the ice.

"It was him, I'm sure. We don't think it could be anyone else. It fits with where he was working."

Flora nodded, feeling—absurdly, after all this time—tears needling her eyelids.

"I went back with them. We searched around the whole bay. We buried him up there, on the beach. If you want, I will show you."

With misgivings settled in her throat like stones, Flora went with him. They took a kayak and paddled up the fjord. The paddle was carved of a smooth, close-grained wood, and fitted her hand like an old friend. It was one of those rare, windless days that come like blessings in late July: the water as still as a pond, the kayak drawing a dark feather across the mercury-glass surface. The sun was just visible through a veil of cloud, a nacreous disk of blurred light. The sky was like the inside of a shell.

Sorqaq grounded them on a small beach backed by crimson cliffs—a lonely spot that sloped down to the water, embraced by rocky headlands. The water in this bay would always be calm; the number of people who would ever set foot here, vanishingly small. He led the way up toward a heap of larger stones that stood proud of the gravel. It was plain that something had disturbed it: probably foxes. Unmistakably, there was something white showing among the stones. Sorqaq stopped and looked at her, distressed.

"I'm sorry, Fellora. I didn't know it would be like this. Will you wait here?"

"No, it's all right."

They walked up the beach and stopped by the scattered heap. She couldn't tell what she was looking at. She couldn't associate that flash of white with the man she had known.

"Was there . . . Were there any clothes, or anything?"

"No. The bones had been in the water and were washed up near here."

(He had kept her letters. *Here.*)

She dropped to her knees in the gravel and began to gently excavate.

Sorqaq, discreet as ever, walked toward the cliffs and began to search for tripe-de-roche.

The whiteness—up close, an ochered, polar-bear whiteness— belonged to the front of a skull: the forehead, smooth and apparently intact. She touched it with her bare fingers.

("Shh. I'll always come back.")

"Sorqaq . . . How can you be sure it's him?"

"There was some hair."

He touched the back of his head.

"It was white and . . ." He undulated his hand to indicate waves. "No *inuk* has hair like that. So we knew. The skull was broken . . . I cannot say whether that happened before he died, or when he fell, or long after. It is impossible to know, Fellora."

She looked at him to see what he meant, but he looked away.

"He was never careless. You know that."

Sorqaq nodded.

Kneeling, she began to move the gravel from around the skull, exposing more of its curve. She cupped her hand over it: the echo of a caress. No warmth there, and it seemed too small to have contained all that he was. She kept burrowing until she felt under her fingers a wad of something fibrous. She asked Sorqaq for the knife he carried. He handed it to her, and she cut off a piece, a hank, a lock . . . and held it. The hair was gray, with a slight curl (he hated, she loved, the way it waved when it grew long). She rubbed it between her fingers. It was matted, gritty, dry—but surprisingly supple. It felt—almost—alive.

A few years ago, while moving house, she had cleared out a linen drawer and come across an old handkerchief—one of a set given to her by Iris. It was folded but unwashed, the silk crisp and brittle with a whitish substance that cracked and flaked from the creases as she unfolded it. For a minute, she could not think what it was, was about to throw it away—and then she remembered.

"Fellora. Are you all right?"

She nodded.

"We'll build the grave better—a proper *kallunat* grave. We can put up a headstone. Or we can move him. I wanted to ask if he should go to the Christian graveyard. There's one in Thule. Or, if you wanted, you could take him back with you."

Sorqaq watched her quietly for a while, then walked down to the water's edge and filled his pipe. He stood looking out over the bay to where some eider ducks were landing with a hiss and clatter of wings and water: small disturbances, little wakes.

Flora bent down and pressed dry lips to the bone above the eye socket. She had done so many times before. It made her feel . . . nothing. There was nothing of him, there. She sat back, felt foolish, theatrical. But what was the right thing?

"You don't have to say now, Fellora."

"He should stay. He loved it here."

Sorqaq sucked on his pipe for a minute.

"*Ieh*. He was happy here—and he was happy up there." He jerked his head toward the end of the fjord. To winter's home; the whiteness that is always there, falling with infinite slowness, infinite patience, into the sea.

Chapter 61

The Big Nail, 90°0' N
1948

The sea-ice, which looks so flat and inviting from above, like a cotton sheet, proves to be rough and chaotic. The pilot has to make several passes at low altitude, looking for the smoothest place in the vicinity of the Pole, and in the end has to make do with this field of white boulders—rattling the teeth in their jaws, the brains inside their skulls. As the wheels hit the ice, there are loud bangs, vicious jolts; at one point, the passengers, all of them, seize their armrests as *Arcturus* seems in danger of tipping over and clipping her left wing on a glassy fin of ice . . . She rights herself. The passengers applaud. When the roaring engines stop at last, silence breaks over them like a solid thing.

They set off early this morning, in darkness, and have been sitting for hours in the freezing cabin; keyed-up, expectant, and bored with the monotony of the view. The place they have landed looks exactly like any other they have flown over during the last four hours: an endless, wrinkled plain, ice littered with ice, more blue than white, under a sky empty of cloud.

Zippered into their padded overalls, they stumble stiffly down the steps and on to the ice. Their thighs make squeaking noises as they walk. They adjust dark goggles against the glare that comes from every direction. Bare, brilliant sunlight; relentless cold. The air sucks the moisture out of their nostrils, their mouths. The scientists assemble their instruments as fast as they can in their clumsy gloves, calling out to each other in excitement.

The film crew sets up, cursing. The cameraman removes a mitten and gets shouted at for his foolishness. The photographer, who is with the air force, paces around, looking for angles on the vast whiteness. Only their shadows show them where they are in the world; the sun flings them down, blue on a white ground. They laugh and joke. Snowballs are thrown—or rather, handfuls of white grit that disintegrate, glitteringly, in the air. It is too cold for snowballs. They find they keep turning to look toward the plane to orient themselves, for relief.

What is odd—so strange the eye almost rejects it—is that everything is the same color, everything the same lifeless substance. The entire world, a dazzling monotony. Imagine a landscape where everything is black, or red. There is that about it which defies us.

To Randall, this undifferentiated point on the Arctic Ocean doesn't feel like . . . anything. He trudges about, grasping for some sense of the occasion that he can later pin down in words. Its importance is not negligible . . . God, he can sound pompous. Men laid down their lives for this place. He looks around and thinks, In heaven's name, why?

He does not have the impression that he is standing on a frozen sea—more like a glaring salt desert; a blighted land after some disaster has smashed it beyond hope of repair. His mind crowds with pictures of Hiroshima after the bomb: the flatness and the ruin; a whole civilization turned to powder. Only, this is . . . cleaner—a more complete pulverizing. He looks around him at shattered ridges of ice, white rubble of every size, nothingness in every direction, and has to remind himself that no catastrophe has taken place, that there was never anything here. Nothing has ever taken place, here. He feels very small.

Randall and Flora have no particular job to do. He has brought his pocket camera, and takes photographs, doubting they will look like much. The horizon is flat and endless—or, rather, round and infinite, like a wheel. The sun is to their left—well, it depends. It is south. Everywhere is south. It dazzles, dizzying. Randall watches Flora as she looks around. In her padded suit, hooded and goggled, she could be any age. She catches his eye and smiles—a blazing, girl's grin.

Flora wanders a little way from the others, searching for a good spot. She squats down and takes something white from the slit in her khaki suit. From thirty yards away, she appears to be digging.

Randall turns around, his camera hovering near his face, hearing the climatologist shout, "With wind chill—minus thirty-three!" as the navigators measure, calculate, discuss, and finally position a flagpole at the point they have deemed—as far as anyone can deem, where compasses do not work and where it is impossible to say which time zone you are in because you are in all of them and none—to be the convergence of lines that are not drawn on the earth. He snaps away as the Stars and Stripes is unfurled and attached to the pole. The wind stills and the flag droops. Someone does something to it: inserts a piece of wire to make it stand up jauntily. People are marshaled. Randall turns in time to see Flora pat the ice with her hand, and then stand up, dusting the snow daintily off her gloves.

Commander Soames comes to take her by the arm. They gather in various combinations by the flag, for the cameras. They smile and, for the film camera, wave. Randall takes a picture of the Snow Queen by herself, standing at the North Pole, and gets a scientist to take a picture of them both there, together.

They don't have long, but, at some point, there is a lull—a reverent hush. The flag is up, measurements taken, the first excitement has crested. Randall wanders away a little, looks around him, looks up, and notices that the air itself is sparkling, like crushed and powdered diamonds. He wonders if he is hallucinating. He opens his mouth and breathes in the sparkling dust. It hurts. He listens to his heart beating, the crunch of his boots on hard, gritty snow. If he concentrates hard enough, he seems to hear the faintest of rustlings, as though something is whispering to him.

Epilogue

Onmogelijk Dal, 78°14' N, 88°32' W

Flora lies on her side. Her eyes are shut against the westering sun. Her limbs feel heavy; her hair is loose, tangled. A stone presses into her hip, but she can't be bothered to move. From time to time, she opens her eyelids the merest crack, so that gold light fractures in her eyelashes, making multiple, tiny suns.

They have been in the valley for weeks. Time has blurred, without nights. She feels as though this is the only place she has ever lived. The rest of the world has ceased to exist. She can't imagine leaving, but that morning there was a veil of rime on the inside of the tent: *nilaktaqtuq*. A portent. She turns her head a fraction so that she can see the angle of his shoulder, the smoke coming from his cigarette, his hair, outlined by light.

"I should have prevented his ending up . . . like that."

When he talks about the Eskimos who died, and, in particular, of Ayakou's fate, he becomes incensed. She loves that about him. From lying in a state of sun-stunned and sated languor outside the tent, he has sat up, drawn up his knees, rolled a cigarette, smoked it down, pressed the stub twenty times into the damp soil—all while seeming unconscious of his fidgetiness, and of his nakedness.

Flora is listening to what he says—she is—but a part of her mind is absorbed in watching the interplay of muscle in his body, the cordage of sinew and knobs of bone that make up his joints, the creases of skin at his flexed hips, the folds of flesh in his belly when he bends forward, his knees. The whole warm landscape of his sunburnt skin. She has been thinking, on the one hand, what a strange thing is a human body; such a gangling, awkward compromise of functional parts: feet, really, when you look at them, are very peculiar things, and as for noses and ears—ridiculous. Yet his body is the loveliest thing she can imagine; she could look at it forever. She smiles: she *will* look at him forever. When he is worried, or angry, his forehead and cheeks crease into furrows that, with his gray hair, make her think, This is what he will look like when he is old. But when he laughs, which is often, he seems like a young man, and when his face is relaxed in sleep, he looks like a boy. She loves all of his faces—she has all of him here in the valley—past and present and future: all hers.

She marvels that he can be so unselfconscious under her scrutiny; it is a kind of grace. She could never match it; even now, in the sun, she has one of the blankets half drawn over her: a spurious modesty. Today, the temperature has reached sixty-six degrees, but Ayakou's fate is chilling. It requires, from her, a semblance of decorum.

She says, "You did all that anyone could have done, and more. You didn't know what the museum was doing."

Jakob glances at her. "I try to tell myself he wouldn't have cared. After all, he's gone."

"Before, when you were here, Armitage took bones from people's graves, didn't he? Did you object then?"

Jakob grimaces. "That was different. It seemed different."

"Why? Because of the time that had passed? Because we didn't know them?"

She picks a tiny, pink flower and holds it up between her half-closed eye and the sun, before perching it on his knee: an offering.

"I sometimes think I did wrong in taking the mummies. I had them displayed exactly in the way your museum had Ayakou displayed—to make people gasp and shiver."

"But they were long dead. No one mourned them. No one even knew who they were."

"I wonder if that makes enough of a difference. Ralph hated my doing it. It offended something deep within him. Is it just a matter of degree? I mean, after how long is it acceptable to display a person's body? Five hundred years seems all right; a few weeks is grotesque. Where do you draw the line? At fifty years? Twenty?"

Jakob shakes his head. "I don't know. Perhaps after everyone who knew them is dead?"

"What about descendants? What if it was your great-grandfather?"

"I don't know, Flora. But it is surely a function of time. What you did with your mummies was not the same as the museum boiling the flesh off Ayakou's bones in its haste to put him on show."

He looks at her, frowning. She takes his hand in hers.

"Perhaps not. I thought, then, that the body is a shell . . . an envelope that is discarded. It's not the essence, or the spirit or whatever you call it. Now, I'm no longer sure."

She kisses his scarred knuckles, the battered fingertips. The nails have grown back, but he thinks his hands are deformed and ugly. ("I'm ashamed to touch you with these hands," he once said. She'd replied, "For God's sake . . .")

"With different bodies, we'd be different people."

He smiles. "Would we? I think memories and experiences are more important in making us who we are."

"But with another body, you would have different experiences. If you were fat and ugly . . ."

She suspects she is blushing, because of the way he is looking at her. He pretends to look stern.

"Are you saying you wouldn't love me if I had a different body?"

Flora smiles. "Mm . . . Would you love me if I had a different mind?"

They both laugh, rather awkwardly.

Jakob lies back on the blanket. She is delighted that, for once, it is she who has disconcerted him.

He says, "I can't think like that. I just know that you are you, and that whatever it is that is me is very glad to be here, with you. More than glad. Let's just stay here."

Flora moves to lie with her head in the crook of his shoulder, his arms around her, her leg folded across his thighs. His skin is cool and warm at the same time. She spreads her hand on his chest. She feels his ribs beneath, his heart beating beneath her fingers, the rise and fall. She thinks, This is everything, right here. It can all stop now. Unaware that, at this moment, she is smiling.

A Glossary of Inuit Words

aja!	an exclamation, often of pleasure
angekok	shaman/person with healing powers
angut	woman
ayornamut	a pity, but it cannot be otherwise/it is fated/bad luck
erneq	son
ieh	yes
illu	house of stone (permanent) or snow (temporary)
imaqa	maybe
inuk	Eskimo/Inuit man (singular)
inuit	Eskimo/Inuit people (plural)
kallunat	Westerners (plural)
kamik	bearskin boot
kiffak	menial servant
kiviak	rotten auk meat, a delicacy
kooyounah	thank you
kujappok	sex
marmarai	Mm, it's good
naamik	no
naasut	flowers
Neqi	meat, food; a place name
nilaktaqtuq	the ice that forms on the inside of a tent

ooangniktuq	north wind
panik	daughter
perlerorneq	winter madness
qamiut	sleds
qaniit	snowflakes
qaqulluk	Arctic fulmar (bird)
qatannguh	sibling
qooviannikumut	deep happiness
Siorapaluk	pretty little sandy beach; a place name
tupik	hide tent used in summer
Tutsarfik	roughly, the month of November. Lit. "it is listening"
ulu	crescent-shaped knife used by women
Umingmak Nuna	Land of musk ox/Ellesmere Land
upernallit	whalers, usually Scottish. Lit. "those who arrive in spring"
usuk	penis
Uttuqalualuk	old man; Inuit name for the star Arcturus

Acknowledgments

I owe huge thanks to a number of people for their help during the writing of this book. First, as ever, to my agent, Diana Tyler, for her support, diplomacy, and for being an absolute champ. To Jane Wood, my editor at Quercus, for sound judgment, ideas, and being such a pleasure to work with. And to my lovely beta-readers: Sarah Collier, Paul Holman, Clare Mockridge, Bridget Penney, Jo Penney, Steve Roser, Tanya Trochoulias, and Marco van Welzen, for reading this book to destruction, and much else besides.

I am also in debt to many writers who have shared their insights and experience of the Arctic, both actual and historical, but above all to Barry Lopez, Jean Malaurie, Wally Herbert, and Robert Bryce. I wish I could remember everything I've learned from them.